Sweet Tea & Fireflies

Sweet Tea & Fireflies

Jane W. Rankin

Winfree Oaks

Denver, North Carolina

To:
Elizabeth
Enjoy!

Jane W. Rankin

ISBN: 978-1-0881-0177-3

Book design: Diana Wade

Winfree Oaks Publishing
Denver, North Carolina

Additional Books by Jane W. Rankin

The Rowdy Girls Trilogy
Book 1: Sour Grapes & Sweet Tea (Book 1)
Book 2: Sweet Tea and Fireflies (Book 2)
Book 3: Sweet Tea and Long Ago (2024 debut)

To

Sailor and Daisy

(AKA Rascal and Annie)

Sailor, an old soul, was a one-in-a-million horse. He gave me the courage to challenge myself, would jump anything, and took care of me in and out of the saddle. With an overflowing heart of devotion, Daisy the golden retriever was my constant companion and confidante—listening to my every word and offering a kiss or perhaps a soft nuzzle in response.

They were the best four-footed friends a girl could have. I will love and miss you both forever!

1.

Pushing with one foot and then the other, I glided our porch swing back and forth as angry clouds, fueled by the August afternoon heat, boiled in the distant sky. With Nick's head in my lap, I ran my fingers through his thick sandy blond hair, counting between the streaks of lightning and the claps of thunder, calculating the relief to be about ten miles away. It had been a breathlessly hot summer, and we were in serious need of rain to narrow the cracks in our arid pastures.

"Our quiet porch time is about to expire," I said, spotting our barn manager walking up the hill.

Coy tipped his tattered green John Deere cap. "Sorry, boss, but I need your help. The drag is wrenched tight on the tractor hitch; it's going to be a two-man job to untangle."

"I'll be right there," Nick said, regaining an upright position and giving me a kiss. "Don't move, babe. This shouldn't take long."

"Okay, but remember you promised me a foot rub," I said.

"I doubt you'd let me forget." He laughed. "I'll be right back."

Despite the five-week-long dry spell, to my eyes, the panoramic view of Long Leaf Farm remained equal to the beauty of a Monet landscape and provided the window for my quiet reflection. Over the past three years, my life had been as turbulent as that billowing thunderhead.

That cascade of events began on a very cold day in early February, when my husband of twenty-seven years announced he was no longer in love with me. I sat frozen as he apologized, explaining that he had fallen in love with his chiropractor, Pam. Parker's last sentence was the final nail in the *how did I not see this coming* coffin of disillusionment. Without batting an eye, he added that they had made plans to move themselves, along with his lawn and landscaping business, to New Bern. Ironically enough, the two of us had often considered retiring to that charming city, nestled at the confluence of the Neuse and Trent Rivers.

I was both amazed and curious at his level of organization. In less than an hour, he had stuffed a suitcase and duffel bag with clothes and his backpack with toiletries and several pairs of shoes. How long had he been planning his move? I wondered. Stopping briefly in the hallway, Parker told me once again how sorry he was, then quickly turned and walked out the front door. My immediate reaction to hearing his footsteps hurrying him across the wooden porch floor and down the steps was to utterly collapse. How could I not have known what was going on? Was I truly that blind? But I had no time for self-pity. It was essential that my adult daughters be first on my list of concerns. News like this would travel faster than kudzu in the town of Hadley Falls. Two phone calls had to be made, and I dreaded each.

Emma, the oldest, was the calmer child, so I called her first. She shared a few choice words for her father and his abrupt abandonment. Catching her breath, she asked if I was okay and did I need for her to come home for a few days? I told her I would be fine and needed some quiet time.

Sidney was the more difficult call. She and her father were very close, and this news would be a knife through the heart for her. My youngest assumed the verbal posture of serious fury, and it took a while to quell her anger. In the end, and for now anyway, she agreed when I suggested that yes things had changed, but we three remained the same.

The following day was the first day of my new life—however that would unfold. I came to realize that I absolutely could not stay in what had become a house full of lies.

A prenuptial agreement had been signed before Parker and I were married, thanks to my father's insistence. Therefore I still held the deed to that house and a few other things. When I downsized from my century-old inherited Victorian, it was heartbreaking to see the "For Sale" sign being hammered into the ground, but I needed a fresh start—a place to create new memories untarnished by the past.

My new address would be 528 Brook Street. As a recently separated woman in her late forties, when I stood at the gate of the dilapidated white picket fence that surrounded the crumbling 1920s pale yellow cottage with a wraparound porch, I instantly fell in love. The little house was in need of repair, but I was too, and its resurrection provided the perfect jump-start for finding the *real* Sarah.

All those desperately trying times seemed like ancient history now. Quickly bringing my thoughts back to the present, I watched Nick reappear through the double barn doors while the massive cloud bank of deep charcoal gray engulfed the pastel colors of the afternoon sky.

"What happened to you?" I howled as his mud-laden body grew closer.

Standing at the bottom of the steps, he began to unlace his work boots. "The drag finally gave way, and as you can see, I found the only mud on this farm."

"Which was where?"

"Before realizing there was an equipment issue, Coy had hosed off the tractor as always," Nick said, stepping out of his pants and piling them on the bottom step. "I'm sorry, but your foot rub will have to wait. I'm off to the shower."

I continued to push the swing. "Not a problem. Perhaps I'll 'bank' that promise for another time."

Nick kissed my cheek. "Thanks. How long before dinner?"

"About thirty or forty minutes. Take your time."

⊂3⊃

The sky darkened as my thoughts drifted back to the day I'd met my Prince Charming.

It was two years ago at the final hunter pace competition of the season. At our age, a long courtship wasn't necessary. We were in our late forties and already knew what we wanted, needed, and refused to accept in a relationship. Last spring I moved to his farm in Greenway, sold my cottage after only two years living there, and we were married this past June.

I had always dreamed of having a house the country with horses in the closest pasture, but Long Leaf Farm eclipsed my wildest fantasies. Stretched out before me was an amazing piece of property encompassing well over a hundred acres, with each space having a purpose. Outlined by black slat fencing, grazing horses dotted the blanket of pristine pastureland, and most evenings just before sunset, it was forage for white-tailed deer. A pebble-bottomed creek ran in and out of the tree line, offering a botanist's buffet and a natural habitat for amphibians, reptiles, and waterfowl. Dense forests of towering longleaf pines anchored the azure blue North Carolina sky.

Dragging my bare feet across the smooth wooden porch floor, I stopped the swing, slipped on my Top-Siders, and along with our two dogs, made my way to the kitchen. From the window above the farm sink, I watched as the rain began to pour from the sky, while the wind whipped through the branches of five white oaks standing arrow straight down the long side of the fenced-in outdoor riding ring.

CR80

The rain, and the breeze that lingered, left the summer air clean and fresh, so dinner on the patio was a treat. Sitting down to our supper of shrimp salad and fresh vegetables from our garden, Nick rested his napkin in his lap and took a sip of his wine. "First let me say, dinner looks delicious."

"Thanks." I smiled. "And second?"

"I'm not complaining...but after my shower I had some difficulty finding my clothes."

Searching for the right reflective look of surprise, I said, "Really?"

"Don't play coy. I love what you did with my closet, with all the colors in rainbow order, short-sleeve shirts in one group and long in another—thank you."

"You're welcome. This morning I was looking for hangers for your clean laundry, and...well...in my estimation, that space was a wreck. I had a wonderful time, but if you don't like it, feel free to change it."

"Funny." Nick smirked. "But since I've been a bachelor for decades, perhaps we could talk things over before just jumping in? And when is it that you go back to school again?"

"I hear what you're saying—honestly—but old habits die hard. And ha ha. Monday, August sixteenth, is our first teacher workday. The students return the following Monday. Now, different topic. I went to the attic in search of a box of table linens—dear Lord—there are so many boxes up there! That space is piled high with mostly my stuff, some of your things, and cartons belonging to the previous owner of my house on Brook Street. Depending on what I find, I guess I should reach out to her."

"I imagine the former owner left it because she didn't want whatever was up there. What do you know about her?"

"Not much. Iris Broadmoor owned the house, but her sister lived there too. I think they moved to a senior living facility near Shallow Neck. It's silly, but for some reason I just couldn't throw it all away without going through it myself, and I'd never had the time. However, the mystery will have to wait until cooler weather."

"Sarah S. Heart, girl detective. I'll bet you ten bucks you can't wait until October to see what you might find."

I took a sip of iced tea. "You know me well, but I nearly passed out just opening the attic door. Anyway, I was thinking about having the first post-wedding 'Rowdy Girls' dinner the fourth weekend in August, while you're with your brother. Would you mind? I thought it would be fun if they all slept over and brought their horses too."

"Of course I don't mind. This is as much your house as it is mine.

Sounds like fun. Please be kind to your new husband when you're telling stories of our life together and my seemingly irreversible shortcomings, like messy closets and disorganization."

Leaning over in my chair, I kissed my husband's cheek. "Absolutely. But the jury's still out on the *irreversible* part—time will tell."

2.

The sun had been up for nearly an hour, and just before pulling onto the highway, I got caught up in a renewed spirit of excitement. This was the first day with students and my twenty-ninth year of teaching art at Hadley Falls High School. Nick and our life together owned most of the credit for my happiness, but Long Leaf Farm deserved some acknowledgment—both he and the farm were many of my dreams, all rolled into one.

But I was no longer a twenty-one-year-old teacher, fresh out of college. My world involved heartbeats, wishes, and desires other than my own. My two girls shared the top spot on my list of concerns. The divorce had been difficult on them. Both in their mid-twenties, they had well-developed reasoning skills, but I'm sure my being married to someone other than their father was strange for them. The move to Nick's farm was "our move," not just mine. In his wonderfully patient way, Nick had allowed them the time they needed for us to become a "new" family of four—or five, counting Emma's husband, Scott.

Sidney was single, lived in Raleigh, and the lure of the horses on our farm had her visiting us about once a month. Emma and Scott lived in Providence, Rhode Island, and their visits were at most two or three times a year. Over the summer, Emma came for a week's stay, which proved to be monumentally successful in the arena of bonding with Nick.

On the pet side of the equation, my dog Annie was elated with her newly found free-as-the-wind life on the farm. But my horse, Rascal, was a different ball of wax.

For the past few weeks, I had been working out my riding schedule for Falling Creek Farm, where Rascal boarded. My handsome chestnut gelding was twenty-four years old, and moving him would have been very disruptive. He and Louie, my friend Margaret's horse, had been the "dynamic duo" forever, and it seemed unkind to separate them. Add to that the guilt I felt for having fun riding the horse Nick had gifted me.

Margaret owned Maggie's Alley, a quaint bookstore in the Historic District of Hadley Falls, and had more workday flexibility than I did. Her one employee could close up in the afternoons so she could come to the barn. We would ride every Tuesday and Thursday after school and on Saturday mornings before Betsy and I went to the farmers' market.

Betsy and I had met more than twenty years ago as a result of our youngest daughters and the show barn where they rode. We'd helped each other weather many a storm. I spent the night before my wedding at her farm, and we made a pact not to allow this move to change anything beyond my address.

Thirty minutes down the highway and stopped at the first traffic light in Hadley Falls, I dialed Betsy's number. "Good morning—can you talk?"

"Sure. Are you on your way to school?"

"Yes—just four blocks away and for the twenty-ninth year, if you can believe that. I've had an idea. Nick is going to be with Jack in Manhattan and Martha's Vineyard from next Wednesday through the weekend, so I thought it would be the perfect opportunity to have a Rowdy Girls dinner at the farm. What do you think?"

Betsy cheered. "How fun! Rose will be back from England, and I know Jennifer and Elizabeth are around. I guess you already know that Margaret can come?"

"Yep. She's in town, so let's get together. I even thought everyone could trailer in their horses Friday afternoon, spend the night, and we could ride Saturday morning after breakfast, before it gets too hot."

"What a great idea! I'll work on getting in touch with everyone else while you're at school."

"Perfect! Quick question—have you heard from Rose? I think she's up to something."

"She called two days ago, checking on her horse, and squeaked out a little something. I asked her to continue, but she refused. Our favorite Brit did offer that she would prefer a group reveal, so our sleepover might be the perfect platform for whatever happened."

"She's English and 'stiff upper lip or soldier on' to the core, but I'll bet it has to do with her worthless French ass of a man friend, Henri du Bois. What a leech! Leave me a message, please, when you know if everyone's a yes."

Betsy said, "Will do, and yes, Henri is all of that. I've never understood the fascination, but forget him. Have a great day, and be sweet to the children."

"Well, as sweet as I can be with a bunch of hormonal teenagers." I laughed.

Tossing my cell phone in my purse, I whispered, "Mornin', God. It's Sarah. Here we go again. Give me the strength to navigate the next 180 days without losing my cool. The older I get, the less restraint I seem to have. You and I have spoken often concerning my intolerance of stupid behavior, fundraisers, decorations for school dances, school plays, and homecoming posters and my disdain for glitter. Not to mention the core teachers who think all I do is color! Please take my hand when the first coach asks me to make a banner in the last fifteen minutes of class for the opening home football game. Especially Coach Dixon; he's only alive because correctional-institution orange is not in my color wheel and few women look good in a black-and-white, wide-horizontal-striped, one-size-fits-all jumpsuit. Amen," I said, pulling into the faculty parking lot and putting my car in park.

The first day with students was always an easy one: a review of the rules, seating charts, handing out the syllabus, calming the fears of the ninth graders, and standing firm with the upper classmen. With my computer softly playing my favorite piece, "Für Elise," by Beethoven, I explained that seldom did I ever sit at my desk but preferred the corners of the art tables and that classical music would almost always fill the background of our space. The boys rarely said a word, while the girls, writing in purple ink with their daisy-topped pens, giggled to each other while taking notes throughout the period.

Aside from the two junior boys added to my already too full second period, everyone was accounted for and seemed happy enough, considering that school was back in session and their summer vacation was over.

CR80

With day one in the books, I was back in my car, checking my phone for Betsy's message. I scrolled down the list—there it was, and yes, we would all be together.

Everyone was now on board for the overnight and the Saturday-morning ride two weeks from now. Everyone, that is, except our kind and gentle barn manager, Coy. Listening, he raised his eyebrows and nervously rearranged his cap as I disclosed that his sanctuary was soon to be invaded by five women and five horses—six, including Rascal. It did soften the blow a bit that he had over a week to prepare.

CR80

The following Monday, as I drove home down the shaded lane to our house, I noticed a dramatic change to the outdoor ring. I knew it was the handiwork of Nick, Coy, and most probably Nancy and Linda, who rode and boarded their horses at LLF. The freshly washed jumps and new artificial posies in flower boxes under each jump were a dead giveaway to the input of those two ladies. Potted arborvitae or Carolina hollies stood in matched pairs at the base of each set of standards, and the footing had been dragged to perfection.

My car barely came to a stop before I jumped out. "This is amazing! What a great surprise!"

Nick and Coy stood proudly with their rakes in hand. "We're glad you like it," Nick said.

Ever the art teacher, I said, "You two look like our version of

American Gothic."

"Only you would think of that," Nick said. "Anyway, Coy and I planned to spiff up the ring, but this over-the-top idea belongs to Linda and Nancy. They stood firm that your girlfriends were not going to look at 'their farm' with a disapproving eye. I assured them that would never happen, but they weren't convinced. I'm glad we did it—it looks very smart, I must say."

"I love it! We should take the first ride tonight after supper." Annie rounded the corner with stalactites of crud swinging from her golden retriever fur. "What happened to my clean dog?"

Nick smiled. "She and Caesar had a great time helping."

"Once they dry, all that dirt and sand will fall off," Coy said, returning to raking the footing.

Nick and I changed clothes after dinner and made our way to the barn. This was a first for us—we had always ridden in the morning, but the cooling temperatures and early-evening quiet offered the perfect backdrop for an easy ride.

I came to have my new horse Buddy by the strangest of circumstances. Less than a year before, he had been abandoned in a meadow just down the road from my favorite place to ride, Moss Creek Farm, which is nestled in the rolling hills of Virginia. The lady who found the beautiful paint was Susan Tillman—owner of that amazing farm and trainer extraordinaire. After all the legal details were settled around Buddy's ownership, Nick bought him and he became my horse.

It had been strange to ride any horse other than Rascal, but we were finding our rhythm and learning to trust each other. He was not at all bothered at being out past his usual bedtime, and together he and Nick's horse, Chance, seemed to enjoy the ride as much as we did.

Autumn purple ash trees lined the back of the barn and hosted cicadas, singing in full chorus and giving rhythm to our brushes as we groomed our horses. The heat of the day had surrendered to a cool and refreshing evening breeze.

"Good Lord, it was hot today. I don't think the school air-conditioning ever stopped running," I said.

Nick looked over the half wall in the wash stall. "I'm such a clod. I forgot to ask—how was your day?"

Brushing my sweaty bangs away from my eyes, I responded, "You're not a clod; school was great! It's slow going the first two weeks back from their summer vacation. Day two, I review the proper use of equipment from pencils to the potter's wheel. Once I hand out the sketchbooks, they stop listening to my teacher blah, blah, blah and go straight to work creating their cover designs. All the while and without notice, they find their 'art groove' and we move on from there.

"I put up the same bulletin boards every year. What a waste of time, but apparently their existence is written in the finer print of classroom necessities. Did you know, I only have one real class rule?"

"Which is?" Nick asked.

"Because I said so! It has served me well over the years. There are others, of course, but it's the only one that really counts. In my opinion, no one in high school should require a review of what is acceptable behavior. My ninth graders are falling right in line, but it takes a while to get the upper grades to recall whose name is printed on my North Carolina teaching certificate."

"Did that extremely gifted boy sign up for art again this year?"

"Yes, he did, and he has an amazing talent, but what a mouth! He'll take it to a higher level now that he's a senior, I'm sure. And you don't have to be mean or hateful to achieve order and kindness in the classroom, but you do need to erase the possibility of accepting anything less on the very first day of class. 'We are fortunate to live in a democracy, but room 112 is a monarchy, and I wear the crown!' is the first sentence in my welcome-back-to-school speech. My students always laugh, and I'm glad about that, but they also know I'm dead serious."

"You'll get 'em straightened out," Nick said. "You look hot."

"Yes, I'll need a shower before bed."

As we returned our horses to their stalls, he said, "Me too, and because I believe in conserving our natural resources…"

"Nicholas Heart!"

"At your service. Come on, dogs." Nick took my hand as we walked toward the house.

The shower was amazing!

3

On the hunt for serving dishes, I made yet another trip to the third floor's towering inferno of an attic. Nick's house was over two hundred years old, and all the plumbing and electrical were in good standing downstairs, but this single lightbulb attached to the end of cloth-wrapped wire had obviously been overlooked. *Note to self*, I thought. *Necessary upgrade or death by electrocution.*

I had labeled the packing cartons, but the movers had created stacks at least four boxes high, so it was a struggle to find the one I needed. To make things even more difficult, Iris Broadmoor's discards were intermingled with my treasures. I did own the blame for that. I hadn't thought to color-code the boxes. For the insanely organized person I am, I paused to scold myself for that obvious lapse in judgment.

The box I needed was at the bottom of the stack. As I carefully tugged the very old, crumbling top cardboard carton, it began to give way. I quickly wrapped my arms around the box, trying to cradle the remains.

Through holes in the disintegrating newspaper, I could see framed pictures. I gathered what was left in the dilapidated box and tucked the trash from the packing out of the way. Stacking the photos from big to small, I placed the pictorial pyramid outside the attic door. I couldn't see anything in the faint light of the swaying single bulb.

Finally locating my Bubble Wrapped brown antique transfer-ware, I descended the steep, narrow steps to the second floor and continued my journey down the much wider, and lovely, hand-hewed staircase to the first floor and into the kitchen. Then, after working my way back up the two flights of stairs, I collected the stack of photos.

Hmm…now, what do we have here? There were seven sepia-brown pictures of random sizes, but due to their unusual shape, the bottom four captured my attention. Resting the twelve-by-fourteen-inch photos on the kitchen table, I took a closer look. The family members were all dressed in what appeared to be their Sunday best with the Cape Hatteras Lighthouse in the background. *Funny,* I thought. *Sunday clothes and high-heeled shoes in the sand—my, how times have changed.* Most of the thin brown finishing paper had crumbled away, and rusty nails held the discolored tag-board backing in place. With the help of needle-nose pliers and thankful for my recent tetanus shot, I carefully removed enough brads to wiggle the photo free from the frame.

"Mr. and Mrs. Otis Cromwell with daughters Iris (13) and Olivia (10)—Cape Hatteras, NC—April 21, 1935" was written on the back of the picture. *Look at it back then,* I thought, *so close to the shore. Good thing the lighthouse was moved to safer ground. That length of coastline has earned its "Graveyard of the Atlantic" title.*

Engrossed in my find, I jumped when my cell phone rang. "How's my handsome husband!"

Nick chuckled. "Hey, babe. I just called to check on you. Is everything all right?"

"Everything's fine. Are you in Martha's Vineyard?"

"Yes. Jack and I got off the ferry about an hour ago. You sound funny. Is anything wrong?"

"No, but I owe you ten dollars. I made another trip to the attic searching for my transferware serving dishes and found some interesting pictures belonging to Iris Broadmoor."

"I have no idea what 'transferware' is—but for now, tell me about the pictures."

"I've only looked at one, but it shows Iris Cromwell—now Broadmoor—her sister, Olivia, along with their parents, at Cape Hatteras in 1935. Wait—just—a—minute!" I exclaimed. "Oh my gosh. Olivia—Olivia Cromwell. I know that name."

"Who?"

"For three years prior to my marriage to Parker, Olivia rented my house on Washington Street in Hadley Falls. You remember the old Victorian I sold after Parker left? Holy cats! I just realized, when Olivia moved out, she went to live at 528 Brook Street. Olivia and Iris are sisters. The plot thickens. I love the intrigue of attics—buried treasure and family secrets that perhaps date back to 1935."

Enthusiastically, Nick said, "The Rowdy Girls will have some fun with this during your sleepover tomorrow night. Is everyone coming? Is Coy having a stroke getting organized?"

"Yes, he is, and yes, everyone's coming. Coy brought in reinforcements—two of his cousins showed up yesterday as I was leaving for school. Those three men pruned shrubbery, limbed trees, and spread fresh mulch all around the barn and the house. I don't know where he found them, but there's now one Chippendale bench on either side of the barn doors. It's gorgeous around here."

"I can't wait to see it. I told Coy he had full rein to 'fancy things up' as he called it."

"He had a minor meltdown when your giant beast of a dog jumped right in the middle of the Liverpool water jump. Apparently, Caesar's romp in the standing muddy water ended with Coy having to wash the standards, the poles, and the dog."

"Oh no. But that Newfoundland does love the water, especially in this heat. I'll be home late Sunday afternoon. I miss you more than you know."

"Ditto! Before we hang up—how's Jack? What did the doctor say? Is Reagan there?"

"She came in yesterday and says she's not going to photograph any more horse shows—Jack will need her. The doctors gave him several options to prolong his life, but even that's only slightly. It's very sad, but I honestly think he's ready. The liver disease and failing kidneys are winning the battle. He's decided to let nature take its course."

"I'm so sorry." I sighed. "Give him my love, and Reagan, too. I can't wait for you to come home."

"Have a Rowdy Girls good time. I'll see you Sunday."

4

Friday afternoon I sat impatiently perched on the edge of one of the newly placed benches, watching for all five of my friends. "There they are!" I said to our dogs. The gravel in front of the barn crunched under the weight of my friends' truck tires as each rig pulled into the lot. Coy choreographed the parking

I smiled with delight. "Hi, guys!"

"Sarah, the farm looks beautiful!" Rose said, climbing out of Betsy's truck.

I glanced in Coy's direction. "Thanks, but I can't take any of the credit. This kind man and his band of elves have worked tirelessly this week to make Long Leaf Farm shine like a new penny."

Jennifer unclipped her horse from the interior crossties of Elizabeth's two horse trailer. "Well, it's paid off. I can't wait to ride in the morning."

"Let's get unloaded, and then we can look around," Margaret suggested, from the back of her slant load while lowering the ramp.

I was ecstatic to be backing Rascal off the trailer. "How's my best boy? Come on, you're going to love this barn." With all four hooves securely on the ground, Rascal took a minute to inhale the essence of this new place. He snorted and blew out but returned his head to normal as we walked along. Margaret's horse, Louie, followed close behind.

CR8O

With the feed, tack, and horses in place, we six walked along the path toward the back porch. "Your wedding was so beautiful in that garden," Margaret said, glancing over the three-foot pierced brick wall.

As I led the way up the back steps to the screened porch, I said, "It was, wasn't it? And made even better by you five surprising me and being my attendants."

"I'll never forget the look on your face when we appeared in your bedroom doorway with dresses in hand," Elizabeth said. "It was priceless."

I opened the kitchen door. "It was perfect!"

"Wow, Sarah! Something smells divine!" Rose said, gently waving her hand in the air, bringing the aroma closer.

Rose was a master cook, so a culinary compliment from her was always appreciated. "Thanks, but remember I'm back at school—so it's just chicken and mushrooms in the Crock-Pot, with wine and cream sauce."

Margaret placed her leafy treat beside my fancy macaroni and cheese—tonight's meat substitute. She was our vegetarian, and she also made the best spinach casserole you've ever devoured.

"Where shall I put the hors d'oeuvres?" Rose asked.

I pointed to the side table. "Over here would be great."

Elizabeth followed, resting her dessert beside Rose's appetizer.

Betsy and Jennifer added their contributions to the table, and we went to work preparing for our first dinner in my new-to-me house.

Our conversations were never short of a topic. Rose was holding something back about her most recent trip across the Atlantic, though, but wasn't quite ready to open up. Respectfully, we all yielded to her hesitance. We knew she'd spill the beans—all in good time.

Margaret shared some troublesome news about her horse, Louie. Her voice quivered like a tuning fork as she spoke. "The vet came this morning, and after some testing and X-rays, the results and diagnosis concerning his front right leg aren't good. Jacob said not to worry too much at this point and to just lighten his riding schedule for now."

Margaret gently wiped away a few tears, we all offered our heartfelt sympathies. Louie would be able to go for a long while yet, with just easier rides and good meds. But still, we all knew how hard it was when a horse started to decline.

Everyone asked about Nick and how things were going between us. I replied that it truly couldn't be better, partially thanks to my psychologist, Dr. Deborah Baxter. My visits began two years ago, when I was in full-on crisis over my divorce, but now our talks were more about the changes in the lives of my children and myself. Recently I began to question my reasons for going.

Betsy smiled. "Do you still have your hot pink folder? Are there to be more Dear Debby letters?"

"Absolutely on the letter question, but I think perhaps lime green for my newly married status." I paused for a second. "'Newly married'—does that sound ridiculous at the one year past the half century mark?"

"No. Don't be silly," Margaret insisted. "Besides, I'm also fifty-one, so feel free to drop the half-century reference, thank you!"

Rose lifted her eyebrows. "I want to hear about the honeymoon. Did you wear the fetching lingerie we gave you?"

Jennifer rolled her eyes. "I still insist fetching lingerie is not worth the price tag and nekked is hot. So, how was it?"

Blushing crimson, I said, "Scotland was beautiful, and the riding was amazing. The six of us should consider taking a trip there. I brought home some 'excursion package' brochures."

"You're dancing around the question," Margaret said, sipping her wine, "but as usual, your cheeks have given you away,"

"Well...is he still Mr. Wonderful?" Jennifer asked.

"Yes, and I'm just beyond happy, which I'll admit is a bit scary. You know, like it's a dream and I don't want to wake up?"

"We're thrilled for you, Sarah," Elizabeth said. "Now, let's have dessert."

Elizabeth was uncovering the cake when Betsy spied the stack of old pictures. "Sarah...what are these?"

"Oh, this is very interesting," I said, resting the pictorial stack on the corner of the kitchen table. "The other afternoon I was rummaging around in the attic, looking for things for tonight's dinner, and found these. Take a look."

Watching as I laid out the photos, Jennifer asked, "Who are these people?"

"I'll try to be quick, but you need a little background: I was a sophomore in college when my aunt Lucy died. I've mentioned her before—my dad's sister. She was single—we rode horses together at Grammy's farm, and she left me her old Victorian house on Washington Street?"

Frustrated, Betsy put her hands to her face. "I may shoot myself!

Yes, we remember—move along!"

"All right, all right, but do you also remember my telling you that, with my dad's encouragement, I used that house as rental property before I married Parker?"

"Again, yes," Margaret said impatiently.

"Okay, now hold on—my one and only renter was Olivia Cromwell, and there she is, ten years old, standing right beside her sister."

"Wow," Betsy said. "But how did these pictures get in the attic on Brook Street?"

"I don't know for sure, but it has something to do with Iris Broadmoor."

Jennifer moved around the table. "Who's Iris Broadmoor?"

I pointed to the older sister in the photos. "I bought 528 Brook Street from Mrs. Iris Broadmoor, and there she is!"

"Are you sure?" Elizabeth asked.

"Yes. When the sisters moved out, the attic remained piled high. I asked my Realtor about all that stuff, and her answer was: 'Iris said it was yours to do with as you please.' I knew her sister lived there too, but I didn't know her name was Olivia Cromwell."

"Holy Christmas!" Rose said. "What an interesting twist—talk about six degrees of separation. You actually knew everyone all along."

"It is an interesting twist." I shivered.

Standing beside me, Betsy started moving the photos around on the table. "Let's see if there is an order to these pictures."

"There is—look at the lighthouse. These four pictures were taken a handful of minutes apart. The Cromwell family piece is just ho-hum, but I find the middle ground very curious. The lady has just come out of the lighthouse, and the man is still in the doorway. Then, in the next two pictures, they're both walking quickly toward the parking lot. Now look at the final one. Her head is down as she's getting into the car. Y'all look and tell me what you think."

Stepping back from the group, I gave my friends time and space to examine the curious quartet.

Betsy's eyes moved back and forth. "In the first one, they're too far away to make out faces, but it's the same striped dress as the lady in the other three. And you're right, her posture doesn't reflect having had a wonderful day at the beach."

"If they were having an argument, surely someone would have heard," Rose said. "In the last one, they weren't too terribly far away."

Elizabeth pointed to the crashing waves. "It's high tide, and with that rough sea, it would have been difficult to hear."

"Let's take the backs off the other three pictures. There's writing on the first one, so there might be something hiding behind the others," Betsy suggested.

Margaret agreed, adding, "But why go to the expense of framing four pictures of the same thing?"

"They're the same topic, but the family is doing something different in each picture," I said, handing Margaret the pliers. "Maybe Mrs. Cromwell liked groupings of four, like Audubon's or botanicals—all birds or flowers, but each different in their own way."

Jennifer picked up the last picture in the group. "I'm leaning toward a series of four photos of a Cromwell family day at the beach. Hatteras is a public place with all sorts of visitors; I doubt they even knew those other two people."

"I want to know who took the pictures," Rose insisted.

"Good question," Betsy said. "Probably a tourist—a passerby who just happened to catch the other two people as well."

Elizabeth nodded. "I agree. From the four different angles and to get the lighthouse in each photo, those two would also be in every frame."

When Margaret removed the final piece of cardboard, there was a piece of newspaper stuck to the back of the picture. "Look at this!" Margaret said, carefully peeling it away and reading aloud.

HADLEY FALLS HERALD—TUESDAY, APRIL 23, 1935
PROMINENT DOCTOR'S WIFE DISAPPEARS

Mrs. Lilith Carter Wentworth was last seen Sunday, April 21, at the First Presbyterian Church in Hadley Falls. She was wearing a navy blue and white striped dress, navy shoes, and a red straw hat. Lilith is five feet six inches tall, medium-length light brown curly hair, and was slight of frame.

If anyone has any information concerning her possible where-abouts, please contact the Hadley Falls Police Department. Your tips can remain anonymous.

"Well, that changes the complexion of the whole thing!" I said.

"Why do you say that?" Margaret asked.

I pointed to the lady. "Because Lilith is described as wearing a navy blue and white striped dress. In a sepia-tone picture, that pattern would come off as a light beside a dark. So, ta-da—there she is! The newspaper article was printed forty-eight hours later, but these pictures were taken the day of her disappearance. I'll bet you dimes to doughnuts the Cromwell sisters don't have a clue about this. They were young girls in 1935, and I doubt they read the newspaper at that age. So for some reason, one or both of their parents put the article behind this picture."

Margaret glanced at the article. "*Disappearance*—that's what the Hadley Falls police called it and what the newspaper printed, but I think she just simply left town, and with that man."

"I'm too curious for my own good, and my imagination occasionally clouds my better judgment. But I need to know the real story, and there's only one way to find out," I said, restacking the pictures. "I need to locate the sisters and see if they know anything about this. I'll work on it, starting Monday. When I get an address, who wants to go with me?"

Margaret spoke up immediately. "I'm sure we all do, but Agnes Anne is on vacation for two weeks, so I have to work all day, every day, Monday through Saturday. Sarah, I can only ride on Sunday afternoon."

"I have two weddings to cater—one being the Alberts' 'got rocks' affair," Jennifer said with a sparkle in her eye.

Betsy wiped her dusty hands. "I wouldn't miss this for the world. Let me know when you find out where they are. If they're close, we can go visit—hopefully next Saturday or Sunday. I hope they're still living and remember this."

Rose clapped her hands together with excitement. "I'll host the next dinner, and we can listen to what you found out together. We'll give you two weeks—three tops—to get the scoop. Modern technology can be a wonderful thing."

"Awesome, and perhaps then you'll be ready to tell us all about your most recent trip to London?" I suggested.

Taking a sip of her wine and a deep breath, Rose said, "Perhaps."

"Who wants cake?" Elizabeth cried, setting out the plates. Five hands flew into the air, and it was back to fun as usual.

5

Nick pulled in late Sunday afternoon, looking emotionally and physically exhausted from his visit with his brother. I helped him with his things as our dogs bounded their way to the back porch. Before taking the first step, Nick turned to me. His hug lifted me off the ground, and the kiss that followed was passionately tender. "You're never allowed to die! It's just too awful what's happening to Jack."

I looked at him lovingly. "I promise to hang around as long as I possibly can. This has been very difficult, hasn't it?"

"Difficult isn't the word. You know what troubles me most?"

"Tell me."

He rubbed his brow. "That my brother and I wasted decades disliking each other over idiotic stuff. Now here we are—Jack already looks so gray and hollow—and it won't be an easy time going forward."

I sighed. "Let's get you inside," I said.

He set his bag at the doorway to the hall. "God, I missed you. Hey, I realized on the flight home I forgot to ask what Rascal thought of our farm."

"He was perfect as always, but, man, was it hard to walk him back onto Margaret's rig. The tears streamed down my cheeks until the trailer disappeared."

"I know, but he's with his best friend," Nick said, glancing over

29

at the side table and the stack of antique photos. "What's all of that?"

"Oh, it's Exhibit A in the puzzling Sunday-afternoon family visit to Cape Hatteras—the possible connection with Lilith Wentworth, the newspaper article, and Miss Olivia Cromwell."

Nick uncorked a bottle of merlot. "That's right—I forgot about your attic discovery. Tell me all about it and your Rowdy Girls sleepover."

"Where to start?" I said, handing him a wineglass. "First, we need to have an electrician work on some lights in the attic before that exposed wire burns the house down. But the dinner and sleepover were so fun, and the morning ride was even better. Especially since I had Rascal! Everyone was very complimentary of the farm, and Coy beamed with pride. After our ring work, we took a trail ride out to the creek, and no one wanted to head back."

"I spoke with Coy yesterday; I could tell he was proud of his efforts."

"He should be." I nodded. "Oh—Margaret's positive that this house is haunted because she hears creaking floors when no one's walking around. I told her they've always creaked, to which she replied: 'Duh, you live in a haunted house.' We don't, do we? I mean the floors do squeak when no one's walking up the stairs."

Filling his glass, Nick chuckled. "No. Well, maybe. Don't look like that. I'm just kidding. Besides, ghosts are very selective. They seem to like creepy abandoned hotels, the run-down house on the corner with a rusty wrought-iron fence, or third-generation farmhouses with a family cemetery. The floors creak because our house is two hundred years old. Now, tell me about the pictures."

"Well, okay, but if it's a woman, I wish she'd learn to vacuum."

I winked at him. "Back to Olivia Cromwell. I'm calling it a mystery because of the middle ground—perhaps curiosity is a better word. Clearly the woman in the striped dress is Lilith Wentworth, but it's equally obvious that something untoward is going on. The icing on the cake is the newspaper article. Why is it there?" I said, arranging the photos for him to see.

Nick studied all four as I explained the collective theory of the Rowdy Girls. We agreed that one or both of the parents obviously knew something about the mystery people in the photo—but what?

"Betsy and I are going to visit the sisters if I can find them," I said, watching as Nick's face changed expressions.

"That could make for an interesting day." He nodded, taking a deep breath. "I think I can tell you about Jack now without breaking down. He and Reagan have already made all the arrangements for the inevitable—he's going to be cremated. There will be a very small service at Saint Elizabeth's on the island. We promised to call at least once a week going forward." His voice broke.

Taking his hands in mine, I said, "Good idea. I think it's wonderful that they're tending to things ahead of time."

"It will take a while for all of this to sink in." Nick sighed.

"I understand. Now, dinner's in thirty minutes; here's the ten dollars I owe you for going into the attic before October," I said, laying a Hamilton on the kitchen table.

"Thanks, but I have a better way to collect on our bet." My husband stood and pushed in his chair, collecting his suitcase.

"Shameful," I said as he walked away.

"And you love it!"

"Perhaps." I giggled.

6

September 8, 2010, was my first "newly married" session with Dr. Deborah Baxter. Taking my usual seat in the cozy corner of the beige tuxedo sofa, I brought a lime green folder out of my tote bag. Dr. Baxter took her multicolored reading glasses from the end table and began to review my letter to her. We had used this tool from the beginning. Writing a letter to her helped me organize my thoughts of the issues I wanted to address.

Our discussion started with Nick's reaction to his rearranged closet.

Dr. Baxter folded her hands. "Sarah, you need to remember that while Nick was once married, he has also been a bachelor for decades since."

"You're right. I know, but sometimes I just forget that my way is not the *only* way. I am happy to say that we're truly finding our *just us* path. Little things, like sharing space or giving each other room to breathe, making decisions together. I'm finding it easier now to let go of being so territorial."

"I'm proud of you for your personal insight. Be careful not to fall back into the dark days of zero trust."

"Absolutely," I agreed. "Oh, this is interesting. I realized the other day that I continue to function as if I still lived in the city."

"How so?"

I chuckled. "I still lock my car even though the farm is miles from another neighbor, and I leave the front door locked and bolted all the time. I read too many murder mysteries—you know, murder in the hayloft."

Dr. Baxter nodded. "Safety issues not unlike the attic light. Let's talk about that."

Our conversation wound in and out of that and additional concerns. I felt lighter leaving her office.

It was truly great to see her again, but walking to my car, I experienced a strange feeling. I'd enjoyed our visit, but that was what it was—a visit, not a necessity.

CR8O

Driving down our lane after my appointment, I could see Nick at the barn.

"Hi, darlin'. Come on down," he yelled.

I locked my car. *Funny*, I thought. *I did it again.* As I rested my purse on the porch steps, Annie greeted me with a wiggle and a huge lick. She was without question the most loving dog alive. "Hi, my sweet girl. Where's your cohort in crime and grime?" I asked, walking toward the barn—knowing Nick could hear me.

In the blink of an eye, Caesar appeared, running full throttle. His joy for life always made me laugh. "You are a funny dog." Caesar pressed against my leg, and I wiggled my fingers in the curly black fur on the top of his head.

"He loves you very much." Nick smiled. "How was your day?"

"I love him too. My day went well. My students are getting back into the swing of things and working hard. And it was great to see Dr. Baxter—it's been a while."

Nick's brow furrowed, his brilliant blue eyes darting back and forth, "I know I'm not supposed to ask," he said, "but is everything okay? You know—with us? You have to tell me if things aren't good."

"Everything's fine—no, better than fine. And yes, I would tell you if something was wrong. I don't understand why everyone assumes life is down the rathole when a person seeks counseling. Couldn't it be that things are very right, and that needs discussion? Especially for a person who's always waiting for the other shoe to drop."

"I never thought about it that way—and yes, I guess it could. But you have to swear you'll talk to me if something starts to go sideways."

"I promise. Talking with Dr. Baxter just allows me to take a step back and see the big picture. Now, speaking of pictures—Betsy and I are going to Lazy Willow Senior Living Center next Sunday morning. I spoke with Iris today."

Nick's mouth dropped open. "You and Betsy...the sisters—the photos? Just promise you'll not give them a heart attack. And what did you say to Iris? Did she respond?"

"I reminded her of who I was and that I wanted to discuss her part of our attic. And yes, I'll be tactful. Oh, Iris answered with a cautious 'all right,'" I said. "How much longer will you be down here? I need to know for dinner purposes."

"I'm right behind you. Oh, Linda and Nancy cornered me today about the hunter pace in November and how that's the anniversary of the day you and I met. I do believe women can make any day the anniversary of something. But what do you think about a reenact-ment of sorts? Rascal is still fit enough to go, and you said Margaret's horse isn't out to pasture—so what'd you say about the six of you and the three of us going together?"

I gave his arm a squeeze. "I say hoorah—that would be so fun! Let me text Margaret and see if she thinks Louie can make the trip."

"The best part of this year's competition is that I get to take you to bed when we get home." Nick winked, reaching for my hand. "Last time I had to wait forever."

I felt the heat rush to my face. "Well, Mr. Heart, was it worth the wait?"

"Completely."

"That was such a wonderful day. You were the most handsome man I'd ever seen in your red hunt coat and those gorgeous blue eyes of yours. I almost fell off my horse when you pulled your horse beside mine at the halfway mark. For one brief moment, I was sixteen all over again, and you, my love, were the class dreamboat!"

He laughed. "Dreamboat, eh? I'll take it! I knew the minute I saw you that you were the one."

"Oh, you did not, but I'm glad you made the first move."

"I did indeed. I came to your house the next night. I never gave up, and here we are. So, what does that tell you?"

I pulled him into a kiss. "That I'm a lucky girl!"

7.

Driving due east, down that pencil-straight highway, elevated just five feet above the brackish water, the endless miles of pine forest planted with military precision gave way to dense stands of cattails and the occasional egret. Realizing we were getting closer to the marshlands, Betsy and I rehearsed how our conversation with the sisters might go. With each scenario we became more nervous: how soon would our carefully scripted narrative be reduced to rubble?

This was a strange thing for us to be doing, and that was saying something. Serious finesse would be required to ease into why we were so interested in the pictures. We decided to leave the newspaper clipping out of the equation. After all, they were just children in 1935. We saw no need to point fingers at possible wrongdoings or perhaps tarnishing memories. We simply wanted to know if there was a connection.

We took the final turn onto Creek Side Drive and were greeted by Coastal Carolina at its best. The opposing semicircular stonewalls, with carriage lamps on either end, were the backdrop for a beautifully manicured entrance, full of azaleas, three weeping willows on each side, and a thick border of variegated liriope adding the finishing touch.

Driving beneath an interlocking canopy of giant live oaks, we could see the main house of the Lazy Willow Senior Living Center. It was a beautiful two-story clapboard structure with towering white columns, double chimneys on each end, Essex Green shutters and doors, with a four-sided wraparound porch both up-and downstairs. I slowed down before turning into the parking area so we could read the National Registry of Historical Places plaque: Home of Oliver Q. Banesbury State Representative in the House of Commons. Construction Completed in 1812.

Betsy sat transfixed. "Wow. It's beautiful."

"It is! They did a wonderful job adding those two wings. How smart to have them come off the back corners of the main house. I'm guessing those are the residents' apartments, with maybe a 'great room' in the back adjoining the two. I wonder who owns it."

"I read somewhere that the house and all the property were purchased years ago by some medical conglomerate," Betsy answered. "These old homes are so expensive to maintain, and this place is in east Jesus nowhere. I imagine whoever held the deed deposited the check before the ink was dry. Now, you do all the talking, and I'll be your moral support."

Putting the car in park, I said, "Okay, but if I get in a bind, you have to swear to help me out."

"Deal. Remember, go slowly and give them time to think and digest."

CﾒꙏꙎꙘꙚ

Standing behind an enormous cherry desk with ornately carved legs, the receptionist offered a thick-enough-to-spread-on-toast Southern, "Good Morning. I'm Karen, and welcome. How may I help you ladies today?"

"Morning. My name is Sarah Heart, and this is my friend Betsy. We have an appointment to visit with Iris Broadmoor and her sister, Olivia."

"Yes, they're expecting you. Follow me, please." Walking down the long central hall and stopping just short of the double doorway to the sunroom, our bubbly guide pointed. "Aren't they just too cute?"

I looked in the direction of Karen's extended arm. There they were, spitting images of each other, and just as suggested, absolutely too cute! Both silver-haired seniors, one dressed in soft pink and the other in lavender, rested deeply on matching wicker armchairs with fluffy chintz pillows at their backs.

Juggling the four pictures, I took the first steps in their direction. "Hello. My name is Sarah Sams Heart. We spoke the other day. I'm the woman who bought your house on Brook Street in Hadley Falls."

"Nice to see you again." Iris nodded, glancing in Betsy's direction. "I don't think I know you, however."

"Oh gosh, where are my manners? This is my dear friend Betsy Henderson."

With a slightly gruff tone, Iris said, "I imagine she can speak for herself."

"Yes, she can," I said, placing the pictures on the oversize rattan coffee table and offering a short synopsis concerning the reason for our visit. One at a time they studied and then passed each of the framed photos to the other.

I pointed to the man and the woman in the striped dress. "I know you recognize your family, but do you know either of these people? I could never dispose of any of your family things without asking you first."

Olivia looked up from the photo she was holding and back over at me. "For some reason I think I know you, or at least your name."

"Yes, ma'am, you do. You rented my house on Washington Street over thirty years ago. My father, Russell O'Neil, handled that property for me while I was in college. You moved to Brook Street when my first husband and I got married."

"That's right, I remember your father—very nice man. He always gave me a fit for paying in cash. I thought it belonged to him, but you say it was your house?"

"Yes, ma'am." I smiled.

"Oh," Olivia said, slowly nodding. "You said first husband—do you have another husband now?"

"I do, and that's how I found these pictures. When we got married—"

Olivia interjected. "For the second time."

"Correct. I sold the house on Brook Street and moved everything to his farm in Greenway."

Olivia was obviously still working on the Washington Street information. "Was your first husband that man who mowed yards and left town with the woman chiropractor?"

"Olivia!" Iris exclaimed, sitting timber straight. "Don't be rude."

"I'm just trying to get my mind organized. So, was he?"

Again I answered in the affirmative.

Thankfully, Betsy jumped in and steered us back to the original question. "Look how young you two were when these pictures were taken. And do you know these other folks?"

With an expression I couldn't quite define, Iris took the reins. "Look, Sister. It's Aunt Lily and Uncle Otto. They look like they're having a fuss, but, then, they did that a lot."

Iris pointed to the man. "Before they were married, Uncle Otto, our father's older brother, lived over in Hatter's Corner above his livery stable—he was the best blacksmith around. I believe Aunt Lily was from closer to Hadley Falls. But gracious, that was so long ago, I really don't remember. For a while we'd visit them once or twice a year in West Virginia. Now, what was the name of that town? Olivia, do you remember?"

"No, but I do remember I hated going," Olivia said, wrapping her cardigan more closely around her and looking for the draft. "It was a very long drive and nothing to do while we were there. Our aunt Lily was a terrible cook and tried to make out like she came from tall cotton, which was funny since they lived in some old rundown hillbilly shack stuck on the side of a mountain. I don't think they even had running water."

Iris fidgeted her hands. "Olivia, you're not being kind, but our aunt did put on airs. They had one boy, Stanley, who was terribly shy. Maybe it was just because he was so much younger than the two of us. We stopped going to visit after a while, but we never knew why."

Understanding we had exhausted that line of conversation, I decided to plot a new course.

"How interesting. Did your family always live in Hadley Falls?" I asked.

Iris cleared her throat. "Yes. Daddy was the foreman at the lumber plant, but he got hurt real bad and couldn't work after the accident. Back in those days, doctors made house calls. Mama said old Doc

Wentworth came over to our house almost every week for a while. Olivia and I had moved away from home when Daddy got hurt."

Making big eyes, Olivia announced, "Iris was a child bride."

"I was not! I was almost twenty-one when Douglas and I got married—he enlisted in the Marines a few months later. Olivia was in college studying music, and Douglas and I lived in Manteo. He died serving in the Pacific in 1942."

"I'm so sorry," Betsy said. "Where did your parents live in Hadley Falls?"

Unclasping her hands, Iris answered quickly, "You know we grew up in the house on Brook Street."

Flabbergasted, I said, "Really?"

"Yes. After Mama passed, I moved in to help take care of Daddy and just never left. Like I said, my husband was gone, and it just made sense. I sold my house with everything in it and said goodbye to Roanoke Island. The Brook Street attic was full of our parents' belongings, not ours. What would we do with all that stuff anyway. These apartments are too small for much. If you find something you want, it's yours for the taking—or sell it if it's worth anything."

After a good while, Betsy and I announced we needed to be heading home but that we'd enjoyed our visit immensely. The sisters asked that we come again whenever we could, and they appreciated seeing the pictures. Betsy and I assured them we would schedule another visit, and we honestly meant to try.

Before backing out of the parking space, I said, "I love that Olivia Cromwell. What a hoot! But did you notice that Iris was uneasy? For some reason, I think she knows more about this than she's letting on."

Betsy started laughing, which was her way of releasing tension.

"So now we have a general idea of the story: the lady captured in the four pictures is Lilith Wentworth, who was also their aunt Lily. They recognized her and their uncle Otto right off. And yes, Iris was very careful with her words, but maybe that's just her way."

"Perhaps, but I think she's hiding something. Aunt Lily ran off with Otto while still married to Dr. Wentworth. In fact, I think Iris knows that Lilith Wentworth is Aunt Lily, but Olivia has always been in the dark. Remember the newspaper article was hidden behind the picture."

Betsy looked in my direction. "But it had never been removed, so how would Iris know anything?"

"I have no clue, but I'm certain she does. I also don't think we can let this cat out of the bag just yet."

"I need a strong cup of coffee," Betsy said.

"There's a McDonald's just after we get on the highway. I could use a Diet Coke myself."

Offering me a cookie, she said, "I wonder what happened to Dr. Wentworth."

"Me too. Did he continue looking for his wife, or did he figure out what happened? Now what do we do?"

"More research. Like Rose said, the whole world's online these days," Betsy offered. "The more I think about it, the more I agree with you that Iris is privy to information she chooses not to share."

"For sure, but Olivia seems innocent."

As I drove, I disappeared into some internal thoughts. I was determined to find out what Iris was hiding—though I wasn't sure how. I also had an idea: *This would make a great book. Four interesting pictures…two aging sisters…shady family past. It's a start.*

8

Nick was walking up from the barn when Betsy and I pulled in. "Well, how are the two girl detectives?"

"Hi, Nick," Betsy said. "It's great to see you. Sorry to be in such a hurry. I need a glass of wine and Frank's ear. Oh, and we had such a wonderful time the other weekend boarding our horses here. Everything about this property is heavenly. Sarah, I'll call you tomorrow on your way to school."

Nick opened Betsy's car door. "Thanks, and say hello to Frank for me."

I waved goodbye as she drove down the lane.

"So, it was an interesting visit?" my husband asked.

"Yes. I'm beyond starving. Have you had lunch?"

"I got so busy with paperwork, I forgot to eat."

By the time we finished the last crumb of our sandwiches, I had gone over the course of events.

Pushing back in his chair, he said, "Wow! Interesting stuff."

"I know, seriously, but I need to find the few missing pieces. It'll drive me crazy until I have the entire story."

"When you do have everything, what's your plan?"

I fiddled nervously with my napkin. "Now, don't laugh, but on our way home, I couldn't stop thinking about Olivia, Iris, and our

43

conversation." I paused. "I'm seriously thinking about writing a novel—*Whatever Happened to Lilith?* Or something like that. What do you think?"

Nick smiled. "It'll be a bestseller."

"I'm serious."

"So am I, and sorry for repeating myself, but remember, it's possible a few people still living in Hadley Falls might know who you're writing about."

"True. Very true. But that makes it more of a challenge. And with fiction you can make it turn out any way you want. The true story is my inspiration, but my imagination would write the book. Before fully embracing this project, I need for you to understand something."

He tilted his head. "I'm listening."

"Because I've written two books already, I know it's not an easy task. There's mapping out a story line, writing the first draft, several rounds of edits, and so on. To do it, I'll need to work after school and on the weekends. So I won't always be available, and dinner will be late or possibly nonexistent. Are you sure you can handle that?"

"Yes, but you won't forget about me—or us—will you?"

I squeezed my husband's hand. "I'd never do that. But this will be a new chapter for me. An exciting one. My other books are nonfiction, so I was working from factual information and not weaving a tapestry of make-believe. For now I would also keep this from everyone but you, Betsy, and Margaret."

"Why?"

"Because I don't even have a story map laid out. Plus, you have no idea how hard it is to actually get published. Finding an agent is insanely difficult, and then, if I do get one, there's no guarantee I'd even get a publisher. So it would just be better if this project remains our secret—no, 'private' is a better word—for now anyway."

Nick winked. "I'm excited you're going to give it a try. I'm assuming here, but if the main character in the book has a husband, perhaps he could be a dashing horseman? And if so, I could help you choose his name…"

"Perhaps," I said clearing the table. "What would it be?"

"I'm not sure. I'll give it some thought. But they need to be very passionate, *and* he needs to be a nice guy."

"See, it's already happening. I haven't even started, and you're causing trouble." I laughed, giving Nick a flyby kiss on my way to my computer.

9.

Betsy's name lit up on my phone. "Hi there. So, what did Frank say when you told him about our day?"

"He agrees we should be very careful with our can of worms. How about Nick?"

"Pretty much the same thing, but I do have something I need to tell you in person. Could I drop by after school?"

Clearing her throat, Betsy said, "Of course, but it will drive me crazy not knowing until then. Give me a hint?"

"No, but it's nothing bad. In fact, it's pretty exciting. Now I have to go—my lunchtime is almost over, and I have to cut paper for my two afternoon classes—it's their introduction to Origami."

"Ooh, I love Japanese art."

Holding my phone between my left ear and shoulder, I said, "Me too. Origami is a good icebreaker for the ninth graders and an excellent opportunity for me to see what they learned in middle school. See you in a few hours."

☙❧

After a full day of academics and adolescents, I turned into Betsy's driveway and could see her in the aisle of her barn. "Hey," I shouted, waving my arm.

"Come on out." Betsy motioned for me to join her.

"Are we alone?" I asked, walking through the doorway of her barn.

Balancing the wheelbarrow stacked high with hay, she said, "Yes. Give me a minute to finish this, and we'll go to the kitchen." Walking down the freshly cut grassy path back to the house, she asked, "Want a cup of tea?"

"Yum."

A few minutes later, Betsy handed me my mug and sat down across from me. "Now, what's going on?"

"Okay, here it is: I've been inspired by Lilith's story to write a novel. As you've said many times before, I can make a good story about even a trip to the bathroom. So imagine what I could do with this one. I'm so excited I could wet my pants—no pun intended."

Betsy warmed her hands around her mug. "Hey, that's a wonderful idea. I'm sure I don't need to tell you to invent a fictitious town, characters with different names, and all the rest, do I?"

"No, and that's the exciting part. I started working on it today—just putting some story ideas on index cards. The setting will be in the eastern part of North Carolina. I'm still going to use Cape Hatteras Lighthouse—it's nationally known, and thanks to pirates and sunken treasure, it has always been surrounded by more than a whisper of mystery. Plus, besides 'the sisters' and us, no one living has ever seen the pictures. In my story, the two people in the middle ground are thought not to be related to the family, but that has a dramatic twist later."

I pulled my chair closer to the table. "Remember, this story line is still in the embryonic stage of development, but here's my idea so far: the 'sisterhood' of six—all of whom ride horses—are on a weekend trip to Southern Pines. I could have them play tennis I guess, but horses are very romantic. Anyway, over dinner, our narrator shares having discovered a set of four framed photos in her attic.

"The photographed family is not the curiosity, but the man and woman in the middle ground are. I'm considering espionage or murder for them. My invented version of Olivia has several options, but I'm leaning toward a retired chemist and apparently the only remaining link to the truth. All of this will change many times over, though, as I write.

"But here's the hardest part—for now, absolutely no one besides you can know I'm working on this."

We were alone in her house, but Betsy leaned in and whispered, "Why not?"

"Mainly because I want to make sure I can protect the Cromwell sisters' family past from taking a ride on the Hadley Falls gossip train. That news would travel faster than a nasty rash, and to my way of thinking, it would be disastrous. And what if my story never makes it to the shelves?"

Betsy rested her mug on the table. "I understand 'disastrous' about the sisters, but why a secret that you're writing a book?"

"I'd rather use the word 'private,' and it's just for now. It's sort of like not sharing the news of your pregnancy until after the first trimester. I need to get my story line mapped out, some research completed, and a few chapters written—then I'll know if it's worth pursuing. I'm not egotistical enough to think anyone really cares, but you know I'd rather go to my quiet place and work it all out by myself first."

"That's fair. I think it's very exciting. Wait a minute—you already have a publisher."

"Yes, but she only publishes nonfiction how-to books—not novels. So I'll have to start from scratch and find an agent. They get a percentage of your earnings, but they're the ones who can get your manuscript through the door of publishing houses. But again, the story has to be good enough and different enough to catch their eye."

"You can do it," Betsy insisted. "Take what you know from our visit, the pictures, and the newspaper article, and just run with it. So, how much of this do we share next week when we go to Rose's house for dinner?"

"Nothing about the possible book, but lots about Lazy Willow Senior Living Center. Zero about Lily and Otto—major hush-hush! What do you think?"

Betsy lifted her corgi Olive, or Olive Oyl, as she called her, onto her lap. "Maybe add how funny they were with their banter and that they grew up in the house on Brook Street. Otherwise, it looks like there was no conversation at all. If anyone's suspicious, it'll be Margaret and Rose."

"We can create a great diversion by asking Rose about her last trip to London. I wonder what Rose is cooking."

"Rack of lamb," Betsy said, returning her dog to the floor and taking our mugs to the sink.

"Oh, she makes the best lamb I've ever eaten, but that drives Margaret around the bend. You know, the consumption of baby animals. Or live lobsters reaching for the sky from a pot of boiling water. Would it cause upset if you asked Rose to make her killer vegetarian lasagna?"

"I'll mention it; she's coming over to ride around five this afternoon."

"I'm out of here, then. Off to write! And remember, mum's the word. I'll talk to you tomorrow." And with that I was on my way home to draft the first chapter, maybe two, of my new adventure.

10

Back at home, I grabbed a hammer and tacks from the kitchen drawer and went straight to my office. The repurposed, two-hundred-year-old large butler's pantry just off from the kitchen was home to my computer, and a slight whisper of silver polish and cherry pipe tobacco continued to fill the air. Using the back twelve-foot wall and starting three feet below the thick dentil crown molding, I hung the four pictures in a vertical row, creating my wall of inspiration.

"Okay, Annie," I said, rubbing her velvety ears between my fingers. "You've helped me before, but this is different: book number three is novel number one. We get to invent a story this time."

Annie flopped down on the floor beside my desk chair as I began to type. She was an excellent listener, but Caesar sat looking straight into my eyes. "No barking, big guy. It breaks my train of thought. Now lie down and listen while I read you a story." Caesar stretched out next to Annie, his back feet spilling out into the hall.

As I explained the finer points of a "working title," Annie thumped her tail and Caesar let out a bark that could crack the plaster. "Quiet now—here we go."

☙

The Disappearance of Lucy Butterfield
"Hmm. That's not bad. We can change it later if we think of something better."

I went on to type:

Chapter One

It was an unusually cool Sunday morning for early May, but Mrs. Lucy Butterfield didn't mind. Two months earlier, she had driven herself to Raleigh to shop for several new spring outfits with all the trimmings. She had already worn her Easter Sunday ensemble, which earned her rave reviews, but this one was even more special. As was the style, she wore a hat, and this was the perfect one: pink straw with flowers all around the brim. Though she had no children, it was the pièce de résistance for her Mother's Day dress of deep rose with white polka dots.

After a bit more work and using my notes from the other day, I'd written about five pages. I pressed save, then stretched and pushed back from my computer. "That's a pretty good start, I think." I rubbed Annie's head. "I'm starving. What time do you think it is?"

"It's seven thirty," Nick answered from the den diagonally across the hall. "I hope the past few hours have been successful, but I may pass out if we don't have dinner soon. Would you like to go out to eat?"

"Oh gosh. I didn't hear you come in from the barn," I apologized, rolling my chair back and looking across the hall. "And yes. How about Zorba's in Hadley Falls? We haven't been there in ages."

"Great idea. Grab a sweater, and I'll go tell Coy we're going out," Nick said, walking into the kitchen and grabbing a banana.

"Okay. Meet you in the car."

Zorba the Greek was on the river in Hadley Falls and one of my favorite restaurants. I loved the informal, come-as-you-are atmosphere—not to mention the delicious Mediterranean cuisine. It was also where Nick and I had our first "just us" date. I tried to think if we had been there since but came up short. I did, however, vividly remember that entire evening.

Nick slid into the driver's seat. "Why are you giggling?"

"Zorba's. Do you remember our first real date?"

"Let me think…Do you mean the fact that your youngest daughter came to check me out, you had on that killer new outfit you bought with your best friends and your purchase of matching underwear?"

"Yes. I nearly died of embarrassment when you asked about that, but it was a wonderful first date."

"It was, except for Sidney giving us a curfew. Oh yes—and the interrogation I got from her afterward."

"That was so sweet of my girls to make sure their mother wasn't in harm's way."

"I agree, but it also destroyed my one glimmer of hope to actually see the matching underwear." Nick laughed.

"Nicholas F. Heart!"

"What?" he asked bashful like, as we pulled into the restaurant parking-lot.

☙❦

Over plates of moussaka and grilled lamb, we talked about Nick's upcoming two-week real estate trip to Pennsylvania in early October, which gracefully flowed into my discussion about my writing. "I got lost in my thoughts tonight. Remember I told you that might happen. But while you're away closing the deal on that piece of property, I can make great headway on the book."

"Please know that while you've spoiled me with your amazing cooking and all the rest, I can fend for myself—and feed you, too, for that matter. Just let me know when you're deep in thought, and I'll spread the peanut butter and open a can of soup."

"Thank you...Much appreciated," I said, reaching out to give his hand a squeeze. "We can make this work. Many writers go into seclusion for months. I don't anticipate needing that, but sometimes I'll sort of disappear right in our own home. Are you sure you can handle this?"

"I'm sure," he said. "Now how about some dessert?"

"Absolutely and thanks again for the treat of dinner out. This has been a very long day."

Nick asked our server for the check when she delivered our shared slice of cake.

☙❦

Once home, we let the dogs out and did a night check at the barn, dropping the last flake of hay for the night and topping off the water buckets.

"I'm spent. The hay man is coming in the morning, so I can't sleep late," Nick said.

"I'm tired too. We have a teacher's breakfast tomorrow. It's a ploy of some sort to soften the blow for something we'll all hate."

I was first under the covers.

Turning off the light and rolling over to kiss me good night, Nick said, "Sarah Heart, where's your nightgown?"

"On the floor. I need to do some research for my book if you have the time. Consider it inspiration for your 'make us passionate in the book' request."

Later, slightly winded, Nick flopped back on his pillow. "I absolutely love helping you research. Your guilt for neglecting me might just finish me off, but what a way to go."

"Nicholas!"

Pulling me closer, he said, "What?"

"I thought you said you were tired."

"Yes, but I've somehow been revived."

"You are absolutely shameful!"

"Thank you." He laughed.

11

The core of our gleaming white barn had stood strong for more than two hundred years. Over time additions had been made, including the indoor ring, which came off one side of the central barn. Nick and I had been working together on plans to enlarge that square footage, creating a more usable space, which would attract additional boarders and, in turn, pay for itself over time. But because it was a listed property on the National Register of Historic Places, we were required to submit drawings to their board for final approval. Between the two of us, we decided to just call them the Historic Registry when talking about our quest for approval.

Together we drew out a rough draft with measurements. I found some pictures and ideas in a barn plan book I'd had for years, and that information was added to the paper pile. Ed the architect was scheduled to come late Friday afternoon, but I would be at Rose's house for dinner. Nick said it gave him something to do while I was with the Rowdy Girls. I also think he wanted to talk it over with Ed, tool belt to tool belt.

CR8O

Rose's home was avant-garde in design, with angles in strange places, tall ceilings, and a multitude of towering windows. She had original pieces of art hanging on the walls and antiques everywhere, most of which were purchased on her frequent trips to England and France. Rose's sister, Eloise, was an antique dealer in London and owned a trendy shop on Portobello Road.

Walking into the foyer, I always felt as if a docent should be standing at the ready to take my ticket and lead me on a tour. The indoor atrium was just off from the dining room, where statuary rested quietly on the slate floor, poking their heads in and out of towering trees, ferns of all varieties, and orchids in bloom year-round.

I could smell the lasagna two steps from the front door. Letting myself in with hors d'oeuvres in hand, I walked into the kitchen and was greeted by Betsy, Rose, and Margaret. I apologized for being ten minutes late—I'd miscalculated the distance from my new house. Jennifer and Elizabeth were running behind, as always, so I wasn't dragging up the rear.

Because of the warmth, laughter, and fellowship, there's little to compare with a Rowdy Girls dinner. We'd earned the accolade—and the plaque to prove it—on our second year at horse camp. For seven years now we had gone to Moss Creek Farm in the rolling hills of Virginia for the third week in June. The owner of MCF, Susan Tillman, suggested we try out a new Western-style steakhouse that had just recently opened. So, breaking our own rule of going straight to bed on the first night, we went out for dinner. Unbeknownst to us, it was also ladies' night. This included all-you-can-eat nachos, $1.00 beers, and the opportunity to compete for bragging rights of conquering the mechanical bull.

When asked about the event, our server, with her tone and facial expression, suggested we were perhaps too old and sissified to actually give it a try. That's all it took—standing six abreast at the bar area corral, we each took a turn and were triumphant in that no one fell off.

To this day I think the young man running the controls gave us a break. But we walked away with the hand-carved, ready-to-hang signage announcing we were the "Rowdy Girls."

We treasured our title, especially since none of us was wild or rowdy, at least not since turning thirty.

Over dinner, I brought up participating in the November hunter pace. It was one of our favorite places to ride and not too far from home. "Remember our two boarders—Linda and Nancy? They thought it would be fun if the nine of us could go together to celebrate the day Nick and I met."

"How precious," Rose said, then added, "I'm sorry, Sarah. That sounded terribly sarcastic, which was not my intent."

"It is a little cheesy, isn't it, but we'll have fun. Now, who's in?" I asked.

Jennifer cheered. "We are. In, fact Elizabeth and I printed out all the entry forms before coming to dinner."

Elizabeth pulled an envelope out of her oversize Tory Burch bag and handed each of us a form and a pen.

Sliding plates to one side, we went to work filling in the blanks. "I'll write one check to cover us all and mail them out tomorrow," Betsy offered. "You can pay me later."

From across the table, Margaret asked, "Sarah, are you riding with us, or with Nick, Linda, and Nancy?"

"With you, of course! I've never done a hunter pace with anyone else. Plus, if it's a reenactment, I won't actually meet him until the halfway break."

"We had the best time that day," Betsy recalled. "Wow, a lot has happened since then."

"Speaking of wow," Rose said, "what happened with the sisters?"

"That was some kind of crazy!" I exclaimed. "They don't remember that day in the photographs at all, but get this: they grew up in the house I bought on Brook Street."

"You're kidding?" Margaret said, looking to her left. "But wait— Betsy, you finish the story. It'll be midnight if Sarah does."

"Funny," I said, making a face.

"Well…" Betsy paused to take a sip of wine, and then off she went.

"So they didn't recognize the lady in the striped dress?" Rose asked when Betsy finished the story.

"They were just so young," I replied hurriedly. "So, Rose, how was your trip? You didn't talk about it the last time we got together."

"It was great. And I do have some news. I've kept quiet about this until I had all the details in front of me."

Elizabeth rested her napkin on the table. "Okay, we're all ears."

"I'm thinking of returning to England on a semi-permanent basis."

A deafening hush fell over the crowd.

"No, you will not!" I selfishly insisted. "Why?"

"I've had an amazing offer to do a 'cookery' show, which may be too good to refuse."

Margaret adjusted her chair. "Continue, please, and leave nothing out."

Rose had met with a producer while in London. She also divulged having been back and forth for months with her via the internet and telephone, discussing contracts and such. "I think it would be a fun new page in my book of life experiences. It would involve about five months a year. My sister, Eloise, still has her flat there, so I wouldn't need a place of my own."

Jennifer smiled, but then pouted. "How exciting! But five months—gosh!"

"What's your timeline for signing on the dotted line?" I asked.

"I have until mid-January to make a decision. As for the question none of you are asking, I broke it off with Henri du Bois. On the spur of the moment, I made a quick trip to Paris, walked into our shared flat, and there he was, in bed with another woman. And her clothes were hanging beside mine in the closet."

Betsy shrieked. "Oh my God!"

"That's about the size of it, and we shall never more speak of that man!"

We all sat as rigid as characters in a wax museum.

Elizabeth broke the silence, "How about dessert? Who wants cake? Cake makes everything better."

Margaret held out her plate. "Yes, it does, especially your three-layered chocolate cake."

We had met Henri only once—about four years ago, at a launch party for Rose and her latest cookbook. It didn't take long to see he was an absolute jackass. We had no proof, but by his obvious infatuation with Elizabeth that day, we were sure "monogamous" was not a word in his vocabulary. Over the years, he often pinched Rose for money, and except for being unbelievably handsome, he had zero redeeming qualities that we could see. Henri's becoming past tense was thrilling, but the possibility of losing Rose to the cooking show hung heavy in the air.

12

Somewhere during my early days of researching Lilith's disappearance at the County Hall of Records, I decided to go in a completely different direction with my novel. There were all sorts of documents concerning marriage, abandonment, money, and property—most of which labeled Mrs. Lilith Wentworth as missing or assumed dead, leaving Dr. Wentworth as a sole survivor. Therefore, her name had been removed from everything jointly held.

Lilith's disappearance was never again in the newspaper. There were several notes on police reports to indicate Dr. Wentworth perhaps knew where she was but made no effort to get her back. But my imagination had taken hold and left the Wentworths behind. Lucy Butterfield's story was quickly traveling down a different path.

October 8, 2010
Dear Debby,

This letter will be short. The visit with the Cromwell sisters was very enlightening and warm. Someday I'll need to confess that I was there just to snoop around. But I must say, I left with an entirely different feeling. It was strange how drawn I was to Olivia. It's almost like we've known each other in a different life. She was so easy to talk to, as opposed to Iris, who guarded her words.

Ethan called yesterday to share that Grammy spent the night in the hospital—a heart issue. He said there was no need to panic but just letting me know. I haven't told Nick or anyone—I'm afraid to say it out loud.

See you tomorrow.

With all good wishes,

Sarah

The following afternoon I snuggled into the corner of the beige tuxedo sofa in Deborah's office. I had grown to love this time with my therapist—a quiet atmosphere to organize my thoughts and feelings. We talked for the better part of thirty minutes about the Cromwell sisters, their story, and my decision to chart a new course with my novel.

Resting the legal pad in her lap, she said, "Sarah, you're to be commended for not using *their* story. This new idea might prove to be even better."

"Thanks. I actually felt relieved the second I touched the delete key. This is now my story, not theirs. Granted, the lady in the striped dress is the catalyst, but that's where fiction takes the wheel."

Dr. Baxter intertwined her fingers. "Nick needs to know that you're worried about your grandmother."

"I know—it's at the top of my list."

ভ৪৪৩

Nick called that night and Grammy's episode was our first topic. "I've decided to go to Iron Springs this weekend," I said after filling him in. "Ethan says she's fine, but I need to see that with my own eyes."

"I'll fly home Saturday—we can go together on Sunday. Give Sibby a call, and if your mother gives you any argument, refuse to listen."

I breathed a sigh of relief. "Thanks. I love you very much,"

"I love you too. See you in a few days."

೦೩೮೦

Two days later, I woke up in the middle of the night after having a larger-than-life dream. It was an epiphany of sorts—the road my novel would take was suddenly as clear as a bell. Throwing on my sweats and thick socks, I made a beeline for my computer.

The dogs hopped up from the floor beside our bed and followed me to my office. After a few yawns and deep stretches, they thought it was great fun to be up in the middle of the night. Turning in tight circles, each took their place on the hardwood floor. Within an hour, I had enough down to outline my dream.

As I walked back down the hall to our bedroom, I heard the upstairs floor squeaking. "It's bedtime, Gladys. Knock it off," I whispered. Giving our ghost a name had made her less intimidating somehow. Once again, Caesar let out one of his mirror-shattering barks, and there was no more squeaking, which was actually a bit disconcerting.

CR80

Nick got home on Saturday evening, and we made our way to Iron Springs the next day.

When we pulled into the driveway on Mulberry Street, my mother opened the door and walked onto the front porch handsomely dressed, in her favorite St. John dress and matching Amalfi slingback pumps, her hair perfectly coiffed.

"You see, with my mother," I said to Nick before we got out of the car, "if you say you'll be here around noon, then noon it must be. She's not a fan of tardy and will give you ten minutes on either side, but that's your window."

After giving Mama a kiss, holding our baskets of food, we walked into the large foyer. My eyes flew straight to my treasured grandmother, standing with open arms beside the newel post of the extra-wide stairs.

"There's my favorite granddaughter," she said. "And, Nick, it's good to see you. Thank you for bringing my Sarah."

Nick leaned down and pecked her cheek. "You're welcome."

Grammy's usual sparkle was a bit subdued, and her coloring slightly off, but compared to the visual I had conjured up in my mind, she looked amazing—her cheeks reflected the pink flowers in her Sunday dress. I softly blew out a sigh of relief.

"Let's go to the kitchen," my mother, Sibby, said. "Sarah, I can smell what you've made. How sweet of you."

Using Nick's arm as her rudder, Grammy said, "I'm not sure of much these days, but I know you made your delicious chicken pie and applesauce. I also think I smell green beans. It's a true Southern

Sunday lunch. Lord have mercy, are those yeast rolls?"

"Yes, ma'am—all your favorites." I quickly blotted my eyes—all was well.

Nick took charge of lifting the low-hanging fog of concern. "Grammy, have you been playing bridge lately? How are Millicent, Ruth, and Lydia?"

"They're all fine; Millicent couldn't hear a train coming if it ran over her, and Lydia can't see two feet past her fingers, but we played last week before…before I had my spell."

"Lunch is getting cold," Sibby insisted. "Now, Sarah, you take charge of serving. Nick, you can do the beverages, and we'll go have a seat in the dining room."

"Okay, Mama—I'll need to zap some things in the microwave, but it'll only take a minute."

CB80

Lunch was delicious, if I do say so myself, and full of laughter. I did the dishes while my mother put the leftovers in containers. Nick and Grammy retired to the den and said they would save us a seat. Several hours later, I suggested we needed to go, considering tomorrow was a school day and Nick had just returned from a business trip.

On our ride home, I realized I had never given much thought to the fact that Grammy had lived on Mulberry Street for nearly forty years. After my grandfather died, she leased their farm and moved in with us. I had been either in the fifth or sixth grade, but couldn't remember exactly.

With a sigh, I said, "Today was perfect, but it's caused me to really think about my mother's future. I've realized that Sibby's never lived alone. What will she do?"

"I don't know, but your mother's in great health, so maybe she'd like to travel? From the outside looking in, I think she's quite capable of taking care of herself," Nick said. "We'll just need to make sure she's not forgotten—forgotten is the killer."

"Thank you, and you're right, but let the record show: I don't like this glimpse into my grandmother's future at all...not at all! It's like taking the first step down the slippery slope of ill health."

"I know. Your grandmother's been a huge influence in your life. She's how you got your first horse, and according to your mother, she taught you how to cheat at cards." Nick squeezed my hand. "But what a life she's had, and from what they told us, the doctor was very optimistic about her health. Now, let's change the subject—is the hunter pace a go?"

"Oh, yes. Betsy took care of the paperwork for our group. I printed off the entry forms for the three of you, filled out yours, and asked Coy to give Linda and Nancy theirs yesterday morning. I'll put them in the mail tomorrow along with a check."

"I can't wait, but I wish we could ride together. I'll worry about you."

"You know Rascal will take good care of me. It's funny, there's so much about that day I've never told you."

Nick's tone was inquisitive. "Such as?"

"The Rowdy Girls were like high school sophomores." I laughed. "Asking who you were, how you just happened to be two trailers down, whether you were married, and so on."

With one hand resting on the steering wheel, Nick chuckled. "Well, I'm glad I passed the test."

"I fought my feelings about you for weeks before finding the courage to entertain the notion that you might actually be my Mr. Right—and by the way, you are."

Nick smiled. "Thanks. It was a great day. How can we make this one even better?"

"It already is—we're together."

"True," Nick said, turning down the lane to our farm.

13

The cool air of fall was a welcomed relief from the oppressive heat of summer. As I wiped Buddy down after a quick afternoon ride, my phone rang. "Hello?"

"Good afternoon. My name is Dottie Parks. I'm the director of Lazy Willow Senior Living Center," she said. "May I please speak to Sarah Heart?"

"This is she."

"Mrs. Heart, I'm calling on behalf of Olivia Cromwell. She would like to invite you and your friend to come for a visit as soon as possible. There is something very important she'd like to share."

How mysterious, I thought. "I'm a teacher, so I can only visit on weekends. Let me speak with Betsy, and I'll check back with you tomorrow."

"That's fine," Dottie said, sounding as if she wanted to say more.

I paused, then asked, "Do you know what this is about? Is everything okay with the Cromwell sisters?"

"I have no idea what Olivia wants to discuss, but I can tell you that Iris passed away almost two weeks ago. She had cancer, you know, and that evil disease finally won the battle."

"No!" I said softly. "Oh my gosh. We were there not so long ago and that was never mentioned, and she didn't appear to be at all ill," I stammered. "But I'll call you tomorrow about visiting Olivia."

Dottie said, "It took her very quickly in the end and that's a blessing. I look forward to hearing from you soon."

⊗৪০

The following Saturday, Betsy and I were on our way to Shallow Neck. During the hour-long drive, every possible reason for this summons was tossed back and forth between the two of us. We had absolutely no idea how far to the right of wrong we actually were.

"Good morning, ladies. How can I help you?" the bubbly greeter asked.

"Morning. We're here to see Olivia Cromwell."

"Oh yes, she's reserved a private meeting space for you." Once again she led us down the main hall, but not to the sunroom. Instead we went into a small study or library. "Make yourselves comfortable. I'll tell Miss Olivia you're here."

"I wonder why we're not in the large sunroom?" Betsy whispered as we stepped inside the cozy room.

"We'll find out soon enough—here she comes," I said. I enjoyed the intimacy of the smaller space.

Olivia greeted us with a smile. "It's so good to see you both; thank you for coming."

She took a seat and began fidgeting with what she held in her lap. "All of what I have to tell you happened many years ago, but it became my truth only recently."

"Well, we're eager to hear what you have to say." I smiled. "But first, please know how sorry Betsy and I were to hear about Iris."

"Thank you, but it's for the best. She was so sick. Dottie came to my apartment and told me she had shared Iris's passing with you, so I'll start there. About two days after my sister died, I was going through her things—you know, in an old folks' home, whoever's left standing has just days to clean out the apartment of the dearly departed.

"Anyway, I came across a package wrapped in brown paper, tied in twine, and tucked deep in the back of her closet shelf. I unwrapped what felt like a book. The cover page said, 'This Diary Belongs to: Celia Cromwell'—you'll remember that she was our mother. The first entry was dated February 14, 1923, Valentine's Day. That matters after you read the first few entries."

"How interesting," Betsy said.

"Interesting's not the word," Olivia said emphatically. "I hope you two have some time, because this will take a while."

"We do," Betsy answered, opening her basket and removing a box of shortbread, a thermos of hot tea, and all the accoutrements.

Olivia's eyes brightened, and soon she was stirring a rounded teaspoon of coarse brown sugar into her cup and reaching for a cookie. "Before we go any further, I need to clarify something: our aunt was always called Lily, and that's all Iris and I ever knew. After today, we'll all know that Lilith Wentworth and Lily Cromwell were the same person and not actually our aunt, I don't suppose. Now, let's go back to those pictures you brought over back in September. We told you it was Aunt Lily and Uncle Otto, but what I didn't know was that they were running away together. I'm not sure Aunt Lily actually wanted to, but she had to."

"Really?" I said, certain I already knew the answer.

Olivia squirmed in her chair. "Yes—she was pregnant with his child."

"How do you know that?" Betsy asked, leaning forward.

"Mama wrote that she and Aunt Lily had a long conversation the first time we traveled to West Virginia. And according to this"— she held up the journal—"Aunt Lily reminded my mother that Doc Wentworth was almost twenty years her elder when they got married; they had tried for years to get pregnant but no luck. In fact, Aunt Lily said they hadn't been intimate in years, so she couldn't have said the baby was his. Iris and I were too young to know anything about that at the time, but I'm positive my sister knew everything—long before this past September and your first visit."

Betsy refilled Olivia's teacup. "What makes you think so?"

"Because I found this in her things, and she had marked several entries. Iris knew I'd find it when she passed. I wasn't sure why she kept our mother's journal hidden, but somewhere in the middle, those questions were answered. I do appreciate her sisterly love. I'm not sure how my life would have gone if I knew then what I know now."

Sitting very straight in my chair, I asked, "Did it say something about the pictures?"

"I'll get to 1935 and the pictures in a minute. First I need to go back a little farther to 1923. Remember I told you Uncle Otto was our father's older brother, lived over in Hatter's Corner, and was the blacksmith?"

We both nodded.

"Well, apparently he and my mother were more than in-laws. According to this, their first encounter was at a Valentine's Day party at church in Hadley Falls and quite flirtatious."

"You're kidding," Betsy blurted out. "Wasn't your father there?"

"No. Mama wrote that Daddy had stayed home because of a bad cold." Olivia pressed the cup of warm tea against her lips. "Going by the posted dates, the affair didn't last too long, off and on for maybe a year—but long enough to produce a child. According to this, that child was me. Mama never wrote another word about that, and I do wonder which brother she truly wanted to be with, but either way, she wanted me, and that's all I care about."

Gobsmacked, Betsy and I sat looking at each other and then at Olivia. "Are you sure?" I asked softly.

"Here." She handed me the leather-bound book. "Read it for yourself. In fact, I want you to keep it."

"Me—why?"

"Because, besides myself, the two of you are the only people living who know my family's story, and you can keep it safe. Your curiosity has surely caught the biggest fish in the sea with this one—hasn't it?"

Betsy blushed. "You're right about that."

"Originally, shameful curiosity brought us here," I admitted, "but please understand that neither of us would ever do anything to hurt you or your family name."

Olivia exhibited a slightly crooked smile. "You're quite dramatic, aren't you? What would you do with this if you could?"

"Confession is good for the soul, and I need to do just that. I'm a published author of 'how-to' books about humans and horses."

"Oh, that's nice—do people really read that sort of thing?" Her pinched brow reflected: *Surely not.*

"Actually, yes, but it's a very narrow audience. Anyway, I thought the original information from our first visit would make a wonderful novel. I've already started fleshing out the story line."

Olivia tilted her head sideways. "Is it any good?"

"It's getting there."

"Tell the truth—is it as good as it could be without the information from today?"

Needing no time to think, I said, "No, not at all!"

"Well, here's what I want you to do," she said with conviction. "Start over, or fix what you've already done, and write a whopper of a story! Make up new names and places, of course, but this is my gift to you. We hardly know each other, but I know you have a good heart. Anyone else would have thrown our memories out with the trash, but not you. You don't need my approval, but I give you all the freedom in the world to write your book using whatever part of my life you choose. Tell me"—she turned her attention to Betsy—"can she make up a good tale?"

Betsy offered Olivia a cookie. "She certainly can, but are you sure about this? What about Stanley? Through all of Sarah's research, she found out that he's still alive."

"Oh, he is?" Olivia said, genuinely surprised. "I haven't seen him since I was a young girl—and if it's fiction, he'd never make the connection. And I guess you also realize that Stanley and I have the same father. Uncle Otto must have been a real charmer."

Olivia dipped the corner of her cookie in her tea. "My father found this diary sometime before his accident, and needless to say, that's why we stopped traveling to West Virginia. Mama wrote that Daddy's hate for his brother was becoming overwhelming. I might as well say it: I think perhaps Mama took her own life. Dr. Wentworth put it down as a heart attack, but there's a page in here about her plans to take a bunch of Daddy's pills. I guess we'll never know how she really passed."

"How sad," Betsy said, reaching out to Olivia.

"Yes. If I'd known how depressed she was, maybe I could have helped," Olivia agreed. "I also think Doc Wentworth figured out what happened to his wife from those four pictures. Mama wrote about taking them down from our dining room wall after the first time he came to check on Daddy. But all I choose to think about now is that she wrote repeatedly how she dearly loved her two girls. I never doubted Daddy loved me, and now I know how deeply, because he knew he wasn't my natural father."

"Wow," I said.

"Isn't that the truth? Now we can all understand why Iris kept the journal and the facts about the pictures a secret," Olivia said, smoothing the top of her skirt. "I've come to terms with the truth of my life. I'll always be the child of Celia and Otis Cromwell.

"I know now that Uncle Otto was my biological father, but he never held my hand when I was scared. He didn't help me up and dust me off when I fell down. No, Otis Cromwell was my daddy."

Betsy and I were unable to speak, trying to regain our composure. Sitting across from us was the sweetest little old lady in a mint-green dress with tiny pink flowers, pouring out her darkest secrets to two strangers who, for some reason, she oddly trusted. The world she knew for over eighty years had been catapulted into space, and yet there she was, at peace and totally anchored with her truth.

Olivia smiled as I talked about how much we loved coming to

visit her. She jumped right into listing things she would like concerning her possible part in the book. In particular, Olivia requested the town be located in the eastern part of North Carolina, and she wanted the fictitious family to take trips to the beach, which was her favorite place to be.

Resting her teacup on the table, she said, "You don't have to use this, but Mama's older sister, our aunt Alice, lived in Swan Quarter, and I just loved going there. We'd go crabbin' or dig for oysters, and our cousin Grady had a sailboat. On a good sailin' day, we'd go way out in Swanquarter Bay, and sometimes, accidentally on purpose, slip out into the river, but no farther. We were forbidden to venture on downstream to the Pamlico Sound. Mama said it was too dangerous, and of course she was right."

"Oh, I know Swan Quarter," I said. "My cousin Bertie lived in Bath. In fact, I was in her wedding at Saint Thomas Episcopal Church. It was hotter than 'hello' that day, and those bridesmaids' dresses were god-awful. Seriously, shocking-pink taffeta in July, but everyone had a great time," I said, pulling on the reins of my enthusiasm. "And, yes, I'll work on the Swan Quarter idea."

After some additional light conversation, we said our goodbyes and promised to visit often. I told Olivia how much I appreciated her confidence in allowing me the opportunity to use bits of her family's story. Once again she mentioned my being overly dramatic but went on to ask if she could read the book when it was finished.

"Absolutely!" I said, giving her petite body as strong a hug as I thought she could handle.

14

Before starting my car, I shook my head. "At church—on Valentine's Day—seriously?"

"Amazing." Betsy sighed. "How are you going to write this?"

"I have an idea, but I've got to work through my thoughts. You and Olivia will be the only ones privy to the whole story before it gets dissected by an editor."

Betsy reached for her sunglasses. "Well, write fast. What is she—around eighty-two? If the whole process takes several years, you need to get on with it. Not everyone lives to see their nineties, and failing eyesight is also a possibility—not to mention going deaf."

"It's funny how she knows that I would appreciate her consent to fashion my version of Aunt Lily, her parents, and their loveless marriage. I wonder how she figured that out."

Knowing me as she did, Betsy said, "Who knows, but you'll never find any peace if she dies before you've finished. So tell Nick to take a number and you'll be with him when you can."

"I think a good bit of this will write itself once I get my story line mapped out." My stomach rumbled. "Hey, are you hungry? Let's stop for lunch."

CRER

Two hours later, we pulled into our driveway and spotted Nick walking up from the barn.

"Hi there," he said, opening my car door. "You two must have had quite the day. You've been gone for hours."

I tilted my head. "Didn't you get my text?"

"Yes, but you know how I worry when you visit Olivia. Lazy Willow is the county seat of 'nowhere.'"

Betsy laughed. "How true. Nick, great to see you—you're in for a whale of a story. Sarah, I'll call you tomorrow."

As we walked up the porch steps together, Nick paused and held me tight. "I don't know what I'd do if anything ever happened to you."

"I feel the same about you, but all is well." I smiled, kissing his cheek.

With our dinner cooking away on the stove and in the oven, both dogs laid out on the floor, and a fire roaring in the den fireplace, I began with Olivia's discovery of the journal and ended with her giving me the green light to use whatever piece of her story, if any, in my book.

"Wow!" Nick said. "Are you going to give it a try?"

"Yes, but I have to get this laid out just right. It's fascinating to you and me, but the intrigue has to raise the hair on the back of an agent's neck and then blow a publisher out of their chair. And that's not so easy to do."

"You can," Nick insisted.

Moving the throw pillow to one side, I sat up straight. "Fingers crossed. Continuing with that notion, I've had an idea. When I'm in my repurposed butler's pantry, I go back and forth to the kitchen to stir something, or I go to the laundry room to fold something, or I see dirt tracks on the carpet and end up cleaning. What I really need is a totally detached, zero-distractions space in which to write. And I know just where I would like it to be."

"Where's that?"

"The old toolshed on the south side of the barn would be the perfect writer's retreat. I've always told you how outwardly cute I think it is, and with a new floor, insulation and drywall, internet, and paint, I think it would be the perfect hideout for me to weave this story. It's probably what, about ten by twelve feet? Just the right size for an office."

"I think that would be a sound investment. The foundation, exterior frame, and roof are in good shape, so that will save some money. Draw it up, and I'll get Ed over here ASAP." Nick nodded. "He's almost finished with the blueprints for the indoor ring renovation, so he can add this to his to-do list."

CR8O

Two days later, work began on the old toolshed. The basic "bring it up to code" necessities needed no discussion, but Ed suggested adding two windows and even flower boxes underneath. Naturally I agreed.

I read Celia Cromwell's journal at least twice, shuffled the story line, and reworked the first four chapters of *The Disappearance of Lucy Butterfield*. The diary and my dream were proving to be valuable assets for my imagination.

79

15.

The annual hunter pace was just days away, and the fragrance of black boot polish, leather-cleaning oil, and freshly laundered white saddle pads filled the tack room air in three different barns. The Rowdy Girls were hard at work preparing for our departure. In an effort to save time on travel day, I decided to spend Saturday night at Margaret's.

The Sunday-morning sun rose to a blue-sky, cloud-free, and no-wind day. Thankfully, it was not too cold, considering it was early November. Traveling down the highway, Margaret and I talked nonstop. I shared the story of the Cromwell sisters, leaving out everything to do with the diary and saving my would-be novel news for later. We discussed Rose's possible TV show in England and how desperately we didn't want her to go.

And then came talk about Henri du Bois. "I'm sure the visual jolt of betrayal was tragic, but perhaps that's what had to happen. Henri was such an ass—I'm so glad he's out of her life. He would have wormed his way into her success of the cooking show."

"Henri was a major loser!" Margaret agreed. "And we are shameful about not wanting her to go, but her deadline for signing the contract is two months away—a lot can happen in that amount of time."

80

Margaret geared her truck down to a crawl as we entered the uneven terrain of the open field to make our way to the designated parking area.

"Oh, I just love this place!"

"Me too, but I worry about Louie. If he displays any discomfort, I've decided to pull up and call it a day."

"Good idea. Rascal, too. Now, let's go have a great time. Remember, jumping is optional in our division. Oh, look. There's Nick. Try and park two trailers down from his if you can."

C3⃀⃀

It was a difficult task trying to reenact last year's hunter's pace. After Margaret, Betsy, and I reached the halfway rest area, I watched for my handsome prince. We were in different divisions—each having their own required distance and degree of difficulty. With sand flying, their group of three came down from the gallop, and as the dust settled, I could see his warm smile from across the twenty-yard clearing. Pulling Chance up beside Rascal, Nick reached out for my hand. "Hey, babe. I hope you guys are having fun. But about this reenactment idea, I'm tired of playing. I fell in love with you that day and have never changed my mind."

"I have to agree. Let's forget the 'meeting you in the lunch line' piece and all the rest. You're even more handsome in your hunt clothes than you were last year, and those blue eyes still melt me like butter."

Finishing our provided snacks of juice and cookies, Nick said, "Watch for me at the finish line!"

"I wouldn't dream of missing the three of you take the final twenty-four-feet-from-end-to-end log jump together—what a rush! Oops. Our ten minutes' rest time is up—they're calling our number." I gathered my reins. "Off we go!"

The remainder of the day was terrific. Nick, Linda, and Nancy were once again winners of their division. The first-place blue ribbon and a beautiful wooden bowl were awarded to each. Margaret, Betsy, and I earned second-place honors in our division and took home the red rosette. Jennifer, Elizabeth, and Rose finished us off in third place with the yellow. But this competition had never been about the ribbons—it was about dear friends enjoying a wonderful day on horseback.

Nick and I said goodbye, and I told him I'd come straight home after getting Rascal settled. We kissed and waved to each other as Margaret and I drove away.

ര380

As we pulled up to the barn, our horses whinnied to their stable mates. Margaret maneuvered around the tractor and backed her trailer in line with the double barn doors. With the ramp securely on the ground, she backed Louie off and walked him toward his stall. I dropped the butt bar behind Rascal, unclipped his halter from the crosstie, and slowly began to back him toward the ramp. He became agitated as his rump cleared the trailer and was snorting, which he never did.

"What's wrong with you? Easy," I said, rubbing his face. Out of nowhere, another rider from our barn came tearing around the corner—her horse was out of control. Rascal bolted forward, and I was thrown into the chest bar and then to the floor. The rest was a fuzzy blur, but I knew my head had bounced off the trailer floor and Rascal was standing over me—or was he standing on me?

In the blink of an eye, Curtis, the son of the owner, Inez Biddle, was standing on the other side of the shoulder-high divider wall, looking down and telling me to remain still as he slid the hinged wall to the empty side. The other rider quickly put her horse away and came running out, apologizing with every step. Margaret flew past her and quickly jumped into the trailer. Gathering Rascal's lead rope, she angled him away from my outstretched body and slowly backed him out. Once safely on the ground, Margaret handed the lead rope to the boarder and insisted she stop apologizing and make herself useful by putting Rascal in his stall.

I wasn't sure of anything except my left leg felt like it was on fire and that an elephant was sitting on my head. Slowly, I slid my hand down my leg to the area of excruciating pain and instantly knew it was broken.

Coming in and out of consciousness, I heard Inez calling 911 and asking that they not blow the siren because of the horses. Margaret took my cell phone from my breeches pocket. "Hi, Nick. It's Margaret. Now, don't panic, but there was an accident backing Rascal off the trailer, and Sarah's been hurt. The ambulance is on the way. They'll take her to the hospital in Hadley Falls."

Reaching my arm up, I motioned for her to hand me my phone. "Hi, handsome—don't worry. I'll be okay."

"Sarah!" Nick said, sounding frantic. "Baby, hang on. I'll meet you at the hospital. I love you."

"I love you too," I said, handing the phone to Margaret and feeling myself slipping away.

⋯

Sometime later, maybe hours, perhaps days, I opened my eyes and saw Nick asleep in the reclining chair.

"Where am I? What's that smell?"

"Hey, baby," Nick whispered, jolting up and stroking my forehead. "Just lie still and don't get excited. You're in the hospital. You had an accident getting Rascal off the trailer."

I was still fuzzy and in serious pain. "Oh no! Is he okay? God, my head hurts!"

"Yes, he's fine. Just take it easy," Nick answered, pushing the nurse's call button.

"How can I help you?" the voice asked over the intercom.

"My wife is awake and could use something for pain."

"Someone will be right there."

Within minutes, there were four nurses hovering around me like gnats circling a dirty dog. Two were talking entirely too loudly and too fast. One was shining a light in my eyes, and the fourth was on the computer, charting away. "What's going on?" I moaned, waving my limp hand. "Please, I really need for everyone to be *very quiet* and back off for just a minute."

Nick moved closer and insisted everyone step back, except for one person. She had very kind eyes and a gentle voice. Injecting something into my IV line, she explained what had happened. "Mrs. Heart, your leg was broken, but you've had surgery, and it's all

84

fixed up. It will take a while to mend, but it will. You've also suffered a nasty blow to your head and have a concussion—that, too, will improve. But for right now you just need to rest."

I could feel the effects of the "calm the hell down" medication and was grateful. The pain was seriously out of control. Trying to put on a brave face for my husband, I said, "So, how long before I can ride?"

He struggled to laugh. "Not this week. But there are two people demanding to see you—can you handle that?"

"Sure," I said, with both thumbs up.

Margaret and Betsy came into the room. "Why are you crying?" I asked, seeing their tear-stained faces. "I'm going to be fine. I'll admit every part of me hurts. It feels like I've been run over by a truck."

Betsy shook her head. "No, just a horse."

"Don't make me laugh. Is Rascal okay? Poor baby. He'll be so worried."

"You know I'll watch out for him and give him extra treats. Hey, we can FaceTime him." Margaret smiled. "But we'll wait a day or two until you sound more like yourself."

"You're going to FaceTime a horse?" the nurse asked with an expression of total disbelief.

"Yes!" we three answered in unison.

"Sometimes it's best not to ask," Nick said to the wide-eyed angel of mercy. "You have no idea what you're in for as long as my dear bride is in your care."

Trying not to alarm anyone as to how badly I felt, I said, "I love you all, but I want everyone to go home. I don't even know what day it is, but I'm sure you've been here most of the time. The medicine she gave me is working, and I won't get better with you staring at me or sleeping sideways in the chair."

My two dearest friends were the first to leave, but Nick was taking his time finding the door.

"I'm serious, babe. Go home and stop worrying. I do need you to call my school and tell them what's happened. They'll need to get a long-term substitute teacher. Also, please call my children, but tell them not to worry and that I'll call them later. Now, seriously, kiss me goodbye and let the drugs do their thing. Oh—please get in touch with Ethan, but not Mama. Ethan will need to tell Sibby in person or she'll freak out."

"It's Monday morning and not quite nine o'clock. I've already called everyone on the list. You can expect a visit from Sidney this afternoon, and you two can call Emma. Ethan will be here sometime this week with Sibby in tow. We agreed it would be best to wait until you look and sound more like yourself. And I'll be back tonight around suppertime. Sarah…" Nick's face was unshaven and his eyes, bleary.

"I know, but I'm going to be just fine. What did the doctor say about my recovery time?"

Holding my hand, he said, "It'll take a while."

"I don't like the sound of that," I mumbled, my eyes closing, the drugs winning.

I felt one last kiss and heard the door close as Nick left my room.

16

On the second full day of my stay at Hadley Falls Community Hospital, the morning sun blasted through my hospital room window, blinding my view as someone came into my room.

After he took several additional steps, I recognized the face of Toby Ray, a former art student and now my orthopedic surgeon.

"Good morning, Mrs. Heart." He smiled. "How are we this morning?"

"Marginally better than the absolute blur of yesterday," I said. "At least this morning I know who you are—and you're a doctor!"

Toby laughed while checking my chart, pinching my toes, and moving my leg around. "Everything looks great; I'll be back later this afternoon. Your physical therapist will be in shortly. You need to eat everything on your breakfast tray—food is fuel for healing."

"I'll try," I said, smiling that Tobias Ray was my doctor.

Within minutes, a zealous young man carrying a pair of crutches swept into my room and announced, "Mrs. Heart, my name is Zack and I'm your physical therapist. Today is walking day." Slowly he brought my fully-swathed-in-fiberglass left leg to the side of the bed, stuck the crutches under my arms, and helped me to stand. Electric jolts of pain immediately raced through my body, and I bit my lip to stop from screaming.

"When I come back from the depths-of-pain hell, we're going to talk about this," I said, gritting my teeth and looking straight into his eyes.

Zack, strong as an ox and very determined, explained that he understood, but we had no choice. I was fairly certain he wasn't even old enough to vote, but I was in no position to argue. "Okay," he said, putting another gown on me from back to front to cover up my exposed backside, "but we've gotta get you up and moving. You'll thank me for this later."

I continued to grit my teeth. "Don't bet on it."

"Here we go." He tied a wide strap around my waist and held on tight. "Your goal is to make it to that chair in the corner. Keep your chin up and focus on where you're going—crutches first, then you; don't look down. Use your arms, not your armpits. Easy does it now...Good job. I'll be back in about an hour, and we'll take a stroll down the hall." With one final adjustment to the recliner and pillows, Zack laid a toasty warm blanket over me, smiled, and said he'd see me later.

Ida, my very own daytime Florence Nightingale, who never lost her patience with my complaints or biting humor, came in just as Zack left.

"I know all I've done is whine," I said, "but this intense pain refuses to subside."

Ida squished another pillow down the side of the recliner. "I know it seems like that. But it will—I promise. Moving will help, and before long you'll be headed home. So, I heard you live on a farm?"

"Yes." I beamed, the visual of Long Leaf giving me hope. "And I miss everything on that property. But I really want to see my horse at the barn where the accident happened. He's a funny bird, that one, and he won't be settled until he knows I'm okay. Horses are very intuitive, and accident or not, he knows he hurt me. Once he sees me standing right there, he'll be back to himself."

"How interesting," Ida said, removing the blood pressure cuff. "I don't know anything about horses, but I think they're beautiful. What's his name?"

"Rascal." I smiled. "He's the best horse ever created, and very handsome. Wait a minute—I'll show you." I reached for my phone on the side table and quickly found a picture.

"Oh, he is beautiful," she said, "and really big!"

"Sort of medium big," I replied. "He'll jump anything and takes very good care of me. This was just a freak accident. So I need to get out of here and to the barn—both barns."

"Well, then, you'll need to bite the bullet and get to work. No more than you can stand, but steady hard work will get you back to your farm."

"Hmm, I've always believed I was a Jack Russell in one of my former lives—so I guess this will put that theory to the test."

From that moment forward, there were no brakes strong enough to harness my determination. Ida's challenge gave me a force of conviction I never knew I had. Zack, my unrelenting PT, posted a chart, calling it my "uphill battle," on the bulletin board in my room. He would move the little Bavarian climber dressed in lederhosen and carrying a walking stick up or back the stair-step mountainside, depending on my success for the day.

It helped that I'm very competitive by nature. The patient two doors down with a similar injury and I had a running challenge. He could outdo me in the wheelchair, but I blew him out of the water on crutches. Two of the machines in the gym were particularly difficult for both of us, but we inspired each other in a healthy way.

CB8O

I got approved to go home on Friday. The extra time was due mostly to the severe concussion. The headaches were subsiding, but the dizziness and blurred vision were still my doctor's major concern. Sometimes, when cutting my eyes left or right, it was like looking through a disco ball. Ida reviewed the list of dos and don'ts several times: limited TV time, only light reading, and wearing sunglasses when outside were in the top five.

Just after breakfast and all smiles, Nick walked into my room right on time for my departure. "Hey, darlin', are you ready to come home?"

"Yes, indeed!" I sat perched on the edge of the chair. "Ida will be right back with the wheelchair, and then I'm good to go. I just can't wait to get home, but I need a favor first."

Resting on the corner of my bed, he said, "Anything."

"I need to go to Falling Creek and see Rascal. I have to show him that I'm all right."

"Sure, but you must be very careful," Nick said. "Dr. Ray and I had a long conversation out in the hall, and I have my instructions as well about setting boundaries and goals. You're going home, but you're not even close to healed."

"Dr. Ray—that sounds so funny. The last time I saw Toby Ray before this week, he was eighteen, sitting in my art class, ready

90

to graduate, and had just been accepted to Harvard as a pre-med student. I'm so proud of him. And don't worry, I wouldn't do anything to mess up my progress, but we have to stop by Falling Creek first, please."

Ida came in and wheeled me downstairs while Nick pulled up the car. As she put the brakes on my chariot, I thanked her for the miles of encouragement she'd offered and her patience with me. Using my hands, I slid myself across the back seat with my left leg stretched from door to door. My right foot rested on the floor and was my rudder. It was glorious to be released from the confines of the hospital. Opening a tiny crack in the window, I inhaled the fresh air as the sunlight washed my face.

Looking in the rearview mirror, Nick said, "We need to stop at the pharmacy and pick up your prescriptions, and then we'll head to the barn."

"Please don't even bother—they're addictive. I refuse to take anything stronger than Advil from here on. The pain is only occasional and passes quickly."

"But what if something happens and that's not strong enough?"

"Then I'll admit you were right, but I still won't take it."

My face lit up like Christmas morning when we pulled off the highway and onto the narrow gravel road of Falling Creek Farm. When we hit the first bump, I thought I would die. It rendered such intense pain that I'm fairly certain I met God. Nick apologized while I took some deep cleansing breaths, and the fire in my leg began to smolder. I focused on how nice it was to be wearing real clothes, even if Nick had cut off two-thirds of the left leg of my favorite pair of jeans to accommodate my cast.

Coming out of the final curve, I could finally see the barn, and I knew my sweet boy Rascal was just inside. Nick barely finished opening the car door, when I pushed myself across the seat and secured the crutches under my arms. Traveling at top speed down the aisle, I called his name, and in a nanosecond that beautiful chestnut head with a white blaze came out through the open top half of the Dutch door and nickered back in response.

"How's my boy?" I said with tears racing one another down my cheeks. I kissed his velvet-soft nose. "Hey there, handsome. I've missed you."

When I reached for the bolt, Nick gently placed his hand on the stall door. "Not today, darlin'. Not today. You can talk, hug, and rub from here, but I can't let you go into his stall—it's too dangerous."

"Thanks. You're right," I said, realizing I'd almost allowed my euphoria to eclipse my good judgment.

After about fifteen minutes of reconnecting, I started to feel some pain but refused to let on that I needed medication. With one last kiss and a special horse treat, I told Rascal I'd be back and not to worry.

Nick looked over his shoulder before putting the car in drive. "Are you okay? Your coloring is a little funny. You look like you're in pain."

"Yes, I'll admit this has been a lot, and I do need some Advil, but beyond that I'm really okay. It just breaks my heart that Rascal's been so worried, but he's fine now, and so am I."

"I'll go through the McDonald's drive-through, and we can get something to drink and a snack." Nick winked. "Do you have any Advil in your purse?"

"If I'm alive, I have my purse and Advil. And thanks for not saying 'I told you so' about needing medication."

"Now, babe, why would I say that?"

"Exactly." I snickered.

17.

As we made the final turn off the highway, our barn came into view. I squealed. "What? Look at that! How on earth?"

Parking in front of the former toolshed, Nick beamed with pride, opened my door, and extended his hand to help me out. "Ed had his crews working overtime to get it finished before you came home. We hope you like it."

I carefully worked my way to the steps. "Like it? I love it—it's beautiful! It's a perfect match to the barn. I don't know what to say."

"You don't need to say anything," Nick said, holding on to me. "Now all you have to do is get organized and write. The golf cart is for you to use to travel back and forth from the house, to get the mail, or just go to the barn. I'll worry less about your crutches getting tangled up in tree roots or something."

"How sweet. Do I have to give it back when I'm all fixed up?"

"No," Nick said, his mouth twitching into a smile. "The guy at the shop fitted it with that extension bar out to the side so you can put your leg up. It's your golf cart's footstool. We'll remove it when you lose the cast."

"What a great idea; I feel so spoiled! And, true to your stripes, it's so kind and thoughtful."

Opening the dark green six-paneled door, I saw that Ed had

added a wall-to-wall bookcase and cabinet unit on the barn side and an extra window on the opposing wall. Someone—I'm guessing Linda—had chosen the perfect furniture and a rug covering most of the hardwood floor. Lately she would do anything for Nick. She and our other boarder, Nancy, had boarded at LLF for three years, but this adoration for my husband was new, and I'd planned to address it after the hunter pace, but then the accident happened.

The day of the competition, she glued herself to his side, followed him around like a puppy, and kissed his cheek with they were awarded the first-place blue ribbon. I wasn't sure if Nick had actually caught on or simply hoped she'd give it up. Either way, my being home again for an undetermined amount of time offered the perfect opportunity to solidify my suspicions before saying anything.

"This is amazing. I can't believe we came in on budget. I'm just speechless."

"We were actually over budget, but it wasn't too bad. Linda's cousin owns that high-end reproduction furniture store in Hadley Falls—I can't remember the name."

"Belvidere's," I answered. "I didn't know Callie Banks was Linda's cousin. Interesting. And how much over budget?"

Nick displayed an innocent smile. "I don't know about interesting, but I loved the twenty percent discount she gave me. And to answer your question, about six thousand dollars after I agreed to add the bookcases and cabinets. But the room needed that addition, and they'll last forever."

"Well, they're beautiful. Thank you. I'm completely blown away by the whole thing. Seriously, Nick, it's amazing!" I lowered myself down to test out the new desk chair. "This lovely space has reminded me that we need to discuss another topic."

Nick pulled out the other chair. "I'm listening."

"My hospital stay allowed miles of quiet reflection. Here goes—
I'm thinking about taking the second semester off from school. Who
knows how long I'll be in this cast, and I can't drive with this stick-
straight leg, so all of that is extended sick leave. And..."

"And?"

"I'll never finish my book without serious quiet time. Mr. Thomas
has been my principal for over twenty years, so since it's a sabbatical,
he'll understand. I'll start by blaming my leg and the concussion but
finish with the truth: my book. Dorothy Phillips would be the perfect
long-term substitute—he likes her. You know I could never do this
without spilling the beans. Who knows—I just might end up thinking this broken limb."

"I think it's a great idea, and no, you couldn't move forward without telling the truth!"

⋯⋯

The next day, Annie, Caesar, and I set out on our maiden voyage
to my very own please-do-not-disturb writer's retreat. They loved
bouncing along in the golf cart to the converted toolshed. Between
the two large shaggy dogs, my desk and office chair, and one side
chair, you could only see the beautiful medallion design in the center
of the Oriental rug, but I knew the rest was there. Our dogs became
excellent writing buddies, and it was wonderful to have company
that never interrupted.

Before I knew it, Thanksgiving was two days away. I was free from pain, but the cast and crutches were still a thorn in my side. Between my developing upper-body strength and the golf cart, I was finding it easier to function with my ever-present fiberglass albatross.

The book was well on its way, and I started getting my part of the holiday dinner organized. I had always contributed a large part of the midday meal at my mother's house. Nick suggested I pass the torch this year for obvious reasons, but naturally I refused. He had become an accomplished sous-chef, and we had such a good time working together, chopping, dicing, and stirring.

Sidney, Nick, and I had ridden horses last Thanksgiving morning, and we'd decided to make it an annual event. But this year I would be watching from the gate. Sidney worked for a Raleigh television station and was one of the reporters covering an annual open-door late-afternoon meal at a local Raleigh church, but at least I got to see her for a few hours.

My older daughter, Emma, and her husband, Scott, always spent Thanksgiving with his family in Pennsylvania—creating another void on the seating chart. I knew I couldn't always have first dibs on my children and was required to share, but I didn't have to like it.

Sidney and her giant Doberman pulled in right on time. Excluding horses, very little could entice my youngest daughter to rise so early in the morning. With hugs and kisses out of the way, Nick and Sidney went to the barn and saddled their mounts, while the three dogs madly chased one another across the closest pasture.

Annie always went with me to Iron Springs, but adding another dog to that house full of people would be a tight squeeze. Plus, my mother would not have been at all pleased. According to Coy, he and Caesar had a great time bunking together. It made me smile thinking he probably enjoyed the company of that wonderfully loving giant dog. I fixed two bags of Caesar's food for Coy and dropped it off at the barn, then enjoyed watching Nick and Sidney ride from the sidelines.

Well…enjoyed might have been an exaggeration. I knew I had a long way to go before I could ride again, and occasionally that was a hard pill to swallow. This year Sidney rode my Buddy, and following a wonderful ride, she mentioned her plans to steal my horse. We laughed, but I recognized the look in her eye and suggested she not become too attached.

Before she could volley, I jumped in with a question about the veterinarian she had been dating, who also happened to be our large-animal vet. "So, how's Jacob? It's been a few months since you told me about your first date. Are you two still seeing each other?"

"Yes, we are, but, Mama, I need you to listen to me." Sidney stopped momentarily to put her dog in the car. "I really like Jacob and the feeling's mutual, but you have to leave it alone for now, please. I know he's your vet, but you must resist interfering. Promise you won't meddle."

"I promise, but I like him so much; I think you two are just meant for each other. How about a little hint—are we looking at a springtime engagement?"

"Mother!" she said emphatically, raising her index finger to her lips. "I have to get back to Raleigh, but don't forget, you promised to be good. Kiss Sibby and Grammy for me. I'll call them on my way home."

"All right. Now, be careful. I love you."

Squeezing me with one last hug, she whispered in my ear,

"Always. I love you too."

I couldn't help but feel a bit gloomy that this was going to be it as far as being with my children on Thanksgiving Day. But Christmas was just around the corner. Enough boo-hooing, I thought. We'd all be together then and for more than just a day.

18

"How's my broken baby?" Sibby called as I slid out of the back seat. Annie immediately romped around in the front yard.

Smiling all the way up the sidewalk, I said, "Hi, Mama. I'm fine—nothing hurts anymore."

"Sibby, you look lovely," Nick said, helping me navigate the porch steps. "I think you've done something different with your hair."

"Well, yes, I have! You're so kind to notice. I decided I needed a new look."

Hmm, I thought. It really is pretty, but why after thirty years? Something's going on—I'll ask Ethan about it when he gets here. Thankfully, it was just a new style and she hadn't colored it, because my mother had the most beautiful graying strawberry-blond hair I'd ever seen.

With one whistle, Annie came running and bounded up the steps. Grammy was waiting in the foyer and led us down the wide hall to the kitchen. "Good girl," I said to Annie. "You go out in the backyard and chase squirrels."

After Nick brought in several loads from the car, he said, "Okay, ladies, I think that's it. This casserole dish is still very hot and I don't want to burn the counter," Nick said.

Sibby folded a terry cloth dishtowel over the soft green colored laminate. "Just put it here for now. Sarah, you didn't need to do all of this."

"Mama, Thanksgiving would never be complete without our family favorite—your corn pudding."

"I agree," Nick said. "Seriously good stuff! Ethan and Meg just pulled in, and Alex and Aunt Tess were rounding the corner. Hi, Grammy!" Nick gave her a warm hug.

Quickly leaving the kitchen, I greeted Ethan at the front door. "Happy Thanksgiving! Come in—it's freezing outside."

"Sarah." My brother smiled. "You look great! Do you feel okay?"

"Yes. I'm progressing, but not fast enough to suit me. Hi, Meg," I said, lowering my voice to a whisper. "Before either of you go any farther, I want an honest answer—what's going on around here? Sibby O'Neil has changed her hair for the first time since Reagan took office, and she's wearing a trendy new outfit. So, who is he?" I laughed. "Wait a minute," I said, as my favorite cousin, Alex, and my aunt Tess walked up the front porch steps.

Alex was balancing her sweet potato casserole, nearly dropping the rolls.

Carrying four bottles of wine in a canvas tote, Aunt Tess smiled. "Sarah, you look wonderful. Where's that handsome husband of yours?"

Alex rolled her eyes. "Mother, please—let's take all this to the kitchen. I'll be back in a minute," she said over her shoulder, walking quickly down the hall.

I turned back to Ethan. "Now, to repeat myself—what's going on?"

Ethan looked toward his wife, his eyes begging for her to finish the story.

"Well," Meg answered softly, "she has been seeing someone. His name is Ken Langley, and they've gone to dinner a few times and to the movies."

"What? Why didn't anyone tell me?" I screeched.

"Not so loud," Ethan said, glancing down the hall. "Because Mother asked me not to. She knew you'd have a fit, as she put it—which, incidentally, you *are*—and wanted to wait until she knew if she actually liked the man. Your getting hurt sort of stopped us from telling you."

"I'm not having a fit. I'm just blown away. Ken Langley…how do I know that name? Doesn't he own that enormous soybean farm just outside of town? His son was in your grade at school—Luke, I think it was."

"Yes." Meg nodded, stuffing her Burberry scarf in her coat pocket. "Ken's wife died in a boating accident years ago. You remember that—the family was skiing on the river, and the mother got tangled in the ski rope and drowned?"

My eyes widened. "I do remember. It was horrible! That was his wife?"

"Yes. Apparently, back in October, Sibby and Ken bumped into each other at the Lion's Club Fall Festival. He's coming to dinner."

I pushed up on my crutches. "Today?"

"Yes, and you have to be okay about this, Sarah," Ethan insisted. "Mom's happy, Grammy's health is questionable, and you don't want our mother to rattle around in this house alone forever—do you?"

Feeling very much behind the eight ball, I said, "Of course not! I'm just not happy everyone's waited until now to spring this on me."

"Hi, Ethan, Meg," Nick said, coming up the hall and looking at me. "What's the matter? What's happened?"

"Mama has a boyfriend, and he's coming to dinner."

Nick smiled. "How nice for her. So that explains the new hairdo—way to go, Sibby."

"She does look lovely," I admitted. "But talk about taking someone totally by surprise. You have to agree that this is a lot to absorb at the front door."

Nick turned to me with a look of *listen to me* on his face. "Baby, your mother's been without male companionship for over ten years now. You can't begrudge her having a friend."

"I don't begrudge her anything. I just wish I had known—that's all."

Meg's face became animated. "Funny thing, Thanksgiving must be our family's show-and-tell for new boyfriends. Last year it was Nick's turn."

"That's right, it was," Nick answered, looking right at me.

As Alex walked in our direction, Sibby announced from the kitchen doorway, "The five of you have about twenty minutes to visit before our Thanksgiving feast is ready. Fix yourself a drink and enjoy the snacks in the living room."

While munching on trail mix and shelling pistachio nuts, we launched into a "remember when" conversation of Thanksgivings gone by. Alex and I recounted our fathers' annual argument about how to best carve the turkey and our mothers telling them that they were both wrong. Ethan brought up the year the candles caught the centerpiece on fire and our dad put it out with red wine. We howled that Sibby's reaction to the stained linen tablecloth was far worse than a potentially torched house.

Nick and Meg laughed at our stories, adding some of their own from their families.

"Lunch is ready, everyone," Aunt Tess called.

"Now, happy faces. Here we go," Nick said, just as the doorbell rang and Sibby flew past us to the front door.

Halfway down the hall, Nick moved me to one side. "Remember, it's just turkey, dressing, and pleasant conversation."

"Of course. I'm just so surprised," I said as we went into the dining room.

Alex looked at me from across the table. "What's going on?"

"You're about to find out." I winked.

With her arm linked through his, Sibby brought her tall and rather handsome suitor to the table. "Everyone, I would like for you to meet Ken Langley. Ken, this is my family, short of two grandchildren and one grandson-in-law." In clockwise fashion, with us standing behind our chairs, the introductions began. Mama finished by saying the blessing.

With everyone seated and plates full from the buffet line, the O'Neil family Thanksgiving was full speed ahead. Ken Langley was a pleasant man, and my mother displayed a look of happiness I hadn't seen for years. Between passing her bits of turkey under the table and the pats on her head, Ken seemed to be very fond of my Annie, which added a feather in his cap from my perspective.

Alex, my favorite cousin, and I had been as thick as thieves since birth. When we were small, the two of us spent at least three weeks of our summer vacation at Grammy's farm, riding horses and creating havoc in her otherwise quiet household. Although I can barely recall his face, I still remember our grandfather taking us fishing on Saturday mornings. He died when we were eight or nine.

Alex looked over the cornucopia centerpiece and asked what I had been doing while recuperating. I lied through my teeth, saying I just messed around at the barn, exercised, and worked about four million crossword and jigsaw puzzles. She knew I was leaving something out, but everyone else seemed satisfied.

Over the clatter of silverware, Ethan said, "Alex, I understand you have a new dog?"

"I do. Sophie is a five-month-old Cavalier King Charles spaniel and has eaten nearly everything in my house," she said, shaking her head. "And before you ask—yes, she's being crate trained, but free time has taken on a whole new meaning."

"My son Luke had one of those. It was a birthday present to his oldest daughter. Cute dog and very smart," Ken said, rubbing Annie's head. "But I've got to tell you, this one right here might be the sweetest dog I've ever met. How old is she?'

After a moment's pause, my mother answered, "Sarah got Annie about two years before Russell died. So I guess she'll be twelve on her next birthday. My late husband didn't allow dogs in the house, but that one stole his heart."

"Luke Langley," Grammy said out of the blue. "Ethan, wasn't he in your grade at school?"

"Yes," Ethan said quickly. "He stole my girlfriend in the ninth grade."

Meg turned her head in surprise. "Hey—I thought I was your girlfriend in the ninth grade?"

"What was her name?" Ken asked.

"Becky...Becky Smith," Ethan answered.

"Now, here's a funny thing. She's now Becky S. Langley. They've been married forever and have four children."

"That is funny," Ethan agreed, his face turning as red as his hair.

"Oh goodness, here we go." Aunt Tess laughed. "Pass the wine. This is getting good."

"Nothing is 'getting good,'" Sibby insisted. "Now, I thought it would be fun if we played cards after our dessert. What'd you say—who's up for bridge?"

Nick rubbed his hands together. "I haven't played in years, but I'm in."

"I didn't know you liked to play cards," I said to Nick, delighted. "Until we were in high school, Friday evening was our family game night, and we usually played bridge."

"Well, I do." Nick smiled. "Grammy, let's be partners."

CB80

The afternoon card fest saw Nick and Grammy as the top score holders; Grammy refused to play with anyone else. It was wonderful to see her looking so well and enjoying the afternoon.

Since there were nine of us, we were one person too many for two tables of bridge. Not minding at all, Mama and I switched off holding a hand, cleaning up, and just visiting. We were alike in so many ways but especially when it came to the kitchen. Over the years Sibby had shooed us out of her way, saying she'd rather do it herself. I understood completely. Sometimes a lot of well-intended help was very much in the way.

On her way to the hall powder room, Meg whispered to her husband, "Before today is over, I expect full disclosure of the other girl you dated our freshman year."

To which my older brother replied, "I've loved you forever, darlin'. She was just a wild oat."

Meg and I giggled, knowing how desperately Ethan wished he hadn't mentioned Becky Smith.

Around five o'clock, everyone collected their coats and casserole dishes and thanked us all for a lovely day. Alex and Aunt Tess were staying overnight with Ethan and Meg. Mama made up plates of leftovers for the four of them. Ken told us all how much he enjoyed the day but that he needed to be getting home as well.

☙❧

Following a light supper of turkey sandwiches, chips, and pie, Nick took Annie for her walk while Sibby, Grammy, and I sat around the kitchen table talking about Ken. Grammy was very happy for my mother, and that made it easier for me.

"Sarah, I know this is hard for you because you adored your father, but I really do like Ken and enjoy his company. You know your dad would have approved, and I need for you to be okay with this."

"Mama, I was just so shocked that you have a boyfriend. I'm glad you're happy—truly I am. And I do think I like him."

Giving me a hug, she said, "I'm not sure about using the word 'boyfriend,' but thank you. Now, about your leg and the long flight of stairs. Would you rather sleep on the pullout sofa in the den?"

"I can do the steps. Are we in my old room?"

"Yes." She laughed. "I hope Nick likes pink!"

When Nick returned, he said, "Annie and I are exercised and exhausted. Who's ready to call it a day?"

"I absolutely am!" I said, sliding to the edge of my seat.

"Before you go," my mother said with a tone of *remain seated*, "I was wondering if you're going to ride again after you're all better? Personally, I hope not. You know I've always thought it was too dangerous, and you are getting older."

I took my mother's hand. "Mama, I can't imagine never riding again—it's my absolute peace and passion. I know it makes you nervous, but this was an accident. I promise I'll be careful. Please don't worry; the Rowdy Girls have dialed it back a notch or two. Now, I'm exhausted—I've got to go to bed. Thank you for a wonderful family day. Grammy, we'll see you in the morning."

Grammy's head was flopped over to one side and her eyes were closed. *Was she sleeping, or something else?* Fearing the worst, I called her name once more, and she coughed and opened her eyes.

"I must have drifted off. You young people can stay up if you want, but this old lady is going to bed. See you in the morning," she said, getting up and shuffling her way down the hall.

Nick and I headed to bed as well. Climbing the extra wide stars and stopping at my childhood bedroom door, Nick's eyes opened wide. "Wow, I had forgotten about the pink!" he said, walking in while unbuttoning his shirt. "Last year we weren't married and I slept across the hall in Ethan's old room. It really is every shade of pink!"

"Pepto-Bismol on steroids," I laughed, carefully sliding off my jeans over my cast and rummaging through my duffle bag searching for my nightgown. Once under the covers, I rested my head on Nick's shoulder. "Well, this has been a day to remember. It's not how

I expected our second Thanksgiving in Iron Springs to go."

"You're right about the somewhat rocky start, but let's see if we can smooth out the finish," Nick said, pulling me closer.

I was amazed at the outcome.

19

Last year, the morning after Thanksgiving, Nick and I had pulled out all the Christmas decorations and dressed my mother's house from top to toe. Over breakfast this morning, she dropped several hints about Christmas being just a scant month away.

Nick gave me a wink. "So, Sibby, what would you think about our decorating your house again this year?"

Mama turned from the sink, wiping her hands. "I was so hoping you two could help, but with Sarah's leg, I didn't see how."

"Sibby." Nick chuckled. "We both know I did most of the work last year, and your daughter just told me what to do."

Defensively, I said, "That's not completely true. Well...maybe sort of. But we can get right to work when we finish breakfast. Where's Annie?"

"I put her outside to chase squirrels," Nick said.

Clapping her hands in delight, Sibby said, "Well, if you're sure you can manage, I'd love to get this old house brightened up for the season. Oh, Nick, are you and Ethan going quail hunting again this year?"

"Yes, ma'am, we're leaving on December twenty-seventh, for three days. I have to make sure Sarah's taken care of. With her leg, it might be better if she stays in Long Leaf. We'll talk about it on our way home."

My mother twisted the kitchen hand towel. "Oh goodness, Nick, how rude of me, I forgot to thank you for the invitation to your Christmas party at the farm this year. I must say I was surprised."

"What invitation?" I asked, snapping to attention. "What are you talking about?"

Mama put her hands over her mouth. "Oh dear, I've let the cat out of the bag."

"Don't worry about it, Sibby. She would have found out soon enough," Nick said. Then he looked at me. "Take it easy. The Rowdy Girls are organizing our second annual Yuletide celebration as your Christmas present. I couldn't say no and truthfully didn't really try."

"Another secret," I said. "But how sweet of them and you, too. When is it?"

"December seventeenth. Betsy's in charge, Jennifer's catering, and Elizabeth has the two Hadley Falls floral guys doing their thing. I told them to send me the bill but spare me the details."

I stood up from my chair, suddenly concerned. "Hey, I haven't heard a peep out of Annie. Will you go check on her, please? I don't trust that mean little boy next door."

No sooner had Nick closed the back door than he darted back into the kitchen. "Don't panic, but Annie's been hurt. Call the vet's emergency number, and meet me at the car."

"Oh my God. Please tell me she's still alive."

"Yes, but we've got to get her to the vet. She's been shot with an arrow."

I staggered back against the kitchen sink. "Oh my God!" I repeated.

Sibby called the police while Nick bundled Annie in an old blanket from the closet. I flattened down the back seats, and Nick laid her down in the cargo area. I managed to wiggle into the remaining open space. Annie was going into shock—her eyes were glazed, and her stare was distant. I gently rubbed her soft face as we flew through every traffic light, arriving at the emergency door of the local animal hospital in record time.

An intern met us at the door with a gurney and took my treasured golden retriever straight to surgery. Another woman told us to have a seat in the waiting room and that someone would be out shortly to review the process.

I sat down, my fists curling into balls. "The juvenile detention center will have one more delinquent in house just in time for Christmas."

"Darlin', try to breathe," Nick said. "We don't know how or who did this."

I shook my head. "You know it was that weird kid next door. He'll rue the day he hurt my dog."

"Sarah," Nick said, "there's a chance it was accidental."

"Sure," I said, narrowing my eyes. "I suppose he could have been aiming at the target in his backyard. I can see it now. He pulled back on the string, and just as he let go, the arrow got caught up by a hurricane-force wind, took a hard right, passed through the chain-link fence, then threaded in and out of Mama's Ligustrum hedge, finding its way into the side of my dog. Accident, my ass!"

I gritted my teeth. *How long will it take for us to find out if Annie is okay?*

Less than ten minutes later, several police officers arrived. There wasn't much crime in Iron Springs, with a population of twelve thousand or so, but the police department was quite capable of taking care of what did come along. As the taller police officer finished taking notes and asking questions of us, the vet tech came out with the arrow wrapped in plastic and handed it to the senior officer. She told me Annie was doing well and would be out of surgery in less than an hour.

Before leaving, the younger man in uniform stepped forward. "Mrs. Heart, try not to worry too much. We're pretty sure we have our suspect. Hopefully, the fingerprints on this arrow will support what we already have. We're finished here, but I do have to ask if you plan to file charges."

My jaw still clenched, I said, "I absolutely do!"

"Okay. We'll be in touch in a few days," he said, turning and walking away.

An hour later, the doctor came out to speak with us.

"Sarah O'Neil, how are you? I haven't seen you since we were in high school," the man said, removing his mask.

"Oh my gosh! Richard Burkhart—what are you doing in Iron Springs? But first—how's Annie?"

"She's going to be fine, but I'll need to keep her here for several days. Luckily, the arrow missed her vital organs, but she's lost a great deal of blood. We'll keep her on IV medications and fluids, and she must stay quiet. Let's see...Today's Friday. Barring any complications, you can probably take her home Monday after lunch."

With that, I shattered into a million pieces. I'd been so worried, and at the same time so relieved, that I started crying and could not stop the overflow of tears. Nick and Richard tried to console me but finally decided to just let me cry it out. "I need to see Annie before we leave," I said, making certain my voice left no doubt in anyone's mind.

"Okay, but try to stay calm and even-toned," said Richard, leading the way to the recovery room. "You cannot get her excited."

Thankfully, Annie was still very groggy. Holding her paw, I wept quietly while rubbing her head. Richard gave me about five minutes, then suggested I give my girl a kiss and go. Resting her paw back on the cold surgical table, I took another minute to regain my composure and whispered, "I love you, Annie." She thumped her tail ever so slightly.

Sibby and Grammy were waiting for us back on Mulberry Street. Nick explained about Annie's surgery, Dr. Burkhart's prognosis, and the police.

Finally able to collect myself, I said, "I'll call them every day, probably more than once, but the vet said that Annie had to stay quiet, so obviously I can't go visit. She'll be able to come home Monday. So, if it's okay with you, we'll come back here Monday morning around ten o'clock? After we put up your decorations and enjoy a nice lunch, we'll pick Annie up on our way home."

"Perfect." Sibby smiled. "I'm so relieved that she's going to be okay."

I began to breathe more easily as we packed our things.

With a kiss on the cheek, Grammy told Nick he was her forever bridge partner, and we should all play again over Christmas.

Nick gave her a gentle hug. "You can count on it. Sibby, take care. We'll see the two of you on Monday."

CR8O

Just as we left the city limits, Nick glanced at me in the rearview mirror. "I've given it some thought, and I think I would feel better if you stayed with your mother while I'm in Virginia, hunting with Ethan. I'll worry less if you're not alone."

"Okay. I wonder what she'll find for me to do."

Nick paused. "Maybe nothing. Maybe you three can just hang out."

"You have a very rich fantasy life. The phrase 'free labor' comes to mind. I love to clean and get things organized, but my mother does not, and she tends to take advantage of that. Mama knows that once I get started, I won't quit until the job is done. Dimes to dough- nuts she's already thought of what I can do on one good leg. Oh, things have been so upside down, I almost forgot. Remember I told you the story about my getting a one-day suspension from school for punching that boy in the eighth grade?"

"Don't tell me—Dr. Burkhart's the boy."

"He is." I laughed. "I can't believe I recognized him. They moved away at the end of our sophomore year, and I never saw him again. Do you suppose he remembers our altercation?"

"He certainly remembers you. It was written all over his face, but it wasn't anger. It was fondness. That's not really the right word. It was more like seeing a long-lost love or something."

"Don't be ridiculous. We never even went out."

"That doesn't mean he didn't like you. He had *that look*."

I took a very deep breath. "Speaking of *that look*, this has been bothering me since just after the hunter pace...I need to put it out there. Linda Vance is gaga over you."

Throwing up one hand, Nick said, "Now, talk about ridiculous—
that's ridiculous!"

"No, it's very real. I don't know the catalyst for her affections, but
lately she can't be in the same room without putting herself by your
side. She looks at you with moonlit eyes every time you tell a story
and follows you around like a lost puppy. What I'm about to say will
sound like some crazed wife thing, but she has two choices—she can
either stop it or pack up her horse and go."

"Before you throw her out, I need to actually pay attention to
what's going on. I'm not defending her. I just don't know what you're
talking about. Linda and Nancy have never done much more than
come to the barn, ride, then leave."

"True, but seriously, you haven't noticed?" I asked, surprised.
"And I agree, except for the hunter pace, they've always just done
their own thing. And until my accident, I've never known what they
did, I was always at school."

"Can you give me a 'for instance'? I'm almost always around the
barn but doing something else. I promise I'll pay closer attention,
and if something needs to be done, it will come from me, not you—
understand?"

"Okay...how about her kissing you on the cheek at the awards
part of the hunter pace? But remember my eighth-grade altercation—I can take her out if need be!"

Nick howled. "Now that you mention it, that kiss was odd. And
even with only one good leg, I believe you could take her out, but
there'll be no catfights at the barn. Who knew you had such an
explosive side?"

"I'm sure you've heard the phrase 'don't poke the bear'? I'm territorial and will fight for what's mine, and you, my love, are mine!"

"I feel safer already." He winked.

Getting the Linda Vance situation off my chest lifted my spirits. Annie was going to be fine, and my mother's new love life was, too, but I was grateful that I could disappear into the story in my book, and all would be well.

After we got home, we had an early dinner of leftovers, and then Nick and I went to the barn—he had paperwork in his office, and I needed to write.

Embossed on my brain was Annie lying on the ground with an arrow in her side. That was going to require serious work to expunge. How could anyone be that unbelievably cruel?

Caesar looked for his best friend. "She'll be back on Monday, big guy," I said, rubbing his curly head. Caesar let out one shattering bark, which I took as his response of "Okay."

20

I struggled to find a comfortable position on her couch, and Dr. Baxter could see I was anxious to begin. While she read my most recent letter, I was able to find my quiet.

"This is a great deal to cover in an hour. Would you like to add some time to today's visit?"

"Oh wow—yes! Nick's meeting with our attorney about the boy who shot Annie, and he said he'd hang out in the waiting room until I was finished."

"Good. Whenever you're ready. And please start with Annie—I hope she's home and recovering!"

I was still emotional over nearly losing her, and my eyes brimmed with tears. "Yes! We brought her home this past Monday."

Offering me a tissue, she asked, "Did you have any conversation with the vet you punched?"

"I did. We chatted a bit; he's married, has two children, bought the practice from Dr. Phipps, and has a home in the Historic District."

Dr. Baxter raised her eyebrows. "Did he mention the eighth-grade slugfest?"

"Not directly, but by the amount of his bill for Annie's care, I think he may still harbor some ill will. He mentioned a trip to France over the holidays—I think I paid their business class airfare and perhaps two nights in a five-star hotel!"

Deborah laughed and told me to continue.

"Seriously—major bucks. But there's no monetary cap for saving my dog. Anyway, she is supposed to remain quiet for a few days, and I've tried, but I think it's totally hopeless. I do keep both dogs with me in the house or when I'm writing, but the rest is wild and free!"

"I'm happy she's doing well," Deborah said. "Any news about the young boy who did it?"

I winced. "Not yet."

Later on, I said, "I've come to realize life is like a casserole—it's only as good as the ingredients you choose to stir together."

"Interesting analogy." She nodded. "Tell me more."

Opening the lime green folder, I handed her an additional page. "I made a recipe of sorts out of my life."

Dr. Baxter leaned forward, seemingly intrigued.

"On the left is a list of the bad times—I call them the regrettable ingredients. On the other side are my treasured memories—my favorite flavors. You see, you absolutely cannot make melt-in-your-mouth chocolate icing without the bitter cocoa! Some of the really good stuff would have never happened without that—pardon my French—shitty bitter cocoa."

"How clever!" Deborah said, holding the landscape layout entitled *Life Is Like a Casserole—Bon Appétit*! The recipe of the good and bad and their measured amounts printed underneath.

"I've realized that part of healing comes from honest and unbridled inner truth. As I wrote down each item or incident of importance, I could see the truth of that particular piece of my life. Each part, good and bad, contributed to the life I now enjoy."

"But make no mistake," I said, "I'll kick Linda Vance's ass if she messes with my husband. A gentle nudge in the right direction can be very effective, you know. I also plan to do something—legally—with that child for deliberately hurting my dog."

My therapist straightened her posture. "Take your time with your decision about the young boy—the rest of his life hangs in the balance. And may I have your written permission to use this recipe idea and your reason for doing so? I think it's an interesting concept and might be a great icebreaker with some of my other patients."

"Sure, but no names or my real events, please—and thanks for the extra time today."

CRURO

Turning down the lane to our house, I smiled. *It really is a good life. If I can just get this damn cast off, it'll be great!*

"Hey, babe," Nick said, opening my car door. "Are you okay?"

"I'm fine, but the verbal 'cleansing' process can be unnerving. Memory lane is not always lined with lilacs," I said, collecting my crutches and powering up the back porch steps.

"You know I'm always here. Now, slow down before you fall." Opening the back door, Nick inhaled deeply. "Something smells delicious!"

"I hope dinner's good. I'm trying a new slow cooker recipe for beef stroganoff," I said, taking off my coat. "It'll only take a minute to cook the noodles."

"I can do that. Go sit down in the den, and I'll call you when dinner's ready."

I turned on the evening news. A reporter was standing beside a giant calendar, crossing off the remaining shopping days until Christmas. Suddenly I was reminded that tomorrow was the day for my doctor's appointment. There was an outside chance I would be fitted with a smaller cast, or maybe a brace instead.

"Dinner!" Nick called from the kitchen.

As I sat down at the table, which Nick had already set, he carried in two bowls brimming with steaming-hot noodles and stroganoff. "Yum," I said, taking my first bite. "This is pretty good, don't you think?"

Nick wiped his mouth and took a sip of wine. "It's delicious. Don't lose the recipe."

"Remember, I have an appointment tomorrow with Dr. Ray. It's funny that my physician is one of my former students. Toby once sat at the first art table on my seating chart, and now I'm the fifth name on his patient chart. Fingers crossed for tomorrow."

"Not to rain on your parade, but no cast is a long shot—it's only been a month. And I bet it is strange seeing your students all grown up, but I imagine half the younger adults in Hadley Falls were probably in your class at some point."

"I've never thought about that, but I'm very proud of Toby. Teachers aren't supposed to have favorites, but he was one of mine. I just hate these damn crutches. However, check out my developing set of guns." I flexed my muscles.

Nick reached out, giving my biceps a squeeze. "Impressive. Now, dig in."

"Yes, dear." I giggled. "Oh, and don't forget the police are coming Friday morning with the paperwork concerning Annie's assailant,

Tommy Asheworth. I'm sure you'll want to be here to rein me in, if nothing else."

Rolling his eyes, he said, "Definitely!"

21.

The technician called me back to the exam room. She helped me get situated on the examination table, and the wait began.

Nick and I were reviewing the human skeletal wall chart when Toby whooshed open the door. "Good morning, Ms. Sams—I mean Mrs. Heart. It's strange to call you Mrs. Heart," he said, glancing at my chart. "So, it's been about a month since I saw you in the hospital; how are we today?"

"This 'we' is fine, but I'm beyond tired of this cast. What are the chances it could come off today?"

"We'll need to get an X-ray first, and we can go from there. Do you have any pain or strange sensations in your leg?"

"No pain, but it does itch right here," I said, pointing to the area six inches above my knee. Dr. Ray pushed the call button and asked his nurse to take me to X-ray. Nick stayed behind to guard my purse and speak with Toby.

After my photo op, I returned to room number six and plopped down in the closest chair.

Nick sighed. "Bad news?"

"Probably. I haven't been told anything, but I can read faces, and I'm betting 'we'll see you soon' looms heavy on my horizon of shattered dreams."

Toby opened the door, slid my X-rays in place, and turned on the light box. Standing on either side, we looked on as he explained. "You see the break is healing nicely but not quite well enough to remove the cast. It'll need at least four more weeks, maybe more. But try not to be too discouraged—you're actually ahead of schedule. I'm going to put on a lighter cast, though, and it won't go so far up your thigh."

"Well, that's good news." Nick smiled.

"It is." I frowned. "But seriously—four more weeks?"

"I know, but like you told me in high school, 'Patience is a virtue, Toby—just take your time.'"

"I did say that, didn't I? But really."

Standing in the doorway, Dan, my *Igor* the cast master, took my chart, instructing me to "walk this way."

"If only I could." I laughed as we continued down the hall to his casting lab.

Helping me onto the table, he asked, "What color would you like this time?"

"I'll take black. It fits my mood and will be stunning with my holiday attire."

He fired up the oscillating cast saw. "Black it is. Now, this won't hurt, but you might not want to look at your leg—you haven't seen where they operated yet."

"Thanks for the warning," I said as he started to crack open the cast. "Whoa—I feel very strange. I think I might pass out. What's happening?"

I felt bad for thinking of him as Igor, but he had to be at least six feet four or more and no less than two hundred and fifty pounds with muscles on top of muscles. Lucky for me he was every bit of that, or I would have found the floor in a skinny minute!

He placed pillows behind my back and took my hand to keep me from falling off the table. "Your leg is swelling; this happens sometimes. Close your eyes, relax, and give your body a minute to equalize."

Toby came in to take a look at my incision. Pushing around both sides of the highway of surgical staples, he used his calmest voice. "Sarah, I need for you to look at me—look at me. Focus on your breathing and not on your leg,"

"I'm trying, but it feels like dough rising."

"Just breathe—even breaths…There you go. Better?" Dan said, moving back a bit.

"Maybe, but that was beyond weird."

Dan let go of my hand. "I know, but let's get to work on the new cast."

With a gentle pat on my shoulder, Toby said, "You're going to be just fine. Next time we'll know that might happen, and you'll be better prepared. Now, see if you can slow down your breathing, and I'll send Mr. Heart back."

"Thank you," I said, "and just so you know, I'm very proud of you, Toby."

Placing my chart in the wall-rack he turned to look at me. "You've made my day, and just so you know, you were the coolest teacher I ever had."

Nick came in just minutes after Toby left. Handing me my crutches, he helped me off the table while Dan stood behind the table. He knew without asking that the outcome was at least four more weeks.

Nick opened the back door of our car, I slid across the seat, and he took his place behind the wheel. "I know you're disappointed, but you're ahead of the healing process. And your new cast is smaller, and black is very sexy." He winked at me in the rearview mirror.

"You're so full of prunes," I said, shaking my head. "There is absolutely nothing sexy about any of this!"

Using his Cheshire cat smile, he said, "I beg to differ. Do I need to remind you of just the other night?"

"Nicholas F. Heart." I blushed.

"At your service, ma'am!"

❦

Friday morning, the same two officers we met the day of Annie's injury arrived right on time—with paperwork in hand.

"I hate that you had to drive out here for this," I said, offering them a cup of coffee and a seat in the den.

"We had business at the county courthouse, and your farm is in between. It was just easier to stop by on our way back to Iron Springs," the detective said. "And sometimes these things go better when we can all just take our time to talk things over."

As they presented all the facts, I learned that if I pressed charges, I had no say in what would happen to the young boy. Time had softened my determination regarding Tommy's being placed in a detention center, but I did feel more than a slap on the wrist was necessary.

After hearing all the options, I asked, "Is there any way I can offer to drop all charges if he'll agree to some sort of community service? I would insist on a face-to-face meeting with him and his parents and signed documentation of the agreement by all present."

The detective organized his clipboard. "Yes, but that's between you and the boy's family. I would suggest you arrange a meeting at your attorney's office. Make the offer and have all the paperwork in place before you drop the charges. If you drop the charges first, it's a closed case."

"How much time do I have?"

"Well, the sooner the better," the officer advised.

I'd been so distraught back in November at the animal hospital that their names had completely escaped me. As the taller man moved his arm to one side, I could see the badge clipped to his belt. Above the center of the star, it read Langley, L. "Detective Langley, by any chance, are you related to Mr. Ken Langley?"

With pride, he nodded. "He's my dad. Why do you ask?"

"Well, it's truly a small world. From the report, you know my mother is Sibby O'Neil, and she lives on Mulberry Street in Iron Springs? You and my brother, Ethan, were in the same class in school."

His expression became curious. "And?"

"And my family enjoyed having your father join us for Thanksgiving dinner."

"My father was at your mother's house for Thanksgiving?"

"Yes," I answered, realizing I might have truly stepped in *it* with both feet.

With a rigid posture, Luke Langley adjusted his belt and cleared his throat. "How nice. 'Bout what time was your family dinner?"

"I guess around one o'clock, wasn't it, Nick?"

Cautiously, Nick answered, "I believe so."

"So that's why he said he wanted to have our family meal closer to six o'clock. What else do you know?"

"I'm going to take the Fifth on this one. You'll need to get any additional information from your dad. But I can see you're as surprised about this as I was."

I walked the officers to the door, and we shook hands. "Yes, I am. You folks have a nice day, and let me know what you decide."

And with that Detective Langley and Sergeant Henry were down the front steps and in their squad car, tearing down the lane.

"What in the hell just happened? I've been carrying on about my mother being with a man other than my father, and obviously the other side of that coin feels the same way about his dad. I wanted to say, 'Now look here. This is my mother we're talking about, not your soybean-farmin' dad.'"

Nick squeezed my shoulders. "I have no doubt Luke's headed straight for Langley Farms. The grass will singe beneath his feet walking to the front door, and all the cards will be on the table in five seconds—maybe six. In a way, it's kind of cute—a senior citizen Romeo and Juliet."

"Cute. That's one word for it." I smirked, knowing they actually were.

"I'll make an appointment with David about the papers for the settlement, or whatever it's called in the legal world. I'll ask him to give the parents a call and set up a time to meet in his office."

Flopping down in my favorite chair, I said, "Please ask David to check deeply into that child's past."

"I will. Now, I need to get into my barn clothes," Nick said. "I'll be back in a minute."

I nestled deeply into the chair, thinking. Caesar broke my silence with an earth-shattering bark as Linda Vance bolted into the kitchen.

Jumping up, I said, "Hi there."

"I'm looking for Nick. Where is he?"

"I'm not sure, Can I help you?" I asked, grabbing my crutches.

Looking around, she said, "No, I need Nick."

"Well, hello. What's up?" Nick said, walking into the den.

Linda threaded her arm through the crook of his. "Something's gone wrong with the automatic water bowl in my stall."

"Where's Coy?"

"I don't know. I just know I needed you."

"Well, let's go have a look," he said, catching my glance of *See! What'd I tell you?* "Sarah, can you come too?" he asked.

"Sure. Let me get my coat."

"You know, Linda, my Sarah is the plumber in the family. She's fixed them before."

Snidely, Linda replied, "Well, aren't we fortunate?"

"Yep, I'm the luckiest man in the world. Let me help you, darlin'," he continued, removing her arm from his and grabbing the other side of my coat.

22

Within thirty minutes all was set right again at the barn. Coy had replaced the broken washer on the automatic water bowl and was soaking up the soggy stall floor with extra shavings. I took the opportunity to groom Buddy after Nick led him to the wash stall. Linda hovered around the office area, and from the corner of my eye, I watched her slip through the door.

Oh, to be a fly on the wall, I thought, but I knew by the look on Nick's face the conversation wasn't congenial. He sat perched on the corner of his desk as Linda took a seat. After ten minutes of your-turn-my-turn dialogue, some of which was loud enough to escape the confines of the office walls, Linda flung open the door and stormed out.

As she hurried in my direction, I began brushing Buddy even faster.

"I'm leaving this barn," she said bitterly. "I am not a liar, and I have the evidence to prove it!"

Not saying a word, I continued to groom my horse. What on earth had happened in the past ten minutes to invoke such a response?

Coming out of the tack room, Linda stopped and waved a piece of paper in my face. "I'm going to let you read this, so you know exactly what's going on around here."

Catching the single sheet midair, I demanded, "Don't move. Stand right there and let me read this."

Dear Linda,

I can no longer hide my feelings for you. You've been at my farm for three years now, and my affection for you has grown stronger with every passing day.

I'm not sure how we can manage this, but I needed for you to understand how I feel about you.

With all my heart,

Nick

"Nick didn't write this. It's not his handwriting. And think about it—have you ever heard him speak to anyone this way? I mean really, all these flowery words? Not to mention this handsome business stationery. In fact, I think I've seen this before."

"Oh really, and how would you know that, Miss Marple?"

"Because I gave Nick a box of gray Crane stationary just like this last year. What's going on around here? Why would somebody do this? Come with me," I said, hobbling into Nick's office.

In one heartbeat, my husband's expression went from surprised to wary as he looked up from his hay and grain logbook. "Ladies?" he said with a cautious tone.

"There's something rotten in Denmark," I said, holding up the note.

"Really?"

"Yes. A few days before the hunter pace, Linda found this note in her tack trunk. It professes your love for her and is on what I believe to be your stationary."

"You're kidding," he said, taking the letter from my hand. "It is the same color as mine, but you know I didn't write this."

I shook my head. "Why do people always say 'you're kidding' when you're obviously not? Anyway, I know you didn't write it, but I know a female did. This is absurdly sophomoric! The question is who and why? I'm fairly certain I know the who, but I'm unclear as to the why. Linda, I have to ask, have you noticed a change in things at home?"

"Maybe just a bit. My husband's been working on a difficult case for a while now, and he keeps late hours. Why?"

"Just curious. And until we figure out who came into our house, took the paper, and planted the note, please just go along as if the past few minutes never happened. Can you do that?"

Linda covered her face with her hands, then took a breath. "Yes, but please let me say how sorry I am for all this and for everything I said to you both. I'm so embarrassed! Wallace and I've been married for a hundred years, and life can get pond-scum stagnant after a while. I was like a schoolgirl—flattered that someone else thought I was attractive. I just lost touch with reality. But who would do such a hateful thing?"

Nick patted her shoulder. "Don't worry. We'll figure it out. Now, go take care of your horse."

With slumped shoulders, Linda walked out of the office and down the aisle to the tack room.

Cℨ𝄞ℷ

Leaning against the golf cart, I said, "I'm positive Nancy Wall wrote the letter and put it in Linda's tack trunk. Other than our tack boxes, it's only the two of them in there. But before we accuse anyone, I don't suppose it's out of the realm of possibility that someone else could have slipped in the tack room unnoticed? Coy's apartment is on the back side of the barn, and we're not always here. Stir in the 'under the cloak of darkness' possibility, with no gate at the end of our drive or a lock on the tack room door. But my money's still on Nancy. And as sad as it is, I'm also positive Linda left the office realizing that her best friend for decades had to be the scribe. How devastating!"

Sliding behind the wheel of the golf cart and lifting my leg onto the arm support, I said, "I'm also fairly certain as to Nancy's catalyst for writing the letter."

Nick sat beside me. "If you're right, it is sad. But how on earth could you know any of this? It's been all of what—thirty minutes since you've been on the case?"

"The Rowdy Girls."

"And?"

After getting out at the house, I took one porch step at a time. "Rose hosted the last Rowdy Girls' dinner—remember?"

"Yes. Go on."

"Jennifer mentioned hearing rumors of some turmoil at the legal offices of Hobart, Hathaway, Peters, and Vance. If you want any dirt on anyone in Hadley Falls, go to Jennifer's restaurant for lunch. I'm sure you remember Ian Peters, Elizabeth's husband? You met him last year at the Charity Ball in Virginia."

"I remember Ian—nice guy."

"Yes, kind of nerdy and oddly quiet, but I guess someone has to listen. Anyway, until that dinner, I had never made the connection, but Wallace Vance is the fourth member of that firm, and I'll give you two seconds to guess his wife's name."

"Linda," Nick said, pouring a glass of wine.

"Bingo, and that's not all. Word over River Bend's scrumptious sweet potato pie is some woman's been seen in and out of that firm for about four or five months, always around one o'clock. I'll give you another two seconds to guess who she most probably is."

"Nancy Wall. Again, how do you know all this stuff?"

"Between Margaret's bookstore, Jennifer's restaurant, my teacher's lounge, and Betsy, we don't miss much. If I'm right, she put the letter in Linda's tack trunk to divert attention from her own affair. It would be all over town that you two were fooling around, which would take the heat off her own secret little rendezvous with her best friend's husband."

"Surely they didn't do anything *in* the office? The other attorneys would have put a stop to that."

"She was probably there on some trumped-up legal nonsense to do with her late father's estate, which would make her frequent visits appear legitimate. Linda would never have questioned that. Word has it they met at that 'hot pillow joint' on down the river. Uh..."

Nick laughed. "Ned's Bait and Catch?"

"That's it. Too funny, right? Bait and Catch!"

"How do you know about a 'hot pillow joint'?"

"I just do. But to my way of thinking, the possible affair isn't our concern. Coming into our house, though, and searching your desk for the stationery absolutely is! You only have copy paper at the barn." Taking our dinner out of the microwave, I shuddered at the thought.

Nick pulled out his chair. "Agreed, and this will require deeper discussion, but we both know Nancy will have to leave the farm. But for now let's change subject to our upcoming events. We have our second annual Christmas party on the seventeenth and the Charity Ball in Virginia is..."

"The eighteenth? Oh, wait a minute. That's the day after our party. That can't be right," I said, handing our plates to Nick.

"Yes, it is." He smiled. "This year we'll all go up early Saturday, enjoy the Charity Ball that night, and come home late Sunday afternoon. I was talking to Susan the other day about a horse she's trying, and she's come up with something you all can do."

"Oh, how sweet, but what can we all do with me disabled?"

Nick pulled out my chair and took my crutches. "I have no idea, but Susan said it was a surprise for the six of you. While the Rowdy Girls spend Sunday at the barn, the boys are off to the links."

"We really do have a great time," Nick continued. "And you know you'll love whatever the six of you are doing. Now, about your outfit." Nick winked. "I can't wait to see your party dress. I remember how you girls ripped poor Mrs. Pritchett to pieces for wearing the same bright green dress for the fifth consecutive year. Women...you should be ashamed."

"Perhaps, but we're not. I really will need to think about what I can wear to the dance and to the barn. I hate this damn cast!"

23

Nick and I sat nervously in the outer office of Mr. David Collins, Attorney at Law. Our appointment was thirty minutes before the family of the "accused" would arrive, allowing us time to review David's findings.

"Nick, Sarah, how are you?" our dapper attorney said. David always looked like he'd stepped off the page of a Brooks Brothers catalog. He wore a starched shirt with French cuffs and gold links, polished wing-tips, and a handsome silk paisley tie. A tanned face and a beautiful head of silver hair rounded out the picture. David had such a gentle nature. Walking across the black-and-white marble floor, he reached out to shake our hands. "Come on in, and let's take a look at some things."

David began by sharing his findings concerning the child living next door to my mother. Tommy had long been suspected of cruelty to animals, but this was the first time solid evidence came into play.

Shuffling the papers in the folder, he said, "Sarah, you're the only person who can see to it that this child gets the help he needs."

"How so? If I press charges and he's found guilty, he'll be sent to some sort of juvenile detention center. How does that get him the help he needs?"

"There's a full staff of qualified professionals there, and that child certainly needs help. One of my associate lawyers did extensive research on Tommy, some of which was in Iron Springs—Mulberry Street in particular. Have you noticed that lately most of the houses have fenced-in backyards but no outdoor pets?"

"Everyone had a dog or a cat or both when we were growing up."

"Okay, but since the Asheworths moved in two years ago, have you ever seen a pet other than your Annie on that street?"

I was unable to move for what seemed to be light-years. "Holy Moses—that's true! So you're saying *he's* possibly the reason?"

Before David could continue, his secretary cracked the door open and poked her head in. "Excuse the interruption, but these gentlemen are here to see you."

As the door opened, I recognized Detective Langley and Sergeant Henry. Standing, David shook the hand of each officer. "Gentlemen, I'm sure you know Nick and Sarah Heart. So, what can I do for you?"

"We have some news about the Asheworth boy and his parents," Detective Langley said.

Our attorney offered each of them a chair.

"Thanks, but we'll stand. On the way here, the Asheworths' car drove head-on into a utility pole. Mr. Asheworth was killed on impact. Tommy's mother is in critical condition, and it's not lookin' good for her, I'm sorry to say."

"Oh my God!" Nick blurted out. "And what about Tommy?"

"Vanished," Sergeant Henry answered. "There's absolutely no sign of him anywhere. I'm not at liberty to say much, but Tommy may have had a hand in the accident. The Highway Patrol took charge at the site of the accident. The Iron Springs police are there too. We've alerted the Greenway police to go to your farm, just to be on the safe side."

Luke Langley took the lead. "We're not sure he even knows your name or where you live, but it's better to be safe than sorry. I don't want to alarm you, but we did find a sketchbook tucked under the back seat."

"And?" I asked.

"Tommy drew pages of handguns firing bullets into hearts."

I said, "This art teacher understands the symbolism, and obviously he knows our name. What about my mother and grandmother? He knows them and where they live."

Luke answered quickly. "We have a car cruising that immediate area, but to avoid any unnecessary panic, we haven't told anyone in that neighborhood. There's really no need. It's not a crime scene. He's trying to get away, not go back home."

Sergeant Henry shifted his weight, "Mrs. Heart, I know this is hard, but try not to worry too much. He's only thirteen—we'll find him, probably before the sun goes down."

C3⬝80

Nick and I went home, and the remainder of our morning traveled at the pace of near reverse. We tried our best to go along as if nothing had happened, which was proving next to impossible. Every creak of the floor sent my heart racing, and if the dogs barked, I nearly fainted. "This is insane," I said, putting the potato I had peeled into one giant fry down on the drain board.

"I know what you mean. I can't concentrate on anything," Nick said. "I've read the same page three or four times. I think I'll go to the barn."

"I'll go work on my book. I'll disappear into the story, and the time will fly by. You two have to stay here," I said, looking at two long faces and four sad eyes. "Don't look at me like that, Annie. You need to rest. Caesar, take care of your sister."

Bouncing along in my golf cart, I could see that the two Greenway officers were still sitting on the porch swing. They hadn't moved an inch since we got home. Yesterday Nick had accidentally backed the tractor into the left side of the double barn doors, and Coy was hard at work repairing the splintered trim board. I waved while pulling up to my office, and he returned the gesture. I hobbled to the door, noticing it was slightly ajar. *Hmm. That's weird. I know I closed it yesterday.* "Hey, Coy," I yelled. "Did you go in here today?"

Before he could answer, something hit me like a bolt of lightning and literally flew right across my body, which was now flat on the ground. "What the hell?" I yelled, looking over my shoulder just in time to see Coy level a young boy using a broken piece of one-by-six pressure-treated pine.

The two Greenway police officers, surprised as I was, bolted from the porch swing, and Nick was standing over me, having a stroke.

"Are you okay? Oh my God, Sarah. Are you okay?"

Trying to stand up, I said, "I think so."

"Wait a minute. Don't go so fast. Are you sure you're all right?"

"Yes, I'm sure."

Out of nowhere, three police cars came roaring down our drive.

Detective Langley was first in line and came straight to me. Sergeant Henry slapped handcuffs on Tommy and stuffed him into the back seat of the squad car.

"Well, Sarah," Luke said. "I guess this is one way to get to know each other."

"Yes…How…?" I stammered.

"We were already on our way out here. News travels fast in a small town, especially if you were having lunch at Trixie's Diner on Main Street in Greenway. Apparently the tow truck driver was finishing off his second 'all the way' Super Dog and Yoo-hoo when he got the call from the office dispatcher on his walkie-talkie. She gave him directions to the crash site and told him to be on the lookout for the missing and potentially dangerous boy.

"The fellow who had been sitting next to him heard it all and, luckily, lives about fifteen miles back down this road. So when he stopped at the end of his drive to get the mail after lunch and saw a boy hitchin' a ride on the back of a hay truck, he called 911. He told them what he'd seen and that the truck was headed in the direction of your farm. You see—"

I interrupted. "Please don't tell me any more. At least not now."

Looking over my shoulder, Luke said, "I wonder how Tommy got past the Greenway officers."

Nick glanced in the direction of the porch floor, which now reflected a veneer of peanut shells with Pepsi cans sitting on the arms of the padded swing. Struggling for an answer beyond the obvious "asleep-on-the-job", Nick said, "This is a big farm, and a little boy can squeeze through fence slats like a greased pig."

"I guess so, but we've got him now."

I looked at Luke. "If you go to the Asheworths' house to search Tommy's room for evidence or something, please don't tell my mother or grandmother anything about what happened here. I'll call Mama in a minute, before she hears it on the news or the front-porch-gossip grapevine."

"I understand," he said, reaching to open the squad car door. "There'll be more you have to do about this, but I'll talk to you ahead of time."

Nick offered Luke his hand. "Thanks. We'll talk soon."

Greenway's finest remained quietly off to the side during all the commotion, but now it was their turn. "Mr. Heart, we're real sorry we didn't see that kid. I don't know how he got by us."

Nick scowled. "I'm real sorry you didn't see him too, but I'm guessing my wife is even more disappointed. It's lucky for you she's not hurt. I'm sure there will be some sort of report I'll need to fill out. Now, what should I say?"

"We're real sorry," the tall one repeated.

He handed them the broom and dustpan from Coy's worksite. "I would certainly hope so. Before you leave, be sure to sweep up the mess you made on our porch."

"Yes, sir." They walked quickly back to our house.

"You're wonderful," I said. "That side porch isn't more than fifty yards from the barn. I understand why Coy didn't see him. He was in and out of the barn, and Tommy could have just waited for the chance to dart across the yard. But…"

"We're just going to let it go, but were I a gambling man, I would bet a nap in the afternoon sun came right after they consumed a giant bag of roasted peanuts."

"I guess," I said, taking a deep breath. "I need to call Mama."

24

Betsy came over two days before our second annual Christmas party under the guise of a visit and taking me for an outing. I could no longer continue with my pretense of situational ignorance. "I know about the party; Mama let it slip over Thanksgiving. You guys are so sweet. What's next to do?"

"I'm supposed to take you to lunch and antiquing while the Hadley Falls florists decorate your house, and when we come back in about four hours or so, you'll know the surprise. Rose, Margaret, Jennifer, and Elizabeth will also be here by then."

"Fantastic. Lunch at River's Bend and then antiquing. On the way home, could we please stop and visit Rascal, though? And do I ever have a story to tell you! Well, several stories, actually, and I'll start with the two ladies at the barn."

"Of course to Rascal. Now, what's their story? Sounds juicy."

I opened the back door of Betsy's car. "Nectar-of-the-gods juicy, but kind of sad, too."

Halfway down our drive, Betsy announced, "Okay, you have my attention."

"Here goes, and don't tell me to hurry up. It wrecks my train of thought, and I'll have to start over."

"God forbid!"

"I'll ignore that." I giggled. "I'm sure you remember Linda and Nancy, who board with us, and the Rowdy Girls' dinner conversation about the upheaval at Hobart, Hathaway, Peters, and Vance."

"Yes, and?"

"And..." I continued to lay it all out.

"Wow!" Betsy said after I finished.

"Exactly. Common sense would tell you that words have been exchanged. They still ride here, just not together. But our issue is not the alleged affair. It's that Nancy came into our house and riffled through our things. Nick spoke with her concerning the stationery issue and gave her one month to find another barn."

"One month was generous. Now, what about the boy that hurt Annie?"

"We are completely out of the picture until the trial. All I know is via our attorney. Because Tommy's thirteen and a flight risk, with no living relatives, he'll remain in the custody of the court system for now. I don't really know what that means, but I also don't want to know."

"That is such a troubling situation," Betsy said, pulling into the parking space closest to the restaurant door.

"It is, but let's go enjoy our lunch. I'm starving."

Betsy gave Jennifer a wave as we walked in the door.

Our sisterhood's restaurateur pointed to an out-of-the-way table for the two of us, and my broomstick-straight leg.

Lunch was delicious, and over a warm brownie à la mode, Betsy asked about my novel.

"I'm making great headway; that's all I'm going to say."

"Did you set yourself a deadline?"

"No, but maybe by late spring for the rough draft. I was reading about what a writer needs to do before submitting a manuscript, so I decided to hire an editor. Her name is Ellie Ward, and it's her job to make my manuscript as polished as possible before I send it out. Thankfully, she can also write the perfect query letter."

"Where did you find her, and why didn't you tell me?"

I smiled. "I just hired her. I found her online—the same way I choose wine."

"No way. You don't drink, so you choose the bottles displaying the prettiest labels."

"Correct. Her website is very well done and a little quirky, which caught my eye. She also rode horses when she was little and lives in Raleigh."

"How does it work? Is she expensive?"

"I'm learning as I go along, and yes, it's expensive, but I also don't care. Her expertise is invaluable. Fortunately, I have my own income, so Nick need never know."

"You couldn't keep that a secret if you tried." Betsy laughed. "You'll crack like an egg, and he'll never say a word—especially if you're happy. New topic. Since you still have your cast, what are you going to wear to the Moss Creek Charity Ball Saturday night?"

"Pants. I've actually enjoyed working on that. Margaret told me the other day that her generous husband is going to drive the dealership's minibus so we can all ride together. How fun!"

"Yes, and hopefully Bill won't drive as fast as he usually does."

Antiquing took the better part of the next two hours, and spending quality time with my Rascal was the best part of the day. I had been there at least twice a week since the accident, but it just wasn't the same seeing him without riding. A teenager at the barn was exercising my horse three times a week and doing a great job, though.

Making our way back home, Betsy asked, "Have you checked on Olivia lately?"

"Actually, yes. I called her the other day and asked if you and I could come for a visit before Christmas. I hope that's okay with you? She sounded in great spirits and asked if we'd bring her some Moravian cookies. This is funny—she said, 'Only the ones in the red tin from Old Salem.' I thought we could go next week, but not Monday; I have an appointment with Dr. Baxter."

"I can go Tuesday."

"Perfect," I said, stretching up from the back seat. "Wow…look at our front door. It's beautiful! The garland is amazing and the wreath finishes it off so nicely."

Margaret, Rose, Elizabeth, and Jennifer were standing on the back porch as we pulled in. It was all I could do to slow myself down as I came up to them. "The front door is amazing!" I yelled.

Margaret hurried to meet me. "Slow down. We don't want you to break anything else."

"Thanks. I tend to get ahead of myself. What smells so good?" I said as we all poured into the kitchen.

"We thought we'd have an impromptu Rowdy Girls dinner," Margaret answered. "Nick offered to bow out, saying he had stuff he needed to do in Hadley Falls. So here we are, your house is dressed for the party on Friday, and dinner's almost ready."

"Fantastic!" Taking off my coat, I glanced down the hallway. "Wow—look at that! I do need to confess something. Over Thanksgiving, my mother let it slip about the party, but I know nothing else. Look at the banister and the table arrangement. This is perfect. Thank you! Thank you!"

"We didn't do much of anything," Elizabeth said. "It's once again the handiwork of the Hadley Falls Florists."

"It's lovely, isn't it," Rose said. "Those two men are truly gifted. Oh, did everyone get the message from Susan about bringing nothing but your saddle?"

Everyone answered yes, except for me of course.

Margaret lowered her chin. "Thankfully we're not bring our horses this time. I'm not sure Louie could have made the trip. In fact, I think it might be time to retire that wonderful old bay and go horse shopping. But I can't pay board on two horses."

Knowing we had more than enough room and plenty of pasture, I said, "Bring him here. You can pay something for his hay and grain, but the rest is free."

"I couldn't do that."

"It's not my place to say," Rose interjected, "but that barn is huge, as are the pastures. You could come over and ride him in the indoor ring to keep him moving. I think it would be perfect—LLF rehab for horses and humans."

Margaret beamed. "It's a great idea, but Nick needs to agree."

"We'll discuss it, but I know it'll be fine. Now, who thinks Mrs. Pritchett will wear the same dress this year, and surely Evelyn will not be half-naked?"

Jennifer sighed. "It's funny about that gosh-awful green dress, isn't it? I wonder if she's color-blind. And yes, Evelyn will be half-naked. I hope Mr. Suggs is still alive. He must be in his mid-nineties by now."

"As is his tux." Betsy laughed, and we continued with the Rowdy Girls as usual.

CB&O

Nick got home around eight thirty and joined us in the living room with a cup of coffee and a wedge of cake. "Have you ladies had a good time? I imagine you've torn poor old Mrs. Pritchett to pieces, tarred and feathered Nancy, and rendered a verdict as to the snake-mean, possibly homicidal little boy?"

Emphatically, Margaret replied, "Absolutely, and we've had a wonderful time. Oh—we thought we'd come about an hour early to get everything put together for the party."

"Good idea." I nodded. "I'm so excited. Thanks again for doing all this."

25

Sibby called on Thursday, assuring me that she and Grammy were doing great, but they were going to stay home this year. The drive was too long, and the party would be too late for them. They were missed, but our holiday house was overflowing with the thirty or so who came: our two boarders, school friends, the Rowdy Girls plus husbands, David, Ethan and Meg, and Coy. And, happily, Sidney and Jacob would stay the night so Sidney could ride the next day.

Halfway through the evening, Linda and Nancy found themselves side by side at the buffet table. I had actually debated inviting them but did so thinking that they would both decline. Clearly I was wrong. Linda shot Nancy a death glare that startled even me. Nick and several others saw it too. There were words shared at a whisper, and I knew immediately that Nick's generous offer of one month was now off the table.

"Sarah, I need you to help me in the kitchen," Nick said, taking my elbow.

Once I propped myself against the counter, I asked, "I'm guessing you also saw 'the death stare?'"

"I did. Nancy has to go and now. I'll take her to the side and give her until next Tuesday to find a new barn."

Just then the kitchen door nearly flew off the hinges, and there she stood.

"I'm going, so there's no need for you to berate me in front of everyone," Nancy said, throwing her coat over her shoulder. "You know it's not all one sided, but I guess you've made up your minds and are standing in Linda's corner of this fight."

The veins on Nick's neck were bulging. I swear I could count his pulse.

"We're only looking at the facts, Nancy. You came into our house uninvited, you stole paper from my desk, and you tried to frame me and discredit my name. Our quarrel with you has absolutely nothing to do with your affair with your once closest friend's husband."

"Alleged affair," she yelled, pushing past Nick and slamming the kitchen door on her way down the porch steps.

Nick looked at me. "Holy Christ!"

"Yes and Merry Christmas," I said. "Now, deep breath. We need to get back to the party and work on damage control. No one needs to know what just happened, but I'm certain they heard it all."

When we walked back into the dining room, everyone stopped talking and looked our way.

"Happy faces, everyone. All is well. Seriously, it is," I said.

The Rowdy Girls took their cue and began to divide and conquer, starting up fresh conversations about the food, the decorations, and whatever else came to mind.

Linda worked her way in our direction. "I'm so sorry about all that," she said.

"It's forgotten," Nick said. "Now, this is a Christmas party. Let's have some fun."

꩜

Early Saturday morning, I gave our dogs a kiss goodbye while hand-ing Coy a mile-long list of their care instructions. After taking a quick glance, he stuffed the stapled bundle into his back pocket, gave the dogs a whistle, and the three of them vanished into the barn. With air kisses, I told Sidney to enjoy the ride but to remember that Buddy was *my* horse. We shared a laugh, and she waved goodbye as she cantered toward the first jump. Nick came out of the barn, reporting that Jacob had everything under control and we were ready to go.

꩜

Parking our car at the Ford dealership, we, along with the other ten passengers, piled our duffel and roller bags into the very back storage area of the minibus.

Bill questioned Margaret about her "steamer trunk," as he called it. "Why do you need to pack so much for just one night?"

Margaret stood on her tiptoes and kissed his cheek. "Because I do."

The super-plush minibus had soft leather side-by-side seats that could be adjusted individually. The driver's seat was stationary, but the shotgun seat swiveled. Two tables stood anchored in the middle of the second and third rows. My leg and I took up half of the one long sofa-like seat that finished off the interior.

Buckling in, Betsy carried on about Frank's choice of outfit. Frank was one of my favorite people for several reasons, but mostly because he was so comfortable in his own skin. He didn't care two hoots that the socks he was wearing didn't match or that his argyle sweater had a giant hole in the underarm.

Rose had created a wonderful travel lunch of petite ham biscuits, macaroni salad, and fruit. Adjusting the rearview mirror, Bill watched for fallen crumbs on the thick carpet. Margaret, Nick, and I ironed out the plans for moving Louie to our farm. Nick refused to charge her for anything beyond hay and grain, but Bill insisted they pay some sort of board. The vet and farrier bills would be mailed directly to their address. The deal was sealed with a handshake during our one potty stop. Jennifer and Mickey, along with Elizabeth and Ian, were engaged in a hot political conversation.

Somewhere nearing the middle of our drive, Rose said, "So, Sarah, what's new with Olivia Cromwell?"

I was taken totally off guard. "What?" I hadn't brought her up since our dinner at Rose's house.

With a quiet voice, Rose explained. "Wednesday, while the 'flamboyant florists' were decorating your house and dinner was simmering, we four took a break and walked down to the barn. Margaret recalled that day at Falling Creek when you needed to leave early to meet with the architect who was creating a separate space for you to write. Anyway, the door was unlocked, and we took a peek inside. It's simply lovely."

"Thanks. I agree," I said hesitantly. *Did they look at my book?* "Ed did an amazing job converting a filthy old toolshed into what you saw. Talk about before and after."

"It's so pretty," Margaret said. "I hope it was okay we took a look inside?"

"Of course! Ed actually started on it before I got hurt, but its being finished and furnished was a total surprise when I came home from the hospital. Linda—y'all remember her—decorated the space."

"What a lovely surprise," Rose said. "But even more surprising is what you're actually writing. You've dipped your toe into something other than how-to horse books. Bravo!"

Reading between the lines of my expression, which fell somewhere between panic and upset, Jennifer exclaimed, "I hate this! I knew we shouldn't have been in there, but we were. I swear to you, Sarah, we didn't read any of whatever you're working on, but we did see the bold print on the title page."

Already knowing the answer, I asked, "What bold print?"

Elizabeth replied. "*The Disappearance of Lucy Butterfield.* You don't have to tell us anything if you don't want to."

"Bill," I asked, "how many miles do we have left?"

"About an hour's worth."

I decided *why not?* My original reason for secrecy, protecting Olivia, had passed, so off I went, happily outlining my project.

"The core of my novel is about a sisterhood of six, with a side story concerning the lives of an older lady and the main character. Separated in age by close to forty years, the two women find an unexpected parallel, which instantly connects them." I also mentioned giving my word to Olivia for a read-aloud. "It's funny, she always adds 'before I die' to her requests."

Betsy pretended she didn't already know. "You mentioned a sisterhood. I'm sure one is perhaps a quirky dresser, with tons of shoes, and a cohort in crime. Visualize: tall, and blond, with an hourglass figure."

"If your main character has a single friend"—Rose winked—"she could be at least five years younger than the rest."

Jennifer took her turn. "All sisterhoods have one member who has the goods on everybody in town, and she either owns a restaurant or a hair salon. A restaurant is a great choice—don't you think?"

"One should be very mysterious and from some faraway place," Elizabeth insisted.

"Like California?" Margaret giggled. "And you are mysterious."

"No, like South America—Rio maybe. A headliner at the Copacabana. And I'm not at all mysterious."

I laughed, shaking my head. "Margaret, what do you have to say?"

"A variety of characters makes any novel more interesting. Perhaps one could be a naturalist who raises chickens and goats."

Thrilled with their enthusiasm, I said, "Your suggestions are all duly noted."

Bill cleared his throat to get my attention. "Do the younger women have husbands, and what do they do?"

Raising my eyebrows, I said, "Please don't be offended, but all the husbands are only briefly mentioned. Rose, you look like you have something to say?"

"I do." She smiled, holding the sandwich tin. "Referring back to the single woman—it would add a bit of global flair if she came from an English-speaking foreign country, wouldn't it?"

"Excuse me," Bill said impatiently. "What do you mean by 'briefly mentioned'? Why aren't we—I mean they—not given much space?"

Betsy laughed. "Because they're not important to the story."

"Hey, I'm driving the minibus!"

"Her point exactly," Margaret offered. "Bill, I've loved you since the third grade, but, darling, you're just the driver. Now the Rowdy Girls…Ooh, those adventures could be part of the story."

From his overstuffed copilot chair, Frank swiveled to face us. "Pull over and throw them all out. Nick, you've been suspiciously quiet. Let me guess. Your character is wildly handsome, filthy rich, amazingly thoughtful, and just plain wonderful in every way."

"I have no idea, but I'm enjoying helping Sarah research the main character, her husband, and their passionate marriage."

"How nice," Ian said. "Plowing through volumes of courthouse records is intensely boring."

Elizabeth took her husband's hand. "I love you to pieces, my dear, but sometimes you're as thick as mud. He's not talking about *that* kind of research."

"Oh—well...no...no?" Ian paused. "She has a cast."

"Yes, she does," Nick said. "But now it's only up to mid-thigh."

Fanning my beet-red face, I said, "Oh my God! Okay, we'll just stop right there."

"There's Moss Creek Farm," Bill bellowed. "Let the fun begin!"

附️

Hours later, dressed in our finery, we were standing in the foyer of one of the oldest hunt clubs in Virginia. From the walnut wainscoting and vintage mural wallpaper to the three-tiered crystal chandeliers, the bouquet of antiquity and affluence filled the air. Every year Susan and Roger Tillman hosted a charity ball to raise money to feed the hounds. A year's worth of nourishment for a pack of thirty was expensive.

The silent auction was always a financial success. For hours, folks continued to up their bids, determined to win the all-inclusive trip to Monte Carlo, original artwork, quality tack, the use of someone's boat, or a black-tie dinner prepared by Chef Someone Special.

Running the length of the dining room wall, buffet tables covered in fresh white linens and interspersed with gorgeous flower arrangements supported our evening feast. There were oysters on the half shell and boiled shrimp sharing space in a boat-shaped tub of crushed ice. Lobster bisque with lump crab, crackers, and pita bread was the soup offering, followed by silver trays filled with a variety of stuffed puff pastries. Chafing dishes warming vegetables of all sorts led you to the carving station, with beef tenderloin taking center stage.

Margaret and Bill, both exceptional dancers, boogied the night away. Elizabeth, Jennifer, and their husbands talked politics and current events nonstop. Betsy and Frank knew everyone there and moved from one people pod to the next. Rose was conversationally entangled with a man none of us recognized, but we were thrilled she was enjoying herself.

Nick and I divided our time between our assigned table and the dance floor. When the band played swing music from the 1940s, Nick held on to me and, without the use of my crutches, turned me this way and that. I felt like the twirling, windup ballerina in the jewelry box—it was paradise to be free of my sticks. There was also a barrage of "oh my goodness, what happened to you?" conversations.

Once again, old Mrs. Pritchett wore that ghastly green dress, but this time she added her fox stole. Punxsutawney Phil waiting to see his shadow in the grass came to mind when I saw that poor fellow, his clothespin mouth biting the tail of the next. Evelyn had toned down her outfit just a bit, but Lyle Bayshore still found her irresistible. The past twelve months had not been kind to Mr. Suggs, but there he was and sporting his moth-eaten, polka-dotted tux. We all gave him a bit more attention, thinking that we may not see him again.

At the end of the evening, our limousine driver was waiting outside to take us back to the farm and our guesthouse.

Getting ready for bed, Nick and I reminisced about last year's ball, when we had shared this same bedroom at the top of the stairs. That night, with each of us in a tiny twin bed, we'd opened our hearts and shared our fears about being intimate.

"We've come a long way in one year. Truly, Sarah, I didn't know I could be this happy."

"Me either. I knew life with you would be amazing, but I had no idea just how amazing."

"Sweet dreams, baby," Nick said, tucking me in and getting under the covers of his Tiny Tim twin bed. "Sarah, are you still awake?" he said minutes later.

"Yes. What's wrong?"

"Nothing. I just need to ask a favor."

"Sure?"

"In your book—thinking about what Frank said earlier—will you please make me not too wonderful? I need some flaws."

I tried but failed to harness my giggle. "He does have flaws, my love, but for the millionth time, it isn't you. But I can write intelligently about a fictitious husband because I have a real one...Actually, I've had two."

"I know, but I need for my character to have flaws in your story."

"The husband of the narrator does have flaws, which are already in my story."

He seemed surprised. "Oh, well what are they? I'm not terrible, am I?"

"Good Lord and good night, my love."

"Wait a minute," he said, pulling up on one elbow. "We need to talk about this."

"No, actually, we don't. It's called writer's privilege. It's a novel. It's fiction. It's not really you anyway. Now, sweet dreams."

"But it *is* me," Nick insisted.

"No, it isn't—or me, either—and to set your mind at ease, the narrator also has flaws. You, my friends, the horses, family, and that weird lady who works at the drugstore were the catalyst for bits and pieces, but that's where reality ends. In fact, most of the story came from the wild blue yonder of my imagination. I've never met those people, and many of the places don't exist. And that's what makes writing fiction fun. I can do whatever I want within three hundred and fifty or so pages. Now, if I said Nicholas F. Heart from Greenway, North Carolina, did something that wasn't true, then there's a problem. But if Todd Gooseberry from Nowhere, North Carolina, did the same thing, it's okay."

"Please don't name me Todd."

"The husband's name isn't Todd, but if you don't knock it off, I'll change it in a skinny minute, and I'll tell everyone it really is you. But even in fiction, if you're stating a fact—like when Columbus discovered America—that needs to be correct. Some people read with a highlighter and would love nothing more than to catch the author out on a technicality or a misspelled word. Now, go to sleep—Todd."

Nick whispered, "What's your name in the book?"

"I'm not in the book. Good night."

⊂ॐ⊃

The aroma of bacon, toast, and eggs wafted quietly up the stairs. *Heavenly*, I thought. Betsy always took on the job of making breakfast and said she loved feeding the troops. I didn't know her secret to scrambled eggs, but they were always better than mine.

"Does anyone know what's happening today?" I asked, taking my seat at the enormous round hardwood table with twelve ladder-back chairs.

Betsy spooned the eggs onto a platter. "Susan's brought someone in to work with us on something very different, but I don't know who it is or what we're doing."

"Whatever it is, it will be an adventure. It's rather refreshing to have something new to do," Rose said, passing the bacon.

"Refreshing. We'll see. At least we don't have the possibility of dying in the cross-country field," Margaret said, taking a bite of toast. "Thanks to Sarah, we're safer this year."

"Don't bet on it. Whatever she's thought up will be demanding as always, but I can't imagine how I'll fit into the equation."

⊂ॐ⊃

After breakfast the men were off to the links, and we made our way to the barn. Susan motioned for us to join her in the observation room. For one brief moment we were warm in that nicely furnished, heated space with an efficiency kitchen, the only bathroom, and a huge observation window that allowed us to view the entire indoor ring.

"This year has offered the challenge of doing something that everyone, broken leg or not, can do. So, I would like to introduce Mr. Angus Thatcher. Gus is a top-level hunter-jumper judge, and we're going to have a horse show."

Elizabeth gasped. "A horse show?"

"Yes, the five of you will ride, and Sarah's going to learn how a judge makes his or her selection. They'll both have a card and will compare notes. While you five are getting tacked up, those two will go over the basic rules. Now, one at a time, reach into the bowl and pull out the name of your first horse. Your lesson will be in the schooling ring before you ride each course."

Initially, I was a pouty puss at not being able to ride and feeling out of place judging. But after a few minutes with Mr. Angus "Gus" Thatcher, I was consumed by his tutorial and charmed by his slightly diluted Scottish accent and Highlander demeanor. Gus was stern but in a soft way, and I knew he was strictly business in the judge's box.

Together we went over the basics of marking the card, most of which I already knew from years of horse showing—refusing a jump, knocking down poles, swapping leads, and such. It was the next part—the finer points—I found so interesting. "Don't worry about things too much, and please stop calling me Mr. Thatcher. Just Gus will do. We'll let my card be the final word, so there are no hurt feelings."

Reaching into his dilapidated briefcase, Gus pulled out the drawings of his five course designs and grabbed a retractable tape measure. We moved toward the ring, where Deacon, Susan's barn manager, helped placed the jumps and step off the strides. Deacon, who was rugged and Holy Christmas gorgeous, set polls and, using the tractor—plus attachment, dragged the ring smooth. It was spiritually pleasing to the soul to watch him move. The end result was nine perfectly-laid-out jumps on well-manicured footing. As I pinned a copy of course number one to the board at the in gate, I experienced the oddest sensation. I felt alive again. I was back in the game.

Betsy stood beside me, studying the course. "Well, forget having an easy go of it. Look at this thing—a line—to an in-and-out, then to a rollback, then finish on an outside line. Thankfully this is a big ring, but seriously, Sarah, did *you* draw this?"

"No, but I can't wait to watch you guys ride it. Wait until you see course number two—you do both inside diagonal lines, plus the single, then…" I stopped. "Do you recognize our judge? Isn't he the man Rose spent time with last night?"

"I think you're right. Look at Rose—not now—but her face is flushed, and she's walking our way. I can't decide if she's worried, or smitten."

Margaret came around the corner, grumbling all the way. "Forget what I said about being safer this year. I drew Top Hat. I'm going to die."

Top Hat was Susan's retired Grand Prix horse and could be quite a handful.

"Boo-hoo." Jennifer shuddered. "Danny Boy is so big I'll never turn him to that rollback."

"I'll trade with you," Rose offered. "I pulled Magic Man out of the bowl. I'll never get that Thoroughbred to slow down to make the correct strides."

Betsy waved her slip of paper. "I'm keeping mine. Talk about luck of the draw. I'm on Diamond Girl."

"No trades for me, either. I've always wanted to ride Donatello," Elizabeth said.

"Well, don't worry too much or get too attached. Remember, Susan said for you to pull out the name of your first ride. It's my understanding you switch horses for the second trip, and so on. By the end of the day, you will have ridden all five horses over five different courses," I said above their chorus of groans and moans.

On my way to the judge's box, I asked, "Rose, isn't Angus Thatcher the man you were talking to last night?"

"Yes," she said before hurrying on down the aisle.

I had a great time as an apprentice, and Gus was a wonderful teacher. I shared that I was an art educator and thought his tutorial skills were top-notch. He laughed and thanked me, adding he couldn't even draw a stick figure. The last part of his sentence required serious restraint on my part. Not only was he unknowingly dead wrong, but I desperately wanted to teach him how.

This was not playtime by any stretch of the imagination. Riding five unfamiliar horses over five difficult courses, while being judged, was a true test of skill, requiring serious concentration. There were a few scary moments here and there, but in the end mostly *hurrahs* rang out. I was surprised to say that I had enjoyed my time in the judge's box immensely. Collectively, we saluted Susan on a job well done in finding something we all could do.

While helping to pack the saddles, Susan said, "I'm glad you guys had fun! Everyone rode into the ring on the horse, and everyone came out on the horse. No injuries, just a few sore muscles. No actual prizes, just the thrill of doing something so different so well. It truly was a blue-ribbon day."

With hugs and goodbyes, we said repeatedly how delightful it was to share an overnight at Moss Creek Farm.

26

Margaret winced as she reached to help Rose with our travel dinner back on the bus. "It would have been easier to have ridden in the cross-country field than to have had that horse show. I take back everything I said about Sarah's leg making it easier this year. I actually think it was the hardest ride we've ever had."

Rose agreed, handing out roast beef sandwiches from last night's leftovers.

Jennifer took the first bite. "Yum. These are delicious. How did you score the leftovers?"

"When the staff began to clear the buffet, I snuck into the kitchen and simply asked for a to-go box for twelve of beef and bread. The potato salad and petit fours are a surprise to me as well. Now, Sarah, and perhaps the rest of you, recognized Gus Thatcher as the man I talked to last night. I had no idea who he was at the party and was surprised to see him today. He must actually hate women."

Bill spoke up. "Why do you say that?"

"Because he created five of the most difficult courses I've ever ridden."

"No kidding," Betsy said, offering everyone a bottle of water.

"I won't be able to walk until possibly Wednesday," Margaret said. "Danny Boy was my last mount. His weird canter makes him difficult to ride."

"How about the five-stride first line I did in four and a half on all five horses?" Rose said, shaking her head. "I'll admit, though, that I'm curious about Gus. Last night we just spoke in general chitchat, but who is he?"

Betsy said, "While we were packing up, Susan shared some general information on him. Let me see…He and his family moved to America from Scotland when Gus was ten—he graduated from William and Mary. He was a top rider in his day and is a well-known judge in Virginia, Maryland, and DC. He's single and owns a farm somewhere in the Shenandoah Valley. I think she said he's fifty-four, and now, Rose, don't be mad, but he asked me about you just before we left the barn today."

Rose nearly dumped the box of sandwiches. "*Asked you what?*"

"If you were single or were seeing anyone."

"And you said?" she asked, lifting her eyebrows.

"Yes and no," Betsy answered. "He also asked for your number."

Her face flushed. "Really? Did you give it to him?"

Betsy didn't bother to hide her excitement. "I absolutely did, and I gave him your email, too."

"Oh," Rose said, allowing that one word to hang in the air.

Taking a sip of water, Margaret said, "I think it's wonderful. You two would be perfect for each other. With your stoic English side, half the time we don't know if you're happy or sad, but the Scotsman would understand instantly."

Jennifer reached for another finger sandwich. "He's very good-looking, and a farm anywhere in the Shenandoah Valley would be beautiful."

"He loves horses," Elizabeth added, "and possibly British accents."

I snickered. "He did give you high marks, even when you were wrong to the second jump every time. I actually questioned him about that."

"What'd he say?"

"Something poetic like, 'my mistake,' blushing as he added the hash mark."

Rose sat back in her seat, her face glowing. "I thought he was very interesting."

"Sarah, Susan put us down for a return visit the last weekend in March," Betsy said. "She thinks you'll be ready to go by then?"

"Hopefully this beast of a cast comes off the second week in January—fingers crossed."

Elizabeth pleaded, "Well, don't get back in shape too quickly. We need for you to be somewhat pitiful for Susan to take it easy on us."

"You have a very rich fantasy life, thinking Susan might ever do that," Jennifer joked.

"I just don't think Louie can make that trip." Margaret sighed.

Before she could finish her thought, Nick jumped in. "After you bring Louie to our farm, you can ride Chance until you find a new horse. He'd love camp—he's an easy ride."

"Wow...thanks!" she said.

"Great idea," I said. "Sidney loves to ride Chance. She says he can see his spot from a mile away—oh, last night it just hit me; I'm moving Rascal to Long Leaf with Louie. It's a no-brainer. The only reason I didn't move him before was Louie. Our boys are the dynamic duo. They've been best friends for, golly, I can't remember how long."

Margaret's voice quavered. "Twelve years. Sarah, I love it. I know the boys will be happier to be together."

"Yes, and when you find a new mount, he has a stall too. Now, stop worrying. I can see it on your face. Our two old guys will stable on the south side of the barn and use that pasture. We'll ride them, of course, but for the rest of the time, our two seniors won't care what we're doing—including our riding other horses. The pasture grass will win over us every time."

"Hey, I was wondering about Sidney and our vet Jacob," Betsy asked. "I only ask because last Thursday when I was buying grain, Bunky Elwood said—"

"Well, there you have it," Nick interrupted with a howl. "The gospel according to Bunky Elwood! Jennifer, that feed store is strong competition to your restaurant when it comes to gossip!"

"You've got that right. Men have their nerve talking about women spreading rumors. There's more trash talk passed around the baskets of onion sets and deer corn than you could imagine!"

"I love going to Elwood's Feed and Seed," I said. "It's truly like taking a step back in time. Where else can you scoop loose seeds into tiny brown paper bags and close them with a stapler? But to answer Betsy's question about Sidney and Jacob, I'm not really sure what's going on. I asked over Thanksgiving and the other night at our Christmas party and was told to 'leave it alone.' So, what do you know?"

Betsy frowned. "Not much."

Jennifer raised her hand. "I do. Bunky, along with his right-hand man, uh..."

"Earl." Rose snickered.

"Yes, that's it, Earl." Jennifer nodded. "Those two have lunch at

River's Bend nearly every Wednesday, and last week's topic was Jacob. Apparently, some woman out on Winding Creek Road had a horse emergency. While Jacob was finishing up, she questioned our handsome veterinarian about his love life, adding he wasn't getting any younger.

"According to Bunky, Jacob didn't offer much information, but did say he'd met someone very pretty and tall who loved horses. I'll make a hefty wager he's talking about Sidney."

"Interesting," I said. "But it would be easier to milk a steer than get information out of my youngest child."

Chuckling, Nick dropped his head to his hands. "Where do you get these expressions?"

"I don't know, but you know I'm right."

Betsy added, "Jacob's so cute. They'd look like a matched set of handsome bookends."

"Yes, they would. I adore my first son-in-law. Can I possibly get that lucky twice? Scott's so good to Emma."

Nick smiled. "If they were to get married, maybe he'd give us a discount on our vet bills."

"Don't count on it. Kimberly's husband's a dentist, and I think he actually charges us more." Frank laughed, adjusting his jacket.

"Oh, he does not," Betsy insisted. "But we should discuss a family rate."

⊂⊃⊂⊃

Margaret and I made plans to move "the boys" between Christmas and New Year's. I told her I'd get Coy to set up the stalls and make sure their pasture was ready to go.

Rose continued to ask questions here and there about "Gus the Horse Show Judge," and the rest of us winked back and forth, delighted with her excitement. Perhaps her obvious interest in the Scotsman could renew her faith in men, especially after the Henri du Bois love disaster, and simultaneously move the cookery show to the back burner of consideration.

From the last seat on the bus, I smiled watching my friends and thought, *Damn cast or not, these are truly the best of times!*

27

O nce home from our fantastic weekend, and changed into my "cast rags," as I called them, I walked back into the kitchen. Nick had the Sunday newspaper laid out in front of him on the table.

Looking over the top of his readers, he said, "I got an email from Detective Luke Langley."

My stomach tightened. "Really? What'd he have to say?"

"Tommy's trial is going to start on January the fourth, and we will be required to testify. The prosecution's office will call us some-time this week."

"Goody!" I said with unbridled sarcasm. "This topic makes me so nervous."

"I know," Nick said, refolding the *Herald*. "But this trial is for animal cruelty only, which is an open-and-shut case, don't you think? Oh—this is tragic news. Tommy's mother passed away, so that's two deaths, or perhaps, murders."

"Oh my gosh, that's awful. Are they using the word 'murder'?"

"I'm not sure, but one theory is that Tommy forced the car to leave the road. There's not a curve for miles on that stretch of highway. The coroner's autopsy report said Mr. Asheworth died on impact, as opposed to a stroke or something. Tommy's fingerprints were also on the steering wheel, so it's possible he intentionally forced the car into the pole."

I shook my head. "I can't imagine being in a mindset where you actually did something like that."

"According to Luke, there were fresh shoe prints on the edge of the back seat, adding to the theory of Tommy possibly coming over the back and grabbing the wheel."

"All this heartbreak because he hurt my dog."

"Sarah, don't you dare think any of this is your fault! We may never know what really happened. It truly could have been unintentional—a spontaneous reaction to something his parents said. Who knows? But that child is clearly disturbed and needs help."

I shivered. "That's true, but it will haunt me forever. I don't believe anyone's born mean. Stubborn, argumentative, contrary, yes. But Tommy's absolutely off the deep end."

"My guess is that the juvenile court will see where the cruelty to animals piece takes them, and they'll proceed from there."

"Will you build us a fire while I cook dinner, and we can watch a sappy chick flick after we eat?"

"Yes, but Todd wouldn't do that for you."

"Probably not, but Darrell would." I laughed, opening the refrigerator door.

"Do not name me Darrell, Bunny."

"Bunny and Darrell—I like that. Bunny would have candy-striped wallpaper above the wainscoting in the dining room, with flowery chintz tie-back curtains and an oversize teardrop chandelier."

"No, you don't," Nick insisted.

As I curled into Nick's arms, watching *Bridget Jones's Diary*, I momentarily forgot about the pending trial.

C3℘

The next morning Nick dropped me off in front of Hadley Falls Mental Health & Wellness. "I'll be in the waiting room when you're finished," he said, helping me out of the car.

Choosing a seat in the outer office, I noticed the headline of the *Hadley Falls Herald*: Thirteen-Year-Old to Stand Trial. I tucked the newspaper under my arm.

"Morning," Deborah said. "Where shall we start?"

I handed her the newspaper. "I think here. This situation has me unraveling at the seams. I know I'm not to blame, but the fact I was the one who finally caught him haunts me."

"Actually, *you* didn't catch anyone. Someone hurt your dog. You took Annie to the vet. The police came. And the fingerprints on the arrow proved it was Tommy Asheworth."

"You're right. You know I feel guilty for everything. What if he comes after me years later when he gets out? He'd be able to drive by then."

"You can't live like this; let's keep working on your guilt issues."

As Dr. Baxter and I talked about all the issues I put in my letter, I found I was no longer upset about my mother's dating. Perhaps Luke had helped to round the corners of that situation. Happiness resonated in my every word when I told her about Louie and Rascal moving to the farm.

Dr. Baxter reached over to silence the infernal buzz of the "time's up" alarm. "You must stand fast as these situations resolve. It's a good thing your friends know about the book now—keeping secrets isn't good for you."

"Tomorrow we're going to visit Olivia, and I plan to read her some of what I've written. I'm slightly nervous, but for now Merry Christmas and Happy New Year. I won't be back until—wow—January, 2011."

"I'm sure she'll love the story. So, relax, enjoy your holiday, and I'll see you next year!"

28

"Good morning, Miss Olivia," I said, taking her hand. "You look lovely. Your Christmas sweater is so cute."

"This thing's as old as dirt, but I do love it." She smiled, straightening the large double-breasted buttons that were actually Santa's eyes. "Thanks for coming. It's been very lonely around here with Iris gone and all."

Betsy had created a circle of three chairs in the sunroom and reached into her picnic basket. "I bet it has. Let's have some tea and cookies. Sugar makes everything better."

"Betsy makes the best cookies you've ever eaten," I said, opening the container. "Don't worry. We didn't forget your Moravian cookies. You can save those for later."

"You girls are so thoughtful. What's all that?" she asked, pointing to the bundle of papers in my tote bag.

"It's part of my book. I thought I would read you a bit and you could share your thoughts."

Olivia took another cookie. "How exciting. I'm ready."

"Now, remember, the names and places are figments of my imagination, as is all the dialogue. Our collective real story is the launchpad for this tale of fiction," I said, taking a sip of hot tea. "Here we go."

The Disappearance of Lucy Butterfield

"Oh, I like the title," Olivia interrupted. "It's very mysterious."

I cleared my throat. "Thanks. Me too, but I can always change it if need be."

Chapter One

As I stepped into the darkness of the third-floor attic, something sharp grazed my ankle. I searched for the string to the overhead light. "Ouch!" I shouted, standing very still, my heart racing. I was never quite sure that space was free of coinhabitants.

I prayed my outburst would cause anything with a heartbeat to scurry away. Bending down to check my ankle, I realized the assailant was not a critter but a disjointed stack of framed pictures from my old house in Salty Path, and the former property of Amelia Stein. "Hmm, look at this," I said.

Pausing briefly, I said, "Amelia is the older sister's name."

"I like that. We had a second cousin named Amelia. She lived in a great big, two-story brick house off Oleander Drive in Wilmington. What's my name in the story?"

"Daphne," I answered.

"Oh no, no!" Olivia scowled. "I once knew a Daphne—she was awful! I need a new name."

"Okay, but try to think of one before I leave today. Remember, it's not really you, so perhaps a name you've always liked. Here's a pencil and paper for you to make notes," I said. "Uh, now, let's see…Where was I? Oh yes…"

She was the former owner of my house on Elm Street. When I purchased that quaint bungalow, Amelia said for me to keep any and everything I found in the house—including the attic. I was seriously retro in my taste and loved antiques, so I embraced the offer.

Several times over the next hour, I noticed Olivia blotting the corners of her eyes or enjoying a quick chuckle. It was hard to tell how she felt about the story, but the paper I gave her remained blank. Taking a break, I asked, "So, what'd you think?"

"I like it. No, I *love* it. Keep reading!"

"It's getting late, and to be honest, I'm a little tired."

Olivia pointed to Betsy. "You start reading."

Betsy laughed, but she reached over and transferred the remaining loose pages to her lap, "I'll read for a little while, but then we really must go."

"That'll be fine—or however long it takes you to finish all that," our dear senior insisted.

As Betsy read, Olivia howled out loud, cried softly, and smiled often. She never took her eyes from Betsy's face. With the final page read, Betsy removed her readers and folded her hands one over the other. "So, how do you like it so far?"

"It's just wonderful. I even like the parts about the horses. I'm scared of those giant animals, but you make me want to meet them. I really like the friends and that they do things together. The fox hunting was exciting. I'm particularly fond of their widowed senior friend—the former chemist." Olivia smiled.

Betsy shifted in her chair. "Miss Olivia, there's something you don't know. This is the first time I've heard the story myself, and I'm speechless. Sarah, it's fabulous! I mean it—wow!"

"You really have kept this a secret," Olivia said to me, surprised.

"So, what happens next?"

"You'll have to wait and see. Today's reading was to make sure that you were happy about the story. But I need you to understand it will change after each edit and before it's actually a book."

"Well, you can sleep good tonight. I really do love it. And I've decided I want the lady chemist's name to be Hattie."

Certain there was a connection, I asked, "Hattie it is. Any particular reason?"

"Yes. My grandmother on my daddy's side was Hattie Mae Cromwell. She had a special gift. She could read the loose wet tea leaves in the bottom of your cup. Every morning she would tell you how your day was going to go. I know there was probably nothin' to it, but as children we thought it was great fun. Grams lived two streets over from us in Hadley Falls. Iris and I spent a lot of time at her house. Oh, she could wish off warts too, but I never paid much attention to that."

"How interesting. Going forward the senior character's married name will be Hattie Hayes."

"Wonderful. Thank you. You already know my daddy was the foreman at the lumber plant, but I don't remember telling you Mama worked at Dudley's Dry Goods Store. If we couldn't go to school 'cause we were sick, or over summer vacation, we stayed with Grams on Beechnut Street."

Olivia looked at my leg, stretched across the ottoman. "I'm sorry for not asking sooner, but how's your leg coming along? That cast's been on forever. I remember you called me from the hospital a few days after it happened to explain why you couldn't come visit the day we had planned."

"Thanks for asking. Fingers crossed it comes off the second week in January."

Holding up her crossed fingers, she said, "I'll do just that!"

With one final hug, wishes for a Merry Christmas, and a promise to come back in January, we said our goodbyes.

As I slid along the back seat of Betsy's car, I said, "I hate leaving her all alone; this is her first Christmas since Iris died."

"Me too, but, Sarah, I wasn't kidding. Your story is amazing. What *does* happen next?"

"Thank you. And no, you'll have to wait until our next visit to continue the story. Did you pick up on the fact that Olivia never mentioned a grandfather on Beechnut Street?"

Betsy started her car. "Yes, I did. Is it important?"

"Maybe…I do wish we'd brought her more than a tin of cookies. It makes me sad to think that's the grand sum of her holiday cheer."

"I know…What can we squeeze in? We could bring her a little tree for her room, a few presents, and lunch or something."

Taking a moment to think, I said, "I can't do tomorrow; I promised Nick I would help with the barn remodel. What are you doing early Christmas Eve morning? Sidney's picking Emma and Scott up from the airport around three, and they won't get to the farm until after four o'clock."

"I think I can. Let me check with Frank, but I wouldn't be able to stay long. The Henderson Herd is due to arrive late afternoon. If it's a go, I'll pick you up around nine o'clock. Is our adorable vet, Jacob, coming to the farm with Sidney?"

I sighed. "I've issued an invitation, but she's yet to answer."

The remainder of our drive home was full of talk of how Rose had surprised us all with an invitation—husbands and wives—to her house for dinner and to ring in the New Year. This was a first. We were more than certain there was a reason. We just weren't sure what it was.

29

Like many others, Betsy and I both had a drawer full of "oh crap I forgot her birthday or something else" gifts that we'd collected from boutiques and bargain tables over the years, to have "just in case." Our surprise Christmas Eve visit to Olivia was the perfect occasion to bring something for her. Talking over the phone the night before our trip, we debated through our collective bounty.

I had been given a lovely lavender lap blanket after my accident but had never taken it out of the packaging. Purple, or any shade thereof, was not in my personal color wheel. Betsy found some matching soaps and hand towels and a humorous daily tear-off calendar for next year.

On a quest that was a true labor of love, my crutches and I climbed the two flights of stairs to the attic and rummaged around, hoping to find a box of pictures belonging to the Cromwell sisters or another type of family memento. After no less than an hour's search, I came across two old shoeboxes, packed full of black-and-white snapshots. Carefully sorting through their lifetime, I found a wonderful photo of Iris and Olivia as little girls, sitting on the top step of the front porch of 528 Brook Street.

With a bit more digging, I located my box of spare picture frames, and the gift was now complete. Descending the steep, narrow attic steps on my crutches was beyond frightening, so I took those on my bottom, one at a time, my crutches jouncing freely down every step.

⊂3 ℰↄ

"Good morning, Miss Olivia," we said, standing at her apartment door. "Merry Christmas Eve!"

"You two have done it again," whooped our adopted senior. "Oh my goodness, what have you brought?"

"Some holiday cheer," Betsy answered, resting the three-foot artificial tree on the table in front of her window. "Let's plug it in and see how it looks."

"This is just so kind of you both. Did you bring any more pages of your book?"

I shook my head. "No, I haven't had time to work on it any more since we saw you last, but you can count on a thick stack when we come back in January. Today is just to wish you a Merry Christmas, make sure you have some yummy treats and a few gifts to open."

Olivia glanced at the pile. "Can I open them now?"

"Just one. The rest you need to save for tomorrow. Oh, and this one," Betsy added, placing the wrapped calendar on top of the dresser, "is for New Year's Day."

We pulled up chairs and talked, sharing tea and English shortbread while Olivia tried to decide which gift to open. "I think I want the one wrapped in the shiny holly paper. Great things come in small packages."

The gift in the shiny holly paper was the photo of Olivia and Iris. Glassy eyed, Olivia held the small oval silver frame gently in her aging hands. "Oh my goodness. Would you just look at the two of us? I remember that day. It was Easter Sunday, and Mama made those dresses. Iris and I thought we looked good enough to be on the cover of the Montgomery Ward catalog."

Betsy reached out her hand. "Let me see. Oh, you two are so pretty."

"Iris was the beauty, and I was the brains," she continued. "Have I ever told you the story of how I came to rent your house on Washington Street?"

"No, but I've been curious for years. My father always thought you took in boarders."

"That's not quite right, but he was close. Can you spare a little more time to hear the story?"

Betsy glanced at her watch. "Yes, ma'am, we can, but we'll need to leave no later than eleven o'clock."

"Okay, I'll be quick. Iris got married early and never gave herself a chance to live her life, but maybe for her, that was living. I, on the other hand, was determined to see the world and leave Hadley Falls before the ink was dry on my high school diploma.

"Four years later, I graduated from college in Greensboro, moved to Atlanta, and started teaching music in public school while working on my master's at Emory. After receiving my graduate degree, I was offered a post at Queens College in Charlotte. I rented a tiny little house about four blocks from the campus and settled in nicely."

"That area of Charlotte is very pretty; Queens is a university now," Betsy interjected.

"Yes—progress, I guess. I loved all the big trees in that part of the city. Anyway, along the way, I had several relationships that, for whatever reason, didn't work out. But when I was in my early forties, I met a very special man. It took a while—perhaps a year—for me to realize his intentions were not honorable. He was special all right, just not in a good way.

"He died in the state penitentiary—not another word about that! But I will say it was a learning experience, and one I've kept to myself. You two are the only ones who've heard my true story since I left Charlotte."

"Goodness," I said, trying to catch my breath. "So what brought you back to Hadley Falls?"

Olivia looked at Betsy. "How am I doin'?"

"You have about fifteen more minutes."

After taking a sip of tea, she nodded. "A good number of my colleagues knew what happened, and I don't mind sayin' that made me very uncomfortable. After all, I was a college professor of music who'd gotten the wool pulled over her eyes and almost bamboozled by a complete fraud of a man. I had to go to court, I had to testify, and I decided I had to leave.

"One weekend in the spring, I went to visit Iris and Daddy and saw the for-rent sign in the yard of your house. It was like gettin' struck by lightning and I knew exactly what I wanted to do. So I called your father, gave him the deposit and first month's rent. I finished out the spring term, packed my things, moved home in June, and lived there until you threw me out."

Slightly shocked, I said, "Oh, Miss Olivia, I did not throw you out. Parker and I were just getting married and needed that house."

"If you say so," she said, pursing her lips. "Anyway, while living on Washington Street, I taught private music lessons and had foster children—it was a wonderful three years. I always wanted to be a mother. After you threw me out"—she looked straight at me—"I went to live with Iris. Daddy had passed away the year before. He and Mama are buried in the cemetery beside the Presbyterian Church.

"I retired from giving piano lessons and stopped fostering—the house on Brook Street was too small, and Iris didn't care for children. I filled the void by taking the director of music position at First Presbyterian and creating the youth choral program at church."

There was a brief moment of mysterious silence, and then Olivia slapped her hand on the table and blurted out, "Oh, I'm just going to tell you about that awful man. He had two wives in two different states and planned for me to be number three! There, now you know it all."

Startled, I said, "What?"

"Yes. One day he brought in my mail and some of his papers to work on after supper. We didn't live together, but he came to dinner almost every Sunday, Monday, and Tuesday. He said he was a traveling salesman and away the rest of the week. I guess we know where he really was—selling something two other women had already bought."

"Oh my gosh!" Betsy exclaimed, her hand flying to her mouth.

"That's one way to put it. When he left that night, he forgot his papers, and in the stack was his open bank statement. Picking up his dessert plate, I had to give it a shake 'cause the bottom of the plate was stuck to his paperwork. With a wiggle, it all tumbled to the floor. His canceled checks spilled out of the open envelope, and staring me in the face were several checks cashed by two different women with the same last name—his."

Absolutely floored, I asked, "What'd you do?"

"I talked to my best friend the next day. She was an English professor. We decided I had to turn him in. She went with me to the police station. I never had another male companion, ever! Please don't use any of that stuff in your book—please."

"I promise. Remember it's not you. Hattie the chemist was married to Charles Hayes for sixty years and they lived in Winston-Salem. But I do hope sharing has made you feel better."

Displaying a faint smile, she said, "It really has. Now, I know you have to go, but you and Betsy were so sweet to come visit and bring me a tree and everything. I hope you have a very Merry Christmas, and thank you for making mine the best in years."

"Olivia Cromwell has had one hell of a life!" Betsy said, driving away from the Lazy Willow Senior Living Center. "Remind me of that when I start to whine about something totally insignificant."

"Ditto!" I answered, thinking how lucky I was to have found a good and decent man like Nick.

30

My girls and son-in-law, Scott, arrived right on time and were full of smiles and Christmas cheer. Following hugs and kisses, they went to work unloading the car, singing Elvis Presley's "Blue Christmas." Keeping time to the music, Sidney's long brown ponytail swayed back and forth as Scott tossed her the duffel bags. As they stacked packages wrapped in a kaleidoscope of holiday colors, a set of felt antlers kept Emma's strawberry-blond hair in place.

Nick had fallen easily into his role of stepfather, and my girls, along with Scott, truly did like him very much. Greeting them at the bottom of the steps, Nick joked with Sidney about her lack of parking skills and hugged Emma, causing most of the carefully wrapped gifts to hit the ground. My girls left Nick and Scott to collect the fallen treasures and came roaring into the kitchen with me.

Emma mentioned they were going to meet their dad at the golf club grill for lunch the day after Christmas. I nodded with a smile, saying I thought that would be lovely, and I seriously did. There was no reason why Parker shouldn't see his children.

Sidney kept checking her watch—I knew something was up.

"Are you expecting someone?"

Her shoulders drooped in disappointment as she sat down in front of the picture window. "Yes. Jacob said he would be here around five o'clock, and it's ten after."

"Wonderful, but it would have been nice if you'd let me know he was coming."

"I'm sorry, but he wasn't sure he could get here at all. He had an emergency surgery."

"Okay, but you knew he might come," I said, noticing Nick's sideways stare. "But we're thrilled to have him, and I hope he can stay the night."

Hearing a car door close, Sidney looked out the kitchen window. "There he is. Now, Mama, don't make too much of him being here. Yes, I should have told you, but you carry on so."

"I do not," I insisted, watching Sidney's face explode into a mega-watt smile as she opened the door. "Hi, Jacob. Come in. Come in. We're so happy you're here. Let's see, I don't think you know Sidney's sister, Emma, and Emma's husband, Scott?"

"Nice to meet you," Jacob said with an extended hand. "Sorry to be late," he apologized, handing me an enormous white poinsettia and taking off his coat.

Nick took the lead. "Not a problem—you're not late. Give me your coat and come on in. What can I get you to drink?"

"A beer would be great—any kind," Jacob said.

With the beer in hand, Sidney swooped her young veterinarian away to the den, and the four under thirty-five attendees launched into conversation.

"Sarah Sams Heart, I see your hackles rising," Nick said, kissing my cheek.

"I'm thrilled Jacob's here. I just wish I'd known he was coming. I've got to rearrange the dining room table to add a place, get out more china and silver, and I don't want him to notice or feel bad about that. You know, it's like no one knew you were coming and now you're causing trouble or something. I don't want him to feel embarrassed."

Nick smiled. "I'm sorry; I never thought how he might feel, and you're right. But by the sounds coming from the den, I don't think he'll notice your behind-the-scenes magic-making."

I moved the beautiful poinsettia to the other side of the kitchen. "It's okay, but Sidney—she does this sort of thing from time to time. Anyway, I'm very glad he's here, and they all seem to be having fun. Please go make sure they stay where they are while I add his place at the table?"

"Okay, but we need to talk about one other thing first," Nick whispered.

I dropped my head. "What?"

"Sleeping arrangements. If he's staying over, are you going to lose your mind if he shares Sidney's room—or should I say bed?"

"No, that's fine. Remember, he's stayed overnight before—after the Christmas party." I blushed. "Now go do your job, please."

CR&O

After everyone had gone to bed, I searched through my "oh crap" drawer and was able to find several things to put under the tree for Jacob. The next morning, Sidney was blown away I had produced suitable gifts for him. On my way to the kitchen, I whispered to my youngest, "Never underestimate your mother, my precious!"

"But how?" she stammered, following close behind.

187

"I'm Sibby O'Neil's daughter, and she was a wonderful teacher. She told me at least a million times, 'Never allow yourself to be ill prepared for an unexpected social situation.' I took her words to heart."

"The drawer," Sidney realized, shaking her head. "Thanks, Mom!"

"You're welcome, but imagine how much better it could have been had I known he was coming. We're all just lucky he's gotten anything at all."

⋘⋙

After presents, we had a light breakfast and headed off to Iron Springs. Grammy was in great spirits and seemed much more alert and stronger since Thanksgiving. Sibby was delighted her grandchildren were in attendance and thrilled to meet Jacob. Aunt Tess and Alex pulled in right on time, and Ken Langley was also there. I gave him a hug.

My girls enjoyed visiting with their grandmother's new friend and thought he was charming. Scott mentioned how great it was that Sibby had hooked up with someone. Emma agreed, but added "hooked up" and her grandmother must never share the same sentence again. He refused to rephrase and said she was being ridiculous.

Jacob and Scott sat on the den sofa and took control of the remote switching to the NFL channel. While devouring a bowl of Chex Mix, they found comfort in each other's company amid the female-dominated world of Mulberry Street. A friendship appeared to be in the making. I think my son-in-law enjoyed no longer being the only male under the age of fifty. I was surprised Jacob had made the trip to Iron Springs. In my mind, that was a huge relationship commitment. Could an official announcement be forthcoming?

Nick and Ethan finalized plans for their second annual three-day quail-hunting trip for December twenty-seventh through the twenty-ninth while my brother carved the ham.

We opened gifts, enjoyed a delicious early-afternoon meal, watched some football, and played bridge, and then the six of us headed back to the farm for Christmas evening. Everyone flopped down in front of the fire in the den, with ham sandwiches on paper plates. The kids were to meet Parker at noon the next day for a quick lunch before Scott and Emma's flight back to Rhode Island. Sidney had to be at the television station in Raleigh by four o'clock for the evening news, and Jacob promised to check on Linda's horse.

With our schedules reviewed, bedtime came early.

ଓଃ୫ଠ

Setting the breakfast table with one more plate than usual, I couldn't help thinking, *If Jacob asks Parker's permission to marry Sidney before he asks me, I'm not sure I can handle that.* My thoughts were quickly diverted as the crew settled around the table, and one dozen eggs, a pound of bacon, baked apples, and biscuits disappeared in what could only be described as a shark feeding frenzy.

Nothing makes me happier than people enjoying the food I make for them!

"Whoever ate the most cleans up," I said, as five empty plates hit the kitchen counter and an equal number of full bellies scattered.

I knew a sad goodbye to my Emma loomed heavy on the horizon. She lived so far away that her visits were few and far between. We talked on the phone several times a week, but that wasn't the same. Scott was such a sweetheart, but I always accused him of kidnapping my child. Occasionally, while giving me a hug, he'd whisper that I could have her back. But I knew he was kidding.

Emma Sams Hawkins, English undergrad with a master's in administration, head of fundraising at Brown, didn't care a thing about equine activities. My oldest was a woman who knew her mind, even when she was a little girl. Around the age of four, I put her in the saddle of a very gentle mount, told her to "grab mane" and hold on as I led her around the ring. The second the horse took his first steps, she screamed bloody murder, thus ending her riding career.

On the other hand, Sidney took to riding like a duck to water, and on most days I couldn't get her off a horse.

Since my youngest lived just an hour away, she came to the farm as often as possible. Not to see me necessarily, but to ride and help herself to our refrigerator. I knew exactly how she felt about riding. I could never imagine my life without horses.

Jacob and Coy worked on a lameness issue with Linda's horse, while Sidney and Nick enjoyed a quick ride. I piddled around, trying not to be a pouty puss that the girls were leaving and I couldn't ride. Emma and Scott explored the attic in search of things for their new house.

When Sidney's car packed tight with people and luggage finally traveled down the lane, I struggled to hold back the tears. Nick and I flopped down on the sofa. The past two days had been utter chaos.

"Are you okay?" he asked.

"I guess." I sighed. "I hate it—I just hate it when my children leave. It makes me so sad. Plus, I'm absolutely exhausted, and this damn cast and I are no longer on speaking terms!"

Nick laughed. "I'm sorry, but you're very funny when you've reached your saturation point. All you need is a good night's sleep, and tomorrow we'll be back at Sibby's. The three of you will have a great time, and you can rest up."

I turned my head in his direction. "Rest up? You're absolutely delusional. Trust me, Sibby has a plan for *our* time. I'll cook dinner every night, and why are you looking at me like that?"

"It's probably not the right time to mention this, but I'm starving—what's for lunch?"

I laughed. "For that, all you'll get is a bologna sandwich on plain ol' loaf bread."

"You know, I really do like bologna. Will you fry it first? And do we have that good spicy mustard?"

Hobbling my way toward the kitchen, I called out, "For pity's sake."

"Does that mean yes? I love you very much," Nick said, following in my shadow.

Later, Nick took me out for dinner. I forgave him after he offered me half his chocolate cake.

⊂≋⊃

As usual, Annie traveled to Iron Springs with us, and Caesar stayed at home with Coy. Nick didn't enjoy having canines in his car, so the cargo area of my SUV was packed tight with dog food, duffel bags, and hunting gear, I was lengthwise in the back seat, and Annie was riding shotgun. I chuckled when Nick occasionally batted at a puff of airborne dog hair, adding at least it was clean.

While Nick took my things up to my old room, Annie romped around in Sibby's front yard and I watched, hoping she didn't remember the trauma from Thanksgiving—so far, so good. On Nick's way back, he gave Grammy a kiss and thanked Sibby for the "eats." Mama had packed three days' worth of food, complete with cooking instructions. Ethan turned in just as Nick rested the cooler on the sidewalk.

Nick gave me one final kiss goodbye before he and my brother disappeared over the gentle rise and fall of Mulberry Street. "Well, there they go," Sibby said. "Now we need to get to work."

Turning my head and calling for Annie, I rolled my eyes, thinking, *Here it comes.* "Really?"

"Yes really. You did such a good job with my attic last year, I thought you could tackle downstairs this time."

"Okay, but..." Downstairs—interesting twist. My mother wasn't a hoarder, but she also treasured her memories.

"I know you're not as quick on your feet as you normally are, so that's why I decided to just try to go through things on the first floor. Your grandmother and I will keep you company." She smiled, placing a folded quilt over the oblong mahogany coffee table.

For the next two and a half days, while I cleaned out cabinets, drawers, closets, and knickknack shelves, Grammy rested on the sofa, working crossword puzzles, and from her favorite wing chair, Sibby needlepointed.

After breakfast on the second day, we once again took our places in the one elf workshop.

"Sarah, your dog takes up half the living room floor," my mother said removing her needlepoint project from the seat of her chair.

"I'll never get up all this fur. A quick vacuum before you leave will be fine. And please sit down. I just have to talk to you about something before we get to work."

"Sure. What is it?" I asked, taking a chair.

My mother clasped her hands together. "Sweetie, you're getting so thin, and you barely ate any Christmas dinner. What's the matter?"

I took a deep breath and let it out slowly. "Nothing's wrong, truly. I'm just never hungry anymore. I think it started in the hospital. The pain was excruciating, and I didn't care about food. My stomach shrank, and it just doesn't take much to fill me up now."

Grammy chimed in. "But you have to eat."

"I do eat, just not a lot. I think things will get better when the cast comes off. Plus, I've always been thin, and I was this thin in my earlier years."

"Well, yes, but you were fourteen and not fully grown. Now you're fifty-one years old and five foot ten, so I need a promise that you'll try to gain some weight," Sibby insisted.

Placing my hand over my heart, I said, "I promise. Now, I have some interesting news."

My mother smiled. "What's that?"

"I'm in the process of writing a book—a novel," I said to a stunned audience of two.

Sibby cleared her throat. "Really? That is interesting news. What's it about?"

I went on to explain the basic plot, while my mother and grandmother listened intently.

"Well, I think it's wonderful," Grammy said. "I hope Grace has a loving grandmother?"

"Who teaches her granddaughter how to cheat at cards?" Mama laughed.

"I guess you'll just have to wait and see," I smiled, thrilled by their excitement. "Now, Mama, are you sure about wanting me to vacuum tomorrow? You know, housework burns calories, and I'm still on crutches."

"Yes! I saw you sweeping Christmas Day using only one crutch, and vacuuming is much easier than that," my mother said.

And with that we began sorting through the loot from yesterday, making three separate areas—trash, Goodwill, or keep.

I created one stack for myself, which included my letters home from camp, report cards, Girl Scout badges, and lots of pictures. There were also a number of small antique pieces. Before adding them to my pile, I mentioned their possible value and historical importance. Grammy said they all belonged to her and were mine for the taking. She added that if I fell upon hard times, not to hesitate in selling them but to demand a fair market value.

Mama didn't confess as to why she wanted this done, but I had an idea. Perhaps she was thinking about selling that wonderful old house and moving to a senior community of some sort, which would have a lot less room for all these keepsakes. I wondered how, or if, Ken Langley factored into the picture....

꽁꽁

Our hunters pulled in right on time. Annie bounced out as soon as Sibby opened the front door and went to work creating unbridled havoc with Ethan's hunting dogs in the tagalong dog trailer. I took the steps with purpose and almost lost my balance, but Nick was waiting at the bottom.

"Boy, oh boy, have I missed you!" I said, giving him a serious kiss. Waving from the sidewalk, I yelled to my brother, "Hey, did you boys have a good time?"

Ethan walked closer. "Yes, we did, maybe even better than last year. What did Mama make you do this time?"

"She said if I felt good enough to climb those stairs, I felt good enough to clean out the entire first floor. Meg came over yesterday to collect your stuff."

With a curious expression, he asked, "My stuff—like what?"

"Oh my God, Ethan, Mama's kept everything we ever did—report cards, letters, certificates, badges, you name it."

"Where was it all?"

"Mostly in the drawers of the secretary and the corner cupboard. Nothing in those two pieces of furniture has been touched since it was placed in there in nineteen-something. Oh." I smirked, pulling a letter from my pocket. "Here's a letter from someone I've never heard of—Polly, or so the return address says—and the postmark is the summer you went to band camp. It was in a shoebox full of junk in the hall closet. I gave Meg the rest."

Ethan snatched the letter out of my hand. "Give me that."

"Considering your wife's surprise over Becky Smith in the ninth grade, I'm guessing she knows nothing about tenth-grade band-camp Polly? Ethan O'Neil, you shameful boy!"

"Shut up," my brother said, giving me a hug and kissing my cheek. "I've got to go. Nick, it was a pleasure, and as long as we're standing, we'll be on for our quail hunt this time every year. Take care of my little sister, and we'll see you soon."

"You've got it, buddy," Nick replied, shaking Ethan's hand and slapping his back with the other. "Thanks again."

Nick gave me a squeeze. "Has your mother really worked you to death?"

I rolled my eyes. "Guess."

Mama came over after kissing Ethan goodbye. "Hi, Sibby," Nick said. "I hope you and Grammy are up for an early dinner at the Cutting Board?"

"Oh yes, and we can't wait. Remind me of our reservation time?"

"Six thirty. Let me take a quick shower and get rid of this gamey smell, and we'll be on our way."

Dinner out was a refreshing change for all of us. Mama and Grammy said thank you repeatedly for the treat and demanded we be careful driving back to Greenway. On our ride home, we talked nonstop about our time apart, while Annie left nose prints on the passenger window.

"Have you heard from the girls? Did everyone get home safely?"

"Yes, all's well on that front. Margaret plans to be at the farm around eleven tomorrow morning with Louie and Rascal. I know those two horses were here for the Rowdy Girl sleepover in August, but this trip is forever. Your back-seat bride is very excited!"

Looking in the rearview mirror, he said, "I talked to Coy yesterday. Everything's ready for our new boarders. We decided to remove one stall divider and made two senior suites. I worried about them getting down and not being able to get back up."

"How thoughtful. Margaret will be thrilled—Louie is so big."

"We old guys have to stick together." Nick smiled.

31

Margaret pulled in right on time, with proof that dreams can come true: Rascal and I were finally going to be living on the same piece of property. The next step was for the two seniors to settle into their new digs, and then all would truly be well.

As Nick backed Rascal off the trailer, I realized this was the first time I had thought about the accident in any detail. I could see it replaying in my mind. Feeling dizzy, I steadied myself against the trailer.

"What's wrong?" Nick asked. "You're as white as a sheet."

Trying to catch my breath, I said, "Just give me a minute. Wow. I must have buried the finer points of my accident deep into my subconscious. I didn't realize I remembered so much, and I'm sorry I do." My hand started shaking as I reached to stroke Rascal's face, and frightened, he shied away. "Sorry, big guy," I said, patting his neck.

Nick led Rascal, who walked sideways for a few steps, trying to figure out where he was. After several more strides, my chestnut settled down, realizing he had been here before. Louie, however, remained cautious and never stopped looking from side to side.

Once situated in their stalls, both horses screamed, snorted, pawed the floor, and peed and pooped to mark their territory. Finally settled, they began to munch on their fresh hay. I stood watch while

Nick, Coy, and Margaret unloaded our tack and trunks from her trailer. Occasionally the boys stuck their heads out over either the interior Dutch door or the one leading out to their paddock.

The original builder of that wonderful old barn was an apparent forward thinker. Each pasture-side stall door opened out to an individual covered paddock, then into a joint pasture. With about twelve feet between the two paddocks, the horses could see each other but couldn't touch.

Coy assured us he would work with them every day, and they'd soon learn how things worked at Long Leaf. He was a gifted horseman, and I had every confidence in his abilities. Margaret knew if I said things would be just fine, she could relax, knowing I'd never put Rascal in harm's way.

Walking around the outside corner of the barn, Coy began a one-way conversation with the horses. "Now, boys, this is how we do things around here: I'm in charge and you're not! As long as you can remember that, we'll be the best of friends." Coy slid the bolt to open Rascal's exterior stall door first, then Louie's.

Back in August, all the horses had stayed in their stalls, so this paddock piece was a new experience for them. Each horse stood for a minute or so to take a look, and in the blink of an eye, they trotted out once again, sniffing and snorting. They went from staring at each other over the fence to rushing to the pasture gates.

Coy stroked the length of Louie's neck. "Not today, but tomorrow morning after breakfast, I'll open those gates, and then I'll see you back here at five o'clock sharp for dinner. Listen for my voice, and come a runnin' like the other horses." Louie knocked off his hat. "Stop doing that," Coy said.

Margaret laughed. "Louie hates hats and will try to knock yours off every chance he gets."

"We'll just see about that," Coy said, picking it up and plopping it back on his head. Once again Louie gave it a toss. Returning the well-worn green John Deere ball cap to its original spot, Coy waited to see what the horse would do. Trying a new tactic, Louie came from the side. Coy gently reached for Louie's halter and held fast, saying "bad dog" in a low, drawn-out, and determined tone.

Margaret stared at me.

"That is funny, isn't it?" I whispered. "It won't take long. Soon Louie will love hats, especially that one. We're talking treasured chapeau."

Walking out of the barn, Margaret and I talked about the upcoming New Year's Eve party. What was Rose up to?

"You know I'm terrible at waiting," I said, "and I'm beyond curious. According to Betsy, Rose said it was big news and we would all need to be patient."

Taking a breath, Margaret rested against the truck door. "What do you really think is going on?"

"I'm sure it has something to do with Angus Thatcher. Betsy says she's only been to the barn once to ride Beau and blamed her absence on not feeling well. I don't believe that for a minute. Rose never gets sick, and a fifth grader could make up a better excuse than that."

Margaret chuckled. "I agree. Rose pretended to be angry with Gus and the horse show thing, but that emotion was as transparent as good crystal. For one, she smiled the whole time, and two, her voice was never stern. But I guess we'll find out in less than twenty-four hours. What are you going to wear? To quote Rose: 'It isn't a dressy affair.'"

"Probably my black one-and-a-third-legged pants and a fun sweater. I go back to the orthopedist the second week in January—pray this damn cast is removed that very day! I'll check on the boys before I go to bed."

Margaret nodded. "Thanks, but I think I need to give Louie one more pat before I leave."

"I'm way ahead of you," I said, my crutches in first and headed to second gear.

32

Parson's Path was not really a street at all and aptly named. Rose owned nearly all of the one-lane cul-de-sac, and her house sat dead center at the end of the one-hundred-yard narrow carpet of asphalt.

None of us were sure how she came to have such deep pockets. Her cookbooks, while well received, didn't generate enough money to give her all this. Rose's monthly syndicated newspaper column Tea & Crumpets was also a steady source of revenue, but neither of those things could support the upkeep, utilities, and taxes on this property.

For some reason, I can't recall just why, Elizabeth thought perhaps Rose came from English nobility. An inheritance from the Duke of Somewhere could go a long way to offset the cost of gracious living and world travel. Three or four quality paintings, perhaps a van Dyck, a Gainsborough, a Reynolds, or dare we dream, a Rembrandt could pay for all of it, and forever if the money was properly managed.

But Rose was frugal, always a careful shopper, never boastful, and unless you visited her home, you would have never known how much she actually had.

The twenty crape myrtle trees were perfectly aligned in a row and covered in tiny white lights, and the stone privacy wall had a wreath on every fourth pillar. I stood for a minute before walking toward the door, just to breathe in the beauty of it all.

"This is quite something," Nick said. "You told me her house was amazing, but wow, I never expected this. Did she have it built?"

"No, the house was already here—a very strange, eccentric old man was the original owner. He rarely left the property. The two houses as we turned onto the street were already there, but when he bought this house, he also purchased all the remaining acreage, keeping the outside world at bay. He was really creepy—you know, bodies-in-the-backyard creepy."

Looking at me with a skeptical eye, Nick said, "So I gather you knew him well? Wait. I already regret having asked the question."

"Funny! No, but I did meet him once. One year I volunteered to be the Girl Scout cookie mom—a decision I deeply regretted shortly thereafter. But competitive me was determined that Troop #143 would outsell all the others. So leaving no street—or should I say doorbell—overlooked, I brought my girls here. The whole experience was very Stephen King-esque, and I was positive we were going to become the *daily special* on that man's nightly menu."

Nick shook his head. "It must be very interesting living inside your brain. You decided all of that by one chance meeting? Did your troop sell the most cookies?"

"Actually, he never opened the door. But he did pull back the sheer curtains on the side window, offered a yum-yum smile, and I nearly wet my pants. And, yes, we did sell the most cookies! Later that March, over one thousand boxes were delivered to our house on Washington Street. My living room became a warehouse of

Thin Mints, S'mores, and all the rest. That entire experience ended my cookie mom career, and for reasons unknown, Mr. Scary Man Parson moved that summer."

As we made our way up the steps to the front door, I said, "Rose bought this house later that fall, had the wall put in, and all the gardens were her doing as well. Actually, she has a gardener/property manager I guess you'd say. Robert lives here, and everything on this property is his full-time job. Which is good, since she's away so often. But this is small potatoes, because the inside will blow you away. Come on, you're in for a treat!"

A sign attached to the door asked that we allow ourselves in. When we stepped through, Nick's mouth dropped open. "Wow! You weren't kidding, were you? What interesting architecture."

"Amazing, isn't it? I can't fathom having to wash those windows," I said as I looked at the two full stories of glass. "Give me our beautiful Georgian Revival any day. But it's a very cool house. Oh, there's Betsy and Frank," I said, wiggling out of one sleeve of my coat.

Grabbing the collar and other sleeve, Nick suggested I hold on for at least one minute before falling flat faced on the foyer floor. I smiled and thanked him for his unwavering patience.

The food was exceptional, as one would expect from a cookbook author: a variety of hors d'oeuvres, a meat and bread tray with condiments, a carved pineapple with a skirt of other fruits, petit fours covered in chocolate or vanilla icing, and spirits of all sorts. And yes, there was Mr. Angus Thatcher, the apparent *catch of the day*! Susan and Roger Tillman had also been invited and were spending the night. That tidbit of information sealed the deal on our thoughts of "big news" to follow.

At half past eleven, we were asked to gather 'round in the living room. Rose placed herself at the corner of the massive fireplace and tapped repeatedly on her champagne glass. Gus joined her side, with the roaring fire behind them. "Quiet, please, quiet. I'm—no, *we're*— so glad all of you were able to join us in ringing in the New Year. This year has been wonderful, even with its bumps and bruises, and we hope next year will be even better, bringing good health and prosperity to us all."

Looking around and surveying her audience, Rose continued. "I would also like to make an announcement."

Grabbing Margaret's hand, I said, "Here it comes," I squeaked.

"As I'm sure you all remember, Gus and I met at the charity ball weekend." Rose smiled.

Margaret looked at me. "Oh my gosh, she's blushing."

"What's she going to say?" Betsy whispered over her shoulder.

Rose looked at her Scotsman. "So, here we are. Gus and I have been seeing each other ever since, and our relationship has grown into something quite wonderful. Because we live so far apart, we've decided to divide our time between Hadley Falls and Bellomy Farm in Virginia."

"If I may interject," Gus said, holding up his hands, "I can see the look of surprise and, perhaps, disbelief on everyone's face, but I promise not to steel away one of the Rowdy Girls just yet."

Just yet! Which clearly meant eventually.

"Well, Virginia is better than England, but only marginally." I sighed, looking at Betsy and Margaret. "Don't misunderstand. I'm very happy for them, but I'm sad too."

Elizabeth and Jennifer hurried their way from two rows back

straight toward us. "Did the three of you know about this?"

Betsy drew a deep breath. "No, and that's the truth. I wonder what their plans really are. She hasn't said a word about moving Beau or having me exercise him while she's away. No, tonight's announcement was to drop the bomb and let the dust settle over an abundance of champagne."

"Rowdy Girls dinner at my house next Friday!" Elizabeth said, leaving no room for debate.

Using her "hostess of the soiree" voice, Rose once again tapped her glass. "Everyone—everyone—we're just minutes before midnight. Find a glass, and let's get ready to welcome in the New Year."

Standing in disjointed rows, arm in arm with our significant others, glasses held high, we began the countdown to midnight. Nick held me around the waist and kissed me gently at the stroke of midnight, "Happy New Year, darlin."

"You too, my love," I answered. "This past year together was extraordinary—let's make the new one even better."

CB&O

With Gus and Rose standing at the front door, the odd guests and business acquaintances were the first to leave. Susan and Roger Tillman took kitchen duty while the Rowdy Girls and their husbands helped to clear the buffet table, collect the trash, and have the after-party scavenger hunt for dirty glasses. From the kitchen door we told the Tillman's good night, then gathered our coats. Standing in a group, we thanked Gus and Rose for the evening, and they thanked us all for coming.

Nick said, "Rose, Sarah's told me many times about your house, but I must say seeing is believing. It's amazing, as are your gardens and the whole property!"

Before she could say a word, Gus said, "I agree; imagine my surprise when I came here for the first time. I thought she was an heiress or something and was a bit intimidated."

"No, no dear," Rose insisted, tugging on his arm.

Paying no attention, Gus continued. "But as only she could do, my Rose explained about the life-insurance payout following the death of her husband. There were also smaller holdings, stocks, bonds, and properties. Being the clever woman she is, she has maintained a handsome investment portfolio. She's done quite well, wouldn't you say?"

Gus's words rendered the Rowdy Girls speechless. *Her husband? Died? We didn't know she'd been married. Ever!*

"I agree," Nick said, breaking the silence of the overwhelmed. "Most young people don't have that degree of insight to invest so wisely."

Her face sheet-white, Rose looked as if she might faint. "Oh, my dear, what's the matter?" Gus asked, taking her hand.

"She'll be fine," I said, "but what you don't realize is that none of us knew anything about a husband, and now we do."

"Rose, please breathe," I said, patting her arm. "It's okay. It might take a day or two, but you'll feel much lighter now that we know."

Trying to catch her breath, she shook her head. "I doubt it."

"Yes, you will," Betsy said. "We're going to have a Rowdy Girls dinner Friday night at Elizabeth's, and you can share whatever you choose to then."

Rose nodded. "I'll see you all on Friday."

At the bottom of the front porch steps, I whispered to Betsy, "Good Lord!"

"No kidding—a husband? I'm astonished!"

Margaret stopped midway down the walk. "I wonder why she never told us. The reason must be terrible. You know, perhaps how he died."

"Maybe not," Jennifer said. "Maybe it was something else."

Frank, being Frank the psychologist, said, "Here's an idea. Why not leave it all alone and let Rose tell you when, and only if, she wants to. Obviously, she had hoped you'd never know. Whatever the reason, it's extremely deep for her. You five need to pay very close attention to your friend from across the pond."

I looked curiously toward Rose's house. "I have no real reason to be suspicious, but I think I'll have my cousin Alex—the private detective—check Gus out. Let's make sure 'the horse show judge' is on the up-and-up. From their announced plans, I'm guessing the cookery show is now an absolute no. But before they start moving furniture, a little background check couldn't hurt. This will be a secret from Rose."

"Fantastic! Our very own Nancy Drew. Stress to Alex that we need the information by Thursday before our dinner on Friday," Elizabeth insisted. "Margaret, please make your spinach casserole, Betsy, your twice-baked potatoes—yum—and, Sarah, one of your sinfully delicious desserts?"

"Okay," we chorused in unison.

On the drive back to Greenway, Nick actually agreed that I should ask my cousin to run a background check on Angus. How tragic it would be to find out, and maybe too late, that Gus was a charlatan with the poorest of intentions who was after our well-to-do friend. Granted, he was a close personal friend of Susan and Roger Tillman, but they wouldn't necessarily know everything about the Scotsman.

Nick sat up straight. "On a different topic, I forgot to tell you, David sent me an email. The prosecutor's office will make contact on Monday and give us the schedule. I do think we'll need to be there for a great deal of the trial. Everything that happened centers on Mulberry Street, you and me and Annie and ended at Long Leaf Farm. Coy got a summons, and I'll bet the veterinarian did too. Hopefully, it will be over quickly, and that will be that."

"Did we actually receive a summons?"

He shook his head. "Jesus, I forgot that too. It was dropped it off when you and Margaret were getting the boys settled into the barn. I laid it on the hunt board in the kitchen, and I guess it's still sitting there. We can look at it tomorrow when there are no distractions."

"Dear Lord! What a way to start the New Year."

33

"Do I have time to shower before dinner?" Nick asked, walking into our bedroom.

Sliding coat hangers across the metal rod in my closet, I said, "Yes. Dinner won't be ready for at least another hour."

"Great. I'm filthy. Coy and I spent all afternoon stacking hay. What are you doing?"

"I never dreamed I'd be trying to decide on a courtroom outfit. I want to get this figured out before tomorrow morning," I said, leaning against the closet door. "Pants with one leg partially cut off, a black cast, and these damn crutches—'News 2 live from the courthouse steps: Mrs. Heart, did that boy beat you up?' 'No I got run over by my horse.'"

Nick howled. "Everything will be just fine. Only you would worry about what to wear to a trial."

"I just want to look nice while sitting in the courtroom. I've worn those abbreviated sweatpants, the one pair of jeans, and these cargo pants since the accident. My witness-stand outfit will really require some serious thought. Elizabeth told me that Ian's secretary calls all their clients the day, maybe two, before they're scheduled to take the stand and tells them exactly what to wear. Anyway, what'd you think about these pants, this top, and my black jacket?"

Unbuttoning his shirt, he said, "Daytime—all business, yet stunning!"

"I'm serious."

"Me too," Nick said, kissing me on his way to the shower.

CB80

Eight thirty the next morning, I was dressed and ready to go. Sliding myself across the back seat of the car, I worked to find some calm for the first day of Tommy Asheworth's trial.

"Everything's going to be all right," Nick assured me from the driver's seat. "I've been reading up on this. Because it's a Class H felony—Cruelty to Animals—and he's a juvenile, there's no jury. It'll just be in front of a juvenile court judge. Don't quote me on this, but it's being broken up into two separate trials, I guess you'd call it. This one is to establish probable cause, and depending on what happens, the judge can either sentence him or send it on to a higher court, which would have a jury. Most judges don't allow a gallery for juvenile court, but there must be a reason this time. Personally, I'm glad, because I'd like to hear it all."

"Tommy's so young and disturbed. Truthfully, I'm having trouble pinpointing my inner struggle with this whole thing."

"Try not to worry about it too much. If the case is sent on and he's on trial for sending the car into the utility pole, we'll have no part in that piece. The judicial system will do its job."

The first day of the court proceedings pulled me in two different directions. On one hand, all the initial legal dialogue rendered a degree of boredom just one step before rigor mortis. On the other,

210

the thirteen-year-old kept looking at me over his shoulder and would occasionally raise his shackled hands and smile. It was beyond creepy! The hate in his eyes was unforgettable.

Morning two there was witness testimony regarding neighbors' accusations against Tommy and the disappearance of their pets. The prosecutor rested a large bar graph chart on an easel, which chronicled the frequent relocations of the Asheworth family and Tommy having been on the class roster of many different schools. As a teacher, I knew that would leave him miles behind the educational curve, probably without friends, and lacking in social skills.

Over the course of testimony, it was disclosed that the father, Mr. Asheworth, could not hold down a job and had done some jail time due to petty theft and spousal abuse. *Hmm,* I thought, *now we're getting to the meat of the problem.* Leaving the courtroom for lunch, Ted, the prosecutor, told us the afternoon would be spent plowing through records and laying the groundwork for the next day. Nick and I decided there was no reason to stay.

CB80

Sitting at our breakfast table on day three, Nick asked, "Did you get a call yesterday concerning your 'witness' outfit for today?"

"Yes." I laughed. "There's no need to go shopping, but cleavage and skirt length were mentioned. How about you?"

"I did. The lady said, 'You need to look nice and neat' and 'Ties are optional.'"

Clasping my hands together, I said, "I can't wait to be done with this. My only true worry about testifying is that I'll forget to just simply answer the question. You know me. Why use five words when twenty-five are so much better? Especially when they ask me about Annie. At that point, I may start to levitate from the anger I have over what that boy did to our precious dog!"

Nick smiled. "Well, you'll need to try to keep focused, but I think everyone would understand."

CR8D

Entering the courtroom, I could see today was going to be quite a contrast. The gallery was about half-full, and Coy had saved us seats. Hobbling my way down the aisle, I noticed Dr. Richard Burkhart, and I assumed the striking woman seated to his right to be his wife.

Our eyes met as I gathered my crutches to slide into my seat on the opposite row. Looking in my direction, Richard nodded, offered a smile, and quickly returned to stoic courtroom behavior.

The judge slammed the gavel against the block—a tsunami sound engulfed us all.

Dr. Burkhart was the first to be called to take the stand, and his testimony concerning Annie's injuries left me angry all over again. He was excused after about twenty minutes—the defense had no questions—and the Burkhart's left the courtroom.

The bailiff stepped forward to call Nick's name. Before standing, he squeezed my hand and gave me a warm smile. I listened as my husband calmly answered each question he was asked, praying I could do the same. Again, the defense declined the offer to cross-examine.

Coy followed Nick on the witness list. I was very proud of our barn manager and the way he conducted himself. He was extremely professional and did a wonderful job. Luke, in full police uniform, then took the stand with absolute authority. This was not his first courtroom rodeo, clearly, and after perhaps ten minutes, he was also excused with no questions from the defense. Coy and Luke left the courtroom, disappearing to the other side of the beautifully carved double doors.

A county official was last up on the morning list, and that inquisition lasted until the lunch break. Nick noticed our attorney, David, from across the room and waved as we stood up. David motioned for us to stay put and that he was coming over.

Standing at our side, he said, "Hi. How are you two doing? Sarah, how's the leg?"

"It's coming along, but the bigger question is, what's on your mind?"

"Remember this morning when Luke was questioned about his first meeting with you, then in my office, and how the climate of your concern took a dramatic one-eighty?"

"Yes."

"Well, Ted, the prosecutor, and I need to talk with you over the lunch break. We just want to take a minute to go over a few things."

"Such as?"

David shifted his weight from left to right. "The defense is going to try to use the fact that initially you were thinking about going easy on Tommy for shooting Annie, but you changed your mind after you learned about his past."

"How does that make any difference?"

"All the testimony in regard to his unprovoked attack on Annie and possible harm to other animals shows his tendency toward violent behavior. But your initial reaction of rehabilitation, added to the testimony regarding his father's abusive nature, could possibly open a window to a bit of leniency from the judge's side of the bench," David said. "It's a long shot, but except for his being thirteen, it's all the defense has."

"Oh," I said thoughtfully.

Moving toward the back of the room, David asked us to follow him, adding that Ted was bringing in lunch. We spent the next hour discussing what I might be asked and how I should respond. The two attorneys continued to remind me that I was not the one on trial, and the truth was all I needed to say. We even had a short mock cross-examination, for which I was grateful. When I would stray from Ted's actual question, David would bring me back to center.

With a light tap on the door of our private room, a young woman peeked in announcing that we needed to return to our courtroom seats. Walking down the center aisle, I noticed very few people remained and was happy for that. I could teach a thousand students with total ease, but I didn't feel at all comfortable in this environment.

The bailiff's words echoed in the near hollow space as he called me to the stand. After I was sworn in, Ted took his place in front of me.

"Mrs. Heart, on the morning of Friday, November 26, 2010..." Getting all the particulars out of the way, Ted surprised me by asking what we had just rehearsed. "Mrs. Heart, is it true that you first considered not pressing charges?"

Realizing the true reason for the tutorial, I answered, "Yes," with a relaxed tone.

"And why was that?" Ted asked. And off I went with what we had practiced just an hour prior. Fifteen minutes later, he announced, "I have no further questions for this witness."

Judge Quincy looked at the members of the defense. "You may cross-examine the witness."

Ted had truly stolen their thunder. Looking shattered, the attorney wearing the dull brown suit replied, "No questions, Your Honor."

I was excused and, with the bailiff's help, stepped out of the witness box and down the three steps.

After some legal back-and-forth, court was adjourned for the day. Closing arguments were scheduled for tomorrow morning at nine o'clock.

∞⁶∞

I rested my head in the palm of my hand after dinner. "I wish I could have been as calm as you seemed to be. Nothing about today appeared to rattle your frame."

Nick pushed back in his chair. "You, my love, have some false sense of ownership, or guilt, or something with this whole situation. For the life of me, I can't figure out why you feel that way. Tommy Asheworth is not your fault. Nor is he your problem. I also think you're a little afraid of him for some reason. Are you?"

Nick pulled me close and wrapped his arm around me.

"Yes, I think I am afraid of him. I watch too much television and read too many murder mysteries. In most of those stories, the villain comes back to right his *perceived* wrong, and the main character is saved at the last minute. I just can't seem to shake that notion."

Kissing the top of my head, he said, "I promise I'll save you. I'm not making fun of your concerns, but, darlin', you can't live like this. Tomorrow, if that kid looks at you, try your damnedest not to flinch."

I shivered. "I'll try, but it's that look that horrifies me. I need to tell you something,"

"What?"

"Since the trial began, I've realized I have feelings other than anger. And oddly enough, they're from my teacher/maternal side."

Nick raised his eyebrows. "Really?"

"Yes. You know I have zero ability to be confrontational, but I want to just smack the crap out of that little boy. I know he's messed up, and I imagine abuse has been a regular part of his daily diet, but I'm just spitting-nails mad at him for hurting my innocent dog. But…"

"But what?" Nick said.

"I also want to talk to him. I want to understand why he did that to Annie. That's weird, right?"

Nick hesitated. "Well, maybe. Can you explain a little more?"

"You know I've been upside down over this whole thing. And I think it's because I want to both hit him and hug him. If he did steer the car into the utility poll, I think the catalyst was his finally being brought to justice. Perhaps it triggered a fear in him that he couldn't control. I seriously doubt he meant for his parents to die, but I do think it was an effort to escape the consequences of his actions."

Nick pulled me even closer. "Sarah…"

"I'm sorry I didn't talk about this sooner. But it wasn't until last night that I truly understood how I felt."

Nick took my hand. "Well, darlin', it all boils down to this: The law is the law, and in regard to Annie, Tommy Asheworth has broken the law. Remember, this trial is for animal cruelty only. But I imagine his age will factor in as well. You've always said he needs help, and perhaps this was the only way for that to happen."

"Let's hope so," I said with a lighter heart. "Thanks for listening. I feel much better now."

"We're in this together, babe—always!"

34

I was much more relaxed on our drive to Hadley Falls for the final day of the trial.

The courtroom was nearly empty, but we sat in the same seats on the same row as all the days before. As the key players began to file into the courtroom, I found myself much less rattled. Before taking his seat, Tommy looked straight at me, I returned the glare, and he looked away.

The defense attorney was the last person to take his seat, giving my eyes and mind somewhere else to go. I noticed he was wearing the same suit as yesterday. He had changed his shirt and tie, but the hideous dull brown suit was the same. *Good Lord*, I thought with a giggle.

"Now what?" Nick asked.

I tried to control my nervous titter. "This place unravels me in every direction. I'll tell you later, but it's old Mrs. Pritchett all over again."

Before Nick could respond, the bailiff entered the courtroom. "All rise. Court is now in session. The Honorable James T. Quincy presiding."

With his robes aflutter, Judge Quincy ascended the three steps to the bench, took his seat, slammed the gavel, shattering the respectful silence, and announced we were ready to begin.

Tommy sat very still as each side of the legal coin made their closing remarks. It seemed as if a crushing blow of reality had landed squarely on the shoulders of the thirteen-year-old. Gone was the punk of a little boy who smiled at each witness as they told their story. Gone was the impish grin on his freckled face, and gone was the expression of "you'll never catch me!" Instead, the look of sullen despair engulfed his entire body. He sat utterly dejected, with slumped shoulders and his head bowed in defeat.

Nick reached over and took my hand. He could see that I was not listening to what was being said but was actually watching a frightened little boy drowning in the words of a grown-up's world. "Stay strong."

The Honorable James T. Quincy made a poignant pre-sentencing speech directed solely at the accused. He insisted, going forward, that Tommy Asheworth had total control over the path he chose for the remainder of his life, and for the first time in his life, it was completely up to him. At the end of his passionate preamble, the judge asked the bailiff to clear the courtroom, leaving just himself, the two legal teams, and Tommy.

I paused midway down the handy-capable ramp just outside the courthouse. "I wonder what's being said."

"I don't know, but since he's so young, I'm sure the rules of disclosure are different. And punishment, too, for all I know."

"You're probably right, but this is equal to realizing the final chapter of the best mystery novel ever written has gone missing."

"Understood," Nick said, "but we'll find out soon enough. Let's grab lunch at River's Bend."

"Great idea. Today's Thursday, which means grilled pimento cheese with bacon sandwiches and homemade vegetable beef soup, yum!"

Nick opened my door. "It's Philly cheesesteak and potato salad for me."

Lunch was delicious, and Jennifer gave us the best seat in the house—the bay window table for two.

෫෨෬

Only a mile or so from home, I suddenly remembered my cousin Alex and my request for any information concerning Gus. She promised she'd send something today. I desperately wanted everything to be thumbs-up for Rose and her new romance.

"What's going on back there?" Nick asked, watching as I feverishly checked my phone and gathered my purse.

"I should have an email from Alex today—hopefully good news to extinguish the fire of curiosity surrounding the Scotsman, Angus Thatcher. I love his name. I wonder if he owns a kilt and if he wears... Well, you know..."

"In 2011, he most probably does wear underwear. I wonder if he plays the bagpipes."

"I love the bagpipes."

"Really?" Nick winced.

"Maybe it's because of my Scotch-Irish roots, but it's hard to beat four verses of "Amazing Grace" when the pipers get going."

CS80

Two giant furry dogs were always standing at full attention inside the back door, waiting to say hello. "Good puppies. Now, you two go potty and I'll change my clothes. Then it's off to the office and our computer," I said as they flew out the back door.

Nick hung his coat on the back of the kitchen chair. "I love how you talk to them like they really know what you're saying."

"Why don't you think they do?" I smiled. "Ten bucks says when I walk out that door and whistle, they'll come running and jump in the golf cart."

"You're on."

"When will I ever learn to up the ante on my surefire bets?"

"Okay." Nick nodded. "How about…loser cooks dinner."

"Now you're talking!" Ten minutes later, I was headed down the back porch steps. With one quick whistle, both dogs jumped into the golf cart and waited patiently for me to arrive. Sometimes winning is not always wonderful, though, and I already regretted my enthusiasm. Nick had often professed his inability to cook but that he could make peanut butter sandwiches.

"We'll eat at seven o'clock," Nick shouted from the top of the steps.

CS80

There was an email from Alex with a summary of what she'd found.

As an investment banker, Gus had done very well for himself, which was a plus—not because he had money but because he didn't need money. He had been married for over twenty years. His wife died from cancer fifteen years ago. No children, but he did have two siblings, both of whom lived in Maryland. The rest of the information was just a tack on to what we already knew and, while interesting, was unimportant. It did catch my eye that he graduated top of his class from William & Mary. Rose was brilliant, so his also being *smarter than the average* bear was a plus conversationally.

I let out a huge sigh of relief and sent a thumbs-up group text to the other Rowdy Girls, minus Rose. And a "See you tomorrow night!"

CB80

After a good afternoon's worth of work, I walked into the kitchen, where something smelled delicious.

"I hope you're hungry," Nick said. "It's the only thing I know how to cook. Thankfully, we had leftover chicken from the other night, and I found a jar of sauce in the pantry. The bag of Caesar Salad was an added plus."

"This is delicious," I said after taking the first bite of Nick's chicken Alfredo. "You're on for this dinner every other Thursday night. Excellent, babe!"

"I'm glad you like it." Nick winked, twirling his pasta.

35

Sitting at the falls of the river and just within the city limits, Elizabeth and Ian's home was a restored old gristmill. The millrace kept the wheel turning year-round, and the faint aroma of dried corn, or perhaps oats, greeted you from the small wooden bridge that led to their front door. The foyer opened into an interior of huge timber supports, antiques of rich woods upholstered in classic fabrics, and a breathtaking vaulted ceiling.

Occasionally they rented out the side yard for small weddings or parties. With the waterwheel side of the mill in the background, a two-foot stonewall along the river's edge, seasonal flowers, giant magnolias, and a lawn looking more like velvet than grass, it was a lovely spot. Photographers drooled when given the opportunity to capture the beauty of the bride with Hedgecomb's Mill as their backdrop.

Betsy was kind enough to come to the farm and pick me up. Just a few more weeks and I would hopefully regain my driving wings.

Rose was the last to arrive, joining us in the kitchen, where we were all busy prepping dinner. "Before we enjoy our meal," she said, removing her coat, "I would like to discuss the disclosure concerning my late husband. So, everyone, please fix yourself something to drink, and let's have a seat in the living room, shall we?"

With Jennifer's beautiful charcuterie tray on the coffee table and beverages in hand, our audience of five took a seat and waited with bated breath.

Elizabeth sprang to her feet. "Oops. I forgot the napkins."

Betsy stood up, announcing she needed to use the ladies' room. Margaret switched chairs. I remained planted on the sofa with my outstretched limb running parallel to the rug, and Jennifer took the opportunity to refill her drink. Rose sat tapping her feet with unprecedented impatience—this delay was upsetting.

Everyone now back in place, Rose asked, "Are we all comfortable? Good! I was twenty-two and a recent graduate from the University of Saint Andrews in Scotland. I could have returned home to Sheffield, but my sister, Eloise, suggested I could use the spare room in her London flat while deciding between graduate school, or going to work. Her offer sounded the far better choice: more exciting and grown-up. So two single sisters were we.

"I took a summer job at a rare bookstore to sort things out, but I loved it so much, I stayed on and ended up managing the store. William came in one day, looking for a copy of *Pride and Prejudice*."

"No way," Margaret, owner of Maggie's Alley Bookstore, said.

"Yes. Rather poetic, wouldn't you say? It was a birthday gift for his niece. William, or Will as I called him, was ten years my elder and a financial wizard with an office on Lombard Street. That's London's equivalent of Wall Street. After nearly two years of courtship, we took the plunge and were married. It was a small affair but quite lovely." She paused, taking a sip of wine. "You know I've never liked an all-eyes-on-me situation.

"Life was wonderful. I had truly found my other half in compatibility and passion."

Betsy wiggled to the edge of her seat. "What happened?"

"I have never spoken of this to any of you for the best reason of all—it would have done you no good to know. We're all different in our personalities and in the way we handle things, and I prefer to keep my past just there. What I'm about to tell you lives in the cellar of my saddest memories.

"Will and I were meeting for dinner at an upscale restaurant near his office. He had just come out of his building as I was rounding the corner on the far side of the crowded street. Calling my name, he waved his hand and stepped onto the crosswalk without looking. A double-decker bus hit him head-on, and my husband was dragged at least twenty additional yards. I saw the whole thing, and that visual will remain with me forever."

"Oh my God!" I gasped.

"Precisely," Rose agreed, looking down and shaking her head. "He was dead on impact, or so they said, and hopefully that's the truth. I lived in the land of grief and disbelief for a long time, but eventually I reclaimed my life. That's when I decided to move to Boston. I had a college chum there, and after giving her a brief explanation for my relocating, I vowed to never again disclose that part of my past. I don't want or need any pity or sorrow that comes with this sort of revelation. You know I'm on the fence concerning organized religion, but I do thank the powers that be for the gift of those few years with him and the life Will made sure I had going forward."

Rose tried to compose herself. "Now, one more quick thing before dinner. I have never allowed myself to love this deeply since that tragic day. It was my self-imposed armor, if you will. But Gus truly is the real thing, and I want a life with him. I can't answer the questions your eyes are asking about our future, but I hope there is one. Oh, I nearly forgot—I've decided to pass on the cookery show. Aside from the five of you, I've found the best reason in the world to remain on this side of the Atlantic, and his name is Gus."

We all applauded and cheered. Betsy took the floor.

"I know I speak for all of us when I say, thank you for sharing, and you can trust your story will never leave this room. And we're obviously thrilled with your decision to stay," Betsy said gently.

In a full-blown blush, Rose quickly searched for a new topic. "Thank you. So, Sarah, what happened with the trial?"

"Dear Lord, what an experience! We were asked to leave the courtroom before hearing the judge's decision. I guess the ruling will be in the paper. But I don't really know. It's different in juvenile court. I'm just thrilled our part is over, and I hope Tommy gets the help he so desperately needs," I said as we moved into the dining room.

Elizabeth filled my plate. "Sarah, you sit here."

"Oh, thanks. I could've gotten it."

"I'm sure, but this is a new rug, and I don't want beet stains where you're sitting."

"Understood." I smiled.

Elizabeth's house, beautiful as it was, had terrible acoustics, especially in the living room, and voices above a whisper were magnified five times over. We didn't care. As we ate and chatted, the "loud" provided a much-needed bridge from the tragic tale of our friend's past to the celebration of the Rowdy Girls remaining the sisterhood of six.

As the night progressed, Rose began to transition back to her old self, with a warm smile and funny British quips. It was as if letting go of her most tragic memory and letting us in on it had freed her.

Over dessert Margaret said, "Sarah, your next doctor's appointment is next Thursday at ten o'clock?"

"Yes, why?"

"Because here's what we should do. If that *damn* cast, as you call it, comes off, then let's all meet on Friday at River's Bend for lunch and ice cream, and you can drive yourself to Hadley Falls."

"Excellent idea. Fingers crossed!" I smiled. "I wonder how long it will be before I can really ride. Coy built me the coolest mounting block. It has four deep steps that led to a flat landing. I stand on the landing, slide my right leg over the saddle, and then simply sit down."

Betsy smiled. "He really is the kindest soul who ever wore overalls, isn't he?"

"Yes, he is," Margaret agreed. "Louie loves him, and I do too."

Jennifer gave herself a generous pour of cabernet sauvignon. "How are the boys?"

"They have the LLF routine down pat and spend all day in the pasture. It's perfect. I'll ride Rascal for the duration of my rehab—he's a much easier, safer ride than Buddy."

"Louie's so happy," Margaret said. "He has truly blossomed at Sarah's. I've decided Falling Creek must have some bad juju, but I don't know why."

"Because Falling Creek is run by Inez Biddle!" Betsy said emphatically. "She's without question the most cantankerous woman I've ever met. If she makes it to heaven, she'll light into God that very minute, producing a list of things gone wrong in her life, unanswered prayers, and why it's all his fault."

Margaret howled. "What would be her top five?"

"Hmm…" Betsy thought. "I'll guess the first two husbands, that worthless son of hers, squirrels, and female balding, in that order."

Jennifer held on to the back of the chair, laughing. "Squirrels—what did they ever do to her?"

"To quote Inez, 'Squirrels are just rats with a better-looking coat.' She blames them for everything from tearing up her planters and eating horse blankets to trashing the hayloft and clogging the gutters. Sarah, do you remember the night we came back from Virginia, and I was dropping you and Rascal off?"

"Do I ever!" I said, briefly covering my eyes. "It's hard to forget a woman dressed in a Turkish caftan, unloading both barrels of a twenty gauge into a squirrel's nest in the trees in near darkness. She almost shot us. Betsy called her name, and she whipped around, ready to fire. Inez really is way to the left of center. Have you ever noticed how her eyes get very strange when she's on a tear?"

"Oh my gosh, yes! But, on the other hand, it's a beautiful farm, and that indoor arena was nice," Margaret added.

"Yep, we did have some good—no, great—times there. But we have an even better indoor ring at Long Leaf. Oh, get this. Nick mentioned putting mirrors down one long sidewall and a row on the far short wall. I'm not sure I really want to see myself ride. I think I prefer the visual I've created in my mind."

"Mirrors—NO WAY! Susan always yells at us to sit up straight, and we tell her we are. But if Nick puts up mirrors, then we'll know the truth," Margaret said. "Maybe mention how difficult they'll be to keep clean, and Coy really doesn't need more work."

"Oh, good thinking!" I said with a nod.

36

As the sun crested the pines, I prayed my freedom was just hours away. I had Nick's coffee brewing, and I stood sipping my soda, when my husband walked into the kitchen with tousled hair and sleepy eyes.

"Hello, Miss Mary Sunshine. Why are you up so early?"

Resting my glass on the kitchen counter, I beamed. "I feel like a child on Christmas morning. I don't want us to be running late. Today is going to be the very best day of the year—so far at least. Dr. Tobias Ray is going to read the X-rays and free my leg."

"Well, let's hope so, but he could also say 'just a few more weeks.' If it does come off, you'll probably need to use your crutches for a little bit and some sort of brace. Your leg is very weak."

I shook my head. "I refuse to listen to any negative conversation."

Nick pulled out his kitchen chair. "Okay, then, if it does come off, what's the first thing you want to do?"

"Sit in the front seat with you facing forward! And, with a completely unfettered left leg, enjoy a thirty-minute shower hot enough to steam clams!"

Nick laughed. "I've missed having you ride shotgun—but not your telling me how to drive. There's been much less 'turn here, turn there, and slow down' since you've been sideways in the back seat."

"I don't tell you how to drive. I'll admit that on occasion, though, I have added some color commentary to the fact that we might die at any moment."

"Yes, that's it. I stand corrected." Nick laughed. "Now, let's have a big breakfast. We can make it together. How about two eggs over easy, sausage, and that thick toast you make? You, my love, need to enjoy some real food. You haven't eaten well during all this. I think you're evaporating in front of my eyes. How much weight have you lost?"

Patting my massive cast, I said, "I don't know, but lugging this around is serious exercise. I'll get on the scales when we get home, but only once I've been freed from the bondage of fiberglass. We don't have time for your lumberjack breakfast, but I'll fix you an English muffin with peanut butter and orange marmalade."

"Thank you, but seriously, Sarah, you're becoming so thin. You told me that even Sibby said so over Christmas. Baby, you have to wear a belt to keep your pants from falling down."

"True, but sometimes eating is just too much trouble." I shrugged. "I love your concern, but please stop picking on me and eat your muffin."

⋯

During our drive to Hadley Falls, Nick said, "Oh, here's something interesting I forgot to tell you about it until now."

From the back seat, I asked, "What's that?"

"Remember before Christmas, when we were discussing our going forward, you know, aging, and what we might do with the farm?"

"Yes, and?"

"Yesterday, while you and the dogs were working on your book, I got the mail. It was mostly junk, but one envelope from North Carolina State University caught my attention."

I sat up very straight. "Really? What did it say?"

"It was a general query asking if we would be interested in meeting to discuss a 'Colonial Farm project' and possibly using a piece of our farm. Apparently, they—the university in conjunction with the Historical Society—have been researching registered properties that would qualify for creating a working colonial farm."

"Wow!" I said, intrigued. "I wonder how many properties are in the running."

"If it's to be an early colonial project, all their possible sites would have to be in the eastern part of our state, but I don't know how many. Here we are. We can talk about this after we get home."

"Okay," I said, pushing myself out of the back seat. "Fingers crossed."

CRð

Hadley Falls Orthopedic Center had a wonderful policy. Each patient always saw the same team of specialized caregivers. Gail was my X-ray technician and very good at her job. She was funny, understood I had the patience of a gnat, and took everything I said with a grain of salt.

"This cast has to come off today," I said as she helped me onto the X-ray table. "If the pictures are good, we'll keep them, but if not, we can search for some that are. Surely there's film around here somewhere of a leg that actually mended?"

"Mrs. Heart, you're so funny, and if we don't get good pictures, I'll look around, but you can't tell Dr. Ray. Now, sit still please."

Back in exam room number six, the door flew open. "Good morning. How is my favorite patient?" Toby said, sliding my X-ray under the clip on the light box. "Okay, let's see what we have. Well, there's mostly good news, followed by some you won't like."

"I'll take the good news first."

"Excellent choice. Look here… The bone has completely healed, *but* it needs a little more time to strengthen. It's like fresh paint—dry on the outside but needs time to cure."

Nervously I asked, "And so?"

"And so, I'm going to have Dan remove the cast, but you'll need to wear a brace for at least the next two weeks, maybe longer. I'll have you come back in two weeks, and we'll take some more pictures. To start with, you'll need to continue to lightly use the crutches until you get your balance back. Doris will get you scheduled at the hospital for physical therapy."

"Oh, I'd really love to have Zack for my PT. He took care of me after the surgery."

"I'll see what we can do. Now, here's the part you're going to hate—but you don't have a choice if you want to walk correctly."

"Okay, what is it?"

"You absolutely cannot get back on a horse—not even the toy one outside Walmart—for the next three weeks, and only if Zack agrees based on your progress. Just remember—your paint is dry but needs time to cure. Plus, you'll need time to rebuild your leg muscles."

"That's not too bad. I can deal with three weeks. The brace is removable, correct?"

"Yes, so you can take a shower, sleep without it, and just sit around, but I would strongly suggest you go easy with everything at first. You may also experience some pain for the first week or so. When you start to move around, and you'll do too much this afternoon and tomorrow—everyone does—there will be some pain. An anti-inflammatory should be enough, but if not, just give me a call."

"I'm so excited," I said, fumbling with my crutches. "I promise to do my best. Oh, can I drive?"

"Yes, but I would remind you of the 'Tortoise and the Hare,' and let's think about who won the race and why. Take it slowly. Mr. Heart, you have my deepest sympathies going forward. The next three weeks will be a test of your intestinal fortitude, but I'm sure you're equal to the task."

Nick laughed. "Thanks, Toby. I appreciate your insight."

"You two are a real stitch," I said.

Dan appeared, and we were off to his lab.

"Now, remembering what happened last time," he said, "I'm going to have you sit up a bit. Last time, pulling you up made the dizziness worse. Let me know if you start to feel light-headed." He powered up the oscillating cast saw, and the end result was much better than before.

Glancing down, I could see my whole leg; it wasn't a pretty sight. My skin was a chalky white and the scar a very strange purple. The track of surgical staples was, to my eyes, at least two feet long. Toby came in and started to remove them one at a time, making me nervous. It was a strange feeling, and one or two put up quite the fight relinquishing their grasp on my flesh.

"Just breathe," Toby would say when he came to a stubborn staple.

"How many were there?"

"Eighteen. I like even numbers. Isn't that funny? I wonder why that is," he said, giving me something to think about.

I answered immediately. "Balance. You always insisted on even numbers. I could never get you to understand that compositions with odd numbers allow the eye to travel."

"Look at that beautiful straight incision," Toby said proudly. "I bet you're glad my eye didn't *travel* this time!"

We laughed and gave each other a sincere high five.

Toby left the room, and Dan began to wipe my leg with a solution of something very soothing, causing my skin to tingle. Thankfully, it also removed the smell of the past two months. Added to the overall unpleasant picture was the length of my leg hair.

Dan recognized the look on my face. "Don't worry, my assistant, Sharon will shave your leg and apply a special cream—we'll send you home with a tube of your own. The first time you do this yourself, be very careful. Your skin is extremely sensitive. When you're just sitting around, fresh air is good medicine."

Sharon was very careful and showed me how close to get to the incision without hurting anything. "Before long, your skin will return to normal, but until then, you really do need to take care," she said, realizing I was a bit unglued. "How's your horse—Rascal, right?"

"He's wonderful. In fact, he lives at our farm now. What smells so good?"

"It's the cream Dan told you about; it's full of plant-based oils and will do wonders for your skin, and the lavender fragrance is calming."

"Delicious," I said, inhaling deeply.

Dan fitted me with a serious brace, complete with Velcro closures and a range-of-motion dial and hinge system. It was cumbersome but not nearly as bad as the cast. Best part: it was removable.

"Now you try, and it needs to be as tight as I have it. Also, don't put it on directly following a shower. Give your skin at least five or ten minutes to air-dry. Apply the cream and let that soak in, and then strap on the brace. Now your turn."

I had no problem lifting my leg and getting it aligned with the brace. I was, however, a bit timid tightening the Velcro straps.

"Good job, but pull the top strap just a little tighter. When you're vertical, it will drop, and we don't want that. Good. A little more. Now let's see what happens when you stand up."

"I can tell this is going to take some time to adjust now that my knee is bent. Can I turn the knobs to regulate the angle? Wait, I'm a little light-headed."

"Okay, let's try sitting down in a chair and getting back up slowly. And yes about the angle, but not too much just yet. We need to go easy on those muscles at first."

Before I tried again, Toby reappeared and asked that I come to the lab before leaving the office. On my way down the hall, I could see Nick smiling and leaning against the doorframe of the lab.

"Look at you. How does it feel? Are you okay?"

"Yes. What's going on?"

"Hey, Mrs. Heart," Nora, my favorite lab tech said. "I need to take some blood and get all your vitals before you go. Dan said you felt a little dizzy."

"I did, but I'm fine now."

"Great. This won't take a minute. You'll need to remove your brace, then hold on to the bars and step on the scale."

"On the scale?" I turned my head sharply, narrowing my eyes as I looked at Nick.

"Yes. We need this information for your chart. Okay, one hundred and seventeen pounds. Are you doing okay?" Nora asked.

"Yes, I'm fine."

Organizing her equipment, she said, "Have a seat and put your brace on. I need to get your blood pressure, check your temperature, and take some blood, and then you'll be good to go."

⊂3೮∽

Leaving the office, I looked at Nick, my voice elevated. "I'm so angry with you. I know you had some conversation with Toby about my weight, and all that checkout nonsense was just to get me on the scale."

Nick opened the door. "Just get in the car and we can talk about this. People are staring."

"I don't give two hoots in hell if they are. Let 'em look."

"Sarah, I need for you to just listen to me. I can explain."

Buckling my seat belt, I said, "I don't see what there is to explain, but okay, entertain me,"

Nick backed out of the parking space. "I know you think I didn't trust you to keep your word, but that's only a small part of what really happened."

"But it's a part?"

"Well, yes, but just listen. When Toby returned to the exam room after removing your staples, he mentioned how thin you looked. I swear to God, Sarah, I'm telling the truth. Anyway, I quickly recapped our breakfast conversation, and Toby said he wanted to check your weight and do blood work before we left. Apparently he wants to rule out other things."

"Other things...What other things?"

"I don't know exactly, but mainly to make sure nothing else was compromised when you had the accident."

"Like what?"

"Again, he didn't say. But I think he wants to make sure the horrific blow you took on the trailer floor didn't injure something else—like your kidneys or liver—but I'm just guessing,"

Pulling into the municipal parking lot and putting the car in park, Nick looked over at me. "And I'll just say it, I'm very happy Toby insisted on weighing you and all the rest. I don't give a rat's ass if you're mad at me. Stay that way for as long as you want. But I love you, Sarah, and refuse to apologize for wanting you to be healthy!"

I tried to hold my emotions in check. "I've told you repeatedly, I'm just not very hungry. Yes, I have lost weight, but I think that's normal. I am so angry, but I'm also sorry for yelling at you and that you were concerned something else might be wrong with me. You hear all the time about people who never knew they were gravely ill until it was too late. It's also the first time we've ever had a heated exchange of words. I guess it had to happen sometime."

"I'm sorry about the tone of our conversation, but serious things are seldom discussed at a whisper. Babe, you're a very strong-willed woman with more than an ounce of stubborn coursing through your veins. To be honest, I'm not really sure you would have stepped on the scale at home. So, since Toby hadn't seen you since your last appointment, when he suggested running a few tests to cancel out any possible underlying reason for your dropping over twenty pounds in two months, I applauded his insistence."

I stared out the side window. "I need some time to think about all this."

"I understand. Do you want to go somewhere for lunch?"

"I think I would just like to go home," I said.

"Home it is."

There was a great deal to mentally unpack from this and previous conversations that morning.

Not another word was spoken for the next thirty miles.

37.

Confrontation has always been hugely upsetting to me, as was not being trusted. But in fairness, I couldn't honestly say I actually would have gotten on the scale at home. And then there was the questionable piece—could there be some other reason for my weight loss?

I spent almost as much time replaying my morning as I did writing. But when I did write, it was as if my fingers were electrified. I was at a point in my story where the main characters had hit a rough spot in their relationship, and I think Nick's and my "discussion" added sparks to the printed page. Rereading those two chapters several times, tweaking my additions, and making minor changes, I beamed with delight—I had found the heat I needed to make it sizzle.

Annie and Caesar had become wonderful listeners and got an earful that afternoon. Clicking save, I suggested we take a break and go check on the barn—*go* was definitely one of their understood vocabulary words. While my two furry confidants bounded around the indoor ring, I stood in Rascal's stall, leaning against the bottom of the Dutch door. With a twist of the dial, I straightened my leg to near flat-footed and rested the crutches against the stall wall.

The smell of a barn had always been magically intoxicating to me, as were the aromas of leather tack and the horses themselves. I have never found any place more peaceful or spiritual, and I stood quietly absorbing it all.

Oblivious to the world, I jumped when a woman's voice asked, "Sarah, are you okay?"

It was Margaret.

"Oh, hi. Yes, I'm fine."

"I don't think so," she scoffed. "What is it?"

I sighed. "Where do I start?"

Margaret placed a small bench in Rascal's stall. "How about the beginning? Look at your leg—at least that's good news."

Taking a seat, I gave her a short review of this morning's trip to the orthopedist. "There's more to it than Nick not trusting me. What if there really is something else wrong? Wouldn't I feel bad or something? And my leg—I can't stand to look at it. I'm not a vain person, but check this out," I said, opening the brace and showing her my scar.

Margaret's jaw dropped open a little, and she gasped. "I'm sorry. It just took me by surprise. You know, we never saw your leg that day. You still had on your breeches and tall boots when the ambulance took you away, and then you had the cast."

"I know. I've seen it once before, but I was such a dizzy disaster, I really didn't take it all in. But today I nearly fainted dead away, and I have a cast-iron constitution—or so I thought. I can never wear shorts or a bathing suit again. This scar is only going to get marginally better. But it will generate miles of 'Wow, what the hell happened to you?' questions for the rest of my life."

"Now, you don't know that for sure. You could see what a plastic surgeon could do if it doesn't heal nicely."

"Here's the other thing: Nick hasn't seen it yet. Watching your husband turn green, or throw up, or both, would not be reassuring."

"Nick won't care, and if you don't believe that, then you really don't know how much he loves you. Do you honestly think he would distance himself from you because of a scar? What's gotten into you? You've taken a tumble down the rabbit hole of boo-hoo."

Looking down at my leg, I sighed. "Well, maybe."

"Well, maybe nothing. Here's what's going to happen: I'm going to ride Louie, and you're going to fuss around with Rascal for a few minutes. Then you're going to march—well, use your golf cart—back to your house and straighten this out with Nick. Starting with your saying that while you're not happy about the weight conspiracy, you do understand his concern. I will mention that sex has always helped to soften the edges of an argument at my house."

"Are you suggesting…?"

"I'm not suggesting anything. I'm just laying out options. Oh, look, the boys are trotting back to the barn. How cute is that? Anyway, put your brace back on, and let me get this bench out of the stall. One more thing."

Tightening the Velcro straps, I asked, "Just one?"

"Funny, but you know I'm right, and you've stirred this situation to butter. Now end it. Do it however you choose, but end it!"

CRE80

A half hour later, I gave Rascal one last carrot, whistled to the dogs, and we were on our way back to the house. Margaret waved from the stall window. She was right and I knew it.

Nick was sitting at the kitchen table, sorting through the mail.

"Hi there. How were writing and the barn? I saw Margaret's car."

"The writing went unexpectedly well, Rascal was sweet as always, and Margaret's terrific. I'm going to take a shower before dinner. I need to wash away today."

"Okay. Let me know if I can help."

"Thanks," I said, walking down the hall to our bedroom.

I was excited to visit my old friend the shower. I had tried once putting a lawn and leaf bag over my cast and tying it tightly, but the water still ran down into my cast via every wrinkle in the bag. So for the past two months it had been sponge baths only. But, oddly, today I felt somewhat unprotected, and it took a minute to plan my strategy for a risk-free shower. The two grab bars in the oversize space allowed me the security I needed. With my head tilted backward, I stood under the steaming-hot water and felt myself begin to relax. I also felt a quick burst of cold air. Opening my eyes, I saw Nick standing in front of me.

"I thought you might enjoy a back scrub."

I tried not to smile. "You did, did you?"

"Yes, and maybe I can help you with other things too."

I can honestly say it was the most amazing shower I've ever taken. Toweling off wasn't too shabby either. I held my breath as Nick gently blotted my body and especially my leg, watching as he took the towel down either side of the crimson scar. His expression remained the same—curious, but kind.

"Do I remember Dan saying the incision needed to rest for a while before you put on the brace?"

"Yes."

"Hmm, what should we do while we wait?" Nick smiled, picking me up and carrying me to my side of our bed, then took his place and pulled up the comforter.

The time we spent allowing my incision to air-dry was not only hands-down biblical but also a passionate exchange of "forgive me."

Nick rested back on his pillow. "Sarah, I'm truly sorry. It really did go the way I told you. I simply answered your doctor's question."

I rested my head on his shoulder. "I know, but it was just a lot."

"I agree. I'm sure there's nothing else wrong with you. I will say your color has improved since the shower," Nick said, raising his eyebrows.

"That's good," I said. "It must be from the hot water."

"Mm-hmm. But what I'm about to say will get me into trouble. I'm suddenly very hungry."

"Really? I wonder why."

"Maybe it's because I got so much exercise today. You know, farming is very hard work. So what's for dinner?"

"Not much. I think there's a pizza in the freezer, and I'll make a salad, but dessert has the potential to be amazing."

And it was!

38

O ur farm and one other had become the top two choices for the college-level agricultural program of farming and animal husbandry in the late eighteenth century. Nick was off to Raleigh for a meeting with the folks from the Historical Society and NC State.

The university had one of the best schools in the country for both areas. I didn't know much about the ins and outs of the "treasured past" part of our farm, but I understood nothing could happen without the Historical Society's approval. And they didn't just say "okeydokey" to ideas. There had to be proposals, committee meetings, tours of the site itself, and so on.

The plan was to construct a two-story replica of a Colonial American home on the outside with all of today's modern conveniences on the inside. The main floor, excluding the kitchen, would be reserved for functions or tours and furnished in period antiques or reproductions. There were two downstairs bedrooms: one for the professor and the other held in reserve for additional staff or possible guest lecturers.

The fourteen working students would live upstairs, dorm-room style, with girls on one side and boys on the other. A large lounge area in between would have a TV and comfy furniture.

Over breakfast, Nick and I tossed around how our farm could

continue on if we eventually had to move to a senior community. We both agreed that if Sidney and Jacob were to get married and were interested, they could live in our house and oversee everything. Jacob was, after all, a dyed-in-the-wool Wolfpacker, holding diplomas from both the NC State undergraduate program and its School of Veterinary Medicine. Coy was also a huge consideration, and his job and home were both his for as long as he wanted.

But all of this was miles down the road. Today's meeting was to see who won the bid and, if it was Long Leaf Farm, to fully understand the project—who paid for what, who got the tax breaks, and so on. I desperately wanted to go, but I had deadlines with my editor, Ellie, that I needed to meet.

March was my tentative launch date to send it to Ellie for her first read.

C8∞

The Rowdy Girls decided to postpone the celebratory lunch by one day to give me a little more time to acclimate to getting around in my new setup. I was very grateful. It was proving to be more difficult than I had anticipated. Too much of a bend in my leg was uncomfortable, and too straight wasn't great, either, but the extra day allowed me the opportunity to find "just right." It felt strange to put my foot on the floor and to wear a pair of shoes. I held my breath every time I took an unfettered step. I'm not certain what I thought might happen, but it was scary all the same. I still used both crutches, just in case I got a bit wobbly.

Nick returned home around three o'clock that afternoon. "We

got the bid!" he shouted, walking toward me.

Standing at my office door, with a smile as wide as Texas, I said, "Wow! And yay! Tell me all about it."

"Okay, but can we talk more later, please? It's all good news, but before it gets dark, you should take a test drive up and down our lane. I'm riding shotgun. You get organized, and I'll put these papers and the dogs inside."

"All right," I agreed, realizing it would be different now that I had to deal with my left leg—the brace—and maintaining a set position behind the wheel. Opening the car door and trying to sit down as usual was a real eye-opener. "This was a good idea you've had," I said as Nick reappeared. "Let me think about this for just a minute."

Starting with the driver's seat all the way back helped, and after several attempts I worked it out. How strange to be behind the wheel again. I found a bend to my leg that I could live with. Following two round trips up and down our lane, we moved on down the highway for a mile or two. It was like taking driver's education all over again. Except to say, Nick was far better-looking than Larry from Student Drivers, Inc., in nineteen seventy whenever.

"Tell me all about the meeting," I said, turning the car around at Nelson's Corner Store.

"In a minute. Do you see that eighteen-wheeler coming down the road?"

Using a sassy voice, I said, "The blue one with white letters?"

"You don't need to get smart. Let it go by," he insisted.

CR8O

After dinner we opened the proposal envelope and laid its contents out on the kitchen table. We had been given a month to decide. We were sure we wanted to be a part of this project, but there was a great deal to be considered. We would lease the land to NC State on an annual basis. Students in the School of Design would be offered the challenge of drafting the plans for the house and outbuildings— top design wins. Using grant money, the university would build the house, and area contractors would bid for the job. Senior students in the College of Agriculture and Life Sciences could apply for a semester's internship of Life in the Late Eighteenth Century.

The program would become part of the university's working college program, with the stipulation that if they ever dropped that internship, the property and everything on it would be returned to us. The Historical Society had the right to hold functions and fund-raisers. The ins and outs of the funds and tax issues were complicated but equitable to all involved.

We both agreed that David needed to look over our side of the deal. But we were very excited about the idea.

CR8O

The next morning, I found it impossible to hide how excited I was to be able to take myself somewhere. It had been almost three months since I lost that basic freedom.

Thirty minutes later, using my crutches, I walked my way into the restaurant. Jennifer had pushed two wooden tables together with a navy blue and white gingham tablecloth running the length of both. Due to the bulky brace, I couldn't cross my legs, but I could sit in a chair with both feet on the floor. We toasted my progress. There was some discussion about the pending maiden jaunt to Susan's in late March. I laid out the doctor's plans for the coming three weeks and that I hoped I could get back in the saddle after that.

"Rascal is such an easy ride. I'll be taking him to Virginia. I know I can't jump—but maybe I can trot poles? If there are no setbacks, that would give me about six weeks to at least be able to post at the trot, maybe not canter, but time will tell."

Uncharacteristically ebullient, Rose said, "Sounds wonderful! Now I have a tidbit of news. Gus and I are going to Scotland in late June and then to visit my family in England."

Margaret quivered. "After camp, I trust?"

"Yes. We plan to leave the last week in June. Sarah, we're going to Glen Eagles first and staying at the Gleneagles Hotel. Isn't that where you and Nick had your honeymoon?"

"How sweet—you remembered! That's the most beautiful place. You'll have a wonderful time."

Jennifer asked, "So, is that where Gus is from? He has family there?"

"He has several cousins splashed about. His family left Scotland when he was a young boy, so it's mostly to revisit where he was born."

"How wonderfully romantic," Elizabeth swooned, "over the heather, through the moors, and around the lochs."

"Will you be pushing on to Gretna Green?" I quipped, with my poor attempt at an English accent. "If I recall correctly, it was, and perhaps still is, a town where couples go to elope. The famous blacksmith's shop would be perfect for two horse lovers—it's called an Anvil Wedding. The blacksmith strikes the anvil, forging the lives of two lovers in an unbreakable bond."

Rose just smiled at the five of us.

"Oh, you are! You're going to get married there!" Betsy said.

"No, not really our cup of tea." She shrugged, leaving us somewhat deflated.

I sighed. "How sad. I think it would be perfect. The proper English girl elopes with the handsome Scottish barbarian, and they marry under the moonlight."

Margaret said, "That would be perfect. Does he have a kilt?"

"Yes, and I know where your minds are going. Just quit it!"

I smirked. "Fat chance!"

"Sarah," Rose said, trying to transition, "we'd love to hear about your book and your progress."

"All in good time. I will say that I'm loving my story. Writing is so cathartic. Now, who's excited about going to Virginia?"

Six hands flew into the air.

Just before leaving, Elizabeth asked, "Sarah, did you ever find out what happened to that boy who shot Annie?"

"Yes, but I don't like to think about it," I said. "He was sentenced to five years in the detention center. Apparently, after that time has expired, an assessment will be made for going forward."

"Five years—wow!" Jennifer said.

I took a breath. "I have to be honest. I'm terrified of Tommy Asheworth, and I pray he gets help. But his being released back into society scares the hell out of me!"

Elizabeth pushed her chair back. "You're thinking he might try to hurt you somehow?"

"Maybe," I said. "Sometimes I wish my imagination would take a holiday. Now, I need to be getting home. I don't want Nick to worry anymore that he already has."

With hugs and goodbyes shared in abundance, we all headed in different directions.

39

Nick and I were fifteen minutes early for what I hoped would be my last visit to the office of Dr. Tobias Ray. The test results were back, and I needed one final set of X-rays. I was more than a little nervous. Over the past two weeks, I had spent entirely too much time on the internet, and as such, I had somehow contracted every disease known to man.

"Good morning," Toby said, clipping the film in the light box. "Let's see what we have here. This is the break line, and everything is back to normal."

Nick cheered. "Well, that's good news, isn't it, Sarah?"

"I'm sorry," I said, realizing I hadn't heard a word. "Toby, could we go over the blood test results first? We can come back to the X-rays if need be."

"Yes, we can," he said, pulling three pages out of my folder. "Everything is just fine. You're a bit anemic, but not enough to cause concern. On the subject of your weight loss—according to the chart, you're not in the danger zone, but you're really close."

"I'm proud to say that I dusted off our scale, and I've gained four pounds since then," I said.

"And that's good, but if you could gain at least five more, that would be great. Healthy bones need proper nutrition. Brittle bones tend to break." Toby shuffled the papers. "Now, everything else checks out just fine. According to the blood work, your liver function, kidneys, and all the rest are just where they should be. So I'm cutting you loose, but I'll truly miss not seeing you. Zack's notes say you're rockin' rehab. I'm not surprised. Good job."

"What a relief," I said, giving him a teary-eyed hug. "Toby, I can't thank you enough for taking care of me."

"My pleasure, and call me if something doesn't feel quite right," he said, patting my shoulder.

ᗏᔓᗑ

I could feel the strength returning to my leg, and my whole body for that matter. PT was tough, and Zack showed me no mercy, but I powered through. February 7 was our target date to finish.

"Oh, that's my birthday. Dear Lord, I'll be fifty-two years old. Will you give an aging lady the best gift of all—my ticket to ride?" I begged.

"We'll see how it goes."

That cold February Monday, I was up and ready to go with hope in my heart. I told Rascal the night before this might just be the day, and I needed him to be on his best behavior. Naturally, I wouldn't do anything much more than get in the saddle and walk around, but that would be enough.

Zack greeted me at his office door. "Mornin', Mrs. H. Happy birthday! Are you ready to get to work?"

"Let's do it, and thanks. Now let's pray for the best gift ever."

After about an hour of working out and strength testing, Zack gave me a high five. "I think you've done all you can do here. Hang on to that brace just in case you need it, but I'm setting you free. I realize it wouldn't do much good for me to tell you to take it easy, but if you want our time together to become a distant memory, I strongly suggest you go slow at first."

"I promise," I said, giving him a strong hug. "I also thank you from the bottom of my heart for your time, and especially your patience."

With a schoolboy grin, he said, "You're a trip, Mrs. H.! What time do you plan to ride today?"

Raising both arms over my head, I said, "Before the sun sets. Hallelujah!"

C3&0

The Rowdy Girls came to the farm around four o'clock to cheer me on. Nick stood white-knuckled, gripping the gate to the indoor ring, and Coy paced back and forth in front of the mounting block. Even though I'd put my crutches away ages ago, I still climbed the stairs one at a time. Reaching the landing, I gently slid my right leg over the saddle and rested quietly, sliding both feet in the stirrups. Everyone clapped as tears of joy poured from my eyes.

Rascal was a one-in-a-million horse and knew his job was to protect me from any harm. After I collected my reins, with his sure and easy steps, we began our maiden voyage around the ring. Every time I looked at Nick, his eyes were on me, but Coy found the ability to relax, standing quietly at the gate. After about twenty minutes, my husband insisted I let that be enough for today, adding it was all his heart could take.

On the days thereafter, Coy insisted on bringing Rascal in from the pasture, saddling him up, and holding the reins as I got on. I never argued the point and appreciated his thoughtfulness. I rode every day in the mornings. Riding freed my mind from the daily clutter of living, and I was stronger afterward, both mentally and physically.

CB80

In early March, Reagan called Nick, suggesting that the end was near for his brother. They had seen each other several times over the past six months, but following Reagan's call, Nick booked a flight for the next day.

He told me afterwards how they sat in the bright white Kennedy front porch rockers, and talked through their shared cauldron of concerns on this, their final day together. A sense of peace filled the air as the setting sun reflected a whisper of vivid peach and canary yellow against the deepening denim blue water. Over dinner, Jack asked for this to be their last visit—this was how he wanted to be remembered.

The two brothers telephoned every day thereafter, Jack's voice growing weaker with every call. On the last day, he could barely even mutter a word. The following morning Jack's long-fought battle with cancer was over.

Nick and I flew up to help Reagan. He was cremated as planned, and a small service was held at Saint Elizabeth's on Nantucket. Nick had called Jack's first wife, Paige, the day his brother died, and surprisingly, she and their two girls plus their husbands were in attendance.

During our flight home, we held each other's hands and gave a gentle squeeze from time to time. When we returned to Long Leaf, Nick poured his energy into the arduous task of being the executor of Jack's estate, allowing time to soften the blow of loss.

40

The closing paragraph of any novel is important—it's the author's last chance to make a permanent impression. I always knew when my books or articles conveyed the right message: I'd give a deep sigh of delight, shed some tears, or raise my hands triumphantly above my head.

It was of great importance to me that my readers experienced that same sense of happiness and joy. My pinnacle of dreams would be realized if they closed the book and said, *Wow! I loved that.* Hopefully my readers, if there ever were any, would find themselves somewhere in my story, perhaps not as equestrians but as women with a sisterhood as strong as the Rowdy Girls.

The Disappearance of Lucy Butterfield was ready for my final edit. This meant I would read the whole thing from cover to cover, find and correct mistakes, and make sure it flowed at a steady pace. Every day the dogs and I worked nonstop, adding, deleting, or rearranging. I changed my mind at least a dozen times about how several areas should play out. But in the end, I had to stop fiddling with it and send my manuscript on to Ellie.

I had actually written a novel. My nonfiction books were no less an accomplishment, but this was blindingly different. This was a concoction of thoughts, fantasies, family, intrigue, horses, healing, and the tungsten-strong bond of six women.

Reading the final sentence on the last of 378 pages, I smiled and, taking a deep breath, thought: *This is actually pretty good. Now, what are the chances an agent or publisher will agree?*

Interestingly, each day as I began to weave my story, I became my narrator, Grace Hobbs, for as long as I was writing. The sisterhood of Libby, Cate, Mary, Dottie, and Bess were *her* friends, not mine. The two aging sisters and the photos were where the story began.

I enjoyed the research, and occasionally it was more fun than the story. There was a great deal of time spent checking and rechecking dates to actual days, giving fictitious names to possible real people, highways, towns, and so on. But in the end I decided to let it ride and trust in the disclaimer that would be printed clearly in the front of the novel.

Ellie Ward came over the following Monday, and I was thrilled to actually meet her. Until now we had only talked on the phone or emailed. I watched as she got out of her midsize SUV. Ellie was taller than I thought she would be and had beautiful shoulder-length light brown hair. As I waved from the door of my writer's shed, she returned the greeting and walked my way.

"Hey," I said, grinning from ear to ear. "It's wonderful to finally meet you."

Ellie sheltered her hazel eyes from the afternoon sun and stepped through the doorway. "My sentiments exactly. Oh, this is so cute. What a great place to work. But I have to ask, where are Annie and Caesar?"

I offered her the only other chair. "In the house and angry at me. As you can see, this space isn't big enough to add eight additional legs and feet." I handed her the Flash drive that contained my manu-script so she could save it to her laptop. "I'm a nervous wreck. I know you have to be objective and, occasionally, brutally honest, but I do truly hope you like my story."

"I can't wait to read it," she said, tucking a stray piece of hair behind her ear. "You won't hear from me for a while. I'll start tomorrow, but it takes serious time to read and edit. When I'm finished, I'll send you an email with an attached document, and then it's your turn."

"'My turn.' What does that mean?"

Ellie returned the Flash drive. "The text will be on the left two-thirds of the page and down the right-hand side will be my comments, corrections, deletes, and additions. You will either accept or reject my changes and type your thoughts under my comments. It's easy: my changes will be in red, and yours will be in green."

Over the next hour, we visited and talked about some of my concerns about my book—some of the plot points, the character-izations, and some technical issues, and she was truly listening. It was refreshing to talk about the mechanics of writing a book with someone who understood the challenges. Walking her back to her car, I thanked Ellie for her time and encouragement.

"I've worked so hard to build this story and have invested nearly eight months on just this part, and I know we still have miles to go. If I do find a publisher, can I even handle the reviews?"

Ellie smiled. "What you're feeling is universal. Yes, some reviews will be unkind to your eyes, but you'll learn to accept their honest opinion. It might sting at first bite, but you must not ever respond."

Chuckling, I said, "We'll see. If a review is too ugly, I might actu-ally reply."

"No, you can't let it get to you. Not everyone loves the same book, just as not everyone enjoys the same art or music. But I'm curious—define 'too ugly.'"

"I don't know: 'This novel wasn't worth the paper it was printed on, but you could use it to level your kitchen table or line the bird-cage.'"

"That really is ugly, as you say, but still no. Forget all that! We're still in the early stages here. When I return the document, take your time and really give each comment serious thought. Now, you and Nick should go out for dinner tonight and celebrate. Raise a glass to February twenty-eighth and keep only good thoughts in your heart. Oh, and absolutely *do not* make any changes while I've got the manuscript, because that will get confusing for you. In fact, take a nice break from it."

I'd been curious about meeting Ellie, wondering whether she'd be as kind and understanding as the online version. As she drove away, I headed back to the house to change my clothes. *What a lovely person and the perfect fit for me,* I thought.

CঙৎৎD

Fifteen minutes later I was dressed and ready to ride. Annie and Caesar flew past me and through the half-opened screen door, taking their places in the golf cart. I shook my head. "Nope. Come on," I said, patting my leg, "We're going to walk to the barn this time. I've got to get stronger, and walking helps. This is top secret—I plan to trot today. Nick and Coy are mending the fence down by the creek. Margaret will be here later, but for now I have the outdoor ring all to myself. Bark if anyone gets near the barn."

It was a beautiful day, and I wanted to ride outside. But was it worth it? If Nick got back before I was finished, the possibility of hell to pay hung in the balance. Following two seconds of deliberation, I decided the ride was worth the risk.

Margaret was early and quickly went to work getting Louie ready to ride. Her presence would help me if I got caught. Nick would never have much to say with another rider in the ring.

I looked over my shoulder. "Do you see anyone in the direction of the creek?"

"No, but I can't see anything anymore. Middle age is hitting me hard," Margaret said, riding into the ring.

"I understand; I can't read a word without my glasses. I'm going to pick up the trot, and you can't tell a soul."

"So that's it—I'm the lookout. You don't have the go-ahead to try this by yourself, do you?"

"Well, Nick did mention he would like to be around when I gave it my first try, but I can't waste this beautiful day."

Margaret laughed. "So, in short, the answer's no?"

"That's correct. He might be upset that I tried without his being around. Not to mention our being outside. I don't know why he thinks I'm safer indoors, but he does. Now, I have to get on with this—our Virginia trip is in three weeks."

Gloriously trotting around the far short end of the ring, I spotted Nick clearing the corner of the barn. He stopped in his tracks. "Sarah Heart, what are you doing?"

"Remain calm," I said, returning to the walk. "And before you blow a gasket, please notice everything is just fine. It's a beautiful day,

Margaret's here, and I have to try sometime."

Margaret trotted by. "Don't forget my number-one suggestion to defuse an argument."

"Thanks, but you're not helping." I giggled.

"You and I will dig deeper into this conversation later," Nick said, trying not to smile, "but for now, pick up the trot and stay collected."

After about fifteen minutes, I announced my leg and I had done enough for the day. Margaret continued to ride while Nick, Rascal, and I walked back to the barn.

"How are you doing? The bone has healed, but what about your muscles? I know you're exercising, but posting is a very different beast."

"It's all coming back, but I'm not there yet. I just have to take it slow."

Nick helped me down from the saddle. "Your admission is nothing short of astonishing!"

"Funny." I paused. "I am a little sore, but here's another thing. I know my femur has healed, but deep in my heart, I don't think it's completely sound, if that's the right word. I just don't trust it won't snap again. I'm more careful than you realize."

He took my hand. "Just for a while longer, I really don't want you to ride if no one's at the barn. Actually, I don't think anyone should ever ride alone, but especially not you—not just yet."

"I understand, but between Margaret, Linda, and the new boarders, there should be someone around almost every day. When are the boarders coming anyway? What do we know about them?"

Nick removed Rascal's saddle. "Only what they wrote on the barn release papers. One lady is from Iron Springs—Holly Burkhart."

"No way," I shrieked. "She could only be the wife of Richard Burkhart."

"Who?"

"Annie's vet! Remember?"

"I do," Nick said. "But regardless, we need the income so the barn can pay for itself. Think of it as getting some of Annie's vet bill returned to our coffers."

Brushing Rascal, I laughed. "How true! Now, who are the other two?"

"I don't remember their names. I can only recall Holly because of Christmas. Linda knows the other two from the Hadley Falls Country Club, and she told me they're coming here for the indoor."

"Interesting. I'll ask her tomorrow, but yes, their board will take us up four thousand dollars a month in income. That leaves eight more stalls to fill for a full barn."

"Wouldn't that be nine?"

I paused. "One has to stay empty for Margaret's new horse when she finds it."

"That's right. Oh, Linda spoke to me about a trainer who's interested in coming to give lessons. I think the name was Dianne Hill."

"Oh, absolutely not!" I said. "I know her from horse shows, and she's out of control. A trainer is a great idea—just not her."

"Okay. If she gets in touch, I'll tell her we are taking applications, and I'll be happy to put hers in the stack."

I laughed. "She's crazy as a bat and will destroy the Zen of the barn."

"Our barn has Zen? What's…? Never mind. I need to get back and help Coy."

Margaret had returned to the barn and overheard most of our conversation. "I nearly passed out when Nick said Dianne Hill."

"No kidding. All the new boarders will be bad enough—so much for peaceful Long Leaf Farm—but to add her to the mix is insane. It would be nice to have regular lessons here, though. We need to find someone who'd be perfect for all of us. I'll put together some barn rules, riding times, waivers, and such."

"Please bind it like a handbook. That looks more official and screams 'I'm not kidding.'" Margaret laughed. "It needs to be fully digested before being stuffed in their kitchen junk drawer."

I thought for a minute. "You know, that's not a bad idea, and since my editor has forbidden me to even look at my manuscript, it'll give me something to do."

41.

Two weeks had passed since Ellie had left with my manuscript, when I found an email from her in my in-box.

"Here goes nothin', puppies," I said, clicking on her name. Annie thumped her tail against the floor, and Caesar opened one eye.

Good morning, Sarah,

Just a quick note to say I ABSOLUTELY LOVE The Disappearance of Lucy Butterfield! Don't be upset, but you must find a different title. I'll explain more about that later.

Several places need work, clarification, or are simply unnecessary, but overall it's wonderful. I'll send it back to you in the next few days, after I reread a few places. When you see it, you'll understand what I explained earlier about how to respond to my comments.

All corrections and/or additions must happen in the document I'll send your way. Go slow and take your time.

One last thing—I couldn't stop reading. Well done!

See you soon,

Ellie

‹3∞

"Holy cats!" I squealed, printing out the message, grabbing the paper, and hurrying out the door with both dogs in hot pursuit. "Nick, Nick where are you?" I called out as we entered the barn.

"I'm right here. What's the matter?" Nick said from the feed room door.

Breathless, I waved the paper. "Read this."

Pulling his readers from his breast pocket, Nick quickly scanned the note. "Darlin', this is wonderful! Let's go out for lunch and celebrate. I've never eaten with a soon-to-be-famous author."

"Don't be ridiculous, but yay to lunch." I laughed. "Hurdle number one cleared, but the biggest ones are yet to come. They're like a cross-country log jump—three feet high, three feet wide, and solid as a rock! But for today it's a clean round."

"I'm sure you'll call them to share this news, so if Betsy and Margaret want to meet us for lunch, the more the merrier. Let's say we leave in an hour," Nick said, kissing my cheek. "One question. Now that things are looking up and moving forward, what's my name in your book?"

"I told you before—it isn't you. But *if and when* it's ever published, you'll know the names of both the main character and her loving and I'll add super-hot husband. Now, I have things to do, Todd."

"Sarah!" Nick shouted as I walked toward the house. "You will *not* call me Todd!"

‹3∞

An hour later, Nick and I were on our way to River's Bend. Betsy and Margaret were in and joining us for lunch.

Jennifer took our order, turned it in, and pulled up a chair.

"This is so exciting!" Margaret said. "I doubt anyone realizes what goes into creating the book they're holding. So does the main character have any friends?"

Looking over my water glass, I said, "Nice try. Of course she has friends, but like Rose said, who doesn't?"

CREO

Driving home, Nick and I talked about the Colonial Farm project. We needed to mark off the amount of requested land and decide just where the house should go. Hopefully the other players would agree with our decision.

Nick took one hand down from the steering wheel and reached for mine. "Lunch was fun today. I enjoyed watching your friends as they tried to wriggle the story out of you. Sadly, I haven't been successful either."

"Okay, you win," I said, dropping my head. "The main characters are Ben and Grace Hobbs, and they live on Tall Pine Farm."

"Oh, I like those names. How did you come up with them?"

"I don't know exactly. I've always loved the name Grace—it's soft and gentle. It took a while to find her match, but Ben is perfect in my mind. It conjures up tall and strong, like the Clock Tower—home to Big Ben. It's stood in place for nearly two centuries. He needs that to balance and support his wife."

"So, are they happy? Does everything turn out all right?"

"I won't tell you another thing. Assuming it ever makes it between two covers, you'll enjoy it more if you know nothing. Now, if you can coax it out of Annie or Caesar, you'll get to hear the whole story. They know every word."

42

Betsy and I had been to Lazy Willow Senior Living Center often enough that many of the staff and several other seniors knew us on sight. Olivia had requested the small sunny room for our private reading.

"Good morning," I said to Olivia, who sat waiting for us in the closest of three intimate groupings of tables and chairs. "You look lovely."

"Sarah, you always say that, and thank you, but what I really look is old."

"You do not," Betsy said. "Blue is definitely your color, and I love your hair. Have you always worn it up in a twist?"

Olivia straightened her skirt. "Yes. It's easy to do. I can't stand stringy hair. But I am getting old." Olivia shared with us her most recent visit from the doctor assigned to the center. "I've been having some heart troubles. According to Dr. Isaac, I need to go to the hospital for some tests."

"Goodness," I said, alarmed. "When?"

"This coming Monday, so I'm glad the two of you could come today. Did you bring any more of your story?"

"Yes," I said, thinking *I really do feel more confident reading it now that I know Ellie loves it. Interesting!*

"Well, hurry up. I'm anxious to know what happens."

Betsy opened her picnic basket. "Sarah, you start reading, and I'll pour the tea."

This was the final read.

"Okay, here we go. The end of my story is in sight," I said.

Olivia became withdrawn, shrinking into herself, when Hattie's husband of sixty years passed away. But she found her smile when Hattie moved back home to Salty Path to live with her sister. A few tears rolled down her face when Amelia passed away and Hattie was left alone.

Months after Amelia's death, loneliness began to set in, and Hattie decided to sell the house and move to a progressive senior living facility just on the outskirts of town. While packing, she found their mother's diary.

Taking a sip of tea, I noticed Betsy, too, had red eyes. "Are you okay?"

"Yes. Sarah, this is wonderful, but I hope we get to a happy place soon."

"We do. This next piece is about Julia Cooke's diary and a treasure in the attic. Miss Olivia, I used the last entry in your mother's real journal, where she mentions a black velvet box."

"I don't remember ever *seeing* a black velvet box," Olivia said. "I just love how you make stuff up."

"Yes, but it really was the last statement in your mother's journal. I almost missed it. Her dated entries stopped about halfway through the available pages, but at the bottom of the back page, she copied a note from her father. I love intrigue, so I created my own version for the novel."

"What did the note say?" Olivia asked.

Clearing my throat, I turned to that page. "'To my daughter Celia: On your wedding day, all I have, I give to you. I pray for you a wonderful life as rich as this gift. Hold each other close, and treasure one another always. Forever, your loving father.'"

"Well, that is a mystery," Olivia said. "It makes the hair on the back of my neck stand up. What could it have been? I wonder."

"I guess we'll never know, but I had a great time inventing the *attic find* in my story. You'll see when we get to that part. Here we go..."

Nearing the end of the story, Grace was once again searching for something in the attic on Tall Pine Farm. As she slides a cardboard box out of the way, it falls to pieces. Scooping up old gloves and scarves, she feels something hard wrapped in an embroidered linen handkerchief and tied with a pink satin ribbon.

Upon opening the box, she couldn't believe her eyes. "Ben!" she shouted.

"What—what's the matter?" he yelled, taking the steps two at a time.

Grace turned around, holding a small black velvet box. Gleaming from inside was the most beautiful sapphire and diamond broach she had ever seen. "Look what I found!"

I paused for a minute to remind Olivia that this was fiction.

"I know, and eventually Hattie's going to die. Right?"

"Yes, and if you're okay, I'll keep reading."

"Please."

"All right, now where was I?" I said, scanning the page. With only the final chapter remaining, I told them that we were nearing the end.

Carrying the beautiful blue porcelain urn to the car, Grace placed it between her feet and read the note. Hattie was very clear concerning where she wanted to be "sprinkled," as she called it, and gave strict instructions that Libby was to go as well.

Salty Path, a tiny town not too far down the road, had nothing to offer in the way of hotels. It took some doing to find lodging that summer, but Libby and Grace found a B&B in Bath for two days in late July.

The instructions said: "Take one cup of my ashes to 761 Elm Street—you know where it is. Pour it on the ground around the front porch. It was my favorite place on the property. It's okay with the folks who live there now. I checked."

The second paragraph read: "Take the ferry from Swan Quarter out to Ocracoke Island, and let my remaining dust ride on the wind of the sea as you cross the sound. It might be against the law, but I could not care less. If the two of you don't tell anyone, who will know?

"I love you both!"

It was an hour before sunset when the ferry prepared to dock back at the Oyster Creek Station in Swan Quarter. After the short ride to Bath, the two best friends were mentally and emotionally exhausted and collapsed at the closest table on the patio of the Scotch Bonnet Café.

As the last kiss of the waning sun danced across the ripples on the Pamlico River, Grace raised her glass and said, "Here's to you our dear, dear friend. Rest in peace, and we'll see you on the other side."

⊂⊃

Months passed and things returned to normal on Tall Pine Farm. Grace would think of Miss Hattie from time to time, especially at twilight.

One evening in late May, Grace came across Julia Cooke's diary and decided it deserved a special place on the bookshelf. Reaching up, Grace lost her grip on the hardback memoir, and it tumbled to the floor, landing in an open position. Taking a seat on the needlepoint ottoman, she read both pages.

Julia wrote often about "after-supper evenings" spent with her children. She told them summertime in the South was very special. "Just look how they light up the evening sky. To sweet tea and fireflies," Julia said, offering a toast to simple pleasures. "Girls, it doesn't get any better than this. Promise me when you're all grown up, you won't forget the magic of fireflies and the dreams you had as children."

"We promise Mama," they said, watching as the evening fairies danced just yards above the dew-laden lawn.

It truly was magical!

Betsy and Olivia sat in total silence for what seemed to be forever.

"I guess I should say 'The end.'" I smiled.

Betsy cleared her throat. "I'm speechless. It's wonderful."

"Wonderful is not a good enough word," Olivia offered. "Sarah, I just love it—truly I do."

"I'm thrilled you like it, but remember, we still have a long way to go before it's a book." I glanced at my watch. "Wow, it's getting late, and we really need to be on our way home. I'll call on Monday and see how things went with the visit to the hospital. Stay positive. There's probably nothing to worry about."

Returning my manuscript to the bottom of my tote bag, I thought, *If all I ever get from writing this story is giving Olivia and Betsy joy, it was a job well done.*

43

On Monday, I called Lazy Willow to check on Olivia.

Following several transfers, I reached the on-site nurse, who told me, "Miss Olivia had her test. Don't be alarmed, but Dr. Isaac is keeping her overnight for observation. She's in room 206 if you'd like to visit."

Without hesitation, I said, "Yes, I would. Thanks so much."

I called Betsy as soon as I disconnected the call. She answered on the first ring, and we agreed to meet at the hospital.

With a light tap on the door, we walked into her room. Olivia Cromwell was sitting up in her bed, watching the Hallmark Channel, eating peach ice cream, and chattering on with her nurse. "Well, I never—my favorite two people in the whole world!"

"We can't stay long," Betsy said, "but we needed to check on you."

Olivia smiled and proceeded to tell us all about her day, which included having to stay the night because of her blood pressure. We agreed that it was best to err on the side of caution.

Olivia made a sad face when we told her we had to leave but said she understood.

Walking across the parking lot, Betsy said, "I'm glad we came. She looks great."

"I agree," I said, opening my car door. "I've got to go. Ellie Ward's coming to talk to me about the book, but she didn't say why."

"You said she loves the farm. Maybe she just needs a dose of fresh country air while you two go over her edits?"

"I guess."

Betsy searched her purse, which was large enough to carry an infant, for her car keys. Finding them, she said, "Call me after she leaves, okay?"

"Absolutely!" I responded, sliding behind the wheel.

⋐⋑

Turning from the highway, I could see a two-horse trailer in front of the barn and a huge bay horse being backed down the ramp. Nick came out of the barn and offered the woman his hand and a smile. Remembering having seen her in the courtroom, I knew the striking woman, without a hair out of place, with the beautiful horse was Holly Burkhart. *Seriously. No apparent flaws. That's just perfect*, I thought, though I immediately scolded myself for being so catty!

Nick waved for me to come to the barn.

"I'll be right there. I just need to change my shoes."

Ten minutes later I was front and center at the barn, exchanging pleasantries with our new boarder. With introductions taken care of, Nick turned the indoctrination over to me. It didn't take long for my ruffled feathers to flatten. Holly seemed to be a genuinely kind person.

Relocating to the office, we discussed the hot-off-the-presses "official" boarders handbook. Somewhere in the middle of our conversation, Coy appeared, looking hesitant. I quickly introduced

274

our amazing barn manager and told her that he had total authority over the barn. Coy's posture softened following my announcement. He asked if she was leaving her trailer.

"Yes, if that's all right? Do you have room for it?"

"Sure. I'll go put it away."

Holly nodded, saying the keys were in the ignition. On his way out the door, Coy asked Holly to find him before she left. He had a few dietary and turnout questions concerning her horse.

I mentioned to Holly I was expecting my editor and needed to get ready for her visit. That announcement generated a bit more explanation and curiosity. I did share that I'd written humorous articles for an equestrian magazine, naming a few titles, several how-to horse books that few people had read, but withheld the fact that I'd written a novel.

"So, 'Shavings in my Shoes'—I remember that one. It was very funny and so true! I even sent a letter to the editor."

"It was funny and thanks for the letter! Now, let me show you where to put your tack, and feel free to look around." Walking into the tack room, I said, "Oh, the barn is closed all day on Monday. That time is used for barn repairs, cleaning, and paperwork. Closing time for the remaining days is at six o'clock. No one is allowed to ride alone. It just isn't safe."

I pointed to the wall-mounted dry-erase calendar. "Before you leave, print your name and time in the squares you think you'll ride. It's helpful to know when riders plan to come to the farm. Nothing's written in stone, so if your plans change, that's fine."

"Do you have a trainer?" she asked.

"Not yet, but we're working on finding someone. I'm sorry to run. Don't forget to speak with Coy before you leave, and welcome to Long Leaf Farm!"

"I'll see you tomorrow." Holly smiled.

"I look forward to it," I said, mentally trashing my previous catty thoughts. It would be fun to have a new face in the barn.

44

I heard Ellie's car pull up; I had been so excited after her email that I was positive my bubble was about to be burst.

"Hi," she said at the door of my office. "I've been thinking about this space since the last time I was here. No dogs?"

"No dogs. I'll let them out of the house when we're finished. But be forewarned—they're very friendly and furry. And thank you—I do love this room. Now, enlighten me. I'm surprised you came all this way to discuss my book."

"That's not usually the case, but I'm on my way to Wilmington for an editing seminar and thought an in-person edit might be helpful. Let's start with the search for a better title for your book."

"I'm not arguing, but why?"

Ellie rearranged herself in the chair. "Because Lucy Butterfield really isn't the story. She may have been in your first drafts, but that probably was lost long ago. Grace's finding the pictures of Lucy and the mystery man kick-starts the book, but after the rewrites, any reference to Lucy Butterfield disappeared."

"Hattie's professional life as the only female chemist in the hospital research lab in Winston-Salem and her husband's troubles handling his wife's success is her fraction of the story. Their inability to have children, her returning to Salty Path, and so on, after his death—finishes that part of your novel.

"The horses, the farms, and the sisterhood, though, are the much larger piece of the book. Grace and her friends' travels to the Foundation—I nearly wet my pants laughing about the foxhunt day and the torn breeches. The six women—their individual trials and tribulations—and their sisterhood are the story. The two big surprises—not to mention sex in the boathouse and the thong underpants floating away—ice the cake!

"I do love how your book ends with Julia Cooke talking to her children—and the parallel that creates with Grace's childhood and their shared joy for the simpler things in life."

I nodded in agreement. "Me too, and now I totally understand the search for a new title."

"A book's title is hugely important," Ellie continued. "It needs to pique the reader's curiosity. If it stays the way it is, they'll be disappointed, because it's misleading. This isn't a thriller or a mystery. But don't worry too much about it now. It's not unusual for the perfect title to simply lift from the pages themselves—especially when you're just quietly reading to find mistakes. If we do find a publisher, they may or may not like your title and will change it if they so choose. But for now you need a clever one to help attract an agent."

"Like moths to the flame. My mind will go directly into high gear on this one."

"At first probably so." Ellie smiled. "But as you think of possibilities, write them down. Eventually the best choice will stand out from all the rest. Before I leave, why don't you pull up my email, and I'll show you how to navigate the choppy seas of edits and comments."

There was an intimidating wall of red running down the right side of nearly every page. You don't need to be an art teacher to understand the reaction that red evokes. But after a brief tutorial, I was enthralled with the process and, under Ellie's watchful eye, worked on the first chapter. Confident I understood, she told me it was time for her to leave.

Gathering her purse and jacket, she said, "Take your time with this. Let's allow six weeks for your edits and my second round. We need to get it as perfect as possible before looking for an agent. If it's chock-full of mistakes, they'll reject it as being too much trouble to fix. If we do find an agent who thinks she can sell it, she will work on finding a publisher. Now that you know your job, have fun and go slow. Oh, don't forget your promise of my meeting Annie and Caesar."

As we walked out of my office, I hustled up to the house.

"Hang on to your hat. I'm not kidding," I said, opening the kitchen door. Both dogs bounded out to greet our visitor. Thankfully Ellie was braced against the side of her car. Reaching down, she petted their heads and tickled their backs as they wriggled and rubbed up against her. They were very good dogs but also very big, which could be overwhelming.

Ellie drove away, and I broke into a cold sweat at the work I had to do as my co-authors and I walked back to our office. "Holy Moses, puppies!"

Nick came over from the barn to see how things went. I tried to explain our meeting; apparently writing the book was the easiest part.

"I saw steaks thawing on the drain board earlier. You work for as long as you need, and I'll make our dinner tonight. Come on dogs—

hey, why won't they come to me?"

"Because I'm standing in the doorway, and they know there's work to be done." I laughed. "The three of us will be in the kitchen around six to help you."

45

Over dessert, Nick and I talked about the Rowdy Girls' trip to Virginia the next weekend, our two new boarders arriving the following Wednesday, and the fact that we really had to hire someone to help Coy with the barn and possibly secure a trainer.

Nick laid his napkin on the table. "I have to ask you something."

"Okay?"

"You may say this is none of my business, but I really think it is. If we weren't married, money wouldn't be an issue, but since we are, I think having everything out in the open is better practice for building a solid relationship. I know we agreed to "yours" and "mine" for things we want that need no discussion and "ours" for the big stuff, but we also have a commitment to each other. So here goes—how much is Ellie charging you?"

"I really don't want to tell you." I squirmed. "It's a lot, but I'm using the money from the sale of my house on Brook Street."

"I understand, and it absolutely is your money to do with as you please. I can see you feel like I'm calling you out on something. That's not my intention at all. I just think it would be better if you invested that money."

"I am investing that money—I'm investing it in myself."

"I agree, but I would like for us to do this together."

"Thank you, and that's very kind. How about this: if it becomes a financial burden, I'll ask for your help?"

"Perhaps. But even though you're writing the book, I see it as our journey. One way or another, whatever happens concerning the novel will happen to both of us. So let's use *our* money to pay for this. What do you say?"

"That's very sweet, Todd. I'll think about it."

Nick laughed. "Todd would never want to share this adventure with you, but I do. Now, back to the original question—the going rate of your editor? I have no background to even venture a guess."

I took a breath and a sip of iced tea. "Well, okay, but hold on tight—remember you asked. Ellie Ward is top of the heap in her business, and she charges $140.00 an hour. Her last bill was for nearly two thousand dollars."

"Holy Christ!" Nick exclaimed. "I had no idea. I'm sure it's a fair price, but I would have never guessed. See? I told you I didn't know anything about the editing business. This is equal to the first bill I received from my attorney years ago. It took three or four of those before I could breathe while opening the envelope."

Laughing, I said, "No kidding. My barn board, a set of new tires, or yoga lessons...I never batted an eye—I was accustomed to those things. I nearly passed out reviewing her website. Her rates are posted in black-and-white. So far she's been worth every penny. I really can't do this without her help. Ellie offers another set of eyes and wisdom I don't possess."

"Sleep on this, but I really don't want you to use the money from the sale of your house. I'd rather you invested in something for the children maybe. I don't know, but let's pay for this together."

"Okay, but you do understand it may turn out to be money down the drain. There's absolutely no guarantee of success with this. It's an expensive crapshoot, and that's why if it's my money, I don't have to explain anything to anyone."

"How frightening. I understand your logic," Nick said, giving me a kiss. "But I know it will be successful."

"Really? How so?"

"Because Ellie Ward stated she 'absolutely loved it.' I don't think a professional would use those words if she truly didn't feel that way. She's read thousands of books and must know true potential. So if she's as good as you say, she wouldn't have been so complimentary. Her reputation is paramount, and if she's wrong, false praise falls on the debit side of her credibility."

"Well then, one last thing…If it does well and the royalties start pouring in, do we have to split the proceeds?" I laughed.

"No. You get the money, and I'll take my half out in trade."

"Trade—what does that mean?" Instantly the light came on, and my face turned crimson.

Nick chuckled at my bright red cheeks, and a soft kiss was his response.

46

Margaret and I were hard at work cleaning tack and packing her trailer for our early-morning departure the next day to Moss Creek. While drowning everything leather in saddle soap and oil, I said, "Normally I'm so excited about going to Susan's. I know my leg has healed and I've been given the medical green light, but I'm still nervous."

Margaret wiped her hands on a rag. "That's not surprising. Your accident was nothing short of a train wreck. And while Virginia is great fun, it's also physically grueling. I really do think Susan will go easy on you, though. Everything will be fine. Just try to relax."

"I will. It'll be fun to get off the farm and do something different. I need a break from my book. Oh, did you get the skinny on our two new country club boarders?"

"Yes. According to Elizabeth, they're joined at the hip and are coming from Twisted Oaks Farm. You know that barn—it's out on Shiloh Church Road."

"I do. Why are they leaving?"

"Rumor has it there was some sort of brouhaha, and they were actually asked to leave—that very day."

I rolled my eyes. "Great. That's all we need. At least forewarned is forearmed. First Nancy, and now this. Will I ever be finished dealing with unruly children?"

"Maybe, but apparently not quite yet. Just go all 'teacher' on them the first day, give out the bound handbook, and tell them the big stuff up front. They'll fall in line. I would love to be a fly on the wall. Seeing you in action is astonishing. It's a gift—you never raise your voice or anything."

"You're ridiculous." I chuckled. "But I also think you're on to something about letting these ladies know the lay of the land."

Margaret snickered. "See, I already want to say, 'Yes, ma'am!' Now, don't tell Nick, but I really do love his horse. He was so generous allowing me to ride Chance, but I might not give him back. Depending on how this weekend goes, I think I'll ask your husband to sell me his horse. He can find a new one. What are my 'chances'—get it?"

"Funny, and yes, I get it, but I really don't know what Nick would say. You do look amazing on that big gray. The other day, when you were way too long to the brush jump, Chance took charge and made it work out. Very good boys like that are hard to find."

"How about softening Nick up on the subject?"

"Maybe," I said. "This is really between the two of you, but if the situation presents itself, I'll chime in."

Holly popped into the tack room about ten minutes later to get ready for an afternoon ride. I jumped right into the discussion of a trainer and whether she would be interested in having formal lessons. "The going rate is around eighty dollars a pop and would be included in your monthly board bill."

I took a seat on my tack trunk. "Private lessons would only be for special situations—they're just not profitable. But group lessons of four riders close in ability are the best.

"There would be no cancelation charge for illness or seriously bad weather. Yes, every rule has an exception. Switching your hair appointment wouldn't qualify—well, it would to us but not the trainer. All riders would be expected to take no fewer than six lessons per month. I'm sure you know this, but the barn gets a percentage of the trainer's fee."

Holly agreed it would be fun and beneficial to have lessons, especially group ones, but her participation would depend on the trainer and price. Margaret and I added that those two items were tops on our list as well.

Holly paused. "I need to share this: there is only one trainer I know I just could not ride with. She travels to several barns and gives lessons, but she and I are like oil and water. Her last name is Hill—perhaps you know her."

Trying to avoid an unkind remark, Margaret didn't utter a word, and I carefully searched for mine. "Yes, we do know her, but only from horse shows. When we're ready, Nick and I'll set up a window for applications. When that time's expired, we'll go through the stack, check references, have personal interviews, watch each applicant ride several of our horses, have him or her give our boarders an actual lesson, and then hopefully make the right choice."

"I know a few people who might be interested," Holly said. "Is it okay if I tell them about this possible opportunity?"

"Absolutely," I said, "but make sure you're up front concerning the process. Also mention Long Leaf Farm is an adult barn full of women over thirty."

Margaret laughed. "That'll shorten the line of applicants for sure."

"Probably" I laughed even louder. "A barn overflowing with female hormones constantly shifting with the tides. Now, everything else—lessons, times, pro rides, days off—is pretty much standard at most barns. When we narrow it down, Nick and I'll have a deeper conversation with the applicant.

"Oh, weekends would be held open for free riding, horse shows, and clinics."

"Thanks. I'll add all of that to my conversation," Holly said happily.

47.

To toast my first tip back to Virginia as a rider, Nick and I went out for a nice dinner in Hadley Falls. Somewhere over our dessert, I mentioned how much Margaret loved Chance and asked what it would take for that horse to become hers. Nick smiled and said that would require some serious thought.

With our new boarders, we really did need to hire someone to help Coy. It was more work than one man could handle. Nick agreed and said he'd discuss it with him tomorrow and let Coy do the hiring.

"Great idea," I said, treasuring my last bite of cherry cheesecake. "I do worry about our dogs when I'm away. Are you sure you know what to do?"

"You forget, they're dogs. Check, please," Nick said as our server passed by.

"I beg to differ. They are not just dogs. This morning I printed instructions for their care and portioned out and labeled individual bags of their food. Annie gets a pill every morning, and Caesar needs oil on his dinner. Oh, sometimes Annie—"

"I'm going to stop you right there. Next you're going to tell me how to make the bed."

I squeezed his hand. "How'd you know? But you do remember the biggest pillows go in the back, right?"

"We're leaving," Nick said, shaking his head.

CR&O

Coy and Nick helped hook up Margaret's trailer and load the horses. I was still gun-shy about walking into the trailer—another thing to conquer. It was strange for me to want to go so badly and yet be so scared to leave.

With one final kiss on the top of each dog's head, I paused, drawing in a deep breath. Nick held my face in his hands and kissed me tenderly. "You'll be fine, and we will too. Now get in the truck and have a Rowdy Girls good time."

"Okay. I do love you so!"

"I know, and I love you too."

We pulled into the parking lot of Saint Andrew's Episcopal Church just outside of Hadley Falls to team up with the other two trailers. Betsy was leaning against her dually, enjoying a cup of coffee, and Elizabeth and Jennifer had yet to arrive.

Our stragglers wheeled in ten minutes later, offering their apologies and fresh-baked oatmeal raisin cookies. Any excuse always falls softer when cookies are involved. We tucked the horses' heads back in with a pat on the face and a carrot each, closed the trailer windows, and off we went.

Arriving at Moss Creek Farm around noon gave us little time to chitchat, and we went straight to work. Owner Susan Tillman stood firm on her one o'clock ring time; excuses were wasted breath. Margaret stood watch as I backed Rascal down the ramp with no issues. Our smiles were Mississippi River wide as I metaphorically spit in the eye of that dragon, victorious over my fear. My big red guy found a new joy to his step when he realized where he was. Chance danced a bit sideways but calmed down and walked quietly behind Rascal.

Rose had already arrived from Bellomy Farm and walked to Betsy's trailer to greet us and collect her horse. We were once again the Rowdy Girls sextet!

The afternoon lesson was in the indoor arena, which was huge and gave each horse room to work. Susan had a very interesting forty-minute flat class involving serpentines to lane work, and I was able to do it all without any problem. As the last rider finished the pattern, we were instructed to come down to the walk while she and her seriously hot barn manager Deacon put together a jump course. There was no argument there. Deacon—a modern-day Adonis draped in Carhartt—was a sight to behold! His chiseled features and rock-hard body would have made Michelangelo secure another block of marble and gather his tools.

While changing directions, I mentioned to Margaret and Betsy that I was uneasy about jumping. I didn't think I should participate, but I also didn't want to be a baby.

Betsy whispered, "Just see what she's going to say. You know if you start the conversation, it will be downhill from there."

"Ladies, how are we doing?" Susan asked. "Sarah, are you okay? I need the truth."

Leaving out my nerves, I said, "Yes, I'm fine."

"All right, then, here's what we're going to do…" Susan reviewed the jump course. All the jumps were very small cross rails, maybe eighteen inches high at dead center. "This is going to be a building lesson. You'll start very small, and the jumps will grow in height as we progress. Your jump order is: Sarah you're first, then Margaret, Betsy, Rose, Jennifer, and Elizabeth."

"Why the hell am I always first, especially now?" I asked.

Betsy giggled as I trotted past.

Susan shouted in my direction. "Sarah, is anything the matter?"

"No, ma'am, I'm all good," I lied. I was actually petrified. Although the jumps were very small cross rails, I hadn't done any jumping since the day of the hunter pace in November. But it was just a mind-over-matter situation that I was determined to conquer.

"Great. Now, everyone remember, trot in, canter out, bring your horse back to the trot before the next jump, and repeat for all eight. Are we clear? Good. Sarah, go."

By the third trip through the course, I began to relax and was on top of the world. Rascal was ecstatic to be doing something more than just trotting around in circles. We were told to take the wall again and return to the walk while she and Deacon raised the jumps. Hearing the metal jump cups rattle on the rise against the standards, my stomach soured like month-old milk.

The hurdles now measured two feet three inches where the rails intersected, and that would require a bit more effort. Keeping my weight in my heels and hinging at the waist, just to name a few. I'd done all of it a million times, but this was the first time since the accident. If I was spot-on, all would be well, but if not, and considering I was no longer actually sitting in my saddle, saying hello to the ground was a possibility—remote, perhaps, but still a possibility.

"The order of go is the same, as are the instructions. You'll need to work hard to return to the trot before the next jump. Your horse will truly want to canter on. So, to my six ladies who never sit down after the jumps, put your butt in the saddle and leave it there until the next jump. Are there any questions? Good. Now, Sarah, slow your brain down, relax, and allow Rascal to do his job."

It took all I had to collect my reins and move forward. I'm not sure I took a breath throughout the entire course, but as I returned to my place at the back of the line, I melted into a puddle of euphoric tears.

Susan told Margaret to wait a minute and walked in my direction. "Are you just happy, or does something hurt? I can't tell. I need for you to get it together and talk to me."

"Oh my God, Susan—I'm wonderful! That felt so good! I just need a minute," I said, choking back a sob.

"Okay, but when it's your turn, do you want to ride the course again?"

"Absolutely!"

With two more trips under my belt, I decided to call it a day. I had done more in the past two hours than I had done in what seemed to be forever. "Susan"—I trotted Rascal to where she was standing—"I need to pass on the rest of today. I'm fine. I just know I've done enough."

"All right, but stay in the ring. I'm going to raise the jumps one more time, and then we'll be finished. How do you feel about going out to the cross-country field tomorrow?"

"I'm in. Rascal would never forgive me if we didn't at least try. That's his favorite place on this farm."

"Great. And you're sure you're okay?"

"Positive," I was delighted to say.

48

With everyone showered and dressed in our street clothes, the Rowdy Girls walked up the hill to Susan's sprawling contemporary with an amazing view. It was huge but also inviting—the rich warm furnishings and thick rugs scattered around softened the angles of the exterior walls. With two steps up to the kitchen and three down to the den, it truly looked like it belonged atop the rise and fall of the mountain it occupied.

Not only were we dinner guests, we also wore the aprons of sous chiefs. The six of us sat around the island in the kitchen as Deacon searched for a pot large enough to house his low-country boil. Our task was to work on the side offerings to the entrée. Cutting, chopping, and dicing took on a whole different meaning from our day-to-day 'cooking dinner' routine. What a view!

"God, he's gorgeous," Jennifer said emphatically, the noise of clanking cookware around us softening her voice.

Elizabeth squeezed in and whispered, "He has an amazing ass. You don't notice it when he's wearing his overalls, but in those jeans—hello!"

Rose inhaled deeply. "For years I've searched for a flaw, but there simply isn't one. I wish we knew more about him."

"His mystery is part of his mystique," Betsy said, chopping the cabbage.

Just then Deacon stood up with selected pot in hand and asked me about Buddy and how he was adjusting to our farm. "Uh," I said, trying to maintain my balance as he looked straight at me. "He's wonderful. Thanks for asking. I haven't ridden him since the accident, but I will in a few more weeks. Do you know what happened to the man who turned him out in the meadow for the insurance money?"

"He was convicted," Susan cried from across the room while setting the table, "but I don't remember what the judge gave him."

"Well, at least he didn't just get a slap on the wrist," I answered.

"Here," Deacon said, pushing a basket of fresh hush puppies in my direction. "Dinner won't be ready for another thirty minutes, so please eat some of these. I bet you girls worked up an appetite today."

Over dinner I opened the door to my request that we change our summer camp week from the third week in June to the fourth. I briefly laid out that my book needed work and thankfully everyone agreed to the new plan.

We spent Saturday morning and afternoon in the massive open field, where Susan took us to the beginner cross-country area. Those jumps were unyielding but not quite as intimidating as the bigger ones. It was glorious flying around from hurdle to hurdle, splashing through the water jumps, and up and down small hills.

After about an hour of the afternoon exercise, I excused myself, and Rascal. We had both done enough. Susan understood that my old guy was feeling his years, and my leg was tuckered out. We enjoyed a lazy walk around the perimeter of the field while the others continued jumping for an hour more.

On Sunday we took a trail ride along Moss Creek and in and

out of meadows exploding with spring. My heart swelled realizing that, just as the blossoms and leaves were returning to their once barren limbs, I too had emerged victorious from a winter's hibernation. It was a wonderful way to end a weekend.

49

By the middle of May, Ellie and I had completed our work. I loved the final draft and appreciated her help and the dollars required to get it that way. Somewhere along the way, Ellie Ward had also become a wonderful friend.

Dr. Baxter helped keep me centered and spiritually balanced. We went over my concerns about "If I get published, what will people say about my novel? Will someone take issue or offense? Are the sex parts too much?" I openly admitted to writing those with one eye closed. The language wasn't trashy, but it led the reader's imagination down the correct path.

Everyone who read the book didn't have to love it, but I couldn't bear the thought of being verbally stoned on the village green of criticism. It was not unlike letting go of your child. I had worked so hard and taken such care of my story, I was terrified to offer it to the world.

"Remember," she said, "you can never heal if you have an emotional reaction to everything that is said to you. Not everyone is going to be complimentary, but, as we've discussed before, just breathe and let it pass."

Ellie sent me a list of thirty possible agents, four of whom were North Carolinians, along with a killer query letter. She called it the "first wave." I was given the task of weeding through the list of possibilities to find my top twelve choices. The remaining eighteen names would be held in reserve for the second round, if need be. I decided to give the book one final read before I sent it out.

C3 80

Nick poked his head in the dining room. "Wow! What's all this?" he asked, admiring our dining room table, set with my English bone china, Irish crystal, and silver flatware. "I'll need to change my clothes. Did I forget a big occasion?"

"You didn't forget anything, and we're fine the way we are. But this is a very important day," I said. "This is just for the two of us. My darling Nick, I could never have done this book without you. Your patience and support have been invaluable."

"You have tears in your eyes. What's going on?" Nick said.

"My novel is finished, and the query letters are ready to go. Well, that is, the emails, which are hugely frightening for me. It will probably take me more than a few deep breaths to muster up the courage to hit send, but I'm determined to stare down my fear of technology."

"Oh, babe, that's wonderful. I'm so proud of you! How does it work?"

Lighting the candles, I said, "It varies. Each agent has asked for something different. For example, one required the first three chapters, and another requested the first one hundred pages. They all get a personal query letter with their individual request attached. If any of these people are truly interested, they'll send a return email asking for the remaining pages."

"Can I read it now?" Nick asked, taking his seat.

"Right or wrong, I'm convinced that everyone, including you, will enjoy it much more if it's actually published. Now, are you hungry?"

"Always." Nick smiled, giving me a tender kiss. "Dinner smells delicious."

Our celebratory meal was delicious and fun in our fancied-up dining room.

"I'm guessing you finally settled on a new title?" Nick asked.

"Yes, I did. It came to me in the oddest of ways, with very sweet memories for me and Julia Cooke."

"Who's Julia Cooke, and what's the title—or are they both secrets too?"

"Yes, and only two people know the answer to your question."

"You and Betsy. Wait…Olivia would know too."

"Nope. Just me and Ellie Ward. Please don't waste your time trying to weasel it out of me. The whole novel will be a better read for you without knowing anything beforehand. Now, leave me alone, Todd, and let's have dessert on the patio."

"I thought my character was named Ben. I swear, Sarah, if you've changed my name to Todd…"

"Well, my love, your mother named you Nicholas, and Grace's husband isn't you, so whatever the name, you're safe on that front."

Nick narrowed his eyes in my direction. "You're enjoying this, aren't you?"

"Grab your wine and my tea, please, and I'll join you on the patio with our dessert. And yes, it's hilarious the depth to which the name of the fictitious husband means to you."

⊂ℨ∞⊃

Just after sunrise, the dogs and I tiptoed off to my writer's retreat. I pressed send twelve times: my query letters plus attachments were on their way. I was a sweaty disaster, floating in a full-blown wave of insecurity. This submissions process was going to cause many a sleepless night. Between *Did I do it correctly?* and *What will they say?* I knew I would count the birds on my patterned bedroom curtains night after night, unable to sleep.

"Good morning," Nick said as we three walked in from the back porch. "Where have you been?"

Refilling my glass, I said, "Good morning. I just finished sending out the first query letters, and my possible nervous breakdown is waiting in the wings."

"Well, congratulations, and 'no, thank you' to the breakdown," Nick said. "Everything will be fine. We should do something special in honor of this momentous occasion."

"Thank you for saying that. I was considering a small dinner party with just the Rowdy Girls—husbands, of course. What do you think?"

"That's a great idea, but it will need to be this Saturday. You six go to horse camp on Monday, and Sunday is our anniversary. I really don't want to share that day with anyone but you."

"I'll see what I can do," I said, giving him a kiss. "And I agree, Sunday belongs to just us."

50

For no fewer than twenty years the Rowdy Girls had celebrated everything—good or bad—together. And this occasion was my turn. I kept my fingers crossed that everyone, including Rose and Gus, could come on such short notice. After five phone calls, we were a full house of twelve.

In true Rowdy Girl style, everyone brought a dish to complement my stuffed beef tenderloin. It was a beautiful June evening, so we decided that dessert on the patio was a must, especially considering Rose had made her famous four-layer chocolate cake earlier that day. She and Gus were spending the weekend at her house in Hadley Falls.

With everyone served but before we could take a bite, Nick whooped with excitement. "Would you just look at that!"

"Wow," Betsy said. "There must be a thousand fireflies in your garden."

I shivered. It was like sparks in the sky. Was this an omen or just happenstance? Clearing my throat, I said, "Everyone, quiet, please. I had planned to keep the book title a surprise, but this evening has made that impossible. Would you just look at this twilight summer sky full of nature's glory! Perhaps some higher being is trying to tell me something—so would you all please raise your glass to *Sweet Tea and Fireflies*."

Holding their glasses high, everyone said, "*To Sweet Tea and Fireflies.*"

Nick squeezed my shoulder and said, "You're kidding? Usually your cosmic thinking scares the hell out of me, but not this time."

I took a moment to reflect: *Whatever happens with the book, I am so happy I did it and was surrounded by my friends and had their support!*

Following dessert, the six Rowdies left the guys on the patio and made our way to the kitchen to clean up.

Stacking plates on the counter, Jennifer asked, "How long do we have to wait?"

"I have no idea. It depends on so many things, but I'll guess eighteen months."

Margaret wiped her hands. "Gosh, that's forever. I'll be nearing my mid-fifties before it's a book."

"You will not." I laughed. "We're the same age. Wait a minute. We'll be fifty-four, maybe fifty-five—that is forever."

I understood Margaret's underlying complaint, really I did, but I also wasn't going to let anyone else read the book. What if it was soundly rejected, and nobody but Ellie and I liked it? I needed validation from a publisher first. And that was an uphill battle for any writer. Hundreds of thousands of writers probably tried to get their book published every year. It was impossible to know. But I was proud to acknowledge that I'd set out to tell a story using my imagination, and I'd done it. Now it was time for the market to decide.

51.

The next morning I snuggled into Nick. "Happy anniversary, my love."

Giving me a stubbly kiss, he said, "Happy anniversary to you, too! What a wonderful year, full of twists and turns, this has been."

"I know, right? I'm so sorry about horse camp and my book falling on or near our actual day. The first anniversary is very special, and I feel like I've diminished its importance somehow."

"Well, you haven't. We planned for this possibility months ago, when the Colonial Farm project was added to our list of events."

"Thank you. I can't wait for whatever you've planned for our surprise celebratory trip. Depending on where we're going, the first week in July could be either hot or cold. I do need a hint on what to pack."

"Very little and for July heat," Nick said. "Speaking of heat…"

An hour or so later, the cool shower before breakfast was not only crowded but also refreshing. "Just tell me one more thing," I asked, toweling off. "Do I need to bring anything nicer than average—for dinner, let's say?"

"Yes, but not over the top." Nick smiled. "That's it for hints! Not another question. I know it will drive you nuts, but too bad."

I had decided to bring Buddy to horse camp, since Rascal could no longer handle the rigor of a five-day physical challenge. I was curious to see what Buddy thought about camp, and I was thrilled that he never refused a jump, glided along the long canter runs, and took the water obstacles like a pro. His stellar performance was proof positive that he loved Moss Creek Farm as much as I did.

Chance did equally well and found the jump field to be great fun. His willingness firmly cemented Margaret's conviction to own the big gray.

For dinner we decided to try out a new little restaurant in town. Once clean and changed into street clothes, we piled into Betsy's truck and made our way up the hill. Susan had an SUV capable of holding the first string of a soccer team, and riding together was always the most fun. I took the opportunity to check my email. Apart from junk, there was nothing. No messages from agents.

Margaret watched what I was doing. "At least no one said no one minute after they got your query, right?"

"That is good," I agreed.

CS80

The Thursday-evening menu was always peel-and-eat shrimp. Using his secret recipe, Deacon boiled the shrimp while the six of us made the sides and sauces. We had never figured out his secret ingredient, and he refused to share.

Always in search of new recipes, Rose used her most enticing voice. "So, Deacon, besides water, what exactly are the ingredients in your seafood boil?"

Deacon looked over his left shoulder while stirring the pot. "My grandma taught me how to cook. We lived in the Tidewater area of Virginia and this recipe goes back at least two, maybe three, generations. Even from the grave, she'd have my hide if I ever gave away the family secret. But I'm glad you ladies like my cookin.'"

Elizabeth whispered, "Imagine the lucky someone who might just harness that gypsy spirit and a drop-dead gorgeous man. Plus he can cook!"

After dinner we enjoyed the evening air from Susan's back deck. It was beautiful and overlooked rolling hills as far as you could see.

"Sarah, have you checked your email today?" Betsy asked.

Susan put down her cup of coffee. "Why does Sarah need to check her email?"

Margaret took the floor. "She sent out twelve query letters last Thursday, trying to find an agent for her book."

"Oh, how exciting. I remember back in March your telling me it was nearly finished. Well, have you checked your email?"

"No, I haven't. You worked us so hard today, it never crossed my mind," I said, pulling my phone from the back pocket of my jeans and my readers from the top of my head.

Rose moved to the edge of her cushioned wrought-iron chair. "Well, do you have anything?"

"Wait a minute...Oh my gosh, I have something from two—no three—agents."

Impatiently, Betsy asked, "What do they say?"

"Read aloud," Susan suggested. "Then you won't have to repeat yourself. You know not all of them are going to say yes, so if there's a rejection, we're here for you."

"That's right." Elizabeth smiled. "Now let's hear what they have to say."

The first one thanked me for thinking of them but said it wasn't right for their list. Rose offered a concise explanation of the "list" reference—meaning that the book might not fit in with the type of books they normally represent, and I moved on to the second. He said he liked the story, but with the horse piece, it was too narrow an audience. We all called him stupid, as I opened number three.

"Holy cats!" I screamed, jumping up and sending Susan's two yellow Labs running for cover as my words bounced over the mountaintops. "Uh, let me see...Rachael Covington loves my story and wants the remaining chapters!"

"How much did she ask for when you sent out the query letter?" Elizabeth asked.

"It was something like the first one hundred pages of the book. I remember that number stopped in the middle of a chapter, which sent me sideways, so I finished it out. But most importantly, I remember her bio said she loved horses, and I felt an instant connection." I flopped down in the chair and wilted in utter disbelief. "I'm blown away, but I can't do anything without talking to Ellie first. She said I was to send her any and all responses. I guess I should do that now."

Margaret held up her index finger, "Before you do, are there legal issues with who said yes first, or can you wait until you've heard from all twelve?"

"I haven't the faintest idea, but Ellie will know. I need to call Nick before it gets too late. His hurt feelings will be justified if he's the last to know."

Pacing back and forth with the deck railing at my side, I first forwarded all three emails to Ellie, reminded her I was in Virginia with limited service, but I would check my email when I could.

Nick answered on the second ring, and I recounted my past thirty minutes.

"Wow, babe! What's your plan?"

"Nothing until I hear from Ellie," I answered. "And I really need to be at home and at my computer to go any further. But I guess if it's an emergency, Ellie could send Rachael what she needed—she has my book on her laptop."

"Try not to get frazzled by this and enjoy your last day at camp tomorrow. How's Buddy doing?"

"Awesome! He loves riding in the field. By the way, you've lost your horse: Chance is a serious fan of camp life, and Margaret has fallen madly in love. I've got to go. We're having homemade strawberry ice cream and brownies for dessert."

"You're hanging up on me for dessert?"

"Only because my ice cream is melting." I laughed. "I adore you, and I'll see you tomorrow."

"So, Rose, is your trip to Scotland still on?" Elizabeth asked, breaking the momentary silence.

Susan jumped in quickly. "A trip to Scotland? Could it be in the company of my dear friend Gus?"

"Yes," Rose answered in a jubilant voice. "We're visiting his childhood home and some of my family in England."

Margaret filled her spoon with ice cream. "Sarah, I know the barn will still be open while you're away, but where is Nick taking the two of you?"

"I have no clue about our anniversary destination, but he said it would be July hot. I'm very excited. I just wish I knew exactly what to pack."

Jennifer raised her spoon. "Remember, nekked is hot. And if the weather is, too, you won't need much."

Everyone howled, and the sisterhood of six, plus Susan, scraped the last drops of ice cream from our bowls and finished off the entire pan of brownies.

52

Once home from camp, I called Ellie to discuss the ins and outs of signing on with an agent. She said I probably wouldn't actually hear from all twelve of the people I emailed. If they weren't at all interested, some would simply never reply. If I had more than one yes, I would pick the one I thought was the best fit for me and then notify the others, giving each a final opportunity to pitch their game.

Ellie advised me to send the remaining chapters to Rachael Covington and wait to see if anyone else wanted a full read. "Now, have a great time on your anniversary trip, and don't touch your phone. They won't retract an offer just because you're unable to reply for a few days. Call me when you get home."

"Okay. I'm so excited about having a week away. I've been going like a house afire, and this will be good for both of us."

CB80

The surprise anniversary trip was to the Four Seasons Resort at Peninsula Papagayo in Costa Rica. What an amazing spot! The first day and a half, we did nothing much more than eat, read, and enjoy the view overlooking the Gulf of Papagayo.

Nick had scheduled a day trip into the jungle, and zip-lining was something I thought I'd never do, but what a thrill that was, sailing just above the treetops. A morning hike along the hillsides included the highly advertised seven-hundred-step climb—a breathtaking view. Our spa afternoon that followed was amazing, beginning with a full-body massage that relaxed our sore muscles. Wrapped in a thick terry robe, Nick decided to read by the pool, while I enjoyed the bamboo garden facial with the lavender scrub. Within minutes I found calm and my skin tingled.

Following dinner on our last evening, we strolled along the beach, leaving our footprints in the sand at the edge of the lapping waves. Holding each other closely, we stood and watched as the sun slowly dipped below the horizon. Those seven days were a wonderful way to celebrate our first year together.

CB80

When we returned to Greenway, I checked my cell phone for emails every day, looking for a response. I did laugh at myself and my reaction. *Patience is a virtue*, I would tell myself, knowing in regard to this topic, I possessed precious little.

"There it is," I squealed on the eighth day.

Startled, Nick jumped up from his chair. "There's what?"

"An email from Rachael Covington. She wants to take on my novel. She wants to be my agent!"

Nick looked over my shoulder. "I can't see. Hand me your phone so I can read it for myself. Babe, this is fantastic. Now what?"

"I'm not sure. I've got to get dressed," I said. "I need to get to my computer and figure this out."

After a mad dash down the steps and a quick ride to my office, the dogs took their places and I called Ellie Ward. I needed a bullet list tutorial on what to ask and what to say. Actually, I wished she'd do it for me, but I refused to backslide. This was my book, my job, and my hill to climb. I wrote as Ellie listed the larger pieces of the upcoming conversation.

"You'll be fine," she said, "but truly listen to what she's saying. Call me later."

After a few sips of my soda and a very deep breath, I dialed Rachael's number.

Following the "good morning" pleasantries, we got down to business.

"I'll email the contract and give you time to look it over," she said.

Trying to remain calm, I asked, "How long do I have to make a decision?"

"Three weeks," Rachael said. "If you receive additional offers, please let me know before you sign with anyone else."

"I will, and thank you so much. Have a great day."

"You too," she said, hanging up.

Over the following week, I had three more no thanks; one said that she liked the story but "was not in love" with the beginning, so no, and two were the "not right for my list" issue.

I also had a request from the last agent on my list. Jackie asked for the entire manuscript. With the speed of light, I sent the email straight to Ellie, and her response read: "Send the manuscript, but give her a heads-up that you have an offer pending. Ask if she can get back to you within a couple of weeks with her interest. Usually, if they're serious, they'll respond sooner. Make sure to add your cell phone number."

Jackie Walker replied five days later that she was interested in representing me, but I decided to go with Rachael Covington. She had more years of experience and sales to her name. I enjoyed talking with both women, but Rachael's personality and love for the ride were a better fit for me. I felt guilty about Jackie but told myself this was a strictly business situation.

Nick and I discussed hiring a contract attorney, but when asked, Ellie said that was an unnecessary expenditure. She could talk us through what was in it, and all reputable agents required a standard fifteen percent commission.

When reviewing the contract together with Ellie at her office, she flipped through it and said, "Rachael gives herself a six-month window to find a publisher, and that's okay. And you need to understand—when you sign, you've agreed not to offer it to any other agent."

Nick rested back in the leather armchair. "At the end of six months, is Sarah free to search for another agent if this one is unsuccessful?"

"Yes," Ellie said, "but my guess is that Rachael already has at least six publishing houses in mind of where she wants to send the book, and she knows their lists."

"There it is again—'list.' I find that hilarious," I said. "Fitting someone's *list* is usually unpleasant."

Ellie chuckled. "Agreed, but you most certainly aspire to be on this one. Now that everything is signed and sent, let's all go to lunch, my treat. We can walk. Chez Bart's is only about a block and a half toward Capitol Square."

Beginning with the best she-crab soup I've ever tasted and continuing on with the lunch entrée offerings, Ellie added to what she had told us in her office. It was wonderful to have the additional information in a casual setting—it made it easier to digest. I was especially grateful Nick was there. Hopefully between the two of us we could remember all the important points.

⊂꒰৪�ব৹⊃

The "things take time" piece of publishing was going to require some effort to endure. I knew my manuscript was being emailed out to different publishers, and it might take months for us to get an offer, if at all. I would throw myself into the final days of summer, the barn remodel, the Colonial Farm project, and prepare for the coming school year. Yet I had enjoyed my time at home and was on the fence about teaching.

"After I change my clothes, I need to write a quick Dear Debby letter before we have dinner," I said to Nick as we walked up the back steps.

"Not a problem. I have paperwork to take care of. May I hitch a ride in your golf cart?"

"Sure, but Annie's the one you need to ask. She rides shotgun."

All four of us bounced along to the barn. Annie stood frozen at Nick's feet and stared at him the entire way. "She's actually mad at me that I'm in her seat," he scoffed.

"Apparently, but she's so sweet, all she'll ever do about it is stare. Give her a treat and she'll forgive you. They're in the glove box. Don't forget about Caesar."

Parking the cart, I said, "This won't take long. We can eat around seven."

"Okay," Nick said, offering each dog a Milk-Bone. "You've ruined two perfectly good dogs."

"They're not ruined. They're wonderful," I insisted.

"After supper, we need to look at the plans for the Colonial Farm project and make sure we're okay with it all. We'll roll out the blueprints and match those dimensions to where we think it should go. I hope it looks as good in reality as it does on paper, but I want to make sure all three of the interested parties are in agreement. You know 'too many cooks spoil the stew.'"

"I agree. I'm glad we're in charge of the construction piece. I mean, we do live here, and it is our property. This is going to be fabulous. I can't wait!" I said.

August 8, 2011

Dear Debby,

I have a contract with an agent and that's awesome, but I'm a wreck. Uncharted territory.

Just leave me out of the spotlight. I'll be in my closet. Let me know how it turns out.

School—I really don't want to go back. We have three new boarders, and I like seeing firsthand what's happening around here. Not to mention the Colonial Farm project. All of which brings me to the realization that I feel like the time has come to turn in my classroom keys. But can I retire with full benefits?

The first teacher workday is August 23, and I need to decide by then. I haven't mentioned this to Nick. There's been so much going on.

Maybe tonight over dinner.
See you tomorrow.
With all good wishes,
Sarah

"That was delicious," Nick said, sopping up the last bit of cream and mushroom sauce.

"Thanks. It was yummy. Slow cookers are the greatest invention since indoor plumbing. Before we get into the Colonial Farm project, I need to run something by you."

Nick pushed his chair back. "What's on your mind?"

"I don't think I want to go back to school, but I may have to. I honestly don't know what to do. There might be a monetary hit, but first and foremost, I absolutely cannot lose my health insurance! I love teaching, but I'm the happiest I've ever been living and working on this farm—even when I had that damn cast."

"I'm not surprised to hear you say that." Nick smiled. "You'll need to talk to the retirement person in HR. He or she can put it all on paper, and you can see if the numbers really make a difference. You know, are you looking at a twenty-dollar or a two-hundred-dollar monthly discrepancy? Your health insurance is a key point. You know what I pay for mine, and it's staggering."

"So you don't think I'm crazy?"

"Yes, yes, I do, but not because you want to stay home. If the book is accepted, there will be demands on your time. I'm not sure you can do both. Plus, you'll be beside yourself wondering what our now unsupervised boarders are doing minus your watchful eye."

Laughing, I said, "So true, and don't forget the student interns working the farm project. I'll call the main office tomorrow and make an appointment."

"Suggestion. Wait on calling HR. Sit down with Mr. Thomas first, and talk it out with him. He's your principal and should be the first to know you're thinking about retiring."

"Better idea. Thanks for helping me work through this."

"You're welcome, darlin.' Now we need to look over the plans."

53

My visit with Dr. Baxter was very productive. She helped me think through my concerns over publishing—being patient and trusting my gut intuition in the foreign world of business. Retiring was an even bigger issue since teaching was all I had ever done, and there were financial implications to consider.

With the iron of self-confidence still hot, I dropped by the high school. I knew Mr. Thomas wouldn't be at all happy, but I also knew he would support my decision to retire. His office door was always open, and he looked up as I appeared at his door. After a cheery hello, his expression changed to curious. He knew something was up. He offered me a seat and waited for me to sit down before he sat behind his enormous hardwood desk.

"So, what brings you here today?" he said, crossing his arms over his chest.

I carefully laid out my thoughts and plans. "There's a great deal to figure out, but I needed to speak with you first. I hope you understand."

"I do understand, but it will be a serious blow to Hadley Falls High School if you retire."

"Thank you. That's so sweet, but I think I'm ready to pursue a different path." I reminded him of our conversation, months earlier, concerning my novel.

Mr. Thomas moved from his chair to sit on the corner of his desk. "I'll say okay, but my selfish side doesn't agree. However, I'm very interested to hear about your book and the process. I would also like an autographed copy."

I tried my best to streamline my explanation. "If it's actually published, I might be asked to go to book signings and such. That said, I couldn't dictate those dates and would need to be free to reply, 'I'd be delighted.'"

"Sarah, this is a wonderful opportunity for you. If you have time, consider going to HR today: since school hasn't started, they may be free to speak with you on the spot. Roy King is the man you need to see. I'll give him a call and tell him you're on your way over."

My voice quivered. "Mr. Thomas, I can't thank you enough. I'll miss the kids and the faculty here, but I've grown to love life on the farm and all my projects. But first and foremost, I have to make sure I can actually afford to retire."

"Well, don't worry too much. Talk to Roy and see what he has to say. There might be options we don't know about. Let me know what you decide."

I rested the strap of my purse on my shoulder. "I will, and thank you so much. Fingers crossed."

"For sure, and remember my autographed copy. I would like it hand delivered, please. That way we can say hello."

Giving him a huge hug, I said, "You'll be one of the first!"

CB80

The administration building was just two blocks over from the high school, and parking my car, I had the strangest sinking feeling. Could I really quit teaching? It was all I had ever done. If I packed my things, that would be that. There would be no going back. Could I stay for the fall semester, knowing if the book were to be published, I'd walk right out the door?

"Hi, Sarah, what's up?" asked Judy, my former neighbor and Roy King's secretary.

I smiled. "Hello yourself. You look like you just got back from the beach."

"Yeah, my folks still have that wonderful old house at Nags Head, and the whole family was there. We were bursting at the seams, but it was great fun."

Just before stating my reason for the visit, an office door opened and a very round man with a jolly demeanor greeted me. "You must be Sarah. Come on in and have a seat. Judy, would you get us two bottles of water, please?" he asked, closing the door.

After about an hour, I had more information than I could digest in this one meeting. Thankfully, most of it was printed out in pamphlets, allowing me to review it at my own pace. I told him about the possible book so that the first-semester question made sense.

My first task was to collect all my records from the past twenty-eight—or twenty-nine, counting this one—teaching years and look for any holes in my service. Thanks to HR and my due diligence, we did find a dent in the armor. Ages ago, funding was tight and the arts were cut back to two-thirds of a day. Due to that short period of time, I would need to teach for sixty days into the coming school year to fill the gap.

But I had accrued so many unused sick days that I could give 180 of them back to the state and get credit for an additional year, which, along with the extra sixty days, took me to the golden goose number of thirty years. I decided to put the compensation from the remaining sick days into a 401K, giving me a nice tax-free investment to just squirrel away. My health insurance was free to me until I died, and that gave me a huge sense of relief.

After a week or so of careful planning, asking Roy in HR more questions, speaking with the representative for the state's health care affiliate, and our investment broker, we all agreed that following the additional two-month period of teaching, I would indeed have enough years to receive full retirement benefits at the thirty-year level. I would start the fall semester while they worked to find someone to take my place. Whoever they hired would shadow me for a month or so, and I'd retire on October 26, 2011.

I had always been insecure about money. While I would still have an income, my pension would be a percentage less. For reasons I could never explain and the answer being simply "because I do," I liked having some cash tucked away in the back of my underwear drawer. If I had ready cash on hand, I slept better at night. I upped the ante in the envelope stashed behind my underpants.

Peace of mind can be found in the oddest places.

54

It was strange to be driving to school for what I knew would be the last day I taught art in room 112. I'd grown up in that school, having gone from a wet-behind-the-ears first-year teacher to a senior member of the faculty. Hadley Falls High School was where I taught thousands of children, two of which were my own, to find their imagination and think outside the box. It was like letting go of a huge piece of myself.

Betsy's phone call broke my reflective silence. "How are you doing, my dear friend?"

"Not so good," I squeaked. "Actually, I'm a wreck. I feel like I'm deserting all those kids. You know that preschool child they hired to take my place doesn't know what she's doing. I'm not exaggerating. It took Miss Sink two days to figure out how to read the class schedule cards. Plus, she's only four years older than her oldest students. Don't get me started on her clothes. There was just enough fabric to make a place mat but not nearly enough for the skirt she had on yesterday."

"You are one of the funniest people I've ever known." Betsy chuckled. "Look in the mirror. You were also twenty-two years old when you started teaching."

"That's totally different. I was mature for my age. And I never showed up at school half-naked."

"Really? I remember seeing your first-day-of-teaching photo. You wore a suede fringe vest over a skintight, spaghetti-strap V-neck camisole, a drop-waist black matchstick skirt, and Birkenstocks. Now, stop being ridiculous. Call me on your way home this afternoon."

Once inside, I turned the key to my classroom door, sighed, gave it a push, and switched on the lights. "Surprise!" My colleagues filled the room, faces beaming, and one of my art tables held a beautiful cake with balloons tied to either side.

"We're celebrating now," Laura said, with Molly standing at her side. They were my two closest teacher friends and made every hard day bearable. "You'll be a disaster by noon. Now, no tears, but, man oh man, we'll miss you."

"Don't make me cry," I said, giving my friends a hug. "This is so sweet. It's been a privilege to work with all of you."

"Even me?" George Finch, the chemistry teacher, Nick's cousin, and my nemesis asked.

"Yes, especially you, George! Who's going to be in my business all the time? Who's going to make fun of my clothes, my teaching methods, and the food I eat? I'll miss you all more than you'll ever know. Now, let's dig into this cake." And with that, our usual, beyond-boring-Wednesday-morning teacher's meeting became unusually wonderful.

The morning send-off and the buttercream cake frosting paved the way for my change in lesson plans. *I refuse to have an average last day,* I thought. *I always want to remember the final thing I taught!*

As each class found their seats, their eyes lit up. It was a *paint day*, and that was their favorite! Egg cartons hosting a dozen different colors and art paper measuring twelve by eighteen inches sat waiting to be transformed.

"Today is an adventure for us all," I said, trying to remain collected. "I'm stepping into a whole new world, and so are you. I honestly don't know how to be retired, but I'm determined to learn. I need you to be just as intent in allowing Miss Sink to pick up the torch and carry on. Her way of teaching is nothing like mine, but different is not always a bad thing. Think in terms of Monet and Renoir. Impressionism was the pinnacle of a brave new world in art. As we've discussed many times before, that group of artists took a huge risk with their style and we know how successful that was.

"Now, you have exactly one hour to complete your impression-istic piece. No pencil work first, just brush to paper. Your subject is your choice, and you cannot start over. If it's not to your liking, fix it. Now, have fun, and don't forget to sign your work."

I'll be forever grateful for the sugar rush. This was one of my best spur-of-the moment lesson plans ever!

Throughout the day, students would stick their heads in my room to tell me goodbye. I struggled through the day with my emotions. There was a required assembly in the auditorium for the whole school for the final thirty minutes of the afternoon.

Walking down the hall, I asked Molly, "What's this about?"

"I have no idea, but it gets me out of teaching my fifth-period class, so I'm grateful. Pray it's not about selling fruitcake again."

"Ah yes, fundraisers. I absolutely will not miss that part of school. Promise me you'll keep an eye on my replacement. My third period will eat her alive if she can't get tough right quick."

"I promise. She'll make it, but you are a hard act to follow. I sort of feel sorry for her. Imagine how many times she'll hear 'That's not how Mrs. Heart did it.'"

"I guess." I sighed. "But just please be her friend."

Walking into the auditorium, I saw Laura with her band and chorus assembled onstage under a hanging banner reading Thanks for All the Years! We'll Miss You, Mrs. Heart. *Oh no,* I thought as the floodgates overflowed; my tears, which had been barely contained all day, finally escaped.

Molly helped me find my way to the front row, and there waiting for me were Nick, Betsy, and Margaret. "Hey, darlin'," Nick said, handing me his handkerchief. "Smile. This is going to be fun."

The program they'd made for my retirement was extremely clever. Clearly the seniors solicited the help of my longtime colleagues for some of the "before they were born" information in crafting a tribute to my past thirty years. They listed all the technological improvements and how I fought them tooth and nail, my clothes, and cars (from a two-seater convertible to a station wagon), former presidents, music trends, cobwebs on the art textbooks because I never used them, and my choice phrases to catalog my career. One final remark was spot on: "We know you're not leaving because you're tired of teaching. You're leaving because you've run out of excuses for being away. Now you can go to horse shows with a clear conscience."

I was asked to come to the front and say a few words.

"This is one of the kindest things anyone has ever done for me, and I appreciate it more than you'll ever know," I said. "So you knew about the horse shows?" I asked sarcastically. Everyone laughed, including the group of my former students who were sitting together in the audience. Looking in their direction, I said how proud I was to have been a very small part of their lives. Dr. Toby Ray was there and smiled, gave me a wink, and that finished me off. I was going to pieces.

My voice trembled. "I'll leave you with this: I've loved every minute of my thirty years—well, not the day of the kiln disaster, but all the rest. I treasure all of you and the memories we share. Give your future one hundred percent, and even in my absence, I expect nothing less than your best artwork to leave room 112. Oh, and remember, absolutely no smiley face sun shines—ever!"

A roar of laughter filled the auditorium, and at that moment I knew I could walk away with my heart full. I had done my job to the best of my ability, and it was now the preschool child's turn to ignite the imagination of the next generation.

55

For the first time in my adult life, I was unemployed and free to do whatever I wanted. The sabbatical had been different because it was temporary. Retirement was forever. I was staring at the bedroom curtains, reviewing this life choice, when Nick rolled over. "Well, how does it feel to be footloose and fancy-free?"

"Interesting you should ask. The answer is: I don't really know. But with all we have going on around here, I'm sure I won't be at a loss for something to do. What would you like for breakfast?"

"You."

Sometime later, I took a breath. "Nicholas Heart, that was amazing. What a fantastic way to start my retirement! But now let me rephrase: what can I cook…? What's that noise?" I jumped. "It sounds like a freight train in the front yard. I think the house is shaking."

Nick slipped on his pajama bottoms and hurried to the window. "Apparently the farm project is getting underway a day early. Come see."

Wrapped in our comforter, I watched as earth-removal equipment of various types rode in on the back of a giant flatbed, followed by two dump trucks full of crushed gravel. An army of pickup trucks was parked all over our yard.

We were dressed in less than five minutes, and Nick was down the hall and out the front door. I was a mere two strides behind.

"Good Morning, Mr. Heart," a man said, offering his hand. "I'm Wilson Farr, the project manager. We're going to start on the new entrance this morning, and I need to know if we can cut across this front field. I'll also need to use that area for parking and off-loading supplies."

"Okay," Nick said, "but going forward, please make sure your crew understands that our lawn is not a parking lot."

"Not a problem. It'll take about an hour to off-load the equipment and to get everything organized, but by the end of the day, you'll hardly know we're here." He smiled.

"Good. But by the end of this conversation, all—and I mean all—of those trucks will be moved off my grass."

Wilson motioned to his crew. "Boys, move your trucks over by that ditch and park 'em in a line."

"Holy nightmare," I whispered from just inside the doorway. "I'll go start breakfast. I'm sure you want to stand watch for a while."

Walking into the kitchen, I glanced up and thanked the powers that be for my retirement. I could not have left all this in my rearview mirror as I drove off to school and worried the entire day.

With the sausage sizzling, I sent a text to our boarders explaining the barn would be closed at least until Tuesday, along with a video of the heavy equipment being off-loaded from the flatbed. I added that the horses would need a few days to acclimate to the noise and confusion before any of us should ride them.

Nick spent the next two hours supervising the supervisor, while the dogs and I went to my hideaway. Caesar was terrified of the crashing racket, and Annie barked at the strangers. "You two are not allowed anywhere near the work site," I said, wagging my finger. "We'll drive the cart over every evening after supper, and then you can have a good sniff around. Now we have work to do. Your grandmother has insisted that I be the guest speaker at her book club. This talk will require serious thought: all of Sibby's contemporaries know me as little Sarah O'Neil. So how do I transition to Sarah O'Neil Heart, the adult author of how-to horse books, funny magazine articles, and one hopeful novel? Let's start with my writing process," I said, pulling up a blank screen on my computer.

Yesterday I'd sent Ellie an email about the agent. We weren't nearly to the end of her six months to find a publisher yet, but that window was narrowing—if only by a bit over half. However, my impatience was widening rapidly. Ellie's response was short and concise: *Try to be patient. I know it's difficult, but it's out of your hands at this point.*

Around eleven, Nick stuck his head into my office. "I've got a lunch meeting in Hadley Falls that I cannot ditch. I'll be home this afternoon. Will you be okay with this lot?"

"Of course. They have the plans and the surveyors marked off exactly where the house belongs. I would only be in their way," I said. The dogs and I followed Nick out to his car. Standing momentarily frozen at the sight of our farm, I saw what could only be defined as the beginning of our own private Armageddon. Within a handful of hours, our pristine farm had taken a serious hit. Mountains of dirt were everywhere, earthmovers were belching black smoke as they tore across the landscape, and the Jolly-Potty delivery truck was turning in. "I guess it's too late to change our minds?"

"Afraid so." Nick laughed. "It'll be beautiful when it's finished."

"Will you please pick up something to grill on your way home?

Your choice—surprise me."

cঙৎ

I decided on a laundry and lunch diversion before heading back to our hideaway. Pulling my new jeans out of the dryer, I chuckled, smoothing out both full-length pant legs with my hand. I was doing better with the weight issue, but I was still one size smaller than before. I no longer looked emaciated, as Margaret had once said. I had regained my muscle tone, and the summer sun had washed the gray haze from my skin. Thankfully, everyone had simply gotten used to the thinner version of Sarah. I was still fourteen pounds lighter than before the accident, but to be honest, I liked the thinner me.

Once back at my computer and before working on the book club talk, I pulled up my email. *How many mailing lists could one person possibly be on?* I wondered, running down the line and pressing delete. "Whoa!" I yelled, realizing the last one wasn't junk. It was from Rachael Covington.

Hi Sarah:

Good news! I have a publisher who is very interested in your novel. I'll call you this afternoon around three o'clock, and we'll go over the details. Write back if this time won't work.

Congratulations!

Rachael Covington

CR80

I clicked forward to Ellie and called her at the same time. "I'm about to wet my pants."

Ellie cheered. "I know you're excited. This is wonderful. I can't wait to hear who it is. Call me after you hang up with Rachael."

"Will do."

I was elated but also so very nervous and found sitting still next to impossible. For the second time in twenty-four hours, I was once again a fish out of water—first retired and now possibly being a published novelist. I don't know why it seemed different from my nonfiction books, but it did, perhaps because it was a product of my imagination.

Rachael called promptly at three.

My biggest questions were about the editor and the publishing house. Rachael said she would email me all those details and I could Google them. She added, "Please don't reach out to them. You have an offer, not a contract. But with a little research, you'll have a better idea of who they are and what kind of books and authors they publish."

56

Nick pulled in around five o'clock, and because my golf cart was parked in front of my office, he knew exactly where to find me.

Standing in the doorway, he said, "Hey, babe. Have you been in here all afternoon?"

"Gosh." I glanced at the clock on my desk. "I guess we have. You'll never believe this." Handing Nick the printed email, I told him, "It's not a contract yet. It's called an offer. Thank goodness for Ellie, who explained the terms of their offer. I don't completely understand everything quite yet about the deal, but the great news is they want my book. That's good enough for me! I didn't allow myself to think this would ever really happen!"

Nick's hug lifted me off the floor. "That's amazing! But I'm not at all surprised with how hard you worked on it. Way to go, babe!"

"Thanks. I've spent the past hour researching Vera, the editor in charge of me and my novel, at Covered Buttons Press, and royalty percentages. I'll need to sell a pile of books to realize any substantial money, but it's never been about that anyway. My head is spinning, but I'm so excited! The publishing house is in New York, and I can't remember anything else right now. I'm a joyful wreck—tell me about the meeting?"

He held out his hand. "The meeting was fine, but I need for you to come out here with me."

"Oh my good Lord—what happened?" I shrieked, standing at the door of my office, my eyes surveying the devastation of a once beautiful pasture.

Nick and I stood dumbstruck, wondering if we had perhaps lost our minds in signing on to this Colonial Farm project.

I took a deep breath. "But when it's finished, it will be so wonderfully Williamsburg, right?"

"Look at what they've done to our drive." Nick pointed in the opposite direction. "Wilson Farr and I will have a come-to-Jesus meeting first thing in the morning."

"Oh my gosh—I didn't notice that. It looks like a jigsaw puzzle. They'll have to smash it all back down and pave over the whole thing. But look," I said, pointing to the hot pink marking tape flapping in the breeze. "Even from here you can see where the new road will be and the corners of the house. Go change your clothes. I'll finish up here, and then the four of us can go visit our on-site disaster."

"Okay, but this redefines *from the ground up*. What a mess!"

Caesar and Annie had a wonderful time on their treasure hunt for the construction worker's lunch trash. The designated drive was going to be lovely, and thankfully that entrance was at least half a mile from the entrance to our house. It dropped down a little hill and curved gently around a grove of weeping willows toward the Colonial house, finishing with a circular drive to the front door and then retracing back to the highway. When the landscaping was put in, there would be plantings inside the circle and perhaps a tree. "It's beautiful, but wouldn't a straight drive with the circle have been more authentic?"

Nick ran his fingers through his hair. "If I remember correctly, it had something to do with the county easements for water and sewer."

I had momentarily lost track of our dogs but then spied them feasting on biscuits from a giant Bo Box and several Big Gulps from Nelson's convenience store. "Tomorrow, after you finish with Wilson Farr, it's my turn to have a go at him about trash."

"Go get 'em," Nick said. "In fact, you take care of both issues. I'll just explode, which won't do any good. Do your teacher thing, and he'll never know what happened."

"Not a problem," I said, offering a thumbs-up.

C3℃80

The next morning, Wilson Farr and I came to a meaningful understanding about our destroyed driveway, the trash, and several other issues. Coy found three old fifty-gallon drums in the back of the barn, repurposed them, and placed them on-site—one labeled food trash and the second recycle. The third barrel, filled two-thirds full of sand, was to be for smoking. I confessed to having been a smoker, so I understood the addiction, but Wilson Farr and his workers needed to realize the construction site was sitting in the middle of a field, near a barn, horses, and hay, so there would be absolutely zero smoking allowed except for in the designated area.

I added that this was not an infringement on an individual's rights, a social judgment, or anything of the sort. It was just that I had no intention of watching our farm set ablaze and burning down around us.

Fussing with his camouflage cap, Wilson said, "We've never had rules on a job site before."

"Perhaps not, but the good news is, the sooner you're finished, the sooner you no longer have to deal with me," I said with raised eyebrows. "You'll be fine. A few rules never hurt anyone. Plus, you haven't even thanked me for the tent-covered picnic table."

"That is nice. Thanks. What are the rules for that?" he joked.

"Your mother doesn't work here—clean up after yourself! That rule is tacked to the top of the table. Now, you have a nice morning, and I'll check on you later."

Walking to my golf cart, I couldn't stop laughing. Wilson Farr gathered his employees around the tent and shared the news. His crew nodded, accepting the first two, but the smoking topic was not well received. I overheard Wilson say, "I don't want that woman down here again, so everybody do what she said!"

CB&ED

Thursday morning, United Asphalt was hard at work flattening the surface of our crumbled driveway and adding a fresh hot layer on top. Wilson knocked on the back door and said we couldn't drive on it for a couple of hours. I thanked him, and he mumbled all the way down the porch steps.

Nick looked over his newspaper. "What did you do to that poor man?"

"Nothing he won't get over. We'll be the best of friends in a few days. He just can't stand a woman telling him what to do. Besides, you told me to take care of things; the driveway took only two days." I chuckled.

"Impressive!"

"Yes. If women were in charge, the world would have fewer problems," I said.

57.

I had set up an appointment to talk with, Vera, at Covered Buttons Press just two days after I got my offer. She told me about the production process, and I asked her a bunch of new author questions. Her answers, not harsh but emphatic, left no doubt that going forward I would have very little say about my book. The art department might show me a few of their cover ideas, but ultimately that was a marketing department decision.

The world of publishing was hard and fast and totally foreign to me. They were in the business of selling reams of books to pay for their expenses, and no amount of cookies, iced tea, or *let's chat* could sway their resolve. The reality of a corporate environment fell hard on the soft shoulders of this Southern girl.

I was also beginning to realize that Vera was now my main cheerleader, and Ellie was no longer involved. That observation rocked me back on my heels. I wasn't ready to surrender her support and gave her a call. After our conversation, I took a breath and relaxed, knowing Ellie Ward would always be my friend who just happened to be well versed in every aspect of the publishing world. I felt better after that.

ᏟᏅᏣᏇ

By the first of December, our two-story Colonial house with double brick chimneys running up both sides was coming along. It was all dried-in with windows, doors, fully insulated, Hardie plank siding all over, and safe from the elements.

Wilson Farr took my words to heart and was doing his best to finish the job on time. We had developed a wonderful working relationship, though he still took on a defensive posture in my presence. But by making myself scarce and offering occasional snacks for all, I kept things on an even keel.

Construction was now down to interior work for the most part—drywall, hardwood floors, the entire kitchen, bathrooms, and so forth. The house was your basic five over four, which is builder's talk for five windows upstairs and four down. The front door, with a fan window above, divided the bottom four, leaving two windows on either side of the main entrance. The fan window, my favorite part, was handsomely authentic, with a carved pineapple at the bottom center of the semicircle. I loved the whole project, and on the unfinished front door, I hung a Christmas wreath, sporting a bright red bow.

Work had begun on the smoke house, the chicken coop, and the six-stall barn, all of which were on the backside of the main house. In the spring, an amazing vegetable box garden would occupy the space in between.

I tried to resist, but the other doors looked naked, so I hung a fresh Frazier fir wreath with a red bow on all three doors. Wilson shook his head the next morning, but he gave me a thumbs-up as I waved hello.

◌3 ◌8◌

"Are you sure we can pull off our third annual Christmas party?" Nick asked. "Everyone will understand if we decide it's too much."

"Considering it's catered, and Kenny and Mark will do their thing, I believe we can."

"Okay. I just didn't want you to feel obligated."

"I think everyone would enjoy a firsthand look at what's happening at LLF," I said. "Plus, I just love our party."

"Me too—December seventeenth it is."

◌3 ◌8◌

Two weeks before our annual holiday hoorah, I decided to visit the attic in search of my grandmother's antique soup tureen. I thought it would be perfect for the dining room floral centerpiece.

Passing through the den, I said to Nick, "If you hear me scream, come running please."

"Okay. Where are you going?"

"The attic. I'm looking for a box I brought home from Iron Springs last year."

"I'll go with you. I don't think I've been up there since I moved here."

I laughed. "Well, you're in for a treat."

Nick stopped dead in his tracks when I turned on the light. "Where did all this junk come from?"

"I told you it was a disaster. I can't seem to get around to dealing with all this. Some of it's yours, and the rest is from Brook Street or

Iron Springs. That pile will get shipped to Rhode Island for Emma and Scott's new house."

"I'm just blown away. Look at this stack—the boxes are falling apart. Yikes."

"Maybe I'll take a stab at it after Christmas, but for now I just need to find the boxes from Iron Springs. But be careful. Those old cartons are just barely holding on."

Nick was leaning against the tower of yesteryear. As he pushed himself back to vertical, the whole thing headed straight for the floor. "That's it—this attic is a deathtrap! We're going to say goodbye to most of this today!" Nick demanded.

"Okay. You work from that end, and I'll start over here. Put clothes, pocketbooks, and hats in the same pile. Somewhere in all this are two boxes of china that Sydney wants, and Emma has laid claim to the complete set of Nancy Drew and Hardy Boys books. If you find those, I'll put them in their bedrooms."

"I'll be right back. It'll be more efficient to bag this stuff and only handle it once," Nick said.

When he returned to the attic with a box of garbage bags, I said, "I found the books."

"All is right with the world, then," Nick joked. "Why and how did it get so bad up here?"

"I just couldn't throw away all of the Cromwell sisters' stuff. Look at this task as a treasure hunt. Who knows what we might find?"

"Yes, I can see us on *Antiques Roadshow* with our photograph of Abraham Lincoln, a Civil War saber complete with silver-clad sheath, and Great-Grandma's tea set. The appraiser will tell us their value, and you'll say, 'It will remain in the family forever.'"

I answered lighting fast. "Not true. 'SOLD!' would be my reply."

"Well, here goes nothing. Now that I realize our fortune is possibly buried somewhere beneath the rubble, I have a new attitude about this hellacious task." Nick shook open a lawn and leaf bag and handed it to me.

We decided to take a break after about an hour. Nick took a seat in an old gooseneck rocker, and I turned a galvanized milk can upside down and perched gingerly on it.

Dusting off my hands, I said, "We really have put a dent in all this stuff. I know the Hadley Falls Arts Guild will love the furniture for their annual auction. And Melanie at the Iron Springs Playhouse will be ecstatic with all the clothes for her wardrobe closet. I'll call the fire department to come get that pile for their annual garage sale."

Nick rubbed his stomach. "I'm hungry. Let's have lunch and do the rest later."

"We can't stop now! You know as well as I do that if we stop, we'll never come back. It won't take long, and besides, I still need to find the soup tureen."

"Why?"

"Because I do." I smiled, kissing him on the cheek. "That's what I came up here for."

"All right, but this stack is my last one for today."

As Nick pulled on the top box, the side disintegrated, and the bottom completely gave way, sending everything flying to the floor. "Damn it to hell!" he yelled. "Look at all this junk. It looks like someone simply turned the drawer over and dumped stuff in."

I crouched to the dusty floor, combing through the debris. "Look at all this. It's mostly costume jewelry, hair clips, old coins, and 'perfect attendance' pins from Sunday school."

As Nick stepped over the scattered pile of trinkets, his foot landed squarely on something else. "What's this?"

Standing up, I couldn't believe my eyes. "Impossible—a rectangular black velvet box! Just like in Celia's journal!"

"Who?" Nick said. "Let's open it."

"No, wait," I said, taking the box. "Come on. We need to go downstairs."

"Why?" Nick asked, turning off the attic light and closing the door.

Leading the way from the attic to the den, I said, "You'll find out in just a minute. Now, get comfortable, because this is going to freak you out."

"Sarah, what is it?"

I began to explain. "Do you remember the day I came home from visiting Olivia and she gave me her mother's journal?"

"Vaguely," Nick said.

"Wait a minute. I'll let you read it for yourself," I said, removing the red leather-bound book from the shelf.

Nick read it twice. "Well, have a seat, untie the ribbon, and let's see what's inside. It might be another perfect attendance award."

I swallowed hard. "And it might not." With shaking hands, I gave the ribbon a tug and opened the dusty velvet box. My jaw agape, I turned the box around so Nick could see the absolutely stunning ruby and diamond necklace.

Nick's eyes bulged. "Christ! Do you think it's real?"

"Who knows, but it's beautiful! That ruby's the size of a quarter, and the diamonds are at least a half carat each." I lifted the necklace from the box. "Oh my gosh, here's her father's note. Look on the back page of her journal—same words. *To my daughter Celia: On your wedding day, all I have, I give to you. I pray for you a wonderful life as rich as this gift. Hold each other close, and treasure one another always. Forever, your loving father.*"

Holding the journal, Nick said, "Why would she have kept it hidden away for all those years?"

"I have no idea, but where would she have worn this in Hadley Falls—the Piggly Wiggly or the Soap and Suds? How odd. I just realized Olivia never once mentioned those grandparents. Betsy and I know everything about Hattie Mae Cromwell, from reading tea leaves to wishing off warts, but nothing about Olivia's mother's side of the family."

Nick asked, "What were their names?"

"I don't know, but finding this is so strange."

"Why?"

"After that visit to Lazy Willow, I read Celia's diary several times and kept coming back to this entry," I said, pointing to the final page. "I was so intrigued by the mystery that I crafted a fictitious version of it for my novel—a sapphire and diamond broach. Who knew there really was a black velvet box, and it was in our attic this whole time!"

"Interesting, and so is this," Nick said, running his hand down the fold of the book. "Three pages are missing. They've been carefully removed with something very sharp."

"You're right. How did I miss that? I'll call Betsy—Lazy Willow here we come."

"Invite Betsy and Frank over for dinner tonight. Then the four of us can talk about it."

Pressing Betsy's number, I looked at Nick. "You're wonderful, you know. Hi," I said, interrupting myself. "What are you and Frank doing for dinner tonight?"

Betsy chuckled. "Nothing special, but from the sound of your voice, that's about to change."

"It is, but I don't want to spoil the surprise, so please come to dinner. We're having pot roast. How about six thirty?"

"Okay. I'll bring bread and wine, but give me a clue."

"No. You'll know everything tonight."

CR80

I couldn't keep the treasure from the attic—it wasn't mine. And I couldn't put it back in the attic. No, Betsy and I had to visit Olivia, with the diary and necklace in hand. We'd been to see her a few times over the past several months, bringing treats and visiting. But this would be different—starting with what could have been in the three missing pages and the necklace.

"What about having it appraised?" Nick asked, passing the platter of pot roast to Frank.

"I have to talk to Olivia first, and depending on what she says, we'll know our next step."

"Our 'senior' will confess if she knows something," Betsy said, then paused. "But, Sarah, remember when you read the part from your manuscript about the black box and the note? Olivia remarked how clever you were to make up such a good tale. But she had already read the diary, and the note from her father was there—yes, on the back page, but it was there."

"That's true, so who excised the three missing pages, and when? Was it Iris, Olivia, or their mother? We know she really did read the note, but maybe the three pages were already gone."

Betsy rearranged herself in the chair. "Or perhaps she read it all, and the three pages were so incriminating she cut them out so we wouldn't know. Iris left all the rest for Olivia to read; why would she have taken out those pages? No, I think Olivia was the paper surgeon."

Frank had been very quiet. "Whatever the story, it revolves around her grandparents and their absence. They have completely disappeared from her conscious thought. There's a reason for her silence. You two will need to tread very softly over this one. The shock of seeing the necklace and your faces full of questions might be unsettling for her."

Nick poured more wine. "I agree with Frank, but I also think you have to get to the bottom of this. Hot or not, if it's genuine, it's worth a lot of money, and we've got to address that. I'm dying to know the story behind it."

"Me too," Frank howled. "Nick, my friend, they've worn us down. Ladies, did you notice it says Tiffany and Co. on the back?"

"No!" I squealed, flipping the necklace over to see for myself.

"I wonder what else is in that attic of yours," Betsy said.

"Look out, *Roadshow*. The jewelry guys will be all over this." Nick laughed.

Frank didn't bother to hide his surprise. "No kidding, with Tiffany and Co., stamped on the back, its age, and the note, it's probably worth even more. Plus you have the original box."

Betsy laughed, closing the velvet jewelry case. "You jest, but it's actually true. Now, who wants chocolate cake?"

"*Antiques Roadshow*—imagine that!" I smiled, taking my first bite of cake.

58

I was surprisingly nervous about this visit with Olivia. Did she actually know about the necklace? How did her mother come to have something so grand?

"Good morning," Olivia said, offering us a seat around the sunroom's Christmas tree. "What a surprise. Did you bring me news about your book?"

"Well, I do have good news on that front," I said, noticing we were all alone in that large space, "but first we need to talk to you about something else."

Betsy moved the chairs to form a tighter circle. "Miss Olivia, we're about to ask you a very strange question, but we have to know the truth."

Olivia fidgeted with her holiday necklace. "About what?"

"About this," I said, opening my bag and taking out the black velvet box, followed by the journal.

The color ran from her face as quickly as a bathtub drains. "It does exist!"

"Yes, and you must tell us what you know," Betsy said, gently patting Olivia's hand.

Rattled, Olivia said, "I need just a minute. A glass of water would be good, or some tea if you brought any?"

Betsy lifted the thermos from her bag. "Just take your time and catch your breath. Sarah will fill you in."

"The other afternoon, Nick and I went to work sorting through the mountain of boxes in our attic. When he pulled the top box from the last stack, it crumbled to bits, and all the contents scattered across the dusty floor. Most of the items were things you'd find in the top drawer of a dressing table—hair pins, costume jewelry, buttons, pennies, and so on. Except for one—this black velvet box."

Olivia quietly drew a breath. "I swear to you both, I had no idea of its existence until now. I did read the note in Mama's diary, but I had no idea what Grandpa had given her."

I smiled. "Let's take a minute so you can tell us about your grandparents."

"All right." Olivia sighed. "But I really don't know much. They died from the Spanish Flu in February of 1920, which was before I was born. Mama and Daddy were married in 1918 and our aunt Alice was married a year after that. Remember, she lived in Swan Quarter. Anyway, Iris and I never knew those grandparents, and my mother rarely spoke their names."

I slowly opened the box. "So how do you think your grandfather came to have this?"

Olivia's eyes widened as she looked at the beautiful tear-drop-shaped necklace. "I'm afraid to tell you."

"Don't be upset. Whatever happened was a long time ago, and you're innocent of any wrongdoing," Betsy said, opening the diary and turning to the back cover. "But do you know what happened to the three missing pages?"

Olivia fanned her face. "Yes, but I've never seen that necklace in my life, and I'm positive Iris didn't either. She'd have done something about it, but that really doesn't matter now. Who would have ever thought you'd find the box, or that it was still anywhere to be found?"

Betsy and I refilled the teacups and offered cookies before I continued. "We only need to know because I've found it, and if it was stolen, I have to return it to the rightful owners. But technically it belongs to you."

Olivia gently pushed my hand away. "Well, I don't want it, so it's yours. I threw away the three pages; I was scared they'd cause trouble. But in a nutshell, here's what was written: Mama's mother was from an upper-middle-class family in Richmond, and my grandfather was a lawyer with an office in Court End and heavy into politics. He won a huge trial defending a man of very questionable character."

"And they paid him off with the necklace?" Betsy interrupted.

"Not quite."

"How not quite?" I asked.

"There was a big party to celebrate the verdict of not guilty, and my grandparents were invited. It was a high-brow, black-tie affair, with every guest dressed to the nines. Sometime during the evening, the wife of the questionable gentleman and my grandmother were engaged in conversation, and my grandmother admired the other woman's necklace."

"Two days later, a messenger knocked on their door—they lived in an area called 'the Fan'—handed my grandmother a package, and disappeared down the front steps. It was the box you're holding. My grandfather was bound by law never to divulge any information, but since my grandmother accepted the package, I guess it served to keep her forever quiet as well. I don't know if that's true, but why else would she give her something so grand?"

"Who were these people? Was there a note?" I asked.

Olivia held her hand to her heart. "There were no names in my mother's diary, and if there was a note, it's long gone. Remember, my grandfather's note said, 'All I have I give to you.' Apparently, Grandpa wasn't very good with money, and after they died, what was left went to pay off outstanding debts, and the bank took their house. Anyway, Mama wrote that she never wore the necklace for obvious reasons: Her parents were no longer alive to back up her story, and where would she have worn it in Hadley Falls? Mostly she worried it came from 'ill-gotten gains.' My parents were of modest means, and it would have stirred the pot of suspicion to a boil."

Betsy smiled. "So your mother tucked it in the drawer along with hairpins, buttons, and perfect attendance pins?"

"Maybe, but I think that box full of junk and one treasure went to the attic when we were very small. Neither of us ever knew a thing about it. Iris did read all this, but the possible whereabouts of the box were unknown."

"Wow," I said. "Don't worry about any of this. I'll have our attorney help with the legal end."

Olivia let out a sigh and straightened her skirt. "One last thing. In the beginning, my father didn't know about the necklace. My grandfather gave it to Mama the morning of their wedding day in 1918. She hid it away and never told a soul."

"Jiminy Christmas!" Betsy exclaimed. "Why not?"

"She wrote in those back three pages that she knew Daddy would have insisted on selling it, and she was scared about that. You know—'How did a foreman for the lumber company have something so valuable?' Mama decided they'd eke out a living and raise their children on what they had—and they did."

"Wow!" I said. "But…"

"Remember, Daddy found the diary years later. In the final paragraph, Mama wrote that his finding out about the affair, me, plus her refusing to sell the necklace ended their marriage. So she must have dumped the drawer into a box and stashed it in the attic."

"What a story. Now, let's soften the air and move on to a lighter subject. Book news: let me tell you where we are with *Sweet Tea and Fireflies*," I said, holding her hand.

"Yes please, but first, about the necklace, it really is yours, and what you do with it is up to you. If you do have it appraised, just for fun, I'd like to know its value. How poetic and tragic—for nearly sixty years of a pinto-beans-and-cornbread life, a possible fortune was resting with the hairpins in the attic of 528 Brook Street?"

I agreed. "That is poetic and tragic, and it's been in someone's attic for nearly a hundred years. But truly, thank you for the gift of the necklace. I'm not sure I'll ever wear it—I live on a farm—but it's beautiful."

"Yes, but I think it's a fancy farm with horses who hardly do a lick of work to earn their keep." She winked.

Cʒʒᴆᴐ

Olivia was genuinely interested in the whole publishing process but said they needed to hurry up and print the book before she died. I mentioned the Colonial Farm project, which she found interesting, and she asked to see the pictures I had on my phone. Betsy added we were leaving tomorrow for the annual Christmas Charity Ball, and Olivia remembered old Mrs. Pritchett and her green dress. We three shared a good laugh about that.

Olivia perked up. "You should wear the necklace to the dance."

"Not until I speak with our attorney and have it appraised. But I promise I'll wear it if everything checks out. I think it's magnificent. Now, before we go, let's walk to your apartment and plug in this tree, and yes, there are presents and Moravian cookies."

Her eyes dewy, Olivia smiled. "You two are the dearest things. For the second year, you've brightened my otherwise lonely Christmas."

While we three sat enjoying the cozy space, Olivia asked about our individual family plans, and in return we asked her about the Lazy Willow holiday celebration. Thirty minutes later, following hugs and well-wishes, we left Olivia Cromwell standing in the doorway of her apartment. Except for my grandmother, she was without question the cutest and sweetest little old lady I had ever known. She had a heart of gold and a will of iron. In what began as shameless curiosity, a loving friendship had grown strong.

Backing out of the parking space, I pressed the brakes. "Wait a minute."

"What?" Betsy asked, surprised.

"Iris knew the necklace was possibly in the attic. I'm sure of it. Remember our very first visit when she said they didn't want anything from Brook Street? Adding that if I did find something, I was free to keep it or sell it if it was worth anything. She was talking about the necklace!"

Betsy gasped. "You're right, she was. But until she found the diary, Olivia never knew any of this."

"It's strange, isn't it? All of this started with four pictures and two sisters. It's like some greater power meant for our paths to cross. Sometimes it makes me shiver."

59

Betsy insisted on a tour of the Colonial House building site before she headed home.

"How did it go?" Nick asked as we stopped by the barn to say hello.

"Great," Betsy said, riding shotgun in the golf cart. "Sarah's going to show me the project first, and then she's all yours."

The dogs bounced all around, disturbing the workmen.

Betsy stood in awe. "I'm moving here when it's finished. This is incredible!"

"Wait until you see inside," I gushed.

Wilson looked horrified as I approached, probably thinking I had brought instructional reinforcements. He was in hot pursuit, making it to the front door of the house in time to say hello. "Betsy, this is Wilson Farr, the man who made this magic. Wilson, this is my dear friend Betsy Henderson."

Hellos were exchanged, and Wilson led us on a guided tour. Betsy couldn't believe her eyes as she admired the craftsmanship, and the backyard rendered her speechless, especially the recently cultivated peach orchard. Somewhere between the chicken coop and the smokehouse, Annie found a half-eaten sandwich.

Wilson's face turned beet-red. "I've told them not to eat anywhere 'cept where you said."

"It's okay," I said, "but just this once."

Astonished, Betsy asked, "Does this construction site have some rules?"

"More like a list," Wilson grumbled, walking away, "and some are pinned to the table."

"Sarah, did you really make rules?"

"Absolutely!" I smiled. "So, tomorrow we're meeting at seven in the church parking lot for our weekend at Moss Creek, yes?"

"Yes, and remind Nick all the guys are congregating Saturday around noon at Bill's dealership to ride in the plush bus. Just think, this year you get to wear pants with both legs intact and dance."

CR80

Sitting on the patio after dinner, Nick bent down to light the gas fire pit. "I want to hear all about Olivia and the ruby necklace."

I wrapped a throw over my shoulders. "Good title, but I still like *The Dresser Drawer* best. Vera's last email insisted that book number two should be well underway—I assured her it was. Anyway, you won't believe this story, and stranger still, it's true." I began to recap our visit to Lazy Willow.

He shook his head. "I don't know what to say. I'll call David tomorrow and see when he can squeeze us in."

"I agree, but can you believe this necklace has lived in a box for nearly one hundred years? I haven't done the math—maybe it's longer. Perhaps the man of questionable character—Olivia swears there were no names—legitimately purchased the necklace."

"Maybe, but the gift of it was to ensure her grandmother's silence," Nick said.

"I agree, but if it's *hot* and we have no names, what then?"

"Who knows? And that's why we'll pay David's outrageous rates to see how to move forward. But I do have another idea."

"And what's that?" I asked.

"David will know the legal part, but regardless, the actual necklace must be authenticated. If it's costume jewelry, then problem solved, but if it's not, we'll need to know our next step. I don't know any place around here, but I completely trust my friend in Pittsburgh. Remember him? He's the man who made your earrings and wedding rings?"

"Oh yes—I do."

"After we talk to David, we'll put the rest on hold until January. There is too much going on over the holidays. It's been in the box for a hundred years, so a few more weeks won't matter."

"Then what—in January, I mean?"

"I'd love to show you the farm where I lived before moving here, and we could go to a Steelers game if they're playing at home. I'll check on that. I still have my season tickets. I'll give Pete a call tomorrow, send him pictures along with what little information we have, and see when he can help us. We can keep the necklace in the wall safe in your closet until we go to Pittsburgh."

"I've never been to Pittsburgh. Won't it be really cold?"

"Yes, and there may even be snow. You're always talking about seeing a "serious snow," so here's your chance."

60

January 2, 2012

Dear Debby,

Happy New Year!

It's been two months since my last appointment, and I have so much to discuss—not the least of which are my thoughts on whether now is a good time to end our sessions.

All the upheaval from the divorce has finally found its quiet place in my past. I'm even comfortable with the possibility of Sidney getting married with Parker and Pam the chiropractor in attendance.

It makes me sad to think of leaving the security of your beige sofa. You've become a dear friend, and I think, over the past year, I've been coming just to chat, although your wisdom has always been valuable.

More tomorrow, but I never want to lose your friendship. I just don't need to pay $140.00 an hour to talk.

I've found calm with my story. I did as you said and found "face the world Sarah." I like her.

See you tomorrow.

With all good wishes,

Sarah

Pushing back in my desk chair, I took a breath. This was huge, but I also knew it was the right thing to do. Dr. Deborah Baxter had done her job, and now it was time for me to cut the cord.

As I walked to the kitchen for lunch, I saw Nick in the den. "Hey, babe," he said. "I just got off the phone with Pete; he has us down for this Friday and next Monday. Will that work for you?"

"Yes." I nodded. "Why two days?"

Nick walked into the kitchen, "We'll get the earliest flight to Pittsburgh on Friday, drop off the necklace so Pete has time to do his thing, and come back to Jenson and Sons on Monday to get the results. David was clear about our options: if it's stolen, he'll alert the authorities on our behalf. If it's yours, then you'll need to decide what you want to do. Over the weekend, I can show you around the city and the countryside. The Steelers are in Denver, but snow is in the forecast."

"I'm sorry about the game, but a major yay for the snow," I cheered.

"Can you ski?"

"I did in college, but since that was light-years ago, I'll pass. I don't want another broken anything."

CR8O

The hills of western Pennsylvania did not disappoint. The snow was beautiful, resembling a sheet of marzipan placed gently over the landscape, untouched by man, dotted only with fallen limbs and tracks left by scavengers.

Nick's former farm looked like a Rockwell painting on steroids, complete with a red barn trimmed in white. We stopped in to say hello to the family who had bought the property, and they insisted we stay for lunch. Mr. Oglethorpe and Nick spent an hour or so crunching through the snow, discussing spring planting, while I helped the oldest son with the cows.

Our lodging was a quaint B and B just outside Pittsburgh proper. The owners of the dark green Victorian gingerbread with rusty red trim had just celebrated their sixtieth anniversary. Late Saturday afternoon they offered, and we couldn't refuse, a narrated photo fest highlighting their lives together.

We traveled downtown for a fancy evening meal in our nicer clothes. The restaurant occupied the entire top floor of a building in the heart of Pittsburgh, and what a view: the lights danced along both sides of the river, spreading up and down the hills. The food was amazing, and the crème brûlée by candlelight was the finishing touch to a lovely day.

Sunday morning, we journeyed west out of the city. I was trans-fixed by the quaintness of each little village resting along the banks of the Ohio River. It was "hunt country" for sure. Nick talked about his years as a member of the local hunt, and I suggested we swing by that piece of property to see if anyone was around. Standing in the doorway, Nick was instantly recognized by several of the members. Recounting tales of past hunts and catching up lasted for hours. I enjoyed listening and watching Nick interact with his old friends.

Monday morning came, and we were off for our second visit to Jenson & Sons. Pete was the reflection of his father; they both had rounded faces and steel-blue eyes. Pete was a bit taller than his dad, but both measured somewhere over six feet.

"What's he going to tell us?" I asked as we drove into the city.

Nick pulled into the parking deck. "There's only one way to find out."

The store was in a very old but handsomely refurbished building. Dwarf Alberta spruce in sturdy earthen planters stood sentry on either side of the front door, and a keypad code was needed to enter. The elder Jenson waved from across the room as Pete came out from behind his desk to offer a handshake to Nick and a hug for me. "Good morning. I hope you two have enjoyed your weekend?"

"Yes," I said. "The snow's beautiful."

"Have you ever experienced a snowfall like this?"

"Not since I graduated from college in the Blue Ridge Mountains of North Carolina. I've been told we can't leave Pittsburgh until I've eaten at Primanti Brothers."

"That's right—a culinary institution for sure," he said, reaching into the desk drawer. "Now for the main attraction." Perfectly positioned on a deep ink-blue velvet board, the necklace sparkled under the lights. "It cleaned up nicely, didn't it?"

I gasped. "Holy smokes."

Nick asked his good friend if he had any information about the necklace.

"I do. Using the photos you sent me back in December and Tiffany's identification number on the clasp, two of my colleagues and I have been hard at work for weeks researching this. Actually having the piece in hand, here's what we know for sure: it was originally sold to an English aristocrat—an anniversary gift for his wife. On the trip back to England in 1898, it was lost in a high-stakes poker game."

Nick looked surprised. "How could you possibly know that?"

"Reasonable question—creditable jewelry stores like Tiffany's keep records, and as you know, the piece is numbered," Pete said, pointing to the back of the clasp. "The ruby actually has a name, 'the

Mountain Rose.' Keying that into the computer brought up a front-page article from the *New York Times* of a high-society function and one of the socialites was wearing the necklace featured in a photo. Here, I made you a copy."

"Thanks," Nick said, glancing at the papers.

"The reporter quoted the socialite as saying: 'My husband's very clever and won it in a poker game, lucky me. It's called "the Mountain Rose," though I don't know why, but it's one of a kind, you know.'"

"Lord have mercy!" I said, causing Pete to laugh.

He sipped his coffee. "I love your accent."

"I don't have an accent, but you do." I grinned. "Please continue."

"We checked all the records available and believe this is the same necklace. There's no information concerning how it got to the questionable gentleman in Richmond, but there are no records of theft, so it's yours."

My eyes widened. "Really?"

"Yes, and there's more." Pete continued. "We uncovered some additional information about your deep red showstopper. The stone was actually found in April 1890 by a farmer near Franklin, North Carolina, thus its name. How about that? Homegrown."

"Amazing—and?" I said, struggling to take it all in.

"And, to use the reporter's words, apparently there were some governmental issues regarding moonshine, back taxes, and revenues. But, as if by magic, all signs of trouble apparently vanished after the sale of the stone. I made you a copy of that newspaper article also."

"Thanks—and?" Nick said.

"And the necklace is worth around $180,000 on today's market. The ruby is very rare, and the diamonds are beautifully cut and clear.

I would strongly suggest insuring it for $200,000. We'll also need to register it and give you the appraisal papers."

I sat dumbfounded, as if I really were on *Antiques Roadshow.*

"Sarah, are you okay?" Nick asked.

I nodded dumbly. "Pete, are you absolutely certain about this?"

"I am, but if you decide to sell it, the price would likely skyrocket at auction. I really don't have a hard number, but perhaps triple in value. It's a beautiful piece, and between the New York socialite, the questionable gentleman, and the farmer, it has a colorful past, and people eat that stuff up."

I regained my focus. "Won't I look fine mucking stalls, throwing hay, and driving the tractor wearing my ruby necklace?" I laughed. "Now that we know more about it, how do we get it home? And this is slightly insane, but I hope you still have the original box."

"Ordinarily I would have pitched it, but with vintage jewelry, having the original case increases the value. We'll send the necklace to you if that would make you feel better," he said. "There are special carriers and packaging for this sort of thing."

I looked at Nick. "What do you think?"

"Let's take it with us. Pete can pack it in something inconspicuous."

"Goodness, all my Southern manners have flown right out the window," I said. "I should have said this earlier—thank you for my wedding rings and earrings. I love them both."

"My pleasure," Pete said, holding out his hand. "Why don't you give me your rings and they can be cleaned while we're at lunch? And, Sarah, you're really in for a treat. Primanti's is unique dining. Everything—fries, slaw, and all—are squished between two thick pieces of bread."

As advertised, lunch at Primanti Brothers was delicious and truly unique. Afterward, the three of us walked back to Jenson & Son's to collect the cleverly disguised package and my sparkling rings.

Nick vigorously shook the hand of his good friend. "Thanks so much, Pete. We appreciate all the time you've put into this. It was great to see you again."

"My pleasure," the younger Jenson answered, turning his head in my direction. "Sarah, it was a treat meeting you. Don't be a stranger."

CB&O

Standing in the TSA line at the security check, I clutched my precious package with an absolute death grip. I held my breath as my shoes, purse, and the Mountain Rose traveled through the scanner and watched the security woman's face as she viewed the screen. She glanced in my direction but made only minimal eye contact. I did have the ownership papers in my purse just in case they thought I might be some sort of international jewel thief. The treasure came out the other end with no inspection necessary.

Miss Olivia would say I was being dramatic, and I guess I was. I giggled as I put my shoes back on.

61.

Driving home from the Raleigh airport, I called Betsy.

"It's not stolen; it's mine," I told her. "It has a name, and it's worth $180,000—even more at auction," I said, gasping for air and waiting for a response. "Betsy, are you there?"

"Wow!"

"No kidding. Wait until we have a show-and-tell with Olivia. Maybe you should bring something stronger than Earl Grey tea."

"If you can, let's go tomorrow morning," Betsy suggested.

Early the next morning, we were on our way.

Following a brief overview of our whirlwind trip and hearing what Pete Jenson had to say, Betsy asked, "Now what?"

"First we have to talk to Olivia, tell her the appraised value, and make sure she doesn't want it for herself. Not to wear but to sell. We don't know anything about her financial situation. She said it was mine, but that was before the appraisal. If she doesn't want it, I don't know what I'd do with it," I said, launching into the story of our trip.

Within the hour, we three sat in the cozy little side room talking about the long-lost treasure and reassuring Olivia everything was on the up-and-up. We could see relief in her eyes, and she fell back in her chair when I disclosed the dollar amount of the appraisal.

Shaking her head, she said, "I can't believe it. All those years living from paycheck to paycheck, and Mama knew what was hiding in the attic the whole time. Daddy would have made her sell it. That money would have gone a long way to living a better life."

Betsy spoke up. "Money can't buy happiness."

"No, but it sure can iron out the wrinkles when trouble comes a-callin'," Olivia said, squeezing her hands.

"That's true," I said. "But consider this: her affair with your dad's older brother was early on in your parents' marriage. Your father didn't know about that until many years later, so maybe she held on to the necklace as a safety net. You know, if he ever found out and left her, she'd have something to live on and raise her children."

Olivia tilted her head. "Maybe. The whole thing is difficult to digest. Sarah, it belongs to you. I don't need any money, and you can sell it or keep it. It's up to you."

I scrunched up my face. "Really—you don't want to think about this?"

"Positive! Now, when's your book coming out?"

"Early June, I think. I'll get my copies before then, but when, I don't know."

We talked a little about the latest news at Lazy Willow and what Olivia was enjoying reading. Before we left, our senior said, "Can you believe it, a $180,000 necklace, sitting in the attic of 528 Brook Street—what in the world! I wonder what else was up there?"

"I'm scared to look," I said with a hug goodbye.

"Don't worry," Olivia said. "The rest is probably just junk."

62

Initiated by the Historical Society, we all agreed a Colonial Farm Champagne Inaugural would be appropriate in mid-spring, 2013. It would kick off the society's fundraising season but also offer an opportunity to show donors of both the society and the university where their annual contributions were being spent. The "continuing support" dollars of the Historical Society provided all the furnishings on the main floor, while the university money created a scholarship fund for their satellite-learning program.

Between the members of the society, university officials, and our friends and family, two hundred invitations were mailed, and one hundred and sixty-five answered yes. Kenny and Mark were hired to do the floral decorations, and River's Bend provided the food.

The TV camera crew arrived around two that afternoon, filming inside and out. That piece of the day had been organized so that the professor/dorm dad with each of the fourteen students who took up residency in early January were dressed in their period work clothes, explained the workings of a colonial farm, and offered hands-on demonstrations. By five o'clock, the film crew was packed and on their way back to Raleigh. A photographer would take over once our guests arrived.

Spring was in full bloom, and a cacophony of colors welcomed our guests as they made their way up the brick walk. Everyone looked so smart all dressed up for our black-tie affair. The first floor had the most gorgeous hardwood floor I had ever seen and was furnished in period pieces, with the table set in pewter plates and flatware.

The square box garden was impressive with its twenty boxes, four groups of five each, overflowing with spring lettuce, herbs, and more. A coop full of Lohmann Brown laying hens rested quietly on their nests, while the one puffed-up rooster sang greetings to every guest. But the matched pair of perfectly groomed Belgian draft horses standing in the paddock drew the largest crowd.

The second-semester seniors were the tour guides, strategically placed around the farm to explain the program or answer questions from the guests. They took great pride in announcing that every-thing on the property, including the farm animals, was their respon-sibility. They added that fresh eggs were available for the modest sum of three dollars per dozen and would be available for purchase on the front porch at the close of the evening.

Nick and I had agreed this would be a good time for me to wear the Mountain Rose. On several occasions, we talked about what I would say if asked about the necklace. "I found it in the attic" would be my answer. If pressed for more, I would add, "Interestingly enough, a similar situation lies between the covers of my book *Sweet Tea and Fireflies*—scheduled for release in early June."

The evening was a huge success so far, but outside the Rowdy Girls, the necklace had generated zero conversation.

"I don't think anyone imagines it's real," Margaret said.

Rose agreed. "To their eyes, it's most surely costume jewelry."

I blew a sigh of relief. "On the one hand, I don't need to fumble for an answer, but on the other, I am missing a serious retail opportunity to hawk my book."

An older woman none of us knew wiggled her way into our circle of conversation. "Hello. I'm Beatrice Foxroy. I wanted to say what a wonderful job you've done with this project."

"Thank you," I said, "but I can't take—"

"Right," she interrupted abruptly. "I know I shouldn't—but your necklace is simply stunning. Could I ask where you got it? Quality costume jewelry is next to impossible to find."

"You're right, but this happens to be real," I said, reaching up to make it twinkle.

The Rowdy Girls and I stood quietly waiting for her response.

"Impossible," Bea responded with a tone of unabated affluence. "Aren't you a schoolteacher?"

"Yes, or was…I'm retired now."

"Well, I don't mean to be insulting," she said, though clearly headed in that direction, "but how did you come to have such an amazing piece of jewelry?"

Betsy's nostrils began to flare. "You know Bea, there's a thin line between good taste and tacky, and we're close to erasing it aren't we?"

"It's okay," I said. "Mrs. Foxroy, I found it in our attic—truly I did. But if you enjoy reading, my soon-to-be-released novel, *Sweet Tea and Fireflies*, has an invented twist of what, years later, became my truth."

"Goodness—you wrote a book?" Beatrice asked, as though it was impossible that I had such talents.

Margaret snapped, "Yes, she sure did—actually three."

Rose took charge, and as only she could do, set Mrs. Beatrice

Foxroy straight. "Oh, how lovely—a shameful discussion concerning money and the possibility that Sarah is poor. Beatrice, when we've run the length of that conversation, let's move on to your inference that my dear friend's not clever enough to write a book."

Before Rose could draw another breath, Beatrice Foxroy made a rapid retreat. I think her British accent takes folks by surprise, and they simply never recover. It's like being dressed down by the queen, and people shrink like a violet in the aftermath.

"I think that haughty woman and I should continue our little chat," Rose said. "Have you ever...? She actually suggested you couldn't possibly own something so lovely."

With a sigh, I said, "Well, she's right. I couldn't. Leave it alone, and let's see what happens."

"Just allow me five more minutes," Rose pleaded, hoping to continue the "dressing down" of our audacious guest.

"No. I sincerely appreciate your having my back, but doing anything makes us as shallow as Bea."

Noticing that Bea and her friends were herding a man in our direction, Margaret sounded the alarm. "Look out. Group attack and they've brought reinforcements."

"Good evening, Mrs. Heart...ladies. I'm Harrison Harper with *News-in-Review*, and I would like to ask you a few questions about your necklace," he said, taking a small ring-bound notepad from his inside coat pocket.

"Thanks, but I'm going to decline," I said. "Your viewers don't need to know anything about my jewelry, and I'll probably never wear it again. However, if you would like to discuss our actual reason for being here, I'm happy to oblige."

Harrison turned out to be a very nice man, and we enjoyed our shared conversation. "This is off the record, but please tell me about the necklace."

"The true story is far too long to tell. But the possibility of a treasure in someone's attic was the catalyst for several chapters in my soon-to-be-released novel *Sweet Tea and Fireflies*. I had great fun inventing that piece of the story."

Sounding surprised, he said, "You wrote a book?"

I pressed my lips firmly together. "Why does that statement invoke such an emphatic response of disbelief? But yes, I wrote a novel!"

Returning the small notepad to his breast pocket, he said, "I'd like to add you and your book to the story I'm doing about the Colonial Farm project. We have plenty of footage and pictures, but an interview to make sure all the facts are correct would be great. Could you come to the station this coming Tuesday or Wednesday? Oh, and I never meant to insult you. I'm really quite impressed."

"Well, thank you, and I apologize for my tone. Hadn't you rather wait until it's published?"

"Actually, I think adding your novel to the farm piece would play better. It would grab more attention from our viewers. Something to look forward to."

"Okay, and thanks. Let me check my calendar. Do you have a card?" I asked.

The remainder of our debut evening went off like clockwork. I loved watching our guests go in and out of the house and finding new things to investigate as they surveyed the property. Several groups helped themselves to the porch rocking chairs, chatting away, enjoying a glass of wine, and overlooking the front lawn.

With most carrying a dozen Colonial Farm eggs, all the invitees were on their way home, the caterers packed up, and the students upstairs in their rooms, Nick and I, along with the Historical Society folks and university officials took a seat around the kitchen table of the new "old" house. There was a short recap of the evening and a report on the financial gain from ticket sales. Masses of kudos were extended for everything, and we were all given a folder containing information on every aspect of the project.

It was nearing midnight when Nick took the floor, offering thanks to everyone, adding it was time to call it a night. Before anyone could stand, the distinguished gentleman across the table motioned for everyone to remain seated. Freddy Foxroy, chairman of the board of the Historical Society, clearly had something to say.

"Mrs. Heart," he said, "my Bea tells me you're an author, and the mystery surrounding the necklace you're wearing lies somewhere between the covers of your latest effort."

"Not actually this necklace, but a piece of jewelry," I said. "I can't spill the beans now. How could I make the top one hundred without your buying a copy?"

"Understood," Freddy said, his voice deep and authoritative, "but you're missing a retail opportunity here."

"I am?"

"You are," he answered. "You know we're in the middle of our annual fundraising campaign—this Colonial Farm was our April project—and again, thank you all for allowing us to benefit from the ticket sales. June is North Carolina Artifacts Month, and that event is held at our museum in Raleigh. It includes everything from pottery and period clothing to Revolutionary and Civil War items, to the Lost Colony, pirates, and yes, jewelry and North Carolina writers. Your book could be on display for the month of June."

"Well, that's an interesting proposition. You mentioned jewelry—this necklace is real and the ruby was found over one hundred years ago in Macon County."

"Even better!" Freddy beamed. "So the book and the necklace could be on display. You two talk it over. I guarantee its safety. We'll need a short history of the necklace—a little mystery can generate a great deal of profit, you know. Our gift shop would carry copies of your novel."

My face slightly flushed, I said, "Thanks again. I'll be in touch."

C3 80

The light from a full moon flooded our bedroom. "Good grief!" I said. "What to do?"

Nick pulled me close. "Not to worry. Make a date to visit Olivia—you won't feel comfortable without her blessing. I know your concern is the diary and the troubles concerning her mother. But the history of the necklace has nothing to do with either. And word of mouth has sold many things."

"True," I said, turning over and scrunching up my pillow. *The Mountain Rose and my book on display front and center at the society's museum—wow!* I thought, feeling myself blush.

63

The following Tuesday I was in Raleigh, seated in front of a television camera, and going over the interview process with Harrison Harper. Sidney was there to cheer me on; I loved sharing time with her on her own turf. Occasionally I lost my train of thought, and after regrouping, we began again; thankfully this was not a live interview, and the tape would be edited later. All in all, I was happy with the interview. Harrison said it would be grafted into his story of the Colonial Farm and would air on the Thursday evening slot of *News-in-Review*.

Sidney offered to take me to lunch—at her favorite vegan restaurant.

"I'll eat most anything but not tofu."

"This restaurant is so good, you'll love it all—including tofu." Sidney snickered.

"I doubt that. Do they have salads?"

Weaving her arm through the crook of mine, she said, "Mother, really, you were just on TV for the first time ever. Continue the trend of new experiences."

"All right, but I refuse to eat raw seafood. You call it sushi—I call it bait!"

Sidney was right that the food was delicious, and I decided the time was ripe to ask a few probing questions. "So, my dearest darling, you haven't said a word in forever about you and Jacob. Are you two still serious?"

"Yes, Mama, we are, but we're not quite ready for any announcement."

"May I know why?"

"Yes, but I need you to promise not to tell anyone. I know you'll tell Nick, but please no one else."

I held my tea glass at shoulder height. "You have my word."

"Jacob doesn't want to get married until he is completely debt-free from his college loans and the equipment costs from starting his practice," she said, taking a sip of her green tea. "He's almost paid it all off but not quite."

"How wonderfully admirable! And I'll add that I'm not surprised."

Sidney glowed. "I know. He's amazing, and I totally respect his decision. We are hoping for maybe next year."

I tried to hold my question at bay but lost the battle. "Does your father know?"

"Sort of, but I've been worried about that since you two are divorced. How all of that will be handled. You know, money, who's invited, Dad walking me down the aisle—stuff like that."

"My love, that's the least of your worries. Your father and I will figure that out, and all will be well."

The tears welled in her eyes. "Seriously, Mama?"

"Absolutely. I promise!"

Perhaps for the first time, I truly saw Sidney as an adult. With hugs and kisses, I was on my way back home—smiling all the way.

Betsy and I visited Lazy Willow on Friday to explain the museum situation to Olivia. I had worked off and on for days, crafting a mini history of the necklace. The Richmond piece of the story simply said it was a gift to Olivia's grandmother from a woman whose name had been lost by time. Years later it was passed down to her mother as a wedding gift. My story ended with Olivia giving it to me. I had her father's handwritten note, the newspaper articles, and Tiffany's letter of authentication for the ruby's origin professionally mounted, and they would also be on display.

Reading the brief history aloud, we sat quietly, waiting for her response.

"I like it," Olivia said, relaxing her hands. "Every word is true, and the trouble with my parents isn't mentioned or relevant."

"Wonderful," I said. "Now, Miss Olivia, this is entirely up to you, but Betsy and I would like for you to attend the opening in Raleigh with us. Nick and I would come pick you up and bring you home."

"Oh no, I don't think so." She shook her head. "I don't belong with all those fancy folks. I don't have anything to wear and wouldn't know what to say."

I patted her hand. "All you'd have to say is what I wrote on the story card."

"You'll have a great time," Betsy added, refilling her teacup. "We'll be there, and the rest of the Rowdy Girls will be there too. No one will let anything happen to you. Sarah and I can find you a lovely dress. So say yes, and let's have a night out."

"Well, okay." She smiled. "But you must promise none of the bad stuff will ever come out. Especially about Mama."

"We promise," I said. "In fact, I need to tell you something."

Olivia put down her cup. "Oh, Lord, another confession."

"Yes. I've been worried someone might stumble across your mother's diary. I was going to hide it, but we all know that doesn't work. The three of us are the only people who know the *whole* truth."

Impatiently, Betsy asked, "So, what'd you do with it?"

"I burned it. Diaries are very personal, and all those thoughts were for her eyes only. Your mother had no one to talk to about her innermost secrets, so the journal was her closest confidant. None of us was ever supposed to know anything about that part of her life, and had Iris not kept it, we'd still be in the dark."

Olivia took a deep breath, blinking her eyes several times. "I can't thank you enough. I've been concerned that the truth about Mother and her affair might somehow get out."

"Time has taken care of that," Betsy assured Olivia. "Except for you, everyone involved has passed away. Stanley doesn't count—he never knew anything in the first place. Now, what's your favorite color to wear?"

"I do love light blue." She smiled. "But don't spend too much. I'll never wear it again."

"Light blue it is. I'll speak with the hair salon before we leave and give them the date so you can get your hair done. We're going to have a wonderful time."

"I'm excited, except for that trip to the hospital, I haven't left this property in years."

Betsy cheered. "Well, hold on to your hat...You're stepping out with the Rowdy Girls!"

"I might be too old for that."

"Never too old, Miss Olivia. Never too old!" I assured her.

❦

Our senior insisted that she be the first person to buy a copy of my book and have it autographed. We made our way to the gift shop just before the doors opened to the public, and using her own money, Olivia was my first customer. I was deeply touched and proud to see my book on display. I received my copies a week earlier, but this was different—this was my literary child being offered to the world!

Olivia Cromwell, dressed in her lovely light blue party dress, with her silver-gray hair styled just right, stole the show, with guests standing three deep at our exhibit. The crowd stood glued to her every word about the necklace. She also recounted our many visits over the past nearly two years and hearing the story of *Sweet Tea and Fireflies* unfold.

Olivia briefly mentioned our first visit and my being so conscientious about disposing of her things and how that was the beginning of our friendship.

I beamed with pride as she explained being the thread of inspiration for the Hattie Hayes character in my book. She told everyone who would listen that she had gained at least ten pounds since we met due to tea and cookies, but she'd loved listening to the story.

Olivia held up her copy. "Sarah and Betsy came to Lazy Willow to see two old sisters about some equally old stuff from our attic, and her imagination wrote this. She'll autograph it for you—won't you, Sarah?"

"Yes, ma'am." I nodded, trying not to cry.

The Rowdy Girls enjoyed the book debut as well. Here and there someone would ask, *Which character is based on you?* I overheard Elizabeth say, "I'm sure none of us is literally in the book. But everyone has best friends, and the six of us have been together for a long time."

The men nominated Frank as their spokesperson but were disappointed that no one asked about their part, if any, in the book.

As it happened, Freddy Foxroy was right. Every copy of my book was sold on the first night of the June opening of North Carolina Artifacts Month.

Bill pretended to be quite upset as we collected our coats. "I'm shattered that no one asked about us. I guess we really aren't important."

"I noticed that myself," Frank said.

Everyone howled, and Betsy took the arm of her ego-deflated husband. "You're important to me, dear."

Frank lowered his head. "Well, that's something, at least."

Bill and Margaret had surprised everyone by securing a limousine from their dealership and hiring a driver for the evening. Being chauffeured to and from downtown Raleigh truly was luxury at its best. We all settled into the cushiony leather seats of the stretch limo, took off our shoes, wiggled our sore toes in the thick carpet, and enjoyed the trip back home. Wine and sodas were available and welcomed—it had been a nonstop verbal four hours.

Olivia was the first to be dropped off. Before leaving the limo, she said, "I had a great time, and it was wonderful to meet all of you. Sarah, you're going to sell a lot of books. Nick, you're a lucky man."

"Yes, I am," he said, helping her out of the car. They continued their conversation as Nick escorted Olivia to the front door, and it was another ten minutes before he returned. "I was taken on a tour and then to her apartment. You're right—she's a hoot."

"I told you. I dearly love Olivia Cromwell."

"Me too," Betsy said. "It was great to see her enjoying herself."

"I was rather disappointed that Beatrice Foxroy didn't come over to see us tonight," Rose said, refilling her wineglass.

Elizabeth agreed. "That was strange. Especially considering her behavior at your farm."

"I think we stole her thunder." Jennifer chuckled. "A month or so ago she was trying to put you down, but tonight, and with the help of Olivia, the Rowdy Girls stopped her in her tracks."

Elizabeth leaned in. "Sarah, how many books were sold?"

"All of them. They're packaged twenty to a case, and the curator said she ordered two cases."

"So how many more do you have to sell to make the bestseller's list?" Margaret asked.

"I don't know for sure, but it's in the thousands and in one week. That's why it's a short list compared to the long list of published authors. But I'd fall over dead if I even made the top one thousand. All I truly care about is that whoever reads my book likes it and can find themselves somewhere between the covers."

"Well, here's to you. Good luck!" Jennifer shouted, holding up her glass.

Nick smiled. "You know the old cliché—'luck happens when preparedness meets opportunity.' So, my love, maybe tonight was just that."

"Maybe so. Freddy Foxroy was right. Tonight really was a wonderful way to launch *Sweet Tea and Fireflies*. I hope no one's disappointed when they read my story."

"Not likely," Betsy insisted. "Remember, I was there every time you read to Olivia."

"No fair!" Margaret said.

"Betsy does know the basic story but not the final version. Now, thank you all for doing as I asked and not buying a book at the museum. I'm sure you've guessed why," I said, bringing a shopping bag out from behind the seat. Pulling the books out one at a time, I handed each friend her copy with a personal note written inside. "I've had my copies for a while, but I decided this very special night was the perfect time to share. Please know how much I love you all and how much our sisterhood means to me."

Rose gently rubbed her hand over the face of the book. "It's such a handsome cover. I loved it at first sight in the gift shop. Did you help in the design?"

I tilted my head and laughed. "Not really. The graphic designer allowed my initial input, then basically ignored me. I do love how it turned out, though. Remember, no sharing copies—there's not a dime's worth of profit in sharing."

"That's right," Margaret said, squinting to read the back jacket.

Nick whispered in my ear, "Where's mine?"

"Patience, Todd, it's in the seat of your den chair," I said, squishing closer.

◌৪৩

When we were finally home, out of our fancy clothes, barn checked, and dogs wriggling all around, Nick said, "What a wonderful evening. Cheers to you, my dear. Now under the covers you go."

"Where are you going?"

"To start reading *Sweet Tea and Fireflies*. I've waited long enough. I'm not sure how long I'll last tonight, but you just go to sleep, and I'll see you in the morning."

"Aw, Todd, that's so sweet."

"Funny!" Nick turned out the light and called the dogs to follow.

CB ED

As the sun peeked through the shutters, I woke up to the smell of coffee brewing and a faint whisper of burned toast.

"Morning." I yawned, standing in the doorway of the den. "You didn't come to bed…You're still reading?"

Nick looked over his readers. "Hey, babe. Yes, I love this story; obviously I can't put it down. I did fall asleep for a while, but I picked it back up again. I'm on chapter forty-seven."

Leaning over and giving him a kiss, I said, "I'm glad you can't put it down! Hmm, let me think…Yes, I know where you are."

Nick said, "Hattie Hayes's husband is going to die, or I think so anyway. I love her, so I have to find out what she does after he passes away. She has several options. And Grace, Ben, and the boathouse—hot stuff! Does she get her thong underwear back, or does someone else find it?"

"Keep reading." I blushed, overjoyed by his enthusiasm. "Let me get dressed, and I'll fix breakfast."

"Okay, and thanks, but this will be my day until I finish reading. Seriously, Sarah, if the remaining pages don't drop the ball, your novel really should be a bestseller!"

"Thank you for your totally biased opinion," I said from the hall.

CB&O

Margaret and I were riding that afternoon when my bleary-eyed husband appeared ringside.

"Wow, babe, what a story!"

"You've read the whole thing?" Margaret asked.

"Yes. I couldn't put it down."

"Well, I've only read the first eight chapters, so don't spoil it for me."

"I wouldn't dream of it. Sarah, I made a reservation at the Tinker Inn tonight for dinner at seven. Little did I know the first time we ate there that I was dining with my future wife and a future bestselling author all at the same time."

"Thanks for the special treat—yum!" I said. "But you're also full of prunes."

"Just you wait and see," Nick insisted, throwing up his hands and walking toward the barn. "Just you wait and see!"

64

There had been a great deal of local interest in the book, and I credited Freddy Foxroy and the artifacts evening for the initial sales. With an intense in-house advertising push from the publisher, which incorporated bits of Harrison Harper's interview, it had quickly gone beyond the confines of the museum gift shop. Covered Buttons Press, in partnership with a nationally known bookseller, had organized a tour of twelve larger cities. I was to leave in three weeks for a two-and-a-half-week tour.

The zigzag pattern of book talks stretched across the country, beginning with Raleigh, moving on to Washington, DC, then points beyond. Vera had sent me an email with cities and dates but allowed us two days to check for conflicts. We couldn't both be absent from the farm for that long, so Betsy agreed to go with me for three cities, and Margaret was up for two.

The night before I left, Jennifer hosted a Rowdy Girls bon voyage dinner to toast the adventure.

As we sat down for dinner, Rose said, "I know I've said it before, but I sincerely loved your book."

Blushing, I said, "Thank you! You're not just being kind?"

Rose continued. "Sarah, I would never review any book, not even yours, without honesty. Clouded praise does no good at all. It really is a captivating story."

"Thanks for making the five girlfriends wonderful riders with no visible signs of aging. You were right—it's pure fiction." Elizabeth laughed. "I love the parts about Hattie Hayes. I cried in the end."

"Me too," Jennifer said. "Is it okay if I sell the book in the restaurant?"

"Wow—yes! Thanks."

Margaret and Betsy discussed what they would pack, and the others were sorry they couldn't go.

"They're going with you, not Nick?" Elizabeth asked.

"Nick will be there for the first three cities. Betsy will meet me in Chicago. Margaret picks up babysitting in Phoenix, and Nick will be there for my final leg home. I don't think I can do it all without their help. I just hope I don't mess this up."

"Why would you say that?" Betsy asked. "You can talk all day and never take a breath."

"I'm not worried about the talking piece. I'm worried about sounding too Southern, saying too much or the wrong thing. Yesterday Ellie Ward came to the farm for the day, giving me a tutorial of sorts."

Margaret looked surprised. "How could you not sound Southern? And anyway, what's wrong with that?"

"Nothing at all, but you know, my Southern expressions, turning a two-syllable word into four, and 'bless her heart,' just to name a few."

"You can invent more ridiculous situations to worry about than anyone I've ever known," Betsy said, shaking her head. "Your genuine Southern charm is one of your best attributes. You'll have them eating out of your hand after 'Hello, my name is Sarah Heart.'"

"Let's hope so. But you may have noticed—conversationally speaking, I can jump the rails and start talking about how much I loved my first-grade teacher or something."

Jennifer tried but failed to control her laughter. "How true. We do know a great deal about Mrs. Hudson and your inability to remain in the *family circle*."

"Don't forget seventh grade," Elizabeth added, "and the boy who put tacks in her desk chair."

"I love that story." Margaret giggled. "But having to stand in the corner in third grade tops them all."

"Exactly! Now you see why Ellie's tutorial was important. You know I'm beyond proud of my roots. My problem is getting off topic and losing my train of thought. Ellie and I designed a little talk cheat sheet."

"I loved how you developed a story from tidbits of truth," Margaret said. "I could hear your voice while reading the whole thing. It was like when I was a little girl and my mother took me to story hour at the public library."

"It was like that, wasn't it?" Rose agreed. "Until now, I've never read a novel written by someone I actually knew."

"Jennifer, this looks delicious," Betsy said, passing the green beans.

We feasted on chicken cordon bleu with all the trimmings, and I received welcomed advice for the tour and my talk. Dessert was next, and just before we cleared the table, it happened.

"There will be absolutely no fuss made over this," Rose said emphatically, taking a very long pause…"Gus and I are married."

You could have heard a pin drop.

"Finally! And yay!" I said. "I can't believe you let me talk about myself and the book the whole time when you had this news to share."

"Talk about taking forever," Betsy said, "but who cares? How exciting! We need details!"

"We said 'I do' last Saturday in the gardens at Bellomy Farm." Rose beamed. "Our next-door neighbors were our witnesses, and we all went out for dinner afterward."

"So July 9, 2013, is your anniversary?" I smiled.

Rose blushed ever so slightly. "Yes."

"Could we have a few more details? Is there a ring? Was or is there to be a honeymoon?" Elizabeth insisted.

Rose took a sip of wine. "It was very spur-of-the-moment, and we just went with it. Actually, we were happy living together without the legal paperwork, but the business side of things—deeds and such—worked better if we were married. I do hope you all understand my not calling. I thought it would be more fun to share tonight when we were all together."

Betsy took the floor. "Of course we understand, and it's totally okay! It's your marriage, not ours. In fact, I think it's very romantic."

"It is romantic. Your Scottish barbarian swept you away, after all," Margaret said. "What about a honeymoon?"

"We spent a few nights in Middleburg at the Red Fox Inn and Tavern, but we're taking a longer trip in the fall. Oh, and I have a ring," she said, slipping it out of her pocket and onto her finger.

Wide-eyed, Jennifer said, "It's magnificent!"

We took turns drooling over the extra-wide gold band with the

Rock of Gibraltar sitting in the middle.

Betsy took a closer look. "It's so unusual."

"Thank you. Gus had it made for me."

"Where are you going to live?" Elizabeth asked.

"I think Bellomy Farm will become our permanent address, but it'll be difficult to sell my house. Someone called about a month ago wanting to buy it for the land to build apartments. I said no. I don't think I could stomach its being reduced to rubble."

"Keep it and develop it into a retreat of some sort," Jennifer suggested.

"Interesting idea. Gus and I'll talk it over. Now, Sarah needs to get home. Tomorrow is the start of her big adventure."

I blamed my tears on the excitement of the evening, but it was mostly about losing Rose to Bellomy Farm. We'd continue to meet at horse shows and Moss Creek Farm, but that really wasn't the same— not at all.

65

The next two and a half weeks were a blur, but we managed to meet all our commitments and then some. With the help of Nick, Betsy, and Margaret, I found a rhythm to my thoughts, and except for once, I was never flustered or tripped up. Ellie's tutorial day had proven invaluable, and I frequently reviewed her cheat sheet of acceptable responses to questions asked.

On gap days, we used our time to take a breath. Betsy and I had one entire free day following my commitment in Denver, and we treated ourselves to an all-day guided trail ride with a packed lunch high in the Rockies. The view was breathtaking—especially on horseback.

While in Phoenix, Margaret and I enjoyed a spa day before flying to Saint Louis the following morning. The massage therapist suggested my back contained more knots than the hour could relieve. I volleyed with "Attack the biggest ones, and have I told you about my book?" I watched as she ordered a copy on her phone. When I mentioned that sharing was unacceptable, she laughed. I assured her I was beyond serious. Margaret and I had lunch by the pool and flopped out on loungers the size of twin beds for the afternoon.

Nick was waiting for me in the lobby of the Roosevelt New Orleans. I had never been to the Big Easy, but my husband had. Thus I now enjoyed my own private tour guide. That book talk drew the largest crowd to date. They laughed at all the right places and asked a multitude of questions.

"There's time for one last question. Yes, ma'am," I said to the raised hand in the back of the room.

Stepping into view, the petite woman with a warm smile, wearing a floral Lilly Pulitzer dress, said, "Hi, Sarah. Do you remember me?"

My beautifully scripted, well-practiced, not over-the-top Southern responses whooshed right out the door. "Lord have mercy. Cindy Hager, what are you doing here? Folks, this is my college roommate from a hundred years ago, and we haven't seen each other since—Lord—forever. Bless your heart, you look fabulous!"

Working her way to the front, she said, "I'll take that as a yes. I've already read your book, and I loved it." She turned to the crowd. "Don't leave this building without buying a copy. It's a delightful story, easy to read, and about the unwavering love of sisterhood, new friendships, sex, and family. You won't be disappointed."

Everyone applauded as my talk finished, and the bookstore management began organizing a line. Cindy stayed with me. "It's so good to see you. Shame on us for allowing this much time to pass since we've seen each other."

Holding her hand, I said, "No kidding. I think it was at our twentieth class reunion."

"I guess so, but thank goodness for Christmas cards. Anyway, you know I write for *Biscuits and Gravy* magazine, and I want to do a story on you. But first let me ask—who's this gorgeous man you're with?"

Realizing I had blown right past Nick, I said, "Oh my God, this is my husband. I can't believe I left you standing there. Babe, I'm so sorry."

"It's okay." Nick smiled. "Cindy, I'm Nick Heart—husband of the flustered author. It's nice to meet you."

"Nice to meet you too. Sarah," she whispered over her shoulder, "what happened to Parker?"

"Divorce. How's Mark?"

"Last I heard my ex was somewhere in the Cayman Islands, hiding from the law, and his twenty-two-year-old bimbo went with him. I got remarried last spring. You'll love Kirk."

"Sarah," the manager interrupted, "we're ready for you now."

"Cindy, while my wife signs books, why don't we get a cup of coffee and maybe a scone? You two can pick up where you left off after she's finished," Nick said.

C3&0

Later that evening, we met Cindy and Kirk at an upscale, true taste of New Orleans restaurant and talked for hours. It was decided one more trip to the bookstore would be needed to meet with her magazine's photographer and tie up any loose ends to her story.

The next morning we met at the bookstore's checkout counter and strolled around looking for the ideal spot. Being, in my opinion, totally unphotogenic, I balked at first, but her photographer worked some serious magic. Surprisingly, one picture in particular was quite good. It was of Nick and me sitting on a lovely bench just outside the turquoise front door. With his rugged good looks and the explosion of summer flowers spilling over the sides of terra-cotta pots, I was happy to be the third thing in the photo.

"Publications always leave a few empty spots for unexpected stories," my former roommate said. "We'll squeeze this article into the August issue. This is never done, but because I love you, I'll email you a copy of what I'm writing. You'll have twenty-four hours to read and return."

"Aw, you remember how I worry about everything. I trust you to write a lovely story, but yes, I'd like a quick read before it goes to press. Old habits die hard."

With one final hug, we said goodbye, and I waved out the window as the cab flew into high gear. We really were pushing our boarding time for the next to the last stop of my book tour, and had to run the final thirty yards. "Last call for flight 1622 nonstop to Miami" rang out just as we arrived at the gate.

Nick fell asleep as we taxied along the tarmac, but I was still on a serious high from the past twenty-four hours. Cindy's kind words and the magazine article were greatly appreciated. I couldn't help but think that *Biscuits & Gravy*'s massive circulation would go a long way to promote the success of my novel. *How do you thank someone for that degree of friendship?* I wondered.

66

I loved that time of year when our brutally hot summers gave yield to the glorious colors and cooler temperatures of autumn. The orange, red, and gold leaves of sturdy hardwoods intertwined with the deep green needles of the pines. Pumpkins and gourds in a kaleidoscope of hues sat handsomely piled at the door of our barn and house to greet us and our friends.

Riding along in the golf cart to collect the mail, the dogs began to bark. I turned my head in the direction of their concern and noticed it was apparently moving-in day for our fall semester farmers. On our way back, we took a detour to say hello and welcome. I introduced myself along with our dogs to the new, very enthusiastic class of fourteen senior interns.

The first three weeks of their experience had been spent in their on-campus classroom. They would live on the Colonial Farm project campus until the week before Christmas break. Exams were taken back in their classrooms in Raleigh.

The onsite professor/dorm dad, who held a doctorate in horticulture, was a veteran by this point, having tutored the spring and summer students. He went straight to work, informing his flock that they had stepped into the eighteenth century, and a minimalist way of living was expected. Sometimes "seeing is believing." It was one thing to read about this internship but quite another to actually live this experience. Their faces fell, but they improved when he added that they did have electricity, running water, and internet. He then introduced the woman at his side.

Before summer semester began, Mrs. Applegate had been added to the staff. She was the instructor of all things edible, the kitchen, laundry, and how it was managed over two hundred years ago. Apparently, the spring students had struggled desperately in those areas. One young man wrote home announcing that he was starving to death and his clothes smelled.

The students were expected to eat what they grew and hang their hand washed period clothes on the line to dry. Mrs. A stood about five feet four and had that place shipshape in no time. Her room was off the kitchen, so any two-legged mice in the kitchen after lights out, or someone dragging in after curfew, would not go unnoticed.

A schedule had been developed to accommodate myriad interested groups of visitors, from schoolchildren to garden clubs, on weekdays from nine to five. Those days and times were spoken for every week to the following June. As a former educator, it was important to me that no child, or school, would ever be turned away due to lack of funds. The university agreed, and that cost was significantly reduced to one dollar per child. All other visitors were assessed the full price of thirty-five dollars each, and tickets could be purchased either online or at the door. Reservations were required. Families usually visited on the weekends and were treated to the same experiences as the weekday guests.

All proceeds from ticket sales, and special class fees, went into the upkeep account, which included utilities and so forth. Heart

House was open year-round with working students growing something for every season. Bird watchers and botanists had found the back creek area to be a treasure trove.

Word had spread about the farming endeavor, and a master gardener program had been added. The chickens and horses had welcomed six very cute but mischievous goats whose job it was to produce the raw material needed to make soap. Their addition produced as much chaos in the barnyard as they did milk. But the visitors, be they young or old, enjoyed all the hands-on activities, from helping to make soap and collecting eggs to even walking behind a beautiful draft horse and give plowing a try.

☙❧

On our way back to the house, my phone rang. It was Vera, my editor at Covered Buttons Press.

"Hi, Vera," I answered, quite surprised.

"Hi, Sarah. I'm calling with some very good news. Are you able to talk?"

"Yes," I said, pulling to a stop in front of my office.

"Excellent. It's my privilege to inform you that your book, *Sweet Tea and Fireflies*, has made the bestseller list." Waiting for a response but hearing nothing back, she added, "Sarah, are you there?"

I struggled to speak. "Yes, yes, I'm here. Are you sure?"

"We are. Congratulations! Covered Buttons Press is honored to have you on our list. We will be sending you a plaque reflecting your name, your novel, and bestseller status. Again, congratulations!"

"I just don't know what to say. Thank you so much!"

"You're welcome, but remember, you wrote the book, and people are just loving it," Vera reminded me.

Nick was coming out of the barn and came over to see why we three were just sitting in the golf cart.

"Hey, babe. What's going on?"

My jaw was dropped open. I was momentarily unable to talk or move.

"Sarah?" Nick asked as I got out of the golf cart.

"My book has made the bestseller list," I said, not believing my own words. "My editor just called; the book sold…I can't remember the amount she said, but it was tons of copies last week. They're mailing me a plaque too."

"That's wonderful!" Nick said, lifting me off the ground. "But I'm not surprised."

"Thanks, but I'm blown away. I also need to thank you for accepting all the time this has taken away from us. Before I do anything else, I need to better understand all this. Give me a minute to call Ellie."

I sat back down in the driver's seat while Nick and the dogs filled the others.

"Sarah," Ellie said, after I filled her in, "you need to take a breath and enjoy today. This could be just the beginning."

"Don't be ridiculous." I tittered. "But thanks for all you did to help make my book a success. I couldn't have done it without you. Talk to you soon."

Nick smiled. "You need to call Betsy, and Margaret just pulled in."

"I'll also give Cindy a ring," I said. "I imagine her article went a long way to promote interest. My brain resembles the spin cycle of the washing machine. I've got so many questions flying around."

"Like what?"

"The going-forward ones, like how do you remain on the list? Are all the big reviews in, or will this prompt more? Stuff like that."

"You've had great reviews so far."

I snickered. "Except for one. I'd love to sit down with that woman and have a chat. 'occasional simple verbiage and too Southern…' Really. She all but called me stupid."

"She did not, and it was one out of how many—a hundred or so? I thought you'd moved on. You knew they couldn't all be five stars."

"I have moved on, but seriously—two and a half stars my ass!"

"I'll see you at the house." Nick laughed, getting out of the cart and calling the dogs. "You're impossible."

Margaret stopped riding after hearing the news, and together we called Betsy. We three agreed it was celebration time, and Betsy insisted the Rowdy Girls assemble next Wednesday at her house. Rose, Elizabeth, and Jennifer were next on my list, and they were all a yes.

Margaret went back to work, brushing Chance, and I stepped into the office to call Cindy.

This was a once-in-a-lifetime experience, and I didn't want it to fade. I wondered if famous writers became numb to the phone call I had received less than an hour ago. I couldn't imagine hearing *your book is number one*, or one hundred, ever becoming passé.

I relocated to our porch swing before dialing my mother and giving her the news. Sibby was over the moon and handed the phone to my grandmother. "What great news!" Grammy said. "I never doubted it for a minute. Have you started the next book?"

I chuckled. "Actually, I have. My agent's been after me since she sold this one, and now that my first book is a success, my publisher has started to turn the pressure screws. It's almost ready for the first edit. My working title is *The Dresser Drawer*."

"I'm not surprised. Here's your mother."

"Sarah, I'm so proud of you, sweetheart. I would love for you to come visit as soon as you can, and bring Nick."

"Okay…How's tomorrow? And should I read something else into your request?"

"Yes, you should," she said. "We're getting very close to late-fall, aren't we?"

My mother's cryptic message left no questions in my mind. Time was running out for my treasured grandmother. She always said we were all "just visiting"—a mere dot in time.

My voice quivered. "We'll see you tomorrow. I'll bring lunch."

"Wonderful and a pumpkin from your garden?"

Solemnly, I said, "I'll bring several."

67.

I began twice-a-week visits to Iron Springs after that day, and everyone knew why.

Grammy had become a much weaker version of herself. She slept most of the time, and her appetite was gone. "Sarah," she said, "we both know what's happening, and I demand you not be too sad when I go. I'll give you one week to mourn and the remainder of your life to celebrate the love we've shared. You must promise."

With a catch in my throat, I said, "I promise, but, Grammy, you don't understand how much I'm going to miss you."

"I do understand, but death is the final word in the definition of life. I've now lived one year past the century mark. I'm tired. I'm ready to go home. I need you to pull yourself up and carry on. Your mother will need you. I won't live long enough to read your second book, but in the first one—tell me the truth—who's the real Hattie Hayes?"

My smile broadened. "What makes you think there really is a Hattie Hayes?"

"Sarah, this is your grandmother you're talking to." She laughed, insisting I continue.

"You win. It all started in the attic…"

 C3&O

Two weeks later, Prudence O'Neil passed away, and the hole in my heart was chasmic. The service was lovely, which I always thought a strange adjective, considering it was a funeral, but it was. Grammy was buried beside her husband of sixty-two years, a man I only vaguely remembered. The day before per her request, I decorated the family plot with chrysanthemums and other seasonal flowers. She was emphatic about not having the standard "wreath on a stick" as she called it.

Several days after the service, while pulling dead tomato plants from our garden, an unexpected breeze came directly from the outdoor ring, along the front of the barn, and straight across my body. A faint whisper of star jasmine lingered in the air. I knew it was Grammy saying goodbye.

Collapsing in the rich garden soil, I grabbed two handfuls and wept uncontrollably. The dogs sat beside me, licking my arms. I had always needed my own quiet time to make peace with things, and this was perfect. Grammy was the world to me, from cards to cookies to teaching me how to ride—those memories would live in my heart forever.

C3&O

Sweet Tea & Fireflies remained on the bestseller list off and on for about two months, which was nothing short of amazing. I will admit reading #1 *NEW YORK TIMES* BESTSELLER printed across the top of the cover to the first reprint brought a feeling of pride I never knew I could have.

While the "bestseller" piece was wonderful, I found more delight in my readers' comments. People I didn't know found joy in my words. The number of reviews did increase, and I read each and every one. A few were not so kind, but as they say, "Art is subjective."

Nick and I had decided to postpone our search for a trainer until after the book tour. It would take a while to complete that sort of interview—to watch each applicant ride, teach, and communicate with our existing boarders. Plus he or she would need to coexist with Coy. After working our way through a dozen applications, we settled on six candidates.

In the end, Nick and I found the perfect trainer: Dexter Bentley, or Dex as he preferred, was hired somewhere in the middle of October. He was in his early thirties, boyishly handsome, accomplished, and allowed zero nonsense.

Nick and I had welcomed several additional boarders, and the barn was over half-full of paying customers. Everyone appreciated the larger indoor ring, which allowed lessons and free rides regardless of the weather. But Dex was the true draw card and ran the "instructional" side of LLF with a kind but iron hand.

"This is potentially a dangerous sport," he would insist. "If you want to play, go take a basket-weaving class at the Y."

The art teacher in me found that analogy unacceptable, but I momentarily let it go. That Christmas I gave him a basket-weaving kit—the most difficult one I could find. "Give it a try, and leave your finished piece on my desk."

Nick was laughing as I walked out of the barn office. "Good luck on the basket, buddy. Sarah taught art for thirty years." It became a wonderful barn joke, and the lopsided, half-finished effort sat dead center in the office trophy case. From then on he used "canasta" as his example of play.

C3·80

Jennifer and Elizabeth trailered in for afternoon group lessons with Margaret, and Betsy rode with me and two other women in the mornings. Linda and the first three boarders were a group, and Rose reported that she was working hard at Bellomy Farm in Virginia.

We traveled to different horse shows about once a month, and our fearless leader was tough as nails. Dex allowed Rose to meet us at the showgrounds and was equally demanding of her. He insisted our hard work and preparation would pay off, and he was right. Long Leaf Farm usually pinned somewhere in the top ribbons in our individual divisions, with Champion and Reserve Champion rosettes finding their way home as well. We appreciated the determination of our trainer par excellence. Underneath it all, he was as sweet as sugar. A fact he could never completely gloss over.

Nick and Coy decided that since Dexter practically lived at our farm, he should actually do so as well and serve as the assistant barn manager. Dex agreed and moved into the apartment beside Coy's on the back of the barn.

Every few months, all six of the Rowdy Girls continued to trailer to Moss Creek Farm, and those trips never disappointed!

Ken Langley was a delightful and permanent fixture by my mother's side. Christmas required a twenty-two-pound turkey, as the entire immediate Langley family was invited. Detective Luke sat to my left, and somewhere over dessert, we agreed that our parents' relationship was wonderful.

Sidney and Jacob were engaged over New Year's. He did ask me first, or so I was told, but in the end I truly didn't care. The wedding was set for early June in the gardens of Long Leaf Farm, and I went into planning mode. My daughter knew exactly what she wanted—it was her wedding, not mine. I gave her a budget and full rein—well, almost.

Nick agreed for Margaret to lease Chance. They were a pair made in heaven and won everything there was to win. Louie lost the battle with his lower-leg issue before Christmas and had to be put down. It was inhumane to make him suffer. We buried the big bay in the sunniest corner of the boys' shared pasture.

About six weeks later, just before dinnertime, my Rascal simply lay down in the pasture near Louie's grave and drew his last breath. The cause of death was said to be old age, but I'll always believe it was from missing his best friend of nearly twenty years. He was buried alongside Louie, and they were once again together forever.

In their honor, the other four Rowdy Girls planted a magnolia tree with a marker that said *Rascal and Louie—a friendship always evergreen.* Nick and Coy put in a black fence with a lovely wooden gate around their space, and Coy cut the grass weekly. Margaret and I could never talk about the boys with dry eyes—maybe someday.

To balance out our sadness with joy, Emma and Scott surprised us by announcing they were moving to Durham. Emma had taken an administrative position at Duke, and Scott got on the payroll of a chemical company in the Research Triangle. I was never quite sure what he did exactly. It was always a bit hush-hush. In the depths of my vivid imagination, I thought he was some sort of government spy—our own 007.

The cycle of life has no brakes—potholes, and side trips, yes, but no brakes—and I was truly enjoying the journey.

68

The day of the Sams-Durant wedding, the weather cooperated with cooler-than-usual June temperatures for the South and offered a pleasant, cloud-free sky. Sidney was radiant, and Jacob, her handsome match, was so happy and proud he could hardly stand himself. Dinner and dancing followed the six o'clock ceremony.

Our guest list was an eclectic collection of interesting people, from editors, psychologists, TV personalities, and educators to horse friends galore, family, and two big dogs sporting wedding collars— Annie's had lace and Caesar's a black bow tie. Running the length of the back of our house, the brick patio that gently spilled into the gardens of Long Leaf Farm was bubbling over with joy.

Jennifer scheduled two more catering jobs, and Rose shared she was selling her house in town. Elizabeth beamed with pride when people admired Sidney's wedding picture taken at Hedgecomb's Mill. Betsy took Susan Tillman on a tour of the barn remodel, and Margaret gave a rundown of our boarders' policy to two interested ladies, adding that Dexter Bentley came with the barn package, which was a huge plus.

Midway through the reception, a youngish man began walking in my direction.

"Mrs. Heart," he said, taking the final step to the patio. "I'm Joe

Davenport. Sidney and I are gym buddies. Thank you so much for inviting me. You have a beautiful piece of property."

"Thank you. We're so glad you could come."

"I know I shouldn't talk business today, but I didn't want to miss the opportunity to speak with you personally about your book."

"Well, Joe, today is about Sidney, not me and my work."

"I understand that, but can I please have a few minutes?"

"All right, I'll give you five," I said, my face hopefully reflecting *talk fast*.

"I'm the host of *Page-Turner*," he said.

Smiling, I said, "Yes, I recognized your name on the invitation list, and I watch your show."

"If you're interested, I'd love to have you as a guest author. How about giving me a call on Monday and we'll go from there?"

"Yes, I'm interested, and thank you," I said, looking over my shoulder. "But I must get back to our guests. I'll call you…let's say Monday afternoon, around two?"

"That'll work," Joe said, handing me his card and eyeing the bar.

CB SO

Four days later, things were put back in place and our guests had gone home. I was in my writer's cottage at the computer, reading several emails from Vera at Covered Buttons Press. My new book, *The Dresser Drawer*, was soon to be released, and she was setting up another twelve-city tour. Annie and Caesar were at my feet, and Nick was busy in the barn.

I had always been a tremendous fan of peace and quiet, and its presence was a welcome change after all of the wedding hoopla. This was a great time for me to organize my thoughts on my interview with Joe Davenport. Making notes was a very good practice for me.

69

Three weeks later, I pushed on the brass revolving door, and with one-half of a revolution, stood inside the main lobby of the television station. An information board told me the floor and suite number of the studio for *Page-Turner*, a weekly program on Public Television.

"Good morning, Mrs. Heart," the receptionist said as I walked in.

"Morning. Please just call me Sarah, and just out of curiosity, how did you know my name?"

Holding her copy of the book, she said, "I read your book. Mr. Davenport will be with you shortly. Would you care for something to drink?"

"I hope you enjoyed it. And thanks—water would be great."

Resting her copy on the counter, she said, "I loved it. Will you please sign my copy?"

"My pleasure. Who should I make the inscription out to?" I said, taking her pen and turning to the front page.

"Addison would be great. Let me get your water," she said.

Within minutes, Joe appeared, and off we went to the studio. The set was cozy, anchored by mahogany bookcases and softened with a robin's-egg-blue oval rug at our feet.

"I know you've had lots of interviews since the success of your book, but let's take a minute to review my list of interview questions," Joe said, shuffling his papers.

"Will this be edited?" I asked.

"Yes, ma'am," he answered. "It will air in two weeks on Saturday and Sunday at five o'clock."

With cameras rolling, we began. Joe gave his standard introduction to this week's show by reviewing my book, a bit about my being a native North Carolinian, and finished with my love for horses.

"Sarah—may I call you Sarah?"

"Please," I answered, and the conversation took off.

Halfway through, Joe said, "You seem to have a real love for front porch swings and attics."

With a genuine smile, I said, "I absolutely do! In my world, 'porch' is a verb. There is little more truly Southern than a front porch swing with padded cushions. When I was a little girl, neighbors would walk by, pull up a chair to share space and conversation—all thanks to the front porch. It's like the welcome mat to your home, and no one's ever turned away."

Joe chuckled. "It sounds like the front porch brings you happiness?"

"Yes. Those are some of the best memories life has to offer. Simple pleasures, quiet times, and always, family. I think of it as 'Peace on the Porch.' I can see my mother and grandmother shelling butter beans as my father rocked back and forth, reading the newspaper and complaining about the cost of things. All the while, my best friend and I were running around in the front yard catching lightning bugs in a jar."

Joe asked, "So how do attics fit into your story?"

"I've always thought of attics as the warehouse of someone's life. Usually the next generation is required to plow through the accumulation of just stuff. But occasionally a true gem lies buried beneath that visually alarming crocheted afghan Aunt Eunice made or the box of clothes your mother swears will eventually come back in style."

With a smile, he leaned in. "You know I must ask, did you really find a sapphire and diamond broach in your attic?"

"No. I wrote that entire piece of the novel long before my real attic discovery. My husband and I literally stumbled across the Mountain Rose while on a purging mission in our attic. The ruby in the necklace, it turns out, was unearthed in April of 1890 on a farm just outside of Franklin, North Carolina. How amazing is that?" I said, watching Joe's face ignite with curiosity.

"Very! Tell us more."

"How much time do we have?"

"All the time in the world," he assured me.

Wrapping up the interview, Joe said, "Before we close, tell me a little about your second novel, *The Dresser Drawer*. Where does it begin?"

"It's a sequel. There are familiar names, faces, and places, but new ones too. Ben and Grace have just come home from an event that is life altering. What was it, and what will happen next? You'll have to read it to find out. But true love, sisterhood, family, and the twists and turns of life are the core of my books."

Joe smiled. "Can I add attics and porches to the list?"

"Always and forever!"

"It's been a pleasure having you on *Page-Turner*. Congratulations on your first novel, and continued success going forward."

"The pleasure was all mine," I said. The camera's light switched off.

As we made our way out of the studio, Joe shook my hand. "It was wonderful having you on the show. I think it will be well received. I'll send any and all emails your way. You can answer them if you want, but be careful—there are lots of strange folks out there."

"Good advice. Thanks again," I said, walking across the lobby. I called Nick once I was well out of the city, sharing that *Page-Turner* was perhaps the best interview to date.

70

Miss Olivia Cromwell passed away the following spring. Her absence left a huge hole in my heart, but her memory filled the void. Per her request, holding her copy of my novel, she was buried in her light blue dress beside her sister, Iris. Frank, Betsy, Nick, and I were the only ones in attendance, but then, we were the only family she had left. Betsy and I made a pact to tend to their family plot on a regular basis—while enjoying a cup of tea and cookies, of course.

I never sold the necklace. Instead, I loaned it to the museum for an indefinite amount of time. Freddy Foxroy had a special display case built to hold the Mountain Rose, its story, pictures of Olivia and the Rowdy Girls, and space for my books. The day I dropped off a copy of *The Dresser Drawer*, Freddy said, "Wonderful, and book number three will go right here when it's finished."

"I'm not sure I have another story in me." I smiled, knowing my third manuscript was now in the hands of Vera at Covered Buttons Press, waiting for the first edit. "But I do thank you for stocking my books and launching my success. You know, Freddy, I give you a great deal of credit every time I do a book talk and tell everyone where they can see the necklace."

"Bless your heart," Freddy said. "I'm proud to have had a cameo role in its success."

CR8O

Nearly a year later, Nick and I received an invitation and six tickets to the Historical Society's Grand Opening of a new exhibit at the Artifacts Museum.

Betsy and Frank were up for an evening out, and we collected them on the way to our capital city. Bill and Margaret were already in Raleigh at a Ford dealership event and joined us later at the museum. The six of us had grown into a wonderful couples circle.

Betsy slid into the back seat and winked at me.

"Stop it," I whispered. "This has to be a huge surprise."

When we arrived, we made our way across the lobby and into the main exhibition room.

Confused, Nick said, "I thought you said the new exhibit was upstairs?"

"It is, but I just want to check on the Mountain Rose."

Pulling Frank in the opposite direction, Betsy said, "We'll meet you upstairs."

The custom display case sat squarely in the center of the room, and we could see the necklace twinkling as we walked across the floor.

"Freddy really did a good job planning ahead for your second book," Nick said, stopping dead in his tracks. "Sarah, what's that?"

Standing beside the case, I said, "Book number three."

"You told me you were ghost-writing for someone?" Nick said.

"I kind of was," I said, giving him a kiss. "I really wanted this to be a surprise."

"*From a Distance*," Nick read out loud. "Why a surprise?"

"Because it's a reflective story about us. It's my vision of how our life together might have been had we met in our twenties. If I couldn't get it quite right, it would be another sequel, but I'm happy to say it's my favorite book so far. I loved you the moment I saw you—*from a distance*, two trailers down."

"Sarah?"

"Yes, Todd?"

"I know you didn't name me Todd. But no Ben and Grace? Are the Rowdy Girls along for the ride?"

Taking his arm, I said, "You'll find out when you start reading. Your copy's at home in your den chair. Let's go see what Freddy's up to now."

଼ଞ୨

Once home, Nick was last out of the bathroom. Dressed in his sweats, he held my face in his hands, "Sarah, I'll love you forever, even if you did name me Todd. Now, put yourself to bed. I'm going to read."

"I'll love you forever too, and I hope you like *our* story." I smiled, wiggling myself under the covers. Seconds after Nick turn off the light, I said, "Darrell and Bunny Bigelow were the envy of everyone in Sleepy Springs."

"Sarah!"

"Yes, dear." I giggled as Nick called our dogs. "It's fiction, Darrell."

"Good night, Sarah!" he mumbled, squeezing out the light from the hall when he closed the door.

From across our room, I stared at the window and into the dark abyss of the midnight sky, "Good night, Ben," I whispered softly, closing my eyes.

Jane Rankin

Sibby's Corn Pudding
This is an absolute crowd pleaser!

1 14.75 oz. can cream style corn
1 8.5 oz. can whole kernel corn—drained
2 tablespoons flour
⅓ cup sugar
½ cup evaporated milk
½ cup reduced fat milk
Add salt and pepper to taste
4 eggs—beaten
4 tablespoons butter

Melt butter in 1-1/2 quart baking dish. Mix both cans of corn, sugar, flour, canned milk and reduced fat milk, salt and pepper to taste. Beat eggs until fluffy and fold into mixture. Pour mixture into baking dish. Place dish in a pan of hot water and bake at 375 degrees for 1 hour, or until the center is firm.

Bon Appétit!

Acknowledgments

Although *Sweet Tea & Fireflies* is a work of fiction, I owe a great deal of appreciation to so many of my friends who gave generously of their time, knowledge, and expertise as I wove the tapestry of this novel.

Hadley Falls lies in the eastern part of North Carolina and exists only in my imagination, but it comes to life with the help of many. High Standards Farm, the barn where I board my beautiful Thoroughbred mare, Drew, is home to a treasure trove of inspiration and information. Among the list of boarders are two attorneys, one doctor, two real estate agents, three business owners, a technology whiz, several women employed in the financial world, an absolute gaggle of children, and one fabulous trainer who also owns the farm. I thank you all for your help and encouragement.

The Rowdy Girls are a group of middle-aged women of my own creation as well. Immersed in a kaleidoscope of changing patterns, my life's highway has allowed me to traverse the decades looking through the eyehole of opportunity, adventure, and experiences— good and bad, near and far, equestrian and teaching, neighbors and childhood—and from those golden threads the Rowdy Girls and their story was born.

A heartfelt thank-you to all my family for their love and support. Kinship and friendships are the essence of this novel. Special appreciation to my editor, Betsy Thorpe, my copy editor, Penina Lopez, and my graphic designer, Diana Wade. Never could I have done this without the three of you.

CR&OR

And, finally, to my readers: I sincerely hope you enjoy traveling along with the Rowdy Girls and continue to treasure your ride through life with dear friends!

Sweet Tea & Fireflies